It Happened One Night

STEPHANIE LAURENS
MARY BALOGH
JACQUIE D'ALESSANDRO
CANDICE HERN

It Happened One Night

AVON

An Imprint of HarperCollins*Publishers*

AVON BOOKS
An Imprint of HarperCollins*Publishers*
10 East 53rd Street
New York, New York 10022-5299

ISBN-13: 978-1-60751-076-5

Contents

A Letter to the Reader

What would happen if four authors were each to write a novella for an anthology and it turned out they had all used the same plot premise? Disaster, right? But what if it had been done deliberately? What if the four had agreed ahead of time on certain plot details they would all use and had then gone ahead and written the novellas without further collaboration? Madness, right? All the stories would be basically the same.

Or would they?

For years it has been my conviction that the individual imagination, voice, style, and outlook on life of each author would guarantee a quite unique story no matter how similar the basic plot was to someone else's. I wanted to test the theory, but could arouse no interest in it until recently. And then I was out on a Levy book-signing tour with a crowd of other authors and idly mentioned my idea to Candice Hern and Jacquie D'Alessandro. They were instantly enthusiastic, and we talked of nothing else for the whole of one long bus journey from Chicago to Detroit. We were going to *do* it. But we felt that we needed a fourth member of the group and made a wish list. Candice happened to have Stephanie Laurens's e-mail address with her, and since she was at the top of our list, we wrote to her and had an almost instant acceptance, despite the time difference between Detroit and somewhere in Australia. Our agents also loved the idea—and so did Avon when we pitched it to them.

And so here it is—an anthology of four novellas with the same plot! You can be the judge. Are they so similar that when you have read one, you have read them all?

Or are they as differently fascinating as the four seasons in which they are set?

The plot premise is this: A man and a woman, who have neither seen nor heard from each other in ten years, meet again when they find themselves staying at the same inn for a twenty-four hour period. To make the experiment a real one, we did not discuss our stories at all as we wrote them. The only artificial restriction we placed upon them ahead of time was to take different seasons of the year, since there are four of those and four of us.

Enjoy these very different novellas—even though in one sense they are all the same. Right? Or wrong?

Mary Balogh

The Fall of Rogue Gerrard

Stephanie Laurens

Chapter One

It was a dark, stormy, and utterly miserable night. Rain fell from the sky in unrelenting sheets; whenever Robert "Rogue" Gerrard, fifth Viscount Gerrard, managed to squint through long lashes weighed down by icy droplets all he saw was more rain.

Hunched in his greatcoat on the box of his traveling carriage, he held the reins loosely in one long-fingered hand; he'd stripped off his sodden gloves miles ago. There was no risk of the horses bolting.

"Just a little further," he crooned, urging them on. He doubted they could hear over the drumming downpour, but the coaxing croon was ingrained habit. If one wanted females or animals to do what one wanted, one crooned; in Ro's experience, it usually worked.

The powerful pair, normally arrogantly high-stepping, were disdainfully lifting first one hoof, then the other, free of sucking mud. Their pace was down to a crawl.

Inwardly cursing, Ro peered through the water coursing down his face, trying through the darkness to make out some—any—landmark. It was February. His mother always maintained one should never travel in February; as with many things, she was proving to be correct. But business had called, so Ro had dutifully left the luxurious warmth of the hearth at his principal estate, Gerrard Park, near Waltham on the Wolds, summoned his trusty coachman, Willis, and set out that afternoon for town.

He'd imagined putting up for the night along the way, possibly at the Kings Bells in St. Neots.

As usual, they'd joined the Great North Road near Colsterworth. It was only after they'd swept past Stamford that Willis, glancing idly back, had seen the massive storm clouds rushing down on them from the north. The turnoff to Peterborough had already been behind them; when applied to for orders, Ro had decreed they'd press on with all speed, hoping to reach Brampton. They'd just raced through the hamlet of Norman Cross when the heavens had opened with a ferocity that had instantly made traveling, even on England's most major highway, a nightmare.

They'd limped toward Sawtry, but with the smaller, slighter Willis all but drowned on the box, having increasing difficulty managing the reins, Ro had insisted on trading places. His drenched coachman was now a shivering lump inside the coach, while Ro, also drenched to the skin, but courtesy of his size and constitution better able to withstand the apocalyptic downpour, squinted through the torrent.

They'd reached Sawtry over an hour ago, only to find every possible habitation packed to the rafters with travelers seeking shelter. The Great North Road was the country's busiest highway; mail coaches, post coaches, and private coaches, let alone wagons and carts, had been stranded and deserted all around Sawtry.

No shelter of any sort was to be had, but the deluge had shown no signs of abating; if anything, as the hours dragged on, the downpour had only increased.

That was when Ro had remembered the small but tidy inn in Coppingford. The lane along which it lay met the highway about a mile south of Sawtry. With no real option, Ro had accepted the risk, not just of that extra mile on the highway, but of what he'd estimated as two miles of country lane.

Now, with the night an icy, wet, close to impenetrable shroud around him, with the horses slowing even more with every step, with the deluge rapidly converting the lane into a quagmire, he was seriously wondering if he'd judged aright. Yet quite aside from its seclusion tucked away through woods two miles from the highway, given the sudden onset of the storm and its dramatic impact, he doubted the Coppingford Arms would be full.

Gaining shelter for him, Willis, and his horses was currently his only objective, and both instinct and intellect told him shelter awaited at the Coppingford Arms.

He was debating whether to get down and lead the horses when he caught a glimmer through the dripping trees. Leaden branches drooped and bobbed in the downpour; he blinked, shook his head, sending droplets flying in a vain attempt to clear his eyes, and stared again. A small, weak lamp glowed through the curtain of rain.

It grew larger, its light stronger, as the horses inched along. Through the drowned night the outline of a low, solid, two-story building in gray stone took shape. As well as the single lamp by the main door, flickering light at one window bore testimony to a fire within. The sight made Ro realize just how chilled he was; he quelled a shiver.

A stone archway beside the inn gave access to the stable yard. He turned the flagging horses under it. "Willis! Wake up, man—we're here."

"I'm awake." Willis was out of the carriage before it had rocked to a halt. "Ostler! Get yourself out here! His lordship's horses need tending before they get washed away."

Swinging down from the box seat, Ro saw an ostler come rushing from the stable.

Wide-eyed, he grabbed hold of the leader's bridle. "We can walk them into the stable and unharness there. No need to get washed away ourselves."

Ro nodded to Willis when Willis looked back at him. "Go on. I'll get my bag and bespeak rooms—come in when you're done."

Willis saluted and rushed to help the ostler manage the heavy, drooping horses. Ro stepped to the back of the carriage, opened the boot, and hauled his portmanteau up and out just as the carriage started moving, then strode up the steps to the inn's side door.

He opened it and squelched inside. The sound made him wince; Hoby wouldn't be impressed. "Innkeep!"

"Right here, sir."

Ro looked up. The innkeeper—the same mild-mannered man Ro remembered from years ago—was standing behind a short counter by the stairs, watching the puddle forming about Ro's large booted feet with resignation.

The man sighed, then ran his gaze up Ro's long frame, animation increasing as he took in the quality of the greatcoat hanging from Ro's shoulders and the elegant coat and waistcoat beneath, equally sodden. "A dreadful night, sir. You'll be wanting a nice dry room, I've no doubt."

"One with a fire, and a room for my coachman as well. He'll be in shortly."

Ro's voice brought the man's gaze to his face.

The man blinked. "Why . . . bless me! It's Ro—" He corrected himself. "Lord Gerrard, isn't it? We haven't seen you in quite some years, my lord."

Everyone remembered Rogue Gerrard. Ro managed to summon the charming smile that rarely failed to get him what he wanted. "Indeed. Bilt, isn't it?"

Bilt was flattered to have been remembered; he came

around his counter. "A right beastly night, my lord. Never seen anything like it—all this rain. A night for Noah, it is. We've one of our front rooms vacant. I'll just nip up and get the fire roaring, and have the missus turn down the bed." Eager to please, he reached for Ro's bag. "If you'd like to sit in the tap for a moment, catch your breath, I'll take your bag up and make sure all's ready."

Ro surrendered his bag. He was tired and sodden and wanted nothing more than to get dry. Getting warm would hopefully follow.

Using both hands, Bilt hefted the portmanteau and hurried to the stairs. "You'll remember the tap from before, I'll warrant."

Ro did. He turned to the archway that gave on to the tap, a decent-sized room with a bar along one wall.

The room lay in chilly darkness. It wasn't the room in which the firelight had flickered.

Ro swung his gaze to the door opposite the archway. If memory served, it gave on to a parlor. Crossing to the door, he opened it. Warmth and golden light rolled over him.

"My lord! Ah . . ."

Already over the threshold, Ro leaned back through the door to look up at Bilt, on the landing wrestling with the unwieldy portmanteau.

Bilt looked down at him, expression aghast.

Ro raised a brow. "What is it?"

Bilt swallowed. "If you don't mind, my lord, someone's hired the parlor."

Ro glanced into the room, then looked back at Bilt. "Whoever they are, they're not here, most probably because it's the dead of night. There is, however, a fire still burning. I'm sure it hasn't escaped your notice that I'm drenched, Bilt. To the skin. I'm sure you wouldn't want me to catch a chill while waiting for my room to be made ready—especially as this fire is burning so well and otherwise going to waste."

He smiled at Bilt, but this time the smile held an edge, one mirrored in his silver-gray eyes. "I'll wait here by the fire."

Very few people forgot *Rogue Gerrard.*

Entering the parlor, Ro closed the door and walked across to the hearth. With every step he could feel the welcome warmth reaching for him, engulfing him . . . but only on his face and hands, his exposed skin. The rest of him remained literally chilled to the bone, and that rest was rather a lot.

Halting before the fire, he shrugged out of his greatcoat and draped it over the back of a wooden chair beside the hearth, then mentally shrugging—there was no one around to see—he fought his way out of his coat, not an easy task given the lengths to which Shultz had gone to tailor the garment to his shoulders and back. The waistcoat was easier to strip off, but even his cravat and shirt were more wet than not. He couldn't recall ever being so drenched. The cravat was a yard of limp, creased linen; he laid it over his coat on the chair. His buckskin breeches—thank God he hadn't changed into trousers before setting out—had largely repelled the rain; they were already giving off steam.

He paused, considering his shirt, but was too desperate to feel heat on his iced skin to wait. Pulling the tails free of his breeches, he tugged and wriggled and managed to haul the damp linen off over his head. On the way, his dripping hair wet the fabric even more, but the heat of the flames caressing his chilled chest and arms brought instant relief.

He sighed, closed his eyes. Rubbing his hair with the bunched shirt, he gradually felt the worst of his inner shivering subside. Muscles tight with cold started to ease, to relax. He was still chilled, but no longer frozen.

His marrow might even be thawing.

Opening his eyes, reaching behind him, he mopped his back with the shirt, then dried his arms, rubbing briskly to get the blood flowing. Then he tried to dry his chest; given the state of his shirt, his skin remained damp. Standing before the fire, he let the flames warm him while passing the crumpled linen back and forth across the band of crinkly hair adorning the heavy muscles.

His mood was almost mellow when the door opened. Expecting Bilt, he turned—

And froze.

Across the room, a lady whisked into the parlor, turned and shut the door. Swinging back into the room, looking down, shaking rain from an umbrella, she walked a few paces, then halted.

She was swathed in a heavy cloak, the lower foot of which was wet through and muddy, but she'd pushed back the hood, revealing hair the color of burnished walnut neatly secured in a chignon, and a small oval face with delicate features.

Features Ro recognized, that still held the power to stop the breath in his chest.

She hadn't seen him; she was patently unaware he was there.

He frowned. "What the *devil* are you doing here?"

She jumped. Smothered a small shriek that died away as her gaze rose, locked, and she stared.

Not at his face.

Her gaze had risen only as far as his chest. His naked chest.

He knew perfectly well what it looked like, knew precisely why women, ladies especially, stared at him in that way, but this was Lydia, and her staring at him in that way was definitely not going to help.

Somewhere in the inn, a clock chimed. Twelve bongs; midnight.

His only option was to ignore his half-naked state. It

could have been worse; he might have changed into trousers before he'd left home, and then she'd have swooned.

"Lydia—cut line! What the devil are you doing here? More to the point, where the devil have you been—in a torrential downpour in the dead of night?" The words came out more harshly than he'd intended, a reaction to the unwelcome realization that ten years had clearly been insufficient time to mute the effect she had on him. And all that flowed from that.

An impulse to shake her, given she'd clearly been doing something witlessly dangerous, being just one of his reactions.

She blinked. Her gaze slowly rose over his chest to his shoulders, then up the line of his throat to his face.

Her lips parted even further; her eyes widened even more. *"Ro?"*

Pressing his lips tight, he hung on to his temper. What the devil did she mean by staring at his chest when she hadn't even known it was he? "As you see. Now, if you please—where the deuce have you been, and why?"

Mouth agape, Lydia Makepeace stared, for quite the first time in her life fully comprehending the meaning of the word "dumbstruck," at the gentleman—gentleman rake, gamester, dissolute womanizer, and acknowledged libertine—displayed so delectably before her, all that damp skin just begging to be touched . . . and valiantly tried to harry her wits back into working order. The flickering firelight caressing his chest—that amazingly sculpted muscled expanse—lovingly outlining each ridge of his abdomen, each heavy curve of shoulder and arm in golden light, didn't help.

Her mouth was dry; swallowing, she forced herself to focus on his eyes, on the irritation clear in the silvery gray.

Even as the most elementary ability to think re-formed in

her mind, she saw her plans, her carefully calculated, absolutely vital plans, unraveling. "No."

His eyes narrowed.

She narrowed hers back, tipped up her chin "What I do is no concern of yours, my lord."

He growled, literally growled. "Ro—remember? And for your information—"

Breaking off, he looked past her. The door opened.

Glancing around, she saw the innkeeper. He stood as if poleaxed in the doorway, the smile on his face melting away—he plainly had no idea what expression to replace it with. As she had done, he was staring at Ro, at his naked chest; unlike her, the innkeeper's expression was horrified.

"Oh, for God's sake!" Ro shook out the shirt he carried in one fist, but one glance was enough to confirm for them all that it was so wet, he'd never succeed in pulling it on again.

Looking up, he pinned her with a rapier-sharp gaze. "Wait here while I go up and change. Do not leave this room."

If you do, I'll come after you.

She heard the unvoiced warning clearly. She set her jaw; wild visions of having him taken up by a constable, or at least being thrown out into the night, drifted temptingly across her mind . . . but it was raining cats and dogs—and sheep and goats and horses—out there, and who would do the throwing? The innkeeper and what army?

Lips as thin as his, eyes every bit as narrow, she folded her arms, watched him scoop up his sodden clothes. "I'll wait here."

She knew better than to try to deny him; never in her life had she managed that, and it didn't seem that anything had changed between them.

He nodded curtly and stalked past her to the door. The

innkeeper—still gawping—hurriedly stepped back and Ro went out.

The instant he was out of her sight, some measure of her accustomed acuity returned; her mind literally cleared. Just as well. If she knew Ro, and she did, she was going to need every wit she possessed.

The innkeeper coughed, then whispered, "Miss—if you want to slip away to your room, I'll escort you up. There's a sound bolt on the door. You could move the little chest across it, too."

She glanced at the man, had to search her memory, see-sawing wildly between the past and the present, for his name. She considered, then spoke, her voice cool, calm, faintly imperious. "That's entirely unnecessary, Bilt. You need have no fear. I have more than sufficient years in my dish to deal with his lordship."

She hoped. She most definitely prayed.

A suspicious look entered Bilt's eyes. "You and his lordship know each other?"

She could imagine what tack his mind had taken, what meaning his "know" was intended to imply. "Indeed," she replied repressively. "Childhood friends." When Bilt's suspicions didn't immediately evaporate, she added some-what waspishly, "Oh, do use your wits, man! If our relationship were any other we'd be meeting upstairs, not in your parlor."

It took a minute for Bilt to accept that not even Rogue Gerrard would be likely to prefer a parlor over a comfortable bed. Given Ro's reputation, Lydia couldn't blame Bilt for the hesitation, or his earlier suspicions.

Brusquely handing him her umbrella, she turned back into the room. "Now." Her mind was functioning again. "Lord Gerrard has clearly just arrived, and equally clearly he can't have dined. I regret the lateness of the hour, but if Mrs. Bilt could assemble a meal, both his lordship and I would be grateful." Shrugging off her cloak, she draped it over the chair, then fixed Bilt with a commanding stare. "His temper is always improved by a good meal."

And setting a table and feeding him would keep Bilt about, at the same time assuaging his unfounded fears.

Bilt blinked, then bowed. "Yes, of course, miss. An excellent notion."

The more she thought of it, the more she felt it was; dealing with Ro was going to be difficult, but perhaps there was some way in which she could turn his unexpected arrival to her advantage.

Setting her mind to that task would keep it focused on her goal—her purpose in being there—and away from what had happened the last time they'd met.

She definitely couldn't afford to think about that.

The sodden hem of her dress—only an inch or so; she'd left her pattens by the inn's door—dripped onto her shoes. Noticing, she placed herself before the fire and lifted the hem to the blaze.

And thought about how to conscript Ro to her cause.

He'd always been something of a protector. A white knight riding to her aid whenever she'd needed him. Admittedly that had been more than a decade ago, yet despite the reputation he'd gained over the intervening years, she suspected something of that white knight remained, concealed beneath his glib, sophisticated exterior.

Gentleman rake, gamester, dissolute womanizer, and gazetted libertine—all were labels she'd heard applied to him, all, as she understood it, with good cause. The entire *ton* knew of his countless affairs, of the wild gambling, the incredible wagers won and lost, the licentious dinners and parties that, if the gossipmongers were to be believed, were one step away from outright orgies.

Recollections of tales of some of his more outrageous exploits drifted through her mind; most such tales hailed from more than six years ago, but the perceived wisdom was that with maturity, he'd grown more discreet. Despite all, he'd remained a darling of the *ton*—Gerrard of Gerrard Park, as wealthy as he was handsome—but unfortunately for the matchmakers, his reputation was sufficiently enshrined in the *ton*'s collective psyche to render him ineligible as a candidate for their delicate daughters' hands.

The Bilts arrived with plates, cutlery, napkins, and platters. She nodded encouragingly, then left them to set the small round table they pulled to the center of the room.

Standing before the fire, waving her gown's hem in the warmth of the flames, she frowned. When, over the years, she'd imagined meeting Rogue Gerrard face-to-face again, she'd thought she'd see a different man, one on whom a licentious, hedonistic life had left its mark. Instead . . . when she'd looked at him, all she'd seen was the same man, just ten years older. He'd been striking as a younger man; now he was impressive—larger, harder, with a none-too-subtle edge that only underscored his innate strength.

As a young man, he'd made her heart race.

Now he set it pounding.

She heard his step on the stair. Turning, she discovered the Bilts had withdrawn, leaving all in readiness on the table. They'd laid two places although she'd already dined. Perhaps she'd have some fruit, just to keep Ro company. She crossed to one chair, looking up as the door opened.

Ro filled the doorway.

Not the Ro who had left, but one infinitely more intimidating. He was impeccably turned out, from the shining chestnut hair clustering in damp waves about his head, to the pristine, intricately tied cravat anchored with a simple gold pin, to the severe, almost austere lines of coat and waistcoat.

Dark trousers cloaked his long legs, making him appear

even taller. The aristocratic planes of his face somehow appeared harder, cleaner, more sharply delineated.

He looked at her, then at the table. Then his gaze rose to her face. Arching a brow, he entered and shut the door.

Before he could speak, she gestured to the platters. "We thought you might be hungry."

He was. Ravenous, now food was set before him. Inclining his head in acknowledgment, Ro walked around the table to hold her chair.

Although he steeled himself, it didn't help; awareness rippled through him, just because she was near.

Within arm's reach.

She sat and he stepped away, forced his feet to the other end of the small table. He sat, helped himself to a slice of game pie, then looked across the table and fixed her with a steady stare. "So—what are you doing here?"

She'd thought about spinning him some yarn, but had—wisely—decided against it; he read as much in her serene expression, in the clarity of her fine blue eyes.

Hands folded before her, she met his gaze steadily. "I'm here to retrieve a letter of Tabitha's that unintentionally went astray."

He chewed a piece of pie, remarkably succulent, and studied her. She was going to make him wring the story from her, cryptic utterance by veiled truth. Tabitha was her sister, a year or so younger, a firebrand even when he'd last met her at fifteen. Now twenty-five, Tab was, so he'd heard, a bluestocking of quite amazing degree, one who controversially preached that women, ladies in particular, had little need for men—gentlemen in particular—in their lives, and should think very hard before surrendering their freedom and fortunes into said gentlemen's hands.

Lydia, now twenty-six, six years his junior, had always been the quieter, the more reserved, the steadier and more reliable. Tab, it seemed, had become something of a female version of himself, a notorious and dangerous hellion, at least as far as the *ton* was concerned.

But what neither sister was, was weak.

He reached for the roast beef. "This letter—who has it, what's in it that makes it a threat to Tab, and why are you here trying to retrieve it, rather than she?"

Lydia's lips tightened fractionally, but she drew breath and replied, "The letter was one Tab wrote years ago, when she was seventeen." She paused, her eyes searching his, then went on. "You remember Tab—you know what she's like. How she throws herself into things, heart and soul, and the devil be damned?"

Reaching for his goblet, Ro nodded.

"Well, *before* she became a bluestocking propounding women's rights, and especially our right not to wed . . ." She hesitated.

He finished for her. "She was seventeen—she fell in love." Recalling Tabitha, nothing was more certain.

Lydia nodded. "Exactly. And she wrote to the gentleman involved, and being Tabitha, she wrote *unrestrainedly*. Without exercising the least discretion, and with an enthusiasm that . . ." She drew in a short breath. "Well, suffice it to say that if the contents of that letter became widely known now, she'd be the laughingstock of the *ton*."

Ro raised his brows. "That bad?"

Lydia grimaced. "Actually, it's worse. She'd be shunned by all her friends—the other women who think like her, and all that circle." She paused, then added, "That's her life now, and effectively, because of this letter, she stands on the brink of ruin."

Ro frowned, toyed with a portion of beef. "Why, after— what, eight years?—has this letter surfaced now?"

"Because Tab remembered it, and asked for it back."

Which suggested that the contents really were inflammatory beyond what even Tab, no wilting violet, could imagine facing down. "From the man she'd sent it to." Ro narrowed his eyes. "And he wouldn't give it back?"

"No—he agreed to give it back." Lydia looked exasperated. "Of course he did. If Tab ordered him to jump through a hoop, he would."

Ro blinked. "Who is he?"

Lydia studied him, then made up her mind. "Montague Addison."

Ro opened his eyes wide, struggled to keep his lips straight. "Addison the spineless wonder?"

Lips tight, eyes like flint, Lydia nodded. "Yes. Him."

"Well." Ro pushed away his empty plate; lifting his goblet, he sipped. "That explains a number of things." Including why Tabitha Makepeace no longer favored marriage. If as an impressionable seventeen-year-old she'd considered Montague Addison a pattern card of gentlemanly virtue, it was entirely understandable that she'd subsequently rejected wedlock. Especially to gentlemen.

"So"—Ro focused on Lydia—"Addison agreed to give the letter back. What went wrong?"

"After getting Tab's note, Addison—the *idiot*—put the letter in its envelope in his coat pocket. He said he intended to find Tab at a ball and hand it over—even though, of course, Tab rarely attends balls. And it's February, for heaven's sake! There are hardly any balls in town, and if he'd bothered to read Tab's direction on her note, he would have seen we were at home in Wiltshire. But Addison, being Addison, didn't think of any of that. He went on his usual rounds to a few parties, then, not finding Tab, went on to some hell called Lucifer's."

Ro was starting to get a very bad feeling about what might have happened, and more specifically where Tab's letter currently was. "I know it."

Hearing his clipped tone, Lydia looked at him, momentarily

distracted from her frustration with Addison. "Yes, I daresay you might." She blinked, then returned to Addison's shortcomings with a frown. "Addison lost heavily, as I understand he frequently does. He needed to write an IOU to . . . the gentleman to whom he'd lost, and—I presume he was thoroughly foxed by then—he pulled out Tab's letter and wrote his note of hand on the envelope, and gave it to . . . the gentleman."

And with that, Ro saw it all. "The gentleman being Stephen Barham, now Lord Alconbury of Upton Grange."

Lydia stilled. She held his gaze for a long moment, then reached, slowly, for a grape. "Why do you think that?" She plucked a grape, popped it into her mouth, and studied him, trying to look innocent while she chewed.

Ro smiled—not humorously. "Because Barham is a regular at Lucifer's, because Addison often tries to ingratiate himself with that crowd, because Upton Grange lies across the lane and through the woods"—with one long finger he indicated the direction—"less than a mile away, and because when you came in your hems were wet." His jaw clenched. "You'd been traipsing about the woods during a downpour of biblical proportions in the dark of night . . . why?"

He'd managed through an effort of quite remarkable magnitude to subdue the emotions roiling and welling inside him—roused by the realization of what she was about—enough to make his question reasonably unthreatening.

She still eyed him warily. After a moment, she licked her lips. "You do realize, Ro, that you have no grounds on which to interfere." She tipped up her chin. "My life is my own, and I will do as I please."

He simply looked at her and made no reply.

She drew breath, then confessed, "I arrived this afternoon, before the rain started. I need to get the letter back as soon as possible, before Barham realizes what he has. You know how fiendish he is—once he discovers the letter it'll be all over London." On the table, her fingers linked, twisted. "And on top of that, Tab and Barham have crossed swords before, and Barham came out of it badly. He would like nothing better than to expose Tab and bring her down in the eyes of the *ton*."

She tried to read his reaction in his eyes; he gave her a blank expression, but nodded.

Heartened, she continued, "So I went to look at the house—Upton Grange. To see how big it is, how hard it might be to get inside and search it. I didn't know if Barham would be there or not." Her lips turned down; she met Ro's eyes. "He is—and he's got a houseful of guests."

Ro nodded. "Indeed." He hesitated, then asked, "I assume that means you've realized you can't, at least at present, search Upton Grange for this letter?"

If fate was kind, all would be well, and he could see her on her way back to her home in Wiltshire, safe and sound, the instant the rain ceased and the roads cleared.

Instead, she frowned at him. "Of course not. I have to get the letter back, and sooner rather than later. Every day it remains in Barham's clutches increases the risk of his discovering and reading it. I would have thought that was obvious."

Ro's jaw tightened until he thought it might crack. "Perhaps. What, however, is rather less obvious is why you believe you—specifically you—have to be the one to retrieve this letter. Why not Addison, or failing that, Tab herself?"

Lydia narrowed her eyes to slits. "*That* is even more obvious. It can't be Addison because the only way he could get the letter back without raising Barham's suspicions is to honor his IOU—and he can't because he's halfway up the River Tick. None of us would dream of trusting Addison to search Barham's house and retrieve the letter by stealth—he's a bumbling incompetent. He'd be caught, and the scandal would be even worse."

"And what of Tabitha?"

Ro's eyes were a hard, bleak gray, obdurate and unyielding. Lydia looked into them, then drew a deep, resolute breath, and told him the truth knowing full well he wasn't going to like it. "It can't be Tab because when I left her she was all but irrational. She was in one of her states—she would strangle Addison if she could lay hands on him, and as for Barham . . . well, if she came upon him while searching his house, she'd probably try to strangle him, too, purely on principle. You know what she's like—the idea of her sneaking into his house and retrieving the letter without some major explosion which will result in the scandal of the year is pure fantasy."

Ro opened his mouth; she raised a hand, silencing him. "Being quiet—getting things done without causing a stir—is not Tabitha's strong suit." She held his gaze. "It is, however, mine."

Eyes like shards of flint pinned her. "And what do you imagine will happen when you're caught, as you most likely will be? Do you think the scandal will be any less?"

Calmly confident, she let her lips curve. "Actually, I suspect the tale won't even get an airing."

He frowned. "Why? What difference—"

When he broke off, understanding dawning in his eyes, she let the curve of her lips deepen. "Precisely. While Tab is widely known as the firebrand of the family, the termagant, I'm equally well-known as the quiet and reserved sister, the always perfectly behaved, decorous sister. What the *ton* will believe of Tab, they won't believe of me. If Barham does catch me—and he'll be much less likely to catch me than Tab, who's never been any good at subterfuge—even if he does, and he's stupid enough to try to spread the tale, even and including the contents of Tab's letter . . . what are the odds that anyone will believe him?"

Ro sat perfectly still, his eyes locked with hers. Minutes

ticked by, then he stirred. "You're deliberately risking your reputation in order to save Tabitha's."

She let her smile fade until her resolution shone clearly. "It's the sort of thing a sister does."

Ro held her gaze, his expression unreadable, then he scowled. "Why the devil aren't you married?"

He felt like running his hands through his hair. And tugging. Why wasn't she married and safely ensconced before some gentleman's hearth, said gentleman's responsibility and not his, protected from all danger—protected most especially from him? He could see where this was leading, and it wasn't good—especially for her, let alone him.

She blinked at him, then laughed—a sound he'd forgotten, had tried to forget, had almost succeeded in burying in his memories.

It shivered through him like a caress.

"Oh, Ro—surely you don't imagine I'm risking my chance to make a good match with this?" The look she bent on him was gently patronizing. "I'm twenty-six—I've had my time on the marriage mart, and didn't like any of the offerings."

That was something he didn't understand; although he'd kept his distance, he knew she'd been courted by numerous eligibles, gentlemen as handsome and in some cases even wealthier than he. He'd steeled himself to hear of her engagement, expected the blow to fall a number of times, but it had never happened. The most he'd heard were whispers that she was finicky; even in her rejections, Lydia had been reserved, forever discreet.

She was watching him, that same almost-smile playing about her lips. "I had my choices and I made them, and I don't regret even one. So now I'm all but an ape leader, and thus protecting my reputation is no longer the absolute imperative it once was. If necessary, as it is in this case, I can, and will, put it at risk."

More than anything else, her calm, even, serenely rational tone convinced him just how set on her chosen path—on retrieving Tabitha's letter—she was. She'd thought the matter through, weighed the risks and her chances, and was convinced her course was right.

Neither she nor Tabitha was weak—because, as he knew, they were both bone-stubborn.

Arguing directly against her wasn't going to work.

"Lydia." He glanced down at his hands clasped on the table, marshaling his arguments, controlling his tone—hiding all evidence of the primitive response her "plan" evoked— then he looked up and met her eyes. "You cannot go waltzing into Barham's house and search for that letter—not now, while he has guests there. After they leave . . . it might be possible, but you're going to have to wait until then."

She held his gaze; he could read very little in her eyes or expression—no hint of how she would react. But there was that same calmness, a cool, serene steadfastness that he recognized from long ago . . . for the first time in many years he let himself wonder what she was seeing, what she was thinking, when she looked at him like that.

Then the curve of her lips deepened; she looked down as she pushed back her chair. Then she looked up and met his gaze.

"Tomorrow I'm going to start searching Upton Grange for Tab's letter." She tilted her head, studying him still. "If you wish, you can help me."

She rose, still holding his gaze. "But what you can't do, Ro, is stop me." She paused, then added, "That I won't allow, so please don't try."

With a nod, she turned away.

Ro pushed back his chair and rose.

Reaching the door, she waved him back. "No—stay and have some brandy and get warm." She paused, the door open, looking back through the wavering firelight at him. "Good night. Perhaps I'll see you in the morning."

Stepping through the door, she shut it gently behind her.

Ro stared at the wooden panels, then dropped back into his chair, scrubbed his hands over his face, and groaned.

After a moment, he lowered his hands, sat back; spreading his arms wide, palms up, he looked up at the ceiling. "*Why?*"

No answer came. Disgusted, he reached for the bottle Bilt had left, poured an inch of brandy into his goblet, then pushed his chair around and leaned back, sipping, his gaze on the dying flames.

He couldn't stop his thoughts from racing back through the years to when he and Lydia had last spoken. To that fateful summer ten years ago.

The daughters of the eccentric branch of the Wiltshire Makepeaces, their father a scholar who although born into it largely shunned the *ton*, their mother a well-bred matron who juggled her wifely duties with those of a mother as best she could, throughout their childhoods, Lydia and Tabitha had been sent every summer to stay with their mother's cousin's family, whose estate shared a boundary with Gerrard Park.

Although six years older than Lydia, he'd noticed her instantly. She'd captured his attention, his eye, his imagination, even when she'd been six years old and he a superior twelve. The difference in ages hadn't mattered, not then, or later.

Later, when she'd been sixteen, innocent and untouched, and he'd been an already polished, already experienced twenty-two. The polish and experience hadn't mattered either, not on that day he'd met her in the orchard, as he often had.

They'd walked, talked, as they always had. She'd been

full of plans for her come-out the following year, excitedly looking forward to waltzing and being courted by gentlemen—a strange species she'd had little exposure to hidden away in Wiltshire with her reclusive parents.

She'd asked him, playfully innocent, to waltz with her, there under the apple trees. He'd smiled and obliged, humming a tune with her, never dreaming . . .

The halcyon day had whirled about them, and something else had taken hold, and risen, softly, gently, through him.

He'd stopped humming, slowed; when he'd halted she'd been lost in his eyes, and he in hers.

He'd bent his head and kissed her. Even at twenty-two, he'd known how to steal a woman's wits with a kiss, but that wasn't how he'd kissed her. He'd kissed her gently, tentatively . . . worshipfully.

It was that last that had opened his eyes, that when he'd ended the kiss and lifted his head, had had him looking at her in a completely different light.

There'd been stars in her eyes; he'd seen them, understood—and panicked.

He'd smiled charmingly, made some excuse, left her—and run.

As fast and as far as he could. His twenty-two-year-old mind had been adamant that she hadn't been, could not have been, his destiny.

From his earliest years he'd been set on being the rogue his nurse had named him, a hellion, a scapegrace, a gamester, a libertine. From infancy he'd been called a rogue; he'd never imagined being anything but, never imagined not living up to the expectation.

So he'd run from her, and had forced himself to never look back—never to go looking for her in the orchards again.

Staring into the flames, Ro drained the brandy, closed his

eyes, and sighed. The next four or so years of his life had gone in a whirl of hedonistic dissipation that had established his reputation beyond question. A rogue he'd been named and a rogue he'd become, and had taken a wholly male, wholly unfettered delight in so doing.

But then . . .

Entirely unexpectedly, things had changed. Dissipation had grown boring. The diversions that previously had held his attention had palled. He'd drawn back from the crowd he'd run with, started looking for other activities—activities that could absorb him, that could occupy a mind he'd deliberately suppressed and allowed to stagnate while pursuing his misguided dream.

From behind the rogue a different man had emerged, one he'd spent the last six years learning, developing, evolving.

But he'd been such an excellent rogue, the reputation had stuck, regardless of his absence from the scene.

Even now, those who looked for him in the gaming hells and didn't find him assumed he was at some more exclusive venue. If he no longer attended the scandalously licentious dinners and parties, everyone assumed he was engaged in some secretive affair of even more scandalous proportions.

Many continued to invite him to their country houses for orgiastic revels; when he failed to show, they were entirely convinced he was attending someone else's more exclusive event.

He hadn't been above using his reputation for his own ends, as a shield to repel the matchmaking mamas and their darling daughters. As a deflecting screen that often led those he dealt with in business to underestimate him, always an advantage.

Opening his eyes, Ro stared at the fire, now reduced to glowing embers. The food, the flames, and the brandy had done their work; he was warm again.

He sighed. Setting the goblet on the table, he rose, and headed for the door. As he silently climbed the stairs, he wondered what Lydia would think, how she would view him, if she knew he was now one of the major philanthropists in England.

He hadn't intended that to be his destiny, but fate, circumstance, and coincidence had led him in that direction, and he'd discovered a real talent, a calling, and others who shared it. At first they'd eyed him askance, knowing his reputation, but he'd worked diligently on each project he'd undertaken, and gradually they'd come to accept him. To understand him.

To understand that even more than the rest of them, anonymity was vital to him.

If it ever became known that he—Rogue Gerrard—the most celebrated rogue in the *ton*, had reformed six years ago, he'd instantly be elevated to the very top of the matchmakers' lists. He was thirty-two, with no close male relative, an ancient title, excellent connections, possessed of a large house and significant wealth. They'd come at him in droves.

He still wondered what Lydia would think of him now . . . if she knew the truth.

Reaching his room at the front of the house, glancing at its mate and wondering if Lydia was behind its closed door, he opened his and went in.

Crossing to his portmanteau, he rummaged inside and drew out the stack of invitations his scarifyingly efficient secretary, Martin Camberthorne, never let him leave his orbit without. The cards covered all the events to which Ro had been invited from yesterday through to the end of next week—the period he'd expected to spend in London, meeting with other philanthropists on a proposal to provide basic schooling around the docks.

Standing before the dressing table, using the light from

the single candle left burning there, Ro flipped through the cards, searching . . . until he found the one he sought.

Lifting it from the pile, he checked the inscribed details. Jaw setting, he tossed the card on the dressing table; the rest of the cards in his hand, he turned away.

Fate, circumstance, and coincidence, it seemed, were once again taking a hand in his life.

Chapter Two

The sound of a door closing reached through the fogs of sleep clouding Ro's mind and prodded at his consciousness. But he knew it was early; he grunted and pulled the covers over his ears . . . but the oddity of his being able to hear a door closing, let alone footsteps sneaking past his door, the creak of a stair . . .

He mentally shut his ears, sank into the bed. Tried to wrap his mind in the elusive webs of sleep.

But recollections, and the realization of where he was— not in his bed at the Park but in the Coppingford Arms— dripped, point by point, into his mind.

Then he remembered who else was there.

Abruptly he opened his eyes, tossed back the covers, swung his legs out of the bed, and sat up. Eyeing his closed door, he swore.

The door he'd heard shutting had been the one next door; it had been Lydia who had crept down the stairs.

"Damnation!" Coming to his feet, ignoring his naked

state, he strode to the door, cracked it open, and shouted for shaving water.

He assumed she was breakfasting, but he knew, just knew, that the instant she'd finished she'd be off through the woods to try to break into Upton Grange.

Bilt arrived with steaming water, Ro's boots, and his brushed breeches. Ro took possession, waved Bilt away, then shaved, washed, and dressed in double time. A brief glance out of the window showed a leaden sky, but at least it had stopped gushing.

Ten minutes later, still fiddling with his cravat pin and easing his shoulders beneath his coat, he stepped off the stairs—and paused. From the tap came men's voices, along with the sounds and smells of breakfast; the door to the parlor was shut.

Bilt appeared from the nether regions carrying a loaded tray.

Ro stopped him with a look. "Who else is here?"

"Just two commercial travelers, my lord, stranded just as you were, although they got in before the storm. We'll have your breakfast ready in a jiffy if you'd like to wait in the tap."

Ro's mind raced; he didn't know what name Lydia was using, or if she'd brought a maid, a coachman, how she'd reached the inn. He inwardly frowned. "I'll breakfast in the parlor. The lady won't object."

Turning, he strode for the parlor door.

Behind him, Bilt shifted. "Well, seeing the lady's already gone out, I suppose there's no harm."

Ro halted. He turned, pinned Bilt with a razor-sharp gaze. "When did she leave?"

Eyes widening, Bilt shuffled. "Ah . . . had breakfast in her room early, then left . . . oh, half an hour or so ago?"

Ro swore. "On foot?"

Bilt swallowed, and nodded. "Headed up the lane, she did. To the right toward Buckworth."

Still swearing under his breath, Ro headed for the inn's main door.

"My lord—your breakfast . . . ?"

"I'll be back in half an hour," Ro growled. "You can serve me then. In the damn parlor!"

Pushing through the front door, he paused for an instant on the stoop to gauge the condition of the lane, then stepped down and, avoiding the worst of the churned morass of mud, picked his way across to the verge bordering the wood.

Once on the sodden grass, on firmer footing, he turned left and jogged in the opposite direction to which Lydia had gone.

She wasn't going to Buckworth; as she'd no doubt discovered yesterday, a rarely used rear drive from Upton Grange joined the lane just a little way along. Ro knew of it because he'd used that approach on the many occasions he'd driven down from Gerrard Park to visit his fellow notorious hellion, Stephen Barham, during the days of his misspent youth.

Now Lord Alconbury, unlike Ro, Barham hadn't reformed. Indeed, if the rumors were correct, he'd sunk even deeper into debauchery.

Ro estimated that by now Lydia would be nearing the house. He had to reach her quickly, which was why he was making for the more direct path Barham and his male guests used to visit the inn.

Reaching the path, he turned up it. Overhanging trees had protected it from the worst of the storm, but it was still slippery; striding, jogging, running whenever he could, he tried not to think of Lydia being found by Barham's men and dragged inside to face their master—or potentially worse, being discovered sneaking about the house by one of Barham's lecherous male guests.

Passing through a clearing, he squinted up at the sky. Overcast though it was, it nevertheless confirmed that the hour was, as he'd thought, a ridiculously early one for him—or any of his ilk—to be awake, let alone about. He doubted it was yet seven o'clock.

Lips tight, he dived into the woods beyond the clearing, the last band of trees before the lawns surrounding the house. He slowed as he reached the edge of the trees. Upton Grange lay before him, a squat gray stone pile with few redeeming features, placed in the center of an open expanse. Judging by the overgrown state of the lawns, Barham wasn't as plump in the pocket as he once had been.

Behind the leaded windows, Ro caught glimpses of movement, both on the ground floor and on the floor above, in the bedchambers assigned to guests, and even, he noted, in the master suite.

Inwardly snorting, unsurprised, hands on his hips, Ro looked around, searching along the tree line. Catching his breath, conscious of his heart thudding—knowing it wasn't from exertion alone—he prayed Lydia hadn't been so foolish as to go up to the house.

Finding no sign of her, he debated, then started to follow the trees around the house, keeping sufficiently back under their cover so that no one glancing out from the house would see him. He headed toward the rear drive, quietly searching.

He glimpsed her through the trees from some distance away. The relief that washed through him was shocking. Jaw clenching, he circled around to come up behind her. She was standing just inside the tree line, well-wrapped in a blue pelisse, her furled umbrella held before her, her hands folded over the handle as she stared at the house.

Her expression suggested she was supremely irritated.

Lydia literally leapt when hard fingers closed about her elbow. Yet even before she'd swung to face Ro, she'd known it was he; he was the only man whose touch could reduce her to breathlessness in less than a second.

His face was set, utterly immobile; his gray eyes were hard. "Come away." He turned and proceeded to drag her—haul her—deeper into the woods, away from the house.

"No!" she hissed. She tried to dig in her heels.

His next tug very nearly lifted her off her feet, reminding her how strong he was—deliberately, she had not a doubt. She narrowed her eyes at him, but couldn't stop her feet from stumbling in his wake. "Ro—I warned you—"

"There's nothing you can do at present." He didn't even glance at her. "No need to stand there waiting for someone to notice you."

She glanced back at the house, rapidly receding behind the screen of trees. She frowned, faced forward, and reluctantly started walking of her own accord. He eased his grip on her arm; he didn't let her go but shortened his stride to match hers. His hold on her arm was now more to steady her over the rough ground than anything else.

Frown deepening, still puzzled, she said, "I thought they'd still be asleep—that I could slip inside and start searching while everyone was still abed. Who would have thought they'd be up so early?"

Ro gritted his teeth. "They're not up early. They haven't yet gone to bed." Or, at least, not to their own beds. Not to sleep.

Lydia glanced at him, then her frown was erased by dawning comprehension. "Oh," she said, and looked ahead.

"Oh, indeed." Ro told himself to stop talking; instead he heard himself say, "Can you imagine what would have happened if you'd gone waltzing into that?" The likely outcome didn't bear thinking about.

She sniffed and elevated her nose. "I'm perfectly aware that Barham's entertainments are popularly described as being one step away from an orgy."

"One step away...?" His incredulous tone would have done credit to Kean. Gripping her elbow more tightly, he swung her onto the path to the inn, instinctively steadying her as she teetered on her pattens. "For your information"—he bit the words off—"there is no such thing as being 'one step away from an orgy.' You either have an orgy, or you don't—there are no shades of gray when it comes to orgies. And you may take it from one who knows, Barham's entertainments very definitely qualify as orgies."

He felt her sidelong glance, then she looked ahead.

"You're trying to scare me."

"Am I succeeding?"

"I'm going to search Upton Grange for Tab's letter—you might as well accept that. I won't change my mind."

They strode along the path in silence.

A silence that seemed full of whirling thoughts, plans, hopes, emotions; Lydia wasn't sure what, but she could feel the atmosphere between them thickening with every step.

She'd dreamed of him last night. For the first time in years, he'd come to her in that shadowy world, a figure conjured by her heart, by her deepest yearnings. That, of itself, was hardly surprising; she'd dreamed of him for more years than she cared to count, just not recently. But what had unsettled her about this latest dream was that he had no longer been the twenty-two-year-old who had stolen her heart with just one innocent kiss in an orchard; last night, he'd been as he now was—and his kiss had been anything but innocent.

With a wrench, she hauled her mind from reliving the dream; if she did, she'd blush, and he—far too quick where she was concerned—would see, and very likely guess the cause.

The mortification she would feel didn't bear dwelling on; she'd much rather walk in on a full-blown orgy.

Apropos of which . . . She glanced at him. "When would

be the best time to search Barham's house? The best time *today.*"

His face was already set; it couldn't get any harder. They reached the lane; he turned her along the grassy verge, heading back to the inn. "Later. Early afternoon is usually quietest. The guests are all abed, and the staff have cleaned up, and are back behind the green baize door resting before the evening rush."

She nodded; that made sense. "Very well. I'll go back then—"

"No. You won't." Ro halted. They'd reached a point opposite the inn; the muddy river of the road lay between them and the front step. He met her gaze. "I'll go. I know the house. I know where Barham's most likely to keep any notes of hand."

She looked up at him, entirely fearlessly, as she always had. Studied him in that calm, collected way of hers; then, it seemed, she looked inward.

A frown formed in her eyes, then she refocused on his. She drew in a quick breath, seemed to steel herself a little. "Thank you for the offer, Ro, but this is my quest. I know going into Barham's house carries a certain risk, but I want to do it, to sneak in there, search for Tab's letter, and sneak safely out again. Or at least try. As you said, I'm the sensible sister, the wise, cautious, never outrageous sister." She paused, then said, "This is my time to act precipitously, to be just a little wild—to do something exciting."

She held his gaze, then quietly added, "I suspect you, of all people, will understand that."

He looked down into her clear blue eyes, and wished he could say he didn't. But he did.

Jaw setting, he bent and swung her up in his arms.

She smothered a shriek, then, as he carried her across the mud-clogged lane, she studied his face.

His features felt like stone; he didn't meet her eyes.

Reaching the inn, he set her down on the stoop; while she slipped out of her pattens, he scraped his boots on the bar by the door. She opened the door; he followed her through.

Stopping just inside, she looked into his face. "What did that mean?"

It took a moment before he could force the words out. "It means I'll take you to the Grange. I know how to get you inside."

Her eyes lit. "You do?"

He was quite sure he was insane even to be thinking of it. "Yes." He took her arm. "We can discuss it in the parlor." He propelled her toward the door. "I haven't had breakfast yet and I need to eat. My brain works much better when I feed it."

"Lord Alconbury requests the pleasure of Lord Gerrard's company for revels unfettered to be held at Upton Grange between the 23rd and the 27th of February." Lydia stared at the invitation Ro had pulled from his pocket and handed her. "That's from yesterday to three days hence."

She glanced at Ro, seated at the other end of the small table in the parlor. He was busily consuming a large pile of sausages, eggs, bacon, and ham, washed down with copious drafts of coffee; she'd consented to being served with tea. "What are 'revels unfettered'?"

He chewed, swallowed. "Exactly what they sound like."

Looking back at the card, she raised her brows. Apparently she was about to experience an orgy firsthand.

"If you'd rather not go, I'm sure I can manage by myself."

She looked up to find Ro pushing aside his empty plate. Across the table, she met his gaze. "No, no—as I said, I'm set on excitement, and who knows? It might be quite . . . illuminating."

She wasn't sure but she thought he growled; ignoring the low rumble, she refocused on the card.

Tapping it, she frowned. "This says nothing about any companions. Won't they think it rather odd if you turn up with a lady in tow?"

She glanced up in time to see an odd look pass through his eyes—wary, cautious, and resigned all at once.

He met her eyes, hesitated. She raised her brows higher.

"A lady, yes." His accents were clipped. "But a courtesan . . . no."

She felt her eyes widen. "I'm to pass myself off as a courtesan?" This quest of hers got better and better. Tab would turn green with envy.

Ro's lips, already thin, tightened into a grim line. "As I said, there's no need for you—"

"How do I go about it?" She sat forward, fixing him with eager eyes. "I don't look like a courtesan—no one seeing me would imagine I am. I presume I'll need a disguise, or to at least in some way change my appearance. How are we going to manage it? What should we do?"

The look in his eyes made her feel terribly daring, as if she were baiting a tiger. As long as the table remained between them, she felt perfectly safe in doing so, confident she could hide the effect he had on her enough to keep it from him. When he touched her, was close to her, she found it difficult to think; when he'd swung her up into his arms, she'd had to struggle to relocate her wits, but luckily he hadn't asked her anything while he'd carried her across the road. Interacting with him in this not-quite-acceptable fashion was exhilarating, as if she were flirting, but with something far more dangerous than inconsequential phrases.

As if she were taking a real risk.

Quite why she felt so tempted, why she was giving in to the temptation to tease him she wasn't sure, but she could see from his expression that he wasn't, even now, sure if she was intending to or not. Regardless of what his reputation might suggest, she knew he would never step over the line, never retaliate in any way that would shock or frighten her, not Ro. With her, he would always be the perfect gentleman.

That didn't mean that she hadn't—wasn't—fantasizing over not being a perfect lady with him.

Inwardly she sighed; she looked again at the card. Of course she wouldn't actually *do* anything outrageous, because as everyone knew, she was the sensible, well-behaved sister.

"The first thing we have to do is find you a gown." He spoke slowly, each word distinct. "And . . . we'll need to do something about your hair."

"Oh?" She opened her eyes wide. "What?"

"Lord Gerrard! Good afternoon, my lord—welcome to Upton Grange. It's been some years since we've had the pleasure."

"Good afternoon, Grafton." In the front hall of Upton Grange, Ro smiled, distantly charming, at Barham's butler, and continued in a bored drawl, "I'm sure it will prove a pleasure to be back. Getting here, however, sadly was otherwise— my carriage broke an axle in this atrocious mud."

Ro cast a heavy-lidded look at Lydia, beside him. She was swathed in her cloak and hanging on his arm, doing a reasonable imitation of a petulant pout. Her hood was up, anchored with pins, screening her face from idle observers. "My . . . lady and I had to make do with that cart you see rattling away." He waved languidly back at the drive. "We're hoping the comfort here will eradicate the memories."

"Indeed, my lord. Of course." Grafton, a large, physically imposing, barrel-chested man of limited imagination, signaled to his footmen with exaggerated self-importance. "I trust there were no injuries?"

"My coachman suffered a knock on the head, but is recovering. Our luggage will follow in due course . . . unless I'm summoned back to deal with the situation. Regardless, as after all these years I've finally managed to find time to attend another of Stephen's excellent events—and my lady, having heard tales of these affairs, was eager for the experience—we came on."

"The master will be delighted, my lord. We've a chamber prepared, if you care to go up?"

"Thank you. I believe we will." Ro allowed his gaze to linger, openly lasciviously, on Lydia, then he looked at Grafton. "One thing, however—while the lack of our luggage will not severely inconvenience me, my lady dressed for travel and is therefore without a suitable gown for the festivities. As I recall, Stephen keeps a store of attire for just such emergencies."

"Indeed, my lord. In the Green Room." Grafton bobbed and bowed as Ro strolled slowly to the stairs. "I'm sure the master would be only too delighted for your companion to make her choice."

"Thank you." Ro waved a languid dismissal as he and Lydia started up the stairs in a footman's wake. "Pray convey my compliments to your master when he awakes."

"I will, my lord. Certainly." Halting at the bottom of the stairs, Grafton went on, "I'm sure you recall our schedule, my lord—breakfast will be available in the dining room from four, with dinner to follow at ten o'clock."

"After which the festivities will commence." Ro smiled tightly as he went up the stairs; he had indeed remembered Barham's program—he intended to have Lydia safely back at the inn, with her sister's letter, by four o'clock. "Thank you, Grafton. If we need anything further, we'll ring."

With similar obsequiousness, the footman led them through a gallery and down a corridor to a large bedchamber overlooking the woods to one side of the house.

The instant the door shut behind him, Lydia put back her hood, carefully lifting the material over the knot of sheeny

walnut curls that her maid, under Ro's direction, had fashioned. "Well! That wasn't so hard."

"That," he informed her, his accents clipped, "was the
easy part. The part that comes next, and the one after that,
might not be so much to your taste."

Untying her cloak strings, she opened her eyes at him.
"So what comes next? A gown?"

He nodded. "Wait here. I'll go and fetch a few possible
outfits, and you can select whichever you fancy." He headed
for the door.

"Wait—I'll come, too. I can choose the gown there—it'll
be faster that way."

"No." His hand on the doorknob, he looked back. This entire
plan of his was insane, yet here he was, doing what she wanted.
Indulging her with an adventure. Be that as it may, given the
other items for borrowing for his guests' indulgence displayed in
Stephen Barham's Green Room the last time Ro had seen it, he
wasn't prepared to indulge her that far. "You stay here. The
fewer people who have any chance to see your face, the better."

He didn't wait for any argument, but opened the door and
went out, closing it firmly behind him.

They were safe enough for the moment; Barham and all
his guests would be sound asleep. They wouldn't start to stir
until after three o'clock. He and Lydia had until then—over
two hours—to find her sister's letter and depart.

But first she needed a disguise.

The Green Room was as he remembered it, but choosing a
gown proved more problematic than he'd expected; not one
garment hanging in the big armoire was in any way decorous. In the end, he picked out three gowns; with them draped
over his arm, he made his way back to their bedchamber.

Lydia was standing by the window looking out; she turned
as he entered, then, curiosity in her face, came to join him at
the foot of the bed as he laid the gowns out.

He stepped back. "These were the most . . . normal gowns there."

"This one's pretty." She picked up a sleek gown in cerise silk, reminiscent of something from a sheik's harem with its overlays of gossamer and tulle. He watched as she blinked, then stared as the various layers shook out—revealing that the opaque silk reached barely to mid-thigh, and featured a plunging neckline that would expose significantly more of her breasts than a chemise.

Lydia swallowed. "Perhaps not." She could feel faint color in her cheeks as she laid the scandalous gown back down.

An errant thought swirled through her head: Had Ro imagined how she would appear in each gown? Was that how he'd chosen them?

The second gown was fashioned from the palest of pale green satins. She held it up. It took a moment of puzzling before she worked out that it was designed in the manner of a Roman toga—of sorts. It hung from one shoulder, and the drape covered her breasts entirely—but the back was all but missing, down to well below her waist . . . "I . . . think not."

Laying it back down, she reached for the last of the three gowns, a confection in white silk and dark blue lace, praying for a miracle. She couldn't help but wonder if Ro had deliberately chosen gowns she couldn't possibly bring herself to wear so she would have to, by her own choice, remain in the room while he searched for the letter.

The last of his selections, however, restored her faith in him, at least as far as his willingness to allow her to join him in the search.

Holding the gown up, she studied it, then turned to the cheval glass in the corner of the room and held the gown against her. "Is it supposed to be a milkmaid's dress?" Ro shifted to stand behind her. She looked at his face in the mirror.

Studying her reflection, he grimaced. "More along the lines of La Petit Trianon, I expect."

She looked again at the gown. "You may be right." The gown was waisted in the style of the last century, the skirts quite full with a ruffled petticoat beneath; her legs would be amply screened. The back neckline was high, shallowly scooped and edged with the dark blue lace, perfectly acceptable even though the dark blue lacings down the center back were far more obvious than the current mode—almost an invitation. Both bodice and skirt were constructed of vertical panels edged with the lace; overall it was a very pretty, frothy gown.

The risqué part—there was one, of course—was the upper bodice.

It was scooped, but the white silk was cut wide and low so it framed rather than concealed her breasts. However, the space between was filled with blue lace; fitting the gown against her, she judged that the lace infill was both dense enough and rose high enough to conceal all she needed to conceal.

She nodded. "This one." She made her voice firm and definite; she didn't want Ro trying to argue her out of the adventure. Especially as she was enjoying it—enjoying the excitement, the thrill of the illicit, the unexpected titillation of looming danger.

Glancing up, she saw Ro's face harden. He'd still been studying her reflection. Lifting his gaze, he met her eyes in the mirror—curtly nodded.

Turning away, he looked at the clock on the mantelpiece. "You'd better get into it then. The sooner you do, the sooner we can search."

And the sooner he could end the torture. Ro couldn't believe he'd agreed to this escapade, that he'd actually planned it. He was already in pain, and that was only going to get worse.

Holding the white and blue gown, Lydia looked around, but of course there was no screen in the room. Feeling as if his jaw would crack, he said, "I'll stand at the window and look out. You'll need help with those laces. Tell me when you're ready." He managed not to growl.

With every evidence of cheery enthusiasm—she was patently enjoying every moment—she watched him stalk to the window, then turned to the bed.

Over the rustle of silks, he heard her humming. He tracked what she was doing by the familiar little sounds; he stared out of the window, but saw absolutely nothing of the trees and unkempt lawn.

In his mind's eye, the vision of her in the gown took shape. He saw . . . considered, then decided speaking was the less painful course. "You won't be able to wear a chemise under that."

The sudden silence spoke volumes; even the rustling stopped. But then she made a little huffing sound; a second later, he caught a soft swish—and tried not to dwell on what it meant, not to let his mind form the image . . .

"I'm ready."

He wasn't, but . . . mentally girding his loins, he turned.

She was standing before the cheval glass, the gown's skirts a froth of silk and contrasting lace about her; she was holding the bodice in place with both hands cupping her breasts—and frowning.

He focused on her back—much safer than focusing on her front. The sides of the gown gaped to well below her waist, waiting to be laced up the center, exposing an expanse of naked porcelain skin he tried hard not to see. Halting behind her, he caught the ends of the laces, and started threading them through the eyelets, expertly tugging them tight as he went.

It was a service he'd performed for countless ladies before; he didn't need to think to accomplish the task. He fought to keep his mind blank instead, devoid of lecherous thoughts.

He was succeeding reasonably well until she wriggled and said, "I hadn't realized it was so small."

He glanced up, into the mirror, directly at the delectable ivory mounds more revealed than concealed by the dark blue lace. Swallowing a curse, he immediately looked down at the laces between his fingers; since the age of sixteen, she'd grown—rather more than he'd imagined.

She wriggled and tugged.

"Hold still." When she grudgingly did, he spoke through clenched teeth, "It's supposed to be like that."

Just like the back of the gown; when hanging, the laces could be done up to the top of the back, but when a woman was inserted into it, the laces only closed to lower mid-back.

Leaving the back suggestively gaping, the ends of the long laces dangling . . . he tied them in a tight double knot.

One even he would have trouble undoing.

She humphed, then realized he'd finished. Eyes suddenly wide, she glanced over her shoulder—first at him as he stepped back, then she tried to see down her back. "What . . . ?"

Whisking around, she put her back to the cheval glass and peered over her shoulder. "Oh, good Lord!"

Precisely his thought. Faced with the fullness of his folly, with the fabulous sight of her so enticingly, not to say provocatively displayed, all he could do was grit his teeth and bear it. And try not to stare, or too openly salivate.

In devising this plan to allow her to participate in the adventure of recovering her sister's letter, he hadn't—definitely hadn't—foreseen this.

Not only was the gown a rake's erotic dream, but with her hair up in the artful knot on top of her head, with just a few flirting tendrils hanging down on either side to brush her shoulders, she looked like a lady just begging to be tumbled.

"Yes, well." He heard his voice, the accents hard and clipped. "There you are." Obviously.

Steeling himself, he reached out and grasped her elbow. "Come on—the faster we find that damn letter, the sooner you can get out of that gown."

She threw him a strange, arrested look, but allowed him to lead her to the door.

He opened it and looked out. All was silent, somnolent, no guests or scurrying servants about. Drawing Lydia through the door, he closed it, then took her hand. "This way."

She followed beside and a little behind him as he retraced their steps to the gallery, crossed it, and headed down a corridor into another wing.

Lydia glanced around, taking in the closed doors they passed; very conscious that behind each lay guests she had no wish to meet, she tried to tiptoe in her half boots. That only made the sensation she was trying to ignore all the more intense; she'd never worn a gown, let alone one like this, with no chemise underneath.

With very step, the fine frilled petticoat weighed down by the gathers of the delicate silk and lace skirts shifted and caressed her bare flesh. Above her garters circling just above her knees, she was naked. Despite the gown—or rather in some strange manner because of it—she felt exposed in some titillating, highly illicit, intensely suggestive way.

In demanding adventure, she hadn't imagined this, but she wasn't about to complain. For the first time in her life, she felt truly alive; for the first time in her life, she could perceive what drew Tabitha to bold and outrageous actions.

Reaching the end of the wing, Ro turned down a secondary stair.

Lydia leaned close as they went down, whispered in his ear, "Where are we going?"

"The desk in the library," Ro whispered back. "Barham keeps all his vowels in the drawers."

She thought about that, thought about how unerringly Ro was leading her through Barham's house. "You know him rather well, don't you?"

They'd reached the ground floor; he halted before a door and met her eyes. "Knew." Then he opened the door; her hand still locked in his, he towed her through.

She assumed being towed was the norm for courtesans.

The room was empty. Releasing her hand, Ro turned back and shut the door. When she looked at him, he nodded down the room. "There's the desk."

She turned; her eyes widened. "It's enormous."

"It was his father's and grandfather's—now it's his." Ro crossed to the massive, ornately carved desk planted like a squat oak stump before the middle of the three bay windows. Lydia trailed after him.

The windows sported deep window seats with thick red velvet cushions; they looked out on the same side of the house as the bedchamber they'd been shown to. The desk stood ten feet or so before the central window; an admiral's chair sat between. Rounding the end of the desk, Lydia saw its unusual length was filled with drawers, with only one relatively small kneehole between.

Eyes widening, she counted four sets of five drawers. "Twenty," she said helpfully.

Ro grimaced. "Presumably he doesn't keep vowels in them all." He pulled the top drawer at one end open.

He stared down at the contents, then opened the next drawer, and the next. And the next.

Then he stood back and swore.

He'd presumed wrongly. It appeared that Stephen Barham, Lord Alconbury, had saved every note of hand he'd ever received—and as Ro knew, his lordship was over thirty-five, and had been a hardened gambler for the last fifteen years.

Lydia, round-eyed, stared. "It'll take forever to search through all these."

Ro's face set. He glanced at the clock sitting on the desk. "We have an hour and a half." He pushed the admiral's chair toward Lydia. "You take that side, I'll take this."

And with any luck, they'd either meet in the middle or find Tabitha's letter—before Barham or anyone else found them.

Chapter Three

"This is absurd." Lydia stared at the assortment of notes she'd checked and stacked on the desktop; they'd been working for ten minutes, but she'd barely made a dent in the papers crammed in the top right-hand drawer.

One drawer of the ten it fell to her to search.

"I thought gentlemen returned notes of hand when they were redeemed."

"Most do." Standing beside the chair in which she was sitting, Ro was sorting steadily through the papers crammed into the top drawer to the left of the kneehole. "But there are other ways. Some sign across the original note, signifying it's been paid. Like this." He showed her one such IOU, with Barham's signature scrawled across Rigby Landsdowne's.

"But why does Barham keep the wretched things?"

Ro shrugged. "Some men put deer heads on the wall—think of these as Barham's trophies. He's been a deep gambler for a very long time."

"Clearly." Lydia poked at three notes she'd lined up on the desk. "This one's from Lord Shillingborne ten years ago, and this from a Mr. Swanson five years ago, while this last one is from Viscount Swinborne from three months ago."

Ro humphed, then he paused, staring at the notes in his hands. Then he quickly shuffled through the other papers in the drawer he was ransacking. "Are all your notes from people with names starting with S?"

Lydia glanced at him, then flicked through the notes she'd sorted, then pulled a handful more from the drawer and checked them. "Yes. Everyone is an S."

She leaned across to look at the notes Ro was shoving back into his drawer. "What were yours?"

"People with names starting with L."

"Which means . . ." Suppressed excitement in her voice, Lydia looked along the front of the desk to the first drawer.

Ro shut the one he'd been searching and opened it. He pulled out three notes, looked. "Yes—these are the A's."

"Well at least that makes more sense." Lydia stuffed the notes she'd been sorting back into the open drawer. No need to take care; there was no sense to Barham's jumble within each drawer. "Here—give me some."

First Ro checked the second drawer. "Bs. Good. All the A's are in this one drawer."

He lifted out a pile of notes from the top drawer and set it on the desk. Lydia pounced on it and started flicking through the papers—of all sizes, shapes, and construction. Some had started life as tailor's bills; she found one that was an account from a modiste, and wondered what Lord Avinley, a renowned bachelor, had been up to.

They searched steadily, fired by their deductions.

Then Ro slowed, stopped. Lydia glanced up at him; he was frowning at the piles of notes. "What?"

Ro grimaced. "You said Addison hasn't paid his vowel yet. It won't be here."

Lydia looked at the notes spread before her. "But not all of these notes are countersigned as paid."

"If a gentleman paid Barham somewhere other than here, he'd give the man a card with a few words signifying the amount was paid. Most men would then later destroy the original vowel, but Barham keeps them—here. So these are all redeemed, even if some aren't countersigned." Ro started dropping the notes he'd examined back into the drawer. "There are too many, most are old, and most tellingly, Barham wouldn't keep notes that mean money in such a mess."

Lydia watched him, then pushed her pile across the desk to be stuffed back into the drawer, too. "So where would he keep vowels not yet redeemed?"

Shutting the drawer, Ro stared at the desk; the surface was remarkably clear and uncluttered, a lamp close to one corner, an inkstand to one side of an embossed leather blotter holder. "They *should* be here. I've seen him bring new vowels in here and come out without them."

With one fingertip, he poked at the leather blotter holder. It didn't move. He smiled. "Aha."

Lydia looked from the blotter holder to him. "Aha what?"

He waved her back.

She scooted the admiral's chair back and to the side, out of his way as he went down on one knee before the kneehole to peer, then feel along under the desk. There was space for a drawer above the kneehole, but there was no drawer front.

He found a small lever and pulled. A sharp click sounded. "There." The nearer edge of the leather panel had popped up. Rising to his feet, he reached for it.

Lydia stood to peer around his shoulder as he lifted what was in fact a hinged, rectangular, leather-covered lid; they looked into a box—the hidden drawer. Various writing implements, a penknife, an ornate letter opener, Barham's seals, a candle stub, and wax were all neatly laid within the box— along with a three-inch stack of vowels.

Ro hesitated; no matter what he thought of Barham, he

didn't like trespassing on the man's privacy. But . . . steeling himself, he picked up the vowels, flicked through them, then drew out an envelope.

"That's Tabitha's writing," Lydia said.

Examining it, he nodded. "With Addison's note of hand on the back." He looked inside the outer casing and drew out a single, thin, neatly folded sheet, with every visible surface covered in Tabitha's scrawly script. He handed it to Lydia. "Check that it's what we're after."

He assumed it was, but with Addison the spineless wonder involved, one couldn't be too sure.

Lydia flicked open the sheet, then stepped back, closer to the bow window, angling the crossed and recrossed page to the light.

Ro slipped the envelope bearing Addison's IOU back in the pile in the same position, then replaced the stack of vowels in the drawer exactly as he'd found it. Closing the drawer, he drew the admiral's chair back to its previous position before the desk. He stepped back, scanning, checking; everything was as it had been before they'd started searching.

Lydia was standing before the window utterly engrossed in her sister's letter. He was turning to her when he heard a heavy, lazy footstep in the corridor outside the library.

Seconds away from the door.

He had only those seconds to react, to protect Lydia while creating some plausible excuse for them being there.

His options were limited.

She caught the next footstep, closer, more definite, and lifted her head, eyes widening, lips parting.

He seized her about the waist. Her eyes widened even more as he lifted and swung her around; sitting on the window seat, he juggled her, pushing her skirts up with his knees as he lowered her.

Lydia smothered a squeak. She ended astride Ro's hard

thighs, her skirts rucked up, her stockinged knees sinking into the thick velvet cushions of the window seat.

Facing him, she clutched Tabitha's letter—the amazing and detailed account of her sister's determined dive into intimacy with Addison the spineless wonder—in one hand. Her other hand was on Ro's shoulder; senses reeling, she clutched, vainly trying to steady her wits, thrown into utter turmoil by the feel of his hands hard and hot about her waist, her skin shielded by only the finest layer of silk.

Before she could gather her whirling wits, he released her waist, reached for her face, speared his long fingers through her hair, dragging locks free as he gripped her head, pulled her to him, and pressed his lips to hers.

Forced hers wide, filled her mouth with his tongue, and kissed her as if he were intent on devouring her.

Distantly—very distantly—she heard the faint click of the door latch . . . but then sensation rose up, welled through her and swamped her. Filled her mind to the exclusion of all else.

All else but Ro, kissing her deeply, flagrantly demanding, commanding and insisting on a response—on complete and abject surrender.

His hands framed her jaw, her face—each long searing kiss, each evocative caress, sank to her bones and melted them.

She slumped toward him. She'd stopped breathing long ago, but couldn't spare any wit to wonder at it. All her mind, all her being, was totally focused on him and what he was doing to her.

What he was making her feel.

All he was making her long for.

He broke the kiss to fill his lungs; their lips all but touching, he whispered, "Barham's at the door. He's watching us." He angled his head to trail languidly lazy, erotically tempting kisses along her jaw to her ear. "Pretend to be hungry—starving."

Pretend? Her skirts were a silk froth across his lap; tucking Tabitha's letter beneath the folds, she placed that hand on his chest, then slid it slowly and deliberately—savoring every inch—up the hard planes, over his heavy shoulder, up and around until she could splay her fingers, spear her hand through his silky dark hair, grip his head—and kiss him back.

She was as hungry as he could possibly want. She made no attempt to hide it, easing up on her knees, leaning into him to press her kisses ever more avidly on him.

Only to discover she was engaged in a duel with him, a heated, willful exchange, one that escalated dramatically, fed her greedy hunger until she grew ravenous, yet she still couldn't match his rapacious demands. The more ravenous she grew, the more rapacious he became, the more flagrantly arousing, the more blatantly sexual his actions. The steely need she sensed rising within him in response to her—to her nearness, to her eager kisses—fascinated and lured, and drew her on.

Ever deeper into the spiraling whirlpool of sensations.

Ever more deeply under their spell.

From some way behind her, a fraction to the side, Barham rather pointedly cleared his throat. "Ro, dear boy."

Barham waited until Ro, unhurriedly and with every evidence of reluctance—including a small but audible sigh—drew back from the kiss. Making absolutely no attempt to sit up or shift Lydia back, heavy-lidded, he remained slumped against the padded back of the window seat, looked at Barham, then arched a languid brow.

He kept Lydia's face anchored between his palms, stopping her from glancing around, keeping her face hidden from Barham.

Barham's smile was all masculine understanding. "A pleasure to see you once again within these walls, dear boy. Grafton mentioned you'd arrived."

"Indeed. It's proving a delight to be back, old chap." Ro pitched his voice to a world-weary drawl, his tone that of a man interrupted, distracted from an activity he would much rather be pursuing only by the demands of polite behavior. "Finally having the chance to rejoin you, as you can see, I grasped it. However, not having attended your revels for so long, I wasn't sure who else might be here. I decided it was wiser to amuse ourselves here, within these more exclusive surrounds, at least until you were up and about."

Barham smiled, nodded, the genial host. He'd been studying Lydia, what he could see of her. "I don't believe I've had the pleasure of meeting your new lady."

Ro smiled at him, the cat with the cream. "Indeed, old son. You haven't. But I'm sure you won't mind if we delay the introductions." He lifted his hips, jigging Lydia. "We're rather *absorbed* at the moment."

Barham's smile was the definition of lecherous, but Ro knew he wouldn't object; this, after all, was the principal purpose of his "revels."

"Oh, indeed. Do continue." Barham half turned toward the door. "Join us when you're free—breakfast will be available in the dining room shortly. No doubt you'll both wish to recoup your energies for the evening's games."

Ro let his smile widen, more overtly sexual. "Indubitably. We'll join you there."

Barham saluted and walked to the door.

Ro didn't wait for him to leave, but drew Lydia's face back to his, covered her lips, and plunged back into her mouth, into the hot, forbidden delight, eager—even desperate—for every last taste for her, before his excuse for kissing her disappeared.

Reaching the door, Barham paused, watching.

Taking one hand from Lydia's face, Ro spread his palm over her silk-clad side, gripping, then he slid his hand around, over her back, intending to pretend to unravel the knot securing her laces—only to discover that the laces he'd so carefully double-knotted, being of corded silk, slithered and gave at the lightest touch. The knot unraveled, the laces loosened and eased; the back of her gown parted, gaped . . . he had to follow through and slide his hand beneath the silk, to feel her skin—a hotter silk—against his palm, to caress, to possess . . . to make it and her his.

Barham went out and shut the door.

Ro told himself to take his hand out of her gown, to break the kiss and sit up—to help her up from her blatantly suggestive position astride his hips, with not even the silk skirts between them to shield the hot, tender skin of her inner thighs from his trousers.

He told himself, and kept repeating the message, increasingly stridently—but his body failed to comply.

His body was all hers, caught, trapped in a web of sexual hunger stronger and more powerful than any he'd previously known.

But this was Lydia.

It took immense effort to force himself to draw back from the kiss, force himself to gasp, his voice gravelly and low, "He's gone. We can stop."

Lifting his lids, heavy and weighted, he focused on her face, only inches from his. His hand was still caressing her naked back, which courtesy of those slippery laces was steadily becoming more naked.

Her lids rose a little, just enough for her to stare dazedly at him. She wet her lips; her gaze dropped to his mouth. "I don't want to stop."

But they had to. "Lydia—"

"No. Don't argue." She leaned in and brushed her lips, swollen and shining, over his. "Just kiss me and show me—I want to know."

More an order than a plea; Ro struggled against the promptings of his baser self, only too eager to suggest that if she wanted to, then it would only be gentlemanly to oblige.

He knew his baser self all too well and didn't trust it.

But before he could gather his wits enough to form any cogent argument, she framed his face and kissed him again, this time more deeply, more alluringly—more determinedly sirenlike than before.

Under the heat of that kiss, the deliberate if innocent warmth behind it, the resolution he'd assembled started to melt . . . he pressed back, shifted, broke the kiss. Tried to sit up, but she was leaning over him, her forearms resting on his chest; to sit up he would have to grip her and set her back, but his hand was spread over her naked back—gripping didn't help. He dragged in a breath. "We've got Tab's letter—we should leave."

He inwardly cursed; his voice was hoarse, the words more suggestion than directive.

"Not yet." She pressed down more firmly across his hips, all soft warmth and sleek, silken heat, the promise of a fiery haven between her thighs blatantly explicit; he had to swallow a groan. He was aroused to the point of pain; when he'd jigged her, he'd clearly made her aware of that, and now she was curious.

He could read that in her face.

Lydia looked down at him, and knew beyond question that here, now, was the time. The only time for her—the only chance she might ever have to know, to experience, what she'd dreamed of for years.

Innocent dreams originally, progressively less so, but now . . . after reading all Tabitha had written in her letter, all her younger sister had described in minute and glowing detail, she couldn't live any longer without knowing, without experiencing it all herself.

Here, with Ro, the only man she could imagine being intimate with.

Now, in this room where they knew they would be private, with her in this dress specifically designed for the purpose, designed to arouse and then facilitate the culmination.

Now, when he was momentarily, at least, thinking along similar lines.

And their unusual position gave her some chance of capitalizing on that, of persuading him and overriding his innate honor, his resistance.

"We can leave . . . in a little while." Of its own accord, her voice had lowered to a sultry murmur. Rising up just a fraction, she held his gaze, and slowly, deliberately, took advantage of the loosened laces at her back; crossing her arms over her breasts, putting each hand to the opposite shoulder, she slowly, smoothly pushed the small lacy sleeves of the gown down her arms . . . if she wanted to succeed, drastic actions were necessary. She had to be bold; fortune favored the brave.

His eyes widened, the gray gleaming silver below his long lashes. Beneath her, between her thighs, she felt him react.

Slowly she pushed the sleeves down, then released them and drew her forearms and hands free, let the bodice slump into folds about her waist. She didn't look down at her breasts, fully exposed to his fixed silvery gaze; instead she watched him, watched the silver in his eyes heat, watched the planes of his face shift, hardening, becoming more sharp-edged, watched his jaw slowly clench.

He drew a long, slow, tight breath.

Before he could speak, she murmured, still sultry and low, "Don't try to tell me that you don't like what you see." She shifted, pressed down just a little more, provocatively brushing the rigid line of his erection with her lower belly, the movement displaying her breasts, moving them closer to his face. She felt like a wanton. The hard bulge pressing up beneath the junction of her thighs hardened even more, felt even more like hot marble, even through the fabric of his trousers.

His eyes fixed on her breasts, he swallowed, then licked his lips. "Lydia . . ."

Ro couldn't believe what was happening. Nor could he believe the effort it cost him to lift his eyes from the fabulous ivory mounds presented so blatantly for his delectation. One part of him was frankly amazed he managed it at all. His hand was still trapped against her silken back—held there by the tactile sensation he couldn't bring himself to lose. The other had fallen from her face as she'd moved; it now gripped her waist, but weakly. His arms, his body, seemed to have lost all strength, all ability to act as he kept trying to.

He gritted his teeth, tried to keep his eyes on hers. "We can't do this."

Her big blue eyes opened wide. "Why not?"

His jaw was going to crack. "Because . . ." He hesitated for only an instant, frantically searching for suitable phrases, but she smiled understandingly and helped.

"Because I'm not the sort of lady you customarily engage in such activities as this with?"

He nodded. "Precisely." Thank God she'd grasped that critical point. "That is the reason in a nutshell."

Unfortunately she didn't react to that reason in the way he'd hoped. Pressing his coat wide, sliding the buttons of his waistcoat free, she pushed the halves aside; setting her hands, palms flat, to his lower chest, to the fine linen of his shirt, she ran them slowly upward, pressing down, patently savoring all she could feel.

Her lids lowered; her eyes gleamed cornflower bright. "Perhaps, in the general way of things, that would be an adequate reason for stopping, for not doing what both of us wish to do." Her voice remained soft, sirenlike, a whisper of temptation. "But, Ro, I'm a year or so away from being an acknowledged ape leader, and there's little to no prospect of anything changing that. So . . ."

Her hands had reached his shoulders. Lifting them to his face, she framed it and leaned close, settling on him, her elbows on his collarbones, resting her glorious breasts, naked, on his shirt-clad chest. Through the fine linen, he felt their warmth, their elemental female bounty, felt everything primitive within him stir.

From a distance of mere inches, she looked into his eyes, searched them. He couldn't breathe—couldn't risk even trying to move his hands. If he did, he'd lock his arms around her, lock all that warm and willing female flesh to him—and then he'd be lost. Lost to all reason. Lost to all sane thought.

Lost to her.

He wasn't sure he already wasn't.

She held his gaze, and he couldn't look away, then she quietly stated, "If I'm going to die an old maid, I want this time—at least this one time—for me, with you. Please Ro— don't make me beg."

He told himself he was strong—strong enough to withstand this. To withstand even her. The muscle in his jaw shifted, bunched as he tried to find strength enough to say, then do, what he felt he should.

But then she smiled—a gentle, wistful, oh-so-understanding smile—leaned closer still, closing the last inches, and gently, wistfully, kissed him.

"Please, Ro." She breathed the words over his lips, then drew back just enough to meet his eyes. "For whatever I meant to you all those years ago, when you waltzed with me in the orchard and kissed me . . . please do this for me here and now. Please . . . just show me."

What could he say?

Some inner, wiser part of him inwardly sighed, resignedly, as if this had been inevitable from the start and he should have known.

Should have known that he could never deny her.

That there was no longer any point in doing so, in even trying.

He suddenly saw that not yielding and doing as she wished, giving her all and more than she was asking for, would simply be denying the truth, that truth he'd known for ten long years, and had never been able to escape.

That was the reason he had never wed. Perhaps that was why she, too, had never walked to the altar.

A thought to ponder, but for now, this minute, he had other things to do, other things to which to turn his mind.

"All right." At his gravelly surrender, a fine frisson of expectation raced through her—like a Thoroughbred waiting for the flag to fall. He finally let his hands, palms burning, grip; he savored the feel of her held poised between his hands, then raised his lips to hers. "As you wish."

And more.

He kissed her, and let the caress and the heated exchange that grew from it carry that message, make clear his intentions. She shivered, quivered in his arms, but her grasping hands only tightened, fingertips pressing in, trying to grip his muscles, holding him to her. Urging him on.

He needed no urging.

His hands roved her back, learning the texture of her, the supple planes, the indentation of her spine. Then he reached once more for her head, spilling pins and untwisting the knot, letting her long, silky tresses free to fall and slide and writhe over and through his fingers.

Bringing his hands forward, he framed her face, held her still, angling his head as he plundered more deeply, more evocatively, taking as much as he wished, giving her as much as and more than she'd asked for.

Releasing her face, he set his palms to follow the long lines of her throat, down over the swell of her breasts, fingers artfully trailing while he listened to her breath hitch, catch, lungs tightening as he circled her nipples.

He cupped her breasts, took one firm mound in each hand and kneaded, possessed, knowing full well that that wouldn't be enough, not for her, not now. She gasped through the kiss, then she kissed him—ardent and needy, wanting . . .

Lowering his hands, he grasped her waist and urged her up, releasing her lips to trail his down her throat, following the line his hands had taken, burning a path to the base of her throat where her pulse galloped and raced, then down over the swell of one swollen, flushed breast to the peak.

He traced a circle about it with his tongue, listened to her frantic breathing, then he opened his mouth, closed it over the tightly furled nubbin, and drew it deep. Suckled as she cried out.

She tried to mute the sound. He drew back enough to growl, "No one can hear. The dining room is at the other end of the house."

He'd liked the tiny scream, wanted to hear more, set himself assiduously to draw more from her.

Giving more, taking more.

More, far more, than Lydia had expected. More than she'd dreamed.

But no more than she wanted.

One hand fisted in his hair, eyes closed against the sight of him feeding at her breasts, she held him to her and drank in every sensation, let it sink into her parched, deprived senses, felt them swell, burgeon, and flower.

Opening to him, wanting only more. More of all he made her feel.

More of him.

Every tactile sense she possessed felt heightened, alive;

her nerves were strung tight, quiveringly taut, twanging at each touch, then waiting, expectation stretching, for the next. Heat flushed beneath her skin, welled, swelled, and washed through her, a seductive fire running down her veins, coalescing low in her belly.

She shifted against him, felt him stiffen, then she felt the silk skirts ruffle and lift; his hand, sliding beneath, found her thigh. From her garter just above her knee he followed the back of her thigh higher, his hot hard palm to her skin, until he found her bottom. He caressed, squeezed gently, explored . . . distracting her while his other hand also slipped beneath her skirts, long fingers trailing up the inside of her thigh; he reached her curls, stroked, then reached further.

Touched, caressed, then evocatively probed.

She quaked, felt as if she stood at the edge of some precipice waiting to jump, then he suckled more fiercely, his hand shifted between her thighs, and one long finger pressed into her.

What little air she had left in her tight lungs came out in a soft moan, then his finger took up a repetitive rhythm of thrust and retreat that stoked the flames inside her . . . until they roared.

Until she couldn't wait any longer.

Releasing his head, she placed her hands on his chest and pushed up. Opening her eyes, she looked down, frantically pushing back her skirts to find the buttons holding the placket of his trousers closed.

With his hands trapped beneath frothy layers of silk skirt and petticoat, he couldn't retrieve them in time to stop her from slipping the buttons free—but as she did, he swore, gripped her hips and lifted her forward so she straddled him higher across his hips, unbalancing her so she tipped forward and had to put her hands back on his chest to brace herself.

"*Ro!*" She infused the syllable with all the pent-up pleading in her soul. She knew what she wanted and she wanted it now, wanted no argument—

"Yes, I know." Ro bit the words out, had no idea if she understood, but there was no reason she should look, and possibly decide to ask questions—such as how could this work?—questions he didn't have sufficient brain free to deal with. "Just wait a minute . . ."

She half sobbed with frustration and need, but she was heated and wet, so very ready, and so was he. No point in prolonging the torture.

He positioned the blunt head of his erection against her entrance, raised his hips to nudge a fraction in, as beneath the silk skirts he clamped his hands about her hips, and drew her slowly down.

She gasped, caught her breath on a sob, then followed his direction of her own accord, slowly lowering herself, impaling herself upon him.

He stopped her when he felt the resistance of her maidenhead, eased her up, then guided her back down. The look on her face as, eyes closed, she felt him slide inside her again, stretching her virginal flesh, was one of sheer wonder.

She understood, caught the rhythm; she rose up twice more, then he gripped harder and she plunged down, breaching her maidenhead as she took him fully, as, a cry strangling in her throat, she sank fully down, enclosing him in slick, scalding heat.

A sensation so intense it had him gritting his teeth, muscles locking against the urge to lift her and bring her down hard again, to thrust into her willing and oh-so-tight sheath. But the look on her face, the fleeting tension of pain washed away by sensual delight, was one that struck to his soul.

"Gently," he murmured, guiding her again.

She followed his lead, carefully at first, then with increasing eagerness, increasing enthusiasm as she realized the pain had faded and only pleasure remained.

Pleasure, it seemed, she was intent on claiming, and equally intent on sharing.

She cracked open her eyes, found his. Breathlessly, imperiously, demanded, "Show me how to do this—how to please you."

"You are pleasing me—immensely." But he kept hold of her hips, kept hold of the rhythm, of their joint reins, and set the pace—let it build, escalate, until need broke through and drove them.

On a desperate gasp, she bent forward and found his lips with hers. They kissed deeply, without restraint, tongues twining and probing to the same plunging, insistent rhythm with which she rode him. He thrust upward and met her, gripping her hips and holding her down to penetrate her more deeply . . . until the dam broke and passion's fire poured through and seared them.

Filled them, consumed them.

Until there was only heat and that driving, relentless rhythm. Until reality fractured and they flew through the void, tense nerves unraveling, senses spinning . . .

Until, like a sunburst, ecstasy broke upon them and shattered them.

Leaving them drifting, wracked, sated, buoyed on dreams come true, safe and content in each other's arms.

He'd been taken advantage of. He'd been accused more than once of taking advantage of ladies—usually by the ladies themselves afterward, and always falsely—but now he, Rogue Gerrard, had been seduced.

He'd been swept off his feet and into an act of intimacy he'd never before engaged in. Had been forced to surrender and be ravished.

Gazing up at the ceiling, Lydia a warm bundle of boneless sated female slumped on his chest, his arms locked around her holding her in place, he couldn't stop smiling.

He'd always suspected that those ladies had protested too much.

The sky outside, gray, overcast, heavy clouds louring, seemed to his eyes to be rosy and glowing. All he now needed to make his life complete was to find some way to break it to Lydia that she wasn't destined to die an old maid.

And that, as he'd now accepted, resistance was futile.

Chapter Four

An hour later, Lydia let Ro hurry her across the unkempt lawns of Upton Grange and into the cover of the surrounding trees. It was close to five o'clock and already dark; once swallowed by the gloom of the wood, Ro slowed, and they walked on, his hand beneath her arm as he steadied her over fallen branches and through undergrowth until they reached a path.

Ro turned down it. "This is the way we went back to the inn this morning."

Lydia nodded. Her mind still wasn't functioning in its usual reliable way; she was perfectly aware, yet felt as if she were detached, floating . . . as if none of the day-to-day, ordinary worldly things truly mattered.

Ro said little, making her wonder if he knew of her mental distraction. Perhaps mental disconnection was a well-known aftereffect of the activity they'd so recently engaged in. If so, he would undoubtedly know, although it didn't seem to have afflicted him; he was calm, collected, and decisive.

She looked at him, watched him glance behind them, watched his eyes rake the surrounding trees and the shadows pooling beneath. There was a tension in him, one she recognized as stemming from protectiveness, but it seemed heightened, intensified. She looked forward. Perhaps the effect on males was different.

Regardless, she still felt buoyed, had to fight to keep a silly smile from her lips; she wouldn't have bothered fighting if she'd been alone and able to wallow, to hold the glorious golden glow to herself and examine and delight in it in private.

They'd retrieved Tabitha's letter, and she'd gained an entirely unlooked-for bonus. A thoroughly wonderful and quite elevating—and illuminating—experience, one she wouldn't have missed for the world. And all without any unwelcome consequences or costs; she'd seized the moment, taken a risk, and had come out the winner.

Her only regret was that they'd had to leave the white silk and blue lace gown at Upton Grange. From the moment she'd recovered enough to stand, Ro had been single-mindedly focused on getting her and Tab's letter out of Barham's house safely—preferably without meeting another soul. He'd whisked her back upstairs to the room they'd used, helped her change into her chemise and gown, then wrapped her in her cloak once more, with the hood up.

The last sight she'd had of the pretty white and blue gown, it had been lying on the floor in a silken heap. The gown had made her feel . . . different. Freer. It had brought out a side of her she hadn't until then known existed, but allowing that self out had felt right. More, it had felt *empowering.*

"Empowering" was a word Tabitha often used, one Lydia hadn't paid much attention to—until now. Now she knew what the word truly signified, she had to agree with her sister that empowerment was well worth pursuing.

The white and blue gown now held fond memories, a

symbol of her moment, a memento of the one time in her life she'd broken free of the sensible, reliable mold and reached for what she wanted. The one moment in her life she'd acted on impulse, had let her inner self rule.

Perhaps she could have a modiste make up an identical replacement.

She was considering that when they reached the lane.

Ro turned Lydia to the left. The surface of the lane was still inches deep in mud, but the verges had drained enough to be easily and safely walked upon. Pacing beside her, he looked ahead, into the gathering dusk, then glanced back along the path; no one had noticed them, let alone given chase. "I think we're safe. I don't believe anyone saw us leave—all the guests and most of the staff would have been in or around the dining room, and that's at the opposite end of the house. We didn't actually steal anything—I seriously doubt Barham had realized the letter was there."

Lydia's hand rose to her bodice, wherein she'd secreted Tabitha's letter. "It was only a single sheet."

Ro nodded. "Barham will be surprised and puzzled—and suspicious—to find us vanished, but all things considered, in the end he'll shrug it off, and ask me next time he sees me." And as his and Barham's paths rarely crossed these days, that was unlikely to be for some years, and by then Barham would probably have forgotten. "Only he and his staff saw us, so we don't need to fear that anyone else might have recognized you."

"Hmm."

When Lydia said nothing more, he glanced at her face. In the post-twilight gloom, he could barely make out her features. When, lying slumped on his chest in Barham's library, she'd finally stirred, she'd been gloriously dazed, but that he'd expected. By then he'd realized his first priority had to be to get her back to the inn safely, her reputation intact; he hadn't encouraged her to chatter.

Now, however, with her safety assured and the inn a looming shadow rising up out of the night before them, he was starting to wonder at her silence.

About what it might mean. About how she felt about their interlude, their intimacy—a moment, a happening, etched in his mind as one of the more important of his life. Quite aside from the physical glory, there was that other, indefinable, elusive, but fundamental change that had occurred, one he, certainly, wasn't going to waste time pretending hadn't.

Drawing in a breath, he halted. "Lydia, about—"

"Ro, in the library—" She swung to face him, and broke off.

They'd spoken over each other. He nodded, a trifle tersely, for her to continue.

She drew in a breath and lifted her chin; in his experience, that was rarely a good sign.

"I wanted to make sure we understood each other"—she gestured vaguely—"about what happened in the library."

Through the gloom, he caught and held her gaze. "When we found the letter, or later, when we were intimate?"

Her lips tightened, but she nodded. "The latter. I wanted to assure you that you need be under no apprehension that I will mention the matter again, and I most certainly will not expect you to make, nor encourage any notion of you making, an offer for my hand because of that . . . matter."

Matter. He stared at her. "Didn't you like it?"

She blinked at him, then swiftly searched his face. "What has that to say—"

"Lydia—did you enjoy the moment or not?"

She held his gaze for a long, tense minute, then tipped her chin higher. "Yes. Of course I did. But you knew that—you're an acknowledged expert, so that can hardly come as a surprise to you."

He snorted. "When it comes to you—and your sister—nothing would surprise me. But just so we have the point clear, you enjoyed the interlude."

Her eyes flashed. "If you must know, I found it highly enjoyable. Quite *lovely*, in fact."

Lovely. He supposed he could make do with "lovely," although "eye-openingly, unbelievably, earth-shatteringly glorious" would have been more apt.

"Regardless," she went on, her tone giving warning of rigid determination, "I want to make it absolutely clear that I neither expect nor wish to hear any nonsense about you being obliged to offer for my hand because we were intimate." She turned and started walking on, nose in the air. "I want to hear nothing of an offer having to be made on the basis of honor. Aside from all else, if anyone ever hears of it and tries to press the point, I will make it perfectly plain that *I* seduced *you*, not the other way about."

Wonderful. Ro gripped her elbow, steering her along the verge while he regretfully jettisoned the until-then attractive notion of disguising his offer for her hand as being prompted by the dictates of propriety.

They reached the point opposite the inn. Because they'd arrived at the Grange by cart, she wasn't wearing pattens; he stooped and scooped her into his arms.

She didn't squeak; he juggled her, settling her securely in his arms, then carefully picked his way across the lane, equally carefully mentally assessing his best and least painful way forward with her. He would rather not admit to the real reason he was determined to make her his wife— certainly not aloud in words. There were, however, other ways to undermine her arguments; he wasn't called Rogue for no reason.

He reached the inn's stoop. Her continuing silence registered; the quality of it had him glancing swiftly at her, alert and wary.

The faraway look in her eyes confirmed she was thinking, planning—again, from his experience, never a good sign. Not if one wanted a comfortable life.

"What?" he asked.

She blinked, met his gaze, studied his eyes for a moment, hesitated, then shook her head. "Nothing."

He gritted his teeth. Told himself it didn't matter because he had no intention of letting her out of his sight, not until he'd spoken with her father, then received from her own lips a commitment to marry him.

Stooping, he set her down on the inn's front step, and paused to scrape the soles of his boots. She remained on the step, glancing down the lane—away from the highway, in the direction she would take to return to Wiltshire.

He decided to be helpful. "The mud's still too soft to risk a carriage—not even my curricle." And certainly not his precious pair. "If there's any rain at all overnight, we'll be stranded here at least until the day after tomorrow. Even if there isn't, it's unlikely the surface will be firm enough to chance a carriage before then."

She humphed and glanced the other way—back toward the highway and London.

"It's even worse that way," he told her. "The highway will be better, but there's more than two miles of lane between."

She looked at him as he straightened, then turned and walked into the inn.

He followed, inwardly smiling, and shut the door. He glanced at the counter, at Bilt hovering behind, ready to respond to any order he might give. "We should dine." It was always wise to feed a woman after an afternoon of pleasure, especially if one intended the pleasure to be repeated over the upcoming night.

Bilt looked eager.

Halting, Lydia turned; she looked distracted again, a slight frown in her eyes.

He smiled charmingly, strolled to her, and took her hand.

Raising it to his lips, he kissed—and saw again that dazed expression creep into her blue eyes. Still smiling, he held her gaze. "No doubt you'd like to refresh yourself after our adventure. Shall we say in an hour, in the parlor?"

She blinked, then inclined her head. "Indeed. That will suit."

Releasing her hand as she turned to the stairs, he raised his brows at Bilt. "I expect Mrs. Bilt will be able to accommodate us?"

"Yes, indeed, my lord," Bilt assured him. "In an hour in the parlor—we'll have everything ready."

With an easy nod, Ro slowly followed Lydia up the stairs. She wasn't the only one who could plot and plan.

Ro was waiting in the parlor when Lydia came down for dinner. It was the more intimidating Ro who, arm braced along the mantelpiece while he stared into the flames, looked up, then straightened as she entered, the immaculately turned-out gentleman, exquisitely elegant but with disguised power radiating from him

A gentleman she seriously doubted many others thought to cross.

She let her eyes drink in the sight, then shut the door behind her and moved into the room. Only then did she realize Bilt was there, pouring wine into the goblets on the table set before the fire.

The table was set for two, and it was clear Mrs. Bilt had taken special care. The linen was crisply white; the cutlery gleamed in the light of a single candle in an ornate silver holder in the table's center.

As she came forward, Ro took her hand and led her to a chair. He held it for her. As she sat, he murmured, low, so only she could hear, "No roses, I'm afraid, but it's midwinter, and we're too far from any of my succession houses."

She inwardly blinked, turned her head to study him as he came around the table and sat in the chair opposite. Expression easy, charmingly in control, he nodded to Bilt, who immediately appeared with a tureen and served the soup.

That done, Bilt set the tureen on the sideboard and bowed himself out.

Not quite sure, wondering, Lydia lifted her spoon and sipped. The soup was delicious. She discovered she had a significant appetite, and Ro seemed ravenous. A companionable silence fell as they emptied their bowls.

The instant they had, Bilt was back to clear the dishes away; while he did, he answered Ro's genial question about what Mrs. Bilt had in store for them with a detailed account of the dishes to follow.

Once Bilt left, Ro turned his gray eyes and his smile on her—and asked her about Tabitha. She wasn't at all sure she trusted that smile—outwardly easygoing, yet she got the definite impression that behind it he was intent, focused, predatorily so—but she answered his question, then proceeded at his urging to fill him in on developments in her family over recent years.

Thinking to return the favor, and perhaps distract him if he needed distracting, she asked after his mother, the Viscountess Gerrard, with whom she was acquainted; somewhat to her surprise, Ro answered with more than simple statements, freely elaborating on happenings over recent years on his estate, at his country home, and in London. The last inevitably led to tales of the *ton*, and of those he seemed to have an inexhaustible supply.

Entirely to her surprise, when they paused to allow Bilt to clear the remains of an excellent sherry trifle, she realized she'd laughed quite a lot, and was relaxed and at ease.

That was certainly not what she'd expected when she'd walked into the room. Her first sight of Ro had raised some sort of instinctive defense, a wariness, a need to watch; she'd been sure, in that moment when he'd looked up and she'd met his eyes across the room, that he was up to something— intent on some plan of his own, some purpose, on getting something from her.

What that something was she didn't know, but her suspicions had largely died. He'd been a charming and entirely unthreatening companion; he hadn't even done anything to make her nerves leap.

Now, reaching across the table, he took her hand. "Come sit by the fire. It's early yet."

She allowed him to draw her to her feet, then lead her to a settle angled to the fire. She sat, and he sat beside her; they both stared into the flames.

"Do you remember that time we cut across old Mrs. Swithin's property and she set her terrier on us?"

She grinned. "Tabitha climbed onto your back."

"You grabbed my arm and hid behind me."

While they recalled such earlier innocent escapades, Bilt cleared the table. He offered Ro brandy, which he declined, then Bilt bowed himself from the room.

Lydia felt so much at ease, so comfortable sitting beside Ro—the man who had inhabited her dreams for years—solid and warm and oh-so-real beside her, his masculine strength an almost tangible aura seductively wrapping about her, that she couldn't help but realize the threat. Not from him, but from herself—her other self.

Steeling her sensible self against temptation, she drew in a breath. "Ro." She turned her head and met his gray eyes, then looked down at her hands, fingers twining in her lap. "I spoke to Whishart, my coachman. He said the wind's coming up, and the lanes should be passable by morning." Lifting her head, she looked into the flames. "So I'll be leaving after breakfast."

For a moment, Ro said nothing, then, "Back home to Wiltshire?"

She nodded. "I have Tab's letter." She glanced at him. "That's what I came for." *But not all that I found.*

He met her gaze, then nodded, lips lightly curving. "Do you remember all those times we met in the orchard?"

"Of course." Those moments were the most golden of her girlhood memories.

"The last time we met there, we waltzed—do you remember?"

"Yes." How could she ever forget?

His smile deepened; rising, he caught her hand. "Come, waltz with me again."

She couldn't resist; last time they'd parted, it had been like this—with a waltz to mark the end. As he drew her into his arms and stepped out, humming softly, exactly as he had all those years ago, it seemed entirely appropriate that this meeting, too, should end with a waltz.

Raising her head, meeting his eyes, she let herself flow into the moment; she was a more experienced dancer now— so, too, was he. He whirled her slowly around the room, and she'd never felt so entirely at one with any man. While her nerves might skitter when his hand brushed her back, might tense when he was close, now they'd been intimate, when she stood within his arms her body—nerves, senses, and even her wits—seemed to accept that that was where she should be. They relaxed, and enjoyed, and let the simple pleasure swamp them.

His gray eyes were locked with hers; slowly, step by step, she lost herself in the warmth of his gaze.

Gradually, his steps slowed. He stopped humming. And still she felt held, not trapped but held so gently, as if by fine spun glass. He searched her eyes, then he lowered his head.

Slowly, giving her ample time to draw back if she wished.

When he hesitated, their lips a bare inch apart, she lifted her face, pressed her lips to his, and kissed him.

He responded immediately; the kiss quickly became an all-absorbing interaction. The spreading warmth came again, welling through her. His arms rose and closed around her, locking her to him; she sank into him, into his embrace, eager to feel the seductive strength of him all around her.

She was leaving in the morning.

His hands roved her back, then slid down, shaping her bottom, flagrantly molding her to him so she couldn't help but know how much he wanted her. How much he desired her.

Just the thought sent shivery need lancing through her.

She didn't need to think to know how much she wanted him; the burgeoning warmth turned to heat and poured down her veins to pool low. The soft flesh between her thighs throbbed; an odd, empty ache yawned within. Now she knew how it felt to have him inside her, she knew unequivocally what her body wanted, what it yearned for. What she yearned for . . .

What he was making her feel.

She drew back, struggled for breath as his hands—his clever hands—closed about her breasts. "Ro—what are you doing?"

His lips curved, although the planes of his face were set. "Seducing you. As you said, in the library you seduced me." From beneath heavy lids, his silvery eyes met hers. "Now it's my turn."

He bent his head again and kissed her, long, sweet, achingly ardent. Then he released her lips, whispered in her ear, "Am I succeeding?"

She hesitated, deliberating over what was safe to say, to admit. In the end she sighed. "Yes." Looking into his face, she studied it for an instant, the well-remembered—if she were truthful, well-loved—features. "Yes."

"Good." To her surprise, he lifted his head further. His hands lowered to her waist, steadying her. "Let's go upstairs."

She blinked.

He saw, elaborated, "I want you in a bed, beneath me. I want to show you what pleasure truly is, and for that, we need a bed."

He was the acknowledged expert; who was she to argue? Anticipation tightening her nerves, she nodded. "All right."

Her knees had buckled long ago, but he gave her his arm.

Ro opened the parlor door, and escorted her out. Her skin was delicately flushed, her lips slightly swollen; he looked around for Bilt—and saw him in the taproom, too far away to detect the telltale signs.

Leading Lydia to the stairs, he started up, steadying her ahead of him. They'd reached the landing, and Lydia was out of sight before Bilt reached the bottom of the stairs and breathlessly inquired, "Will you require anything else, my lord?"

"No, thank you, Bilt, we're retiring to our rooms for the night."

From above Lydia called, "I'll ring if I require any assistance, Bilt. Please tell my maid I'll ring if I need her. Good night."

"Good night, miss. My lord."

A second later, climbing steadily in Lydia's wake, Ro heard Bilt's footsteps scurry back to the tap. Inwardly smiling, blessing whoever was in the tap, he led Lydia to her room, opened the door, and held it for her, then he followed her in and shut it behind him.

A single candle had been left burning on a small table beside a large four-poster bed set against the wall directly opposite the door. The hangings were loosened but not drawn, revealing a thick mattress, pristine linen sheets beneath a dimity coverlet, and thick, plump pillows.

To the left, a fire burned brightly in the hearth, casting flickering golden light across the room. Lydia halted before the bed, and turned to him.

He met her gaze; holding it, he unhurriedly crossed the short distance between them, then smoothly drew her into his arms, bent his head—and waltzed her straight back into the kiss they'd interrupted.

Straight back into the flames they'd left smoldering.

Instantly the fire between them leapt to life, as he'd known it would. For the first time in his life, he surrendered to it without thought or hesitation, gave himself over to it, to the steadily escalating heat, to the need that built within it . . . in that moment gave himself wholly and ineradicably to her.

She was no more inhibited than he; he sensed it in her kiss, in the abandoned eagerness she made no effort to hide, even to disguise.

They shed their clothes, hands busy, lips breaking apart only to hungrily come together again. Desire rose, passion in its wake, sending fiery tendrils of flame licking over and through them. Outside the wind howled; inside her room, despite the wintry chill, being naked, heated skin to heated skin, grew to an all-consuming need.

Stepping free of the puddle of her gown and chemise, Lydia gasped as Ro's arm banded her waist, and he pulled her to him, to the glorious expanse of chest she'd uncovered. Hands gripping, fingers tracing his ridged abdomen, she lifted her face and met his lips with hers, tasted the hunger and passion and sheer desire that flared through them both, that had set them both burning.

She pressed into him, bare breasts to his chest, naked hips to his bare thighs. She shifted against him, wantonly inciting, glorying when she sensed his breath catch.

His hand drifted from her breast, from the furled nipple he'd been worshipping; he grasped her waist, then raised his head and broke the kiss.

Only to trail hot, open-mouthed kisses down the line of her throat, over her collarbone, and then lower, over the swell of her breast to her aching nipple, to pay homage there

before he sank lower, trailing light, nipping kisses down her
midriff, over her waist, until he paused at her navel to circle
it with his tongue, then lightly probe.

Sensations lanced through her; her nerves flickered and
jumped. He went to his knees before her, his hot lips pressed
to the taut skin of her stomach. Lids heavy and low, she
laced her fingers in his hair, felt his hands stroke over her
hips, her thighs, then he gripped her garters and rolled down
her stockings, first one, then the other.

Obediently she stepped out of them; she'd kicked her slip-
pers off long before. She waited, expecting him to rise and
join her, to strip off his trousers and—

He raised his head and set his lips to her curls, kissing,
then—

"Ro!" Lids falling, head tilting back, she gripped his
skull—her only anchor in a world suddenly swamped
with sensation. His tongue, too knowing, too clever, touched,
probed. He licked, and her senses quaked; her knees
buckled.

His big hands steadied her; he shifted her back a fraction
so her spine was braced against the bedpost, then he kissed,
licked, laved—lifted her leg and draped her knee over one
shoulder the better to open her, to gain access to the sensitive, private, intimate place between her thighs.

He was thorough, and far too knowing; ruthless and relentless, he sent her senses careening, his ministrations perfectly gauged to send her spinning from this world . . .

His tongue filled her and she screamed, a strangled sound
as she fractured and fell, falling through the void.

But he was there to catch her, to hold her, then he lifted
her up and laid her on the bed.

Naked, already boneless, yet with expectation and anticipation still thrumming through her veins, she waited, struggled to catch her breath while she watched him dispense

with his shoes, then his trousers; she studied the long, muscled lines of his thighs, the thick, rigid rod of his erection
lovingly bathed by the fire's light.

Then he put one knee on the bed, fleetingly considered
her, then crawled across the covers; catching her ankles one
in each hand, he spread them apart, and came to kneel between.

Releasing her ankles, he ran his palms up over her calves.
His eyes followed; slowly he ran his gaze up her legs, to the
heated, swollen flesh he'd already tasted, then his gaze followed a path up her torso to her eyes.

He held her gaze for a long moment; she felt her heartbeat
in her fingertips, all over her body just beneath her skin.
Then he leaned forward, bent, and gently kissed the curls
covering her mons, then slowly trailed his lips higher, steadily,
with both reverence and purpose working his way back up
her body, lowering his hard, hot body to hers.

When his lips finally reached hers she was frantic, more
so than she'd been before. She clutched at him, arched beneath him.

He took her mouth, filled it with his tongue, plundered
and possessed, then he pressed deeper between her spread
thighs, and with one powerful thrust filled her.

In that instant her world teetered on some invisible edge,
then he withdrew and plunged deeper. She gasped through
the kiss, clutched his arms, arching beneath him, nails sinking in as passion crested, then he reached down, caught her
knee, and wound her leg over his hip.

And penetrated her more deeply still.

She sobbed, clung as he started to ride her with a slow,
steady, relentless rhythm. Deep, hard, intoxicating.

A rhythm that gave her, her senses, more than enough time
to absorb every nuance, every little facet of the overwhelm-
ing spectrum of sensations he evoked, and sent crashing

through her. Of the deep, rhythmic, relentless pressure fluctuating within her, of the weight of him holding her pinned to the bed, beneath him as he'd said, of the slick friction as their bodies moved one against the other, of the elemental, indescribable sensation of knowing she was his, that he could do with her as he pleased, and yet . . . all he did, all he gave her, was pleasure.

Soul-stirring, passion-steeped pleasure.

He broke the kiss. Lifting her weighted lids, she looked into his face, close, mere inches apart as he rocked ever more deeply, more completely into her. Joining with her in this most flagrantly intimate way. The candle on the table beside the bed was on the side away from the hearth; its weak golden light fell on them, gilding his features, the harsh angular planes, the passionate, mobile mouth.

His lids were low, lashes screening his eyes, yet they gleamed silver as she watched, then his lids fell.

They were both beyond breathless, their breathing ragged beyond belief. She sensed the inevitable coiling tension, the inevitable escalation to the peak. He picked up the pace, drove even more forcefully into her; her lids fell as she cried out.

And then they were there, whirling through the maelstrom, every nerve alive, every sense they possessed fracturing and shattering under the weight of an elemental pleasure too great to encompass, evoked by a reality larger than them both, too powerful to resist.

Impossible to deny.

Ro clung to her, the anchor he needed, the one he'd recognized and run from long ago. To no avail. As passion washed through him and pleasure wracked him and left his senses razed, he knew that, understood it, accepted it.

As beneath him her body clenched, convulsed, and clutched his, her release calling on and encompassing his, he held her close, and as the last aching gasp was wrung from him and he collapsed in her arms, he did what he'd never imagined he ever would. But for her and only her . . .

He willingly laid his heart at her feet, and gave his soul into her keeping.

Chapter Five

"It's all right! I'm her sister."

Ro blinked awake, lifted his head from the pillow and looked over his shoulder—more by instinct than intention—to the door of Lydia's room.

Just as it swung open and a lady with wild, frizzy red hair swept in.

And stopped, jaw dropping, eyes popping.

Then she made a strangled sound, eventually managed, "*Ro?*" in accents of utter disbelief.

Then her eyes shifted to Ro's left. And widened even further. "*Lydia!*"

That came out as a high-pitched squeak.

Ro groaned and closed his eyes. "*Go away*, Tabitha."

Lydia struggled up from beneath his arm. "Tab? Good Lord!" On her elbow, clutching the covers to her chest, she stared at her sister. "How . . . ?"

Then she stared past her. "Oh God! For heaven's sake, Tab—go away and *close the door.*"

Tabitha, whose expression had been blank for several seconds, blinked, then grinned hugely. "Yes, of course. We'll wait downstairs."

Turning, she went back out of the door—joining the older couple hovering in the corridor.

The door shut.

Ro turned over and slumped back on the pillows. He didn't bother groaning. "That was your parents, wasn't it—the pair behind Tabitha?"

Lydia nodded. She stared at the door, still stunned.

"You left a note, I take it?" His tone was resigned.

"Just to tell Tab not to worry. I told her I would stop at an inn near Barham's house and steal back her letter—I told her to stay at home and leave me to handle things."

"Since when has Tab ever listened to orders—yours or anyone else's?" Ro swung his legs out from beneath the covers and sat up.

Still stunned, Lydia gestured to the door. "I never imagined she'd come, let alone bring Mama and Papa."

Pulling up his trousers, Ro shrugged. He fastened them, then reached for his shirt. His brain was functioning again; it might well be that Tabitha had done him a service. He could settle everything immediately without having to travel to Wiltshire first.

Regretfully, he would have to face the senior Makepeaces without a cravat; tying one would take too long. He'd shrugged on his waistcoat, stepped into his shoes, and reached for his coat before Lydia realized.

She frowned at him. "What are you doing?"

"Getting dressed to go down and speak with your father. Probably your mother as well."

"*What?*" In a mad scramble, Lydia came off the bed. "Don't be silly. What are you going to say?" She swiped up her chemise and dragged it over her head.

Settling his coat, he frowned back. "What do you think I'm going to say? They just saw us in bed together, and with our clothes strewn between the door and the bed, they wouldn't have had to wonder all that hard to deduce what we'd been doing there."

"But—" Lydia broke off to wrestle her gown down over her head. "I'll speak with them—it's nothing to do with—"

Ro wasn't where he'd been. Turning, she saw him going through the door. "Ro! Come back here!"

She nearly tripped on her way to the door. She opened it a crack and shouted, "I *forbid* you to speak to them!"

A hand flattened on the outside of the door and Tabitha appeared. "Much good that will do—he's already on his way down." She pushed through the door, forcing Lydia back.

"Oh, thank God—Tab, help me with this." Lydia's gown had got tangled, hems tucked through the bodice, skirts wrenched the wrong way, sleeves inside out. "I have to get dressed and get down there before he does something stupid."

Tabitha regarded her for a moment, then walked to the bed, sat on it, bounced once, then let herself fall back. She stared at the canopy. "I've never known Ro to do anything stupid." Turning her head, she looked at Lydia. "Why do you think he's going to change and do something stupid now?"

Lydia hissed. "Because he's an honorable man—and the *idiot* is going down there to offer for my hand."

Tabitha nodded. "I expect he is. But why is that stupid?"

"Because he doesn't love me! He's only doing it because he feels honor-bound, now Mama and Papa caught us together."

Tabitha grinned. "Do you know what Mama said?"

"No—what?" Lydia couldn't believe how impossible her gown was being; the more she tugged, the worse it got, as if it had a mind of its own.

"She said, 'Well, dear me—and with Lord Gerrard, too. I always wondered when she'd get to it.'"

Lydia snorted. "You're making that up."

"I swear on her grave. Anyway, you know that's exactly the sort of thing Mama would say."

Lydia didn't bother denying it; aside from herself, her entire family were eccentric beyond belief. Somehow they got away with it; she'd always suspected because the rest of the *ton* found them rather frighteningly amusing. "Tab—for the Lord's sake get off that bed and come and help me! I have to get down there and save him! You know what he's like—once he makes an offer, he'll get stubborn and difficult, and refusing him will be impossible."

Shifting onto her side, Tabitha propped on one elbow and frowned at her. "Why do you want to refuse him? You've always been in love with him—everyone knows that—even, obviously, Mama. Methinks the lady doth protest too much."

With her gown finally straight and the skirts shaken down, Lydia stared at Tabitha, then glared. "That's immaterial. *I* might be in love with *him*, but *he's* not in love with *me*—and that's what counts."

"Don't be silly—he's as much in love with you as you are with him. He always has been."

Lydia growled.

"No—it's true. The year I made my come-out, when you were having your second Season, I used to see him at balls—but he took great care that you never did. He saw you though, and truly, just one look at his face, and even you would have known." Tabitha grimaced. "If you must know, that's why I took up with Addison—because I thought that any day Ro would surrender and speak for you, and of course you'd accept him, and then you two would have each other . . . I wanted someone of my own."

Lydia had stopped frantically tugging at her bodice to stare at Tabitha. "You encouraged Addison because you knew I was in love with Ro, and he was in love with me?"

Tabitha nodded. "But then Ro slunk away and didn't speak, and you know what happened with Addison." She looked up and met Lydia's eyes. "Incidentally, did you find my letter?"

Lydia jerked her chin toward her bag. "It's in there." She'd wrestled the bodice and back of her gown into place, and got her arms down through the sleeves, but the laces defeated her—Ro had pulled them completely out of the eyelets. "Tab—please come and help me with this gown."

Tabitha frowned. "You're not listening to me, are you? You don't believe he's in love with you. I can't see why you imagine he's down there talking to Papa otherwise."

"Because he's Ro, and that's exactly what he would do!" Exasperated, Lydia stamped her foot. "He thinks he's ruined me, or some such twaddle, so—"

Tabitha snorted. "Lydia—we're talking about Ro— *Rogue*—Gerrard. You do know why he's called that, don't you? It's not because he does sweet, roguish things, but because 'rogue' signifies a being beyond control. Uncontrollable. Ro does what he wants and always has. No one and nothing gets in his way. If he wants something, he'll have it, and as he certainly wants you—"

"Nonsense. He wants to do the right thing, but I have a say in this, and I won't have it."

Tabitha shook her head. "He's not going to let you get away this time. Especially now he knows you love him."

Lydia gritted her teeth and tried to thread her laces behind her back. "He doesn't love me, and he certainly doesn't know I love him."

Tabitha stared at her, then looked at the rumpled, severely disarranged bed, then back at her. "Lydia—he knows. Of course he knows."

"Rubbish—I took great care to say nothing at all. Not even in extremis."

"You didn't have to say a word. Great heavens, you're

twenty-six and you haven't been living in a nunnery these past years. You've had countless gentlemen only too ready to marry you or seduce you, whichever you preferred. And yet here you are"—Tabitha waved at the bed—"finally having your first time with Ro—you think he's not going to guess why, after all these years, you decided to give yourself to him?"

Lydia sniffed. "That wasn't the first time. The first time was in Barham's library."

Tabitha's eyes grew round. "In Stephen Barham's library?"

"In a courtesan's gown."

Tabitha's jaw dropped. "When you decided to let your Makepeace streak loose you obviously went to town. You *must* tell me all."

"I will if you'll only help me with these damn laces!"

Tabitha narrowed her eyes, then slumped back on the bed. "No. This has obviously required a huge turnaround in Ro's thinking—he probably could use more time to convince Mama and Papa . . . although, of course, given you're twenty-six anyway, even if they dismiss his suit, I can't see him meekly going away. Perhaps he'll kidnap you, and you'll elope. That would be exciting."

"Tabitha!" Lydia stared at her turncoat sister. "What happened to gentlemen and marriage being the bane of a gentlewoman's life? What happened to avoiding marriage with gentlemen?"

Tabitha lifted one shoulder. "That dictum isn't for ladies like you and gentlemen like Ro—it's for ladies like me, who will never find a gentleman we can trust."

Lydia blew out a frustrated breath. Drew in another—and tried not to think how many persuasive arguments Ro had already brought to bear in the parlor downstairs. "Please, Tabitha—just be useful and do up these laces."

Tabitha looked at her—stubborn against stubborn—and

shook her head. "No. The longer Ro has to talk Mama and Papa around before you get there to try to scupper your own happiness, the better."

Lydia narrowed her eyes at her sister, then nodded. "Very well—be this on your head." Turning, she headed for the door, opened it, then, hands behind her holding her gown together as best she could, she stalked out and down the stairs.

Behind her she heard a gust of delighted laughter, and swore she would sometime in the future find some suitable way to pay back her meddlesome sister.

Reaching the ground floor, she swept down the hall to the parlor door; ignoring the interested—nay, amazed—stares of Bilt and Mrs. Bilt, wide-eyed behind their counter, she paused to draw in a deep breath, then opened the door and went in.

Inside the parlor, standing before the armchairs in which the senior Makepeaces were seated, Ro was congratulating himself on having successfully survived an interview that had unexpectedly been remarkably civil, not to say surprisingly easy, a great deal easier than he'd thought.

He hadn't had to state the obvious—that Lydia was in love with him, something he'd had demonstrated with stunning clarity in Stephen Barham's library, and subsequently had had confirmed over the last hours—and although he'd spoken of his long and deep regard for her, he hadn't had to specifically state that he was irrevocably and irretrievably in love with her, too, let alone admit that he had been since the age of twenty-two.

Lydia's father, as it happened, knew more about him—about his real self and true habits—than he'd supposed, through a mutual friend, Gideon Armistead, a fellow philanthropist. That had made matters considerably easier; he hadn't had to try to explain, let alone prove, that his reputation had for more than six years been a smoke screen left after the fire had died.

Nor had he known that Mrs. Makepeace corresponded regularly with his mother. Although labeled by the *ton* as wildly eccentric, neither of the senior Makepeaces struck him as unreasonable, or lacking in wit—certainly not when it came to their daughters.

Lydia's father had just finished giving Ro his permission to pay his addresses to Lydia, and her mother had capped that with a sweet but edged smile and reminded him that, of course, permissions aside, Lydia's hand was her own to bestow, when the door behind him opened.

He glanced around as Lydia kicked the door shut and advanced into the room, her entrance rendered somewhat awkward by both hands being held at an odd angle behind her back, apparently holding her gown together.

Her expression, however, commanded instant attention. It was set and beyond determined.

She marched up to him, then stepped across in front of him, facing her parents, giving him her back. Turning her head, she muttered over her shoulder, "For goodness' sake, do up my gown!"

He looked down, and obediently set his fingers to the laces.

Lydia looked at her parents, watching the proceedings with transparent interest and, being her parents, no shock whatsoever. "What has he said?" Before they could answer, she held up a hand. "No—never mind. *Regardless* of whatever he's said, regardless of whatever he's claimed, it was my decision entirely, mine alone, and I will not—"

"So you found Tab's letter, heh?" Her father, smiling in his usual vague, scholarly way, blinked up at her through his spectacles.

She paused, drew breath. "Yes. I have it upstairs."

"Excellent." Her mother folded her hands in her lap. "I understand Ro helped you retrieve it."

Lydia pressed her lips together and nodded. Her father

might be vague, but her mother was not. The shrewd blue eyes she'd inherited looked steadily—calmly—back at her. She licked her lips. "We went into Barham's house together."

"It must have been quite an adventure." Her mother arched one fine brow, a knowing smile curving her lips. "I have to say that, given Barham's reputation, I'm very glad Ro was about to see you safely through it. It's one thing to be adventurous, quite another to be witlessly reckless. But I understand all went well, which I have to say is a relief. Now Tab can calm down and stop falling into histrionics, although I daresay she'll now complain that you had all the fun." Her mother's smile grew more openly amused, equally fond. "Quite a turnaround, to have *you* engaging in wild adventure while Tab is the one insisting on us racing to the rescue."

Her mother's eyes shifted to Ro, still behind Lydia, still cinching her laces. "But all has gone well, and it appears Ro has something to say to you, and I recommend you give his words due consideration."

Lydia snapped out of the drugging web of calm her mother had wrapped her in. "No. That is"—she dragged in a breath, searched for the patience her minutes with Tabitha had eroded—"everything *has* ended well, and Ro *might* have something he wishes to say, but I'm here to explain that no matter what he's said, no matter how things might appear, there is absolutely no reason for him to make any offer for my hand."

Her father blinked; then, a puzzled, rather concerned look on his face, he glanced at Ro, then looked back at her. "That's not what Ro told us, dear—perhaps you should hear him out."

"No! I mean, *yes*, I will hear him out, of course—I can hardly stop him from speaking—*however*, I want you to know, to understand, that regardless of anything whatever, I have no intention of allowing him to be forced into marrying me." She planted her hands on her hips and met her parents' fond smiles—why were they smiling? what did they find so amusing in this?—with rigid determination and unbending purpose. "He may ask, but I will not—"

A hard hand clapped over her lips. Ro's arm banded her waist.

"If you'll excuse us for a few minutes, sir, ma'am, I believe I need to explain a few matters to your daughter."

Her mother smiled even more. "Yes, of course, Ro dear—take however many minutes you wish."

Eyes huge, Lydia mumbled frantically; she tried to pry Ro's hand from her lips, but couldn't budge it. She tried to wriggle; his arm tightened and he lifted her off her feet.

Her father, also grinning delightedly, bobbed his white head. "It's late. We can talk more tomorrow—once Lydia understands."

I do understand!

Her frustrated, exasperated reply came out as a series of mumbles as Ro turned and, with her locked against his chest, carried her to the door. He had to take his hand from her lips to open it.

"Ro, if you don't put me down this instant I'll—"

The hand returned, muting her threat to never speak to him again.

He carried her out of the parlor and straight across the hall—under the startled gazes of Bilt, Mrs. Bilt, and Tabitha, the last of whom was, of course, utterly delighted and actually *clapped!*—and into the darkened tap.

It was late, the lights had been doused; there was no one around to see Ro halt by the wall just inside, then release her. The instant her feet touched the floor, she whirled to berate him. He caught her face in both hands, tipped her lips up to his and covered them.

In a kiss that stole her breath, sent her wits reeling,

and—when he finally lifted his head—had reduced her to dazed incoherency.

She stared at him, blinked, then hauled in a breath and set her chin. "I am not—"

He kissed her again, for much longer this time, more deeply, more ardently, until her wits weren't just reeling but flown, until, when he ended the kiss and raised his head, she had to cling to him and brace her spine against the wall he'd backed her into just to stay upright. In the darkened tap, she blinked her eyes wide, trying to regain her mental feet; speech was, at that moment, far beyond her.

Searching her eyes, he seemed to understand as much. "Good." There was a faintly grim set to his lips. "I suppose I should have known that marrying a Makepeace couldn't possibly be so easy—that it wouldn't be a simple, straightforward matter of me offering for your hand and you accepting."

She concentrated and managed a frown. She opened her lips, but before she could speak, he frowned back harder. "No—just listen. You had your turn, now it's mine. Yes, I told your parents I wanted to offer for your hand. I didn't, however, even attempt to use the excuse that I'd seduced you, or that you had seduced me, that we'd been intimate, whichever way you want to state it. I didn't because that isn't why I want to marry you."

He paused, his eyes searching hers. Sensing that he was fighting some inner battle, overcoming some deep reticence over telling her what he was about to say, she bit her tongue against the impulse to ask the obvious question—this was definitely not the time to interrupt.

Then he drew in a deep breath; lips tight, he held her gaze. "I've wanted to marry you for over ten years—ever since that day in the orchard when we waltzed. I knew it then—and it scared me witless. I was twenty-two and knew nothing of love, and had no idea what to do when I discovered I'd found it far, far earlier than I'd bargained for."

Lydia stared into his silver-gray eyes and felt her world tilt crazily, then slowly realign. Slowly re-form into a landscape she'd never imagined she might see.

His lips curved, not humorously. "Yes, I know. That's a long time ago, but . . . I'm now thirty-two, and the only love I've ever known is for you."

Ro reached blindly for her hand, caught it, raised it to his chest, and laid it over his heart. "My heart races for you, and only you. It's always been that way, and always will be. I didn't want to tell you—didn't want you to know—because it makes me feel too exposed, too vulnerable—too dependent."

Closing his hand about hers, he raised it from his chest to press a kiss to her fingers, then another to her palm, his eyes never leaving hers. "I want you as my wife, my viscountess. I need you by my side, and now I know that you want me, too, no matter what you say, I will never let you go. Even if you don't at first agree, I won't go away, or withdraw my suit, or even let you leave here without me. I became yours under the apple trees all those years ago . . ." Holding her gaze, he released her hand and spread his arms. "And now I'm yours to do with as you will. My life is yours, my heart and soul are in your keeping. Nothing you say or do can change that—it simply is."

He sobered, felt all the uncertainties he still harbored rise through him, but he knew her stubbornness, had known he had to admit to the truth and convince her of it or she'd dig in her heels and refuse him. That if he had his pride, so did she, and she wouldn't bend or yield, not unless she believed.

He prayed she now did, that she saw the truth as clearly as he, sensed the power of what linked them as strongly as he did.

Drawing in a tight breath, he forced himself to find out, to say, to ask. "I hope you'll forgive me for keeping you waiting all these years. I'm hoping you can find it in your heart to set those behind us, accept my proposal, and go on from here together." He paused, his fingers once more finding and tightening around hers. "My one and only love—will you marry me?"

Having her as his wife was the one thing in his life he couldn't simply demand, couldn't, one way or another, simply arrange to make his. She had to agree, of her own volition, with her own determination, or it would never be.

His heart slowed, stuttered; as he looked into her wide eyes, their expression unreadable in the poor light, and waited for her answer, for the words he needed to hear her say, he could have sworn his heart literally stopped. Distantly he heard a clock chime, twelve midnight.

Then she smiled, tremulously at first, but the glow only grew until it lit her face and she beamed at him. "Oh, Ro! Of course I will."

She flung her arms about his neck, flung herself into his embrace as his arms closed around her, and kissed him. Soundly. Then she drew back and fixed him with a quintessentially Makepeace look. "You only had to ask." Radiant, she positively glowed.

Relief laced with triumph sweeping through him, Ro grinned and drew her back into his arms.

As he kissed her to seal their pact, a distant part of his mind cynically reflected that it had taken fate a mere twenty-four hours to accomplish the fall of Rogue Gerrard.

When news of the impending marriage of Robert "Rogue" Gerrard, Viscount Gerrard, of Gerrard Park, and Miss Lydia Constance Makepeace, of the Wiltshire Makepeaces, broke upon the unsuspecting *ton*, there was much whispering and speculation as to how Miss Makepeace had managed where all others had failed, and apparently with so little effort. The grandes dames, however, were as one in declaring that it came as no surprise—the lady who had tamed the rogue, despite her earlier appearances as a quiet, sensible, and decorous young woman, was quite clearly as eccentric as the rest of her clan.

Only a lady of significant wildness could, they declared, have brought Rogue Gerrard to his knees.

Naturally Ro heard of their conclusion, but he only smiled. He saw no reason to correct them. But he knew the truth. Carried it enshrined in his heart.

It wasn't Lydia's elusive wildness—although its very elusiveness fascinated and lured him—that had made him her devoted mate. It was love, pure and simple—his for her and hers for him—that had sealed his fate.

Love had been the only weapon involved in his capitulation—in bringing about what the *ton*, with typical histrionic fervor, referred to as "The Fall of Rogue Gerrard."

Stephanie Laurens

New York Times bestselling author **STEPHANIE LAURENS** began writing as an escape from the dry world of professional science. Her hobby quickly became a career. Her novels set in Regency England have captivated readers around the globe, making her one of the romance world's most beloved and popular authors. Stephanie lives in Melbourne, Australia, with her husband and two daughters.

For information on Stephanie and her books, including details of upcoming novels, visit Stephanie's website at www.stephanielaurens.com.

Readers can write to Stephanie Laurens via e-mail at slaurens@vicnet.net.au. Readers can also e-mail that address to be included in the PRIVATE Heads-Up e-mail book announcement list for notification whenever a new Stephanie Laurens title hits the shelves!

Spellbound

Mary Balogh

Chapter One

Nora Ryder was expecting the village of Wimbury to be busy, small though it was. This was the first day of May, after all, and Cowper, Mrs. Witherspoon's handyman, had warned her that the maypole had been set up on the village green and that there was to be a fair about its perimeter. Everyone from miles around would be there, he had told her.

Except Mrs. Witherspoon herself, of course. She never went anywhere.

And except him and the other servants, Cowper had added somewhat wistfully.

Mrs. Witherspoon never celebrated any event—not even Christmas or birthdays or the first snowdrop that poked through the grass to bloom in the springtime. Working as her companion for the past six months had not been a joyful experience for Nora—and that was grossly to understate the case.

It might have been better to choose another day than May Day for going into Wimbury, Nora realized, but really she had little choice in the matter. It was true that she had re-signed from her position and might conceivably have stayed one more day if it had been an amicable ending to her em-ployment. It had not, though. In fact, she had resigned scarcely one whole minute before Mrs. Witherspoon sacked her.

Mrs. Witherspoon had told her she was to leave immedi-ately, and Nora had replied that that was not nearly soon enough. They had settled on the following day.

She had not been paid—not once in six months. There had been various excuses for five of those months. Once it had been the apparently reasonable argument that since Mrs. Witherspoon never ventured beyond her own home and gar-den, then neither did her companion, and so there was noth-ing upon which to spend money. But now, after half a year, Mrs. Witherspoon had informed Nora that her annual wage had been agreed upon at the start of the employment—and that meant it was to be paid annually. Since Nora had seen fit to abandon her post, she was not entitled to be paid. Was it not enough that she had been fed and housed in the lap of luxury all this time?

It would not have been nearly enough even if there had *been* luxury, which there most certainly had not. But Nora, recognizing a hopeless case when she saw one, chose not to argue the point beyond giving herself the satisfaction of in-forming her erstwhile employer just before she left exactly—*exactly!*—what she thought of her.

Eloquence could be marvelously satisfying to one's bruised sensibilities, but did nothing to fill one's purse.

Yesterday Cowper, who had been running an errand for the old lady, had bought a stagecoach ticket to London for Nora—not out of the said lady's bounty, it might be added, but out of the last of the meager supply of money Nora had originally brought with her to Dorset.

The journey itself might prove to be a hungry one, she realized, since she had enough left in her purse to buy perhaps half a cup of tea if it was being sold cheaply, and Mrs. Witherspoon's cook could not be expected to risk her employer's wrath by packing up some choice morsels of food for Nora to take with her. But at least she would be free again and sane again. And woefully penniless—again. Jeremy, her brother, would sigh and favor her with one of his long-suffering looks when he discovered her on his doorstep—again!

She was going to have to search for some new employment, something more permanent this time, it was to be hoped.

She had been saved from having to walk the five miles to the village with her heavy valise when Mr. Crowe, a neighboring farmer, had decided to take advantage of the holiday to visit his daughter ten miles away. Happily for Nora, his journey was to take him through Wimbury. His aged gig had wooden seats that threatened the legs and derriere of the unwary with a thousand splinters. Its squeaky wheels set one's teeth on edge with every turning, and it smelled strongly of manure even when empty of that commodity, as it was today. However, squeezing herself up beside Mr. Crowe's rotund frame was preferable to walking, and Nora had accepted his offer of a ride with heartfelt gratitude.

She was expecting to find the village crowded, then, even though it was still morning when they arrived. What she was *not* expecting was the frenzied press of activity about the Crook and Staff Inn, the very place where she was headed. There were those, of course, who would have taken their places early in the taproom, intent upon imbibing as much good cheer as they could before the day's festivities began in earnest. But they ought to be quietly and respectably ensconced inside.

These people were all outside.

So was the stagecoach, which Nora could see above their heads. It had arrived early. She felt an uncomfortable lurching of the stomach as she sat forward in her seat. What if it went rumbling off in the direction of London before she could weave her way through the crowd and board it? What would she do then? She would have to wait a whole day for the next one—assuming, that was, there would be room for her on tomorrow's coach. Whatever would she do in the meanwhile? She could not go back to Mrs. Witherspoon's. She had certainly burned a few bridges there. Not that she regretted a single one of them.

It quickly became apparent, however, that she was not in imminent danger of losing her ride. The stagecoach was listing at far too sharp a sideways angle to be occasioned by an obese passenger or a particularly heavy piece of luggage stowed too far to one side.

"That thar coach must ha' met with an accident," Mr. Crowe remarked sagely, breaking a conversational lull of ten minutes or longer. And he drew his gig to a halt some distance away, lifted Nora's valise out of the back, held out a massive hand to help her alight, nodded and grunted when she thanked him, and climbed in and drove off just as if he did not possess an inquisitive bone in his body.

Nora picked up her bag and hurried forward into the noisy fray. Crowds of people, doubtless a mingling of the stagecoach passengers and curious villagers, were clustered about the gateway to the inn yard and the coach itself, most of them talking excitedly, several of them doing so at great volume and with wild, even menacing gestures.

"What happened?" she asked the people closest to her.

They all spoke more or less together though none of them turned their heads to look at her.

"There has been a terrible crash. I swear my heart stopped for a whole minute when I heard it. I expected to see at least a dozen dead bodies."

"That coachman did not blow his yard of tin before turning into the inn yard, and he was going too fast anyway. He collided with a perfectly innocent gentleman's vehicle that was on its way out."

"He *did* blow his horn. Are you stone deaf? It came near to deafening *me*. The gentleman was not paying proper attention, that was all."

"Thought he had the right of way just because he had a natty new curricle and pockets stuffed full with half a fortune."

"Three-quarters full, I would wager. Did you catch a look at his boots? He didn't get *them* for ten quid or even twenty."

"The coachman was not looking where he was going, and see what happened as a result. It is good for him no one was killed. He would be swinging for it before the week was out. It was his fault right enough."

"He had his eyes peeled. It was the gentleman who was looking over his shoulder—probably at one of the chambermaids."

"A public vehicle has the right of way."

"No it don't. Where did you get that daft idea? The carriage that is leaving gets to go first."

"The coachman was swearing the air blue just a minute or two ago. You should have heard him. He told that gentleman a thing or two, I am here to tell you."

"That's as much as *you* know of the English language. The gentleman swore rings around him."

"The coach has lost a wheel and its axle has been badly damaged. It may not even be possible to repair it."

"The gentleman's curricle has been smashed to smithereens."

"No, it hasn't. It merely has a split axle. I don't think it's even in as bad a way as the coach."

"And who do they think is going to mend two broken axles and a broken wheel today of all days when everyone is on holiday? They'll expect it, though, mark my words."

Beyond the group closest to her, Nora could hear the stagecoach passengers, their voices raised in appeal and outrage. What were they supposed to do until tomorrow? And what if they could not *wait* until tomorrow to get where they were going? How could they be sure anyway that the coach would be ready to resume its journey even then? *Someone* was going to hear about this. *Someone* was going to answer for it. *Someone* was going to pay.

Nora felt slightly weak at the knees even though it did not appear that anyone had sustained any physical injury.

What was *she* going to do?

Within a few minutes everyone was beginning to drift away in the direction of the inn itself, and Nora was able to elbow her way forward until she stood before the man who must be the stagecoach driver.

"When do you expect to be on the way again?" she asked, realizing the foolishness of her question even as she spoke. She could see the carriage more fully now.

"Tomorrow, if I have anything to say about it, ma'am," he said none too graciously, not even looking at her. "If you have a ticket, you are just going to have to come back tomorrow."

"But what am I to do today?" she asked him.

He shrugged and scratched his head, his eyes on the damage to his vehicle. "Take a room at the inn like everyone else, I suppose," he said. "You had better hurry, though. There aren't going to be any left pretty soon."

It would not matter if there were a hundred rooms left. Nora's mind was humming with the realization that she was well and truly stranded. With nowhere to go and without a feather to fly with.

"Perhaps," she said, "I can have back the price of my ticket."

Though that was no real solution to anything, was it? If she spent that money, then she was going to be stranded here forever and a day.

"It's not possible, I'm afraid, ma'am," he said with surly impatience, bending to peer under the vehicle. "No refunds are allowed."

And so that was that. Somehow she was going to have to stay stranded here for a whole day—and a whole night—before she could even hope to begin the long journey to London.

She did not know anyone here. Even though Wimbury was only five miles from Mrs. Witherspoon's, she had not once before left the house and garden, and there had never been visitors.

It was going to be a long, hungry day. Nora glanced up at the sky as she wandered aimlessly toward the inn entrance, where everyone else had disappeared. She stood just inside the taproom door for several minutes, undecided about what to do or where to go. Other people milled about her. All seemed to have somewhere to go and someone else to talk to.

She felt suddenly and horribly lonely and isolated and—stranded.

A lanky young man wearing a soiled apron and carrying a tray of empty glasses stopped close to her. He was looking slightly harried.

"If you are another of the stranded passengers, ma'am," he said, "you are going to have to make other arrangements for tonight. We are full, what with the May Day fair and the coach crash."

"I—"

Nora was never afterward sure what she was about to say. Someone else spoke first. It was a man's voice, soft and cultured and clearly accustomed to commanding and being obeyed.

"The lady already has a room," he said. "She is with me."

Nora, startled, looked to see to whom and about whom the gentleman was speaking. But clearly he was speaking to the waiter—and he was looking directly at her with lazy blue eyes, above which his dark eyebrows arched.

She had a fleeting impression of tallness and broad shoulders and slender hips and well-muscled thighs, all clad in fashionable, expertly tailored clothing that looked as if it had been molded to his handsome frame. But then other thoughts intruded.

It could *not* be.

Surely—

The light inside the taproom was dim, the windows being small and half covered with heavy curtains. It was impossible to see with any clarity after just stepping inside out of the sunlight.

Even so . . .

It could not possibly be, though.

But it was.

Or rather, *he* was.

Richard.

He was *Richard*.

But she had missed something. He had said something else during the second or two of numb shock she had felt as she recognized him. The words were only now imprinting themselves on her hearing, like an after-echo.

"She is my wife," he had just said.

"Ah, that is all right then, sir," the waiter said as he turned away about his business.

Chapter Two

Richard Kemp, Lord Bourne, had made an early start on his journey. He had left Dartwood Close behind him when dawn still barely reddened the eastern sky. He was going to spend a few days with his grandmother in Hampshire before continuing on his way to London, where he would stay for the rest of the Season.

It was a sunny morning with no appreciable wind—a perfect day for traveling by curricle. His carriage, with most of his baggage and his valet, was to follow him to London in a few days' time.

He made a stop at Wimbury for a change of horses when the morning was already quite well advanced, though he resisted the temptation to step inside the inn for refreshments. The taproom looked crowded, as was to be expected on a holiday, especially as he could see that there was to be a fair here—and the maypole was up. He would surely allow himself to be drawn into conversation if he went inside, and before he knew it an hour or more of valuable traveling time would have gone by. He would relax when he reached his destination. His grandmother would be delighted to have his company.

But what was that old adage about more haste leading to less speed? Old adages had an annoying habit of being right, as he realized when he thought about it later.

If he had started out from home at a more civilized hour, or if he had stopped sooner to change horses, or if he had stepped inside the taproom here for a glass of ale and a pasty, or if he had done a number of things more slowly than he had actually done them, then he would not have been pulling out through the gateway of the Crook and Staff's yard at the exact moment a stagecoach was pulling in. And he would not have been delayed by a whole day as a result.

But that was precisely what did happen.

He was pulling out of the yard with full care and attention upon what he did despite the fact that the maypole with its colorful array of ribbons was directly in his line of vision, when suddenly all hell broke loose. He heard the simultaneous sounds of a horn blasting and hooves thundering and imprecations being shouted—some of them coming from his own lips—and metal and wood crashing and screeching against metal and wood and hysterical screaming. And he saw horses rearing, their eyes rolling in panic, and a florid-faced, gap-toothed coachman hauling on the ribbons from the large box of a stagecoach as it attempted to occupy the same space as his curricle in the gateway.

All his reflexes set him to work bringing his panicked team under control and jumping from his seat before he could be pitched out of it and crushed beneath what was left of his curricle.

He had collided with a stagecoach.

His first coherent thought was that the driver of a stagecoach was supposed to blow his yard of tin *before* turning a sharp corner, not *as* he was doing it—at far too reckless a speed. The warning blast had been a mite useless at that point.

There was a driver, he suspected, who was overeager for his pint of ale.

Passengers spilled from the stagecoach as it tipped dangerously to one side, some of them involuntarily, most notably those who had been perched on the roof. The coachman, swearing horribly, was attempting to control his own horses and prevent the vehicle from tipping completely over while creating further catastrophe.

Men were yelling. Women were screaming. The taproom was emptying of its patrons, most of them still clutching their mugs. Villagers were appearing as if from nowhere.

Miraculously—it was Richard's second coherent thought—there appeared to be no dead or mangled bodies lying around and no blood. He did a quick mental inventory of his own limbs and other body parts and discovered nothing more alarming than a sore ankle, which was very probably not broken or even badly sprained.

There was not a great deal of time for thought or recollection. A score of people—at least that many—were talking or yelling or shrieking at once, most of them claiming to have been eyewitnesses, and enough blame was being slung about to do justice to a mass riot. And since the occupants of his own vehicle were in a minority of one, most of the blame was coming his way.

His horses appeared unharmed, he noted at a quick glance. So were the stagecoach's. Another miracle. His curricle had not fared nearly as well. It had an axle that was very probably broken, and the paintwork was horribly scratched. But nothing was beyond repair, if his guess was correct.

He turned his attention to defending himself. Not that anyone was throwing fists or using life-threatening weapons. But the air was fairly blue with damaging language, most of it issuing from the stagecoach driver's mouth and most of it graphic and uncomplimentary about his pedigree and that of his mother. The man's face was so purple, Richard feared

he had apoplexy and was the only real casualty of this
mishap.

Richard opened his own mouth and gave as good as he
got. The first shock of the collision over with, he was beginning to feel angry. Furiously angry, actually. The curricle
was no more than three months old and had been his pride
and joy. He had been hoping to reach his grandmother's tonight and was now stranded in the back of beyond—without
his valet. And this stagecoach driver with his foul mouth
was *entirely* to blame, as Richard informed him in no uncertain terms and without having to resort to inventing pedi-
grees.

The ire of the passengers began to turn against their own
coachman, and a fierce discussion began on when exactly that
horn had been sounded and how fast exactly the coach had
been going as it turned into the inn yard. The taproom patrons, who had been grinning at the coachman's colorful language, cheered Richard's blistering tirade, and one of them
raised his glass to him. The villagers added their own opin-
ions, entirely uninformed as they were, since it was unlikely
any of them had actually witnessed the mishap—though all
would probably claim to have done so for the rest of the day.

Having had his say and noted that a couple of ostlers were
freeing his horses and leading them away, Richard turned
on his heel and stalked off into the inn, the innkeeper at his
side assuring him that the best room in the house had already been set aside for the gentleman's use tonight.

The stranded passengers crowded in behind him, having
just realized that they, too, would need rooms and that there
might not be enough to go around. A few were loudly indig-
nant and warned no one in particular that *someone* was going to pay for this. Several others were quieter and apparently
resigned to the unexpected delay.

One such person stood inside the door, making no effort

to elbow her way forward to demand a room. She carried a valise and was decently dressed, but something about her drooped shoulders and downcast expression told Richard that finding a vacant room might not be her main problem.

How many of her fellow passengers, he wondered suddenly, might not be able to afford the extra expense the crash had caused them?

He lost sight of her for a moment as he nodded to acknowledge the innkeeper's assurance that his bag had already been taken up to the best room in the house. He turned to follow it up. He would be glad to get out of this hubbub until everything had quieted down. He would go out later to have a good look at his curricle and see what arrangements he could make to have it repaired.

This was all one *devil* of an inconvenience, he thought almost viciously.

He glanced toward the doorway again as he turned. She was still there, that woman passenger. She must be traveling alone. She was turning her face toward the window, and the light shone on her profile.

It was something about the nose. It was not a particularly prominent feature and it was apparently straight when viewed from the front. But there was a slight bend in it just below the bridge that gave her face character and saved her from being just conventionally pretty.

Or so he had once told her when she had wished aloud that it was perfectly straight.

But it *could* not be . . .

He was forever seeing women who reminded him of her, but on closer inspection they were never anything like her at all. There *was* no one like her. *Thank the Lord*, he added silently with a tightening of the jaw.

But he took several steps away from the staircase, frowning as he did so. He had to take a closer look, as he always did.

She had turned her face back into the room and had raised her eyes to a waiter who was returning to the kitchen with a tray of empty glasses.

Oh, devil take it!

She was ten years older, and there was something very different about her. *Many* things, in fact. But there was no mistaking her.

She was Nora.

The waiter was speaking impatiently to her, telling her to leave.

Richard, not even pausing to wonder why that fact should so annoy him, took one more step forward.

"The lady already has a room," he said. "She is with me."

Too late he thought that it might have been wiser simply to have hurried away to his room. He had spoken without even knowing what he was about to say.

She looked startled and her eyebrows rose as she turned her gaze on him. He watched surprise turn slowly to shock as she recognized him.

She certainly had changed. Age—she must be twenty-eight now, three years his junior—had matured her face into a perfect oval, and it had taken some of the bloom of youth from her cheeks. Her eyes, though just as blue as he remembered them, looked larger and deeper, with less sparkle. Her flaxen hair was no longer dressed in curls and ringlets to bounce about her head and face at every movement. It was drawn back smoothly beneath her bonnet and coiled at her neck. The bonnet and the rest of her clothes were serviceable and respectable. All the remembered pastel-shaded frills and flounces were gone.

She looked like someone's governess—and perhaps was.

They were thoughts and impressions that flashed through his head in a second or less.

"She is my wife," he added.

That satisfied the waiter, who continued on his way to the kitchen.

There was a moment's silence—if one discounted the din around them.

"I am not—" she said.

He held up a staying hand as he stepped even closer to her.

"It might be wise not to complete that thought," he said, his tone clipped. "I doubt there are any rooms left, and this is a respectable establishment. You had better come and share my room—as my wife."

She stared at him, clearly feeling just as he felt—that at any moment she would awake from this bizarre dream.

"Sir? Mr. Kemp?" The landlord was at his elbow, indicating the staircase.

Richard broke the spell of gazing at Nora and turned his head. He had chosen not to divulge his title or there would be no end to the obsequious bowing and scraping.

"Have my wife's bag carried up, too, if you will," he said. And he cupped her elbow with one hand and turned her in the direction of the stairs.

"Your *wife*, sir?" The innkeeper sounded surprised.

"She has taken no outward harm from the spill," Richard told him, "but I wish her to rest for a while nevertheless."

"Of course, sir, Mrs. Kemp." The innkeeper's voice had turned brisk and he was clicking his fingers to draw the attention of a servant.

There was still a great deal of noise and hubbub among those passengers who had not yet got a room. Someone was telling them, as Richard maneuvered Nora around them and up the stairs to his room, that they would be billeted with villagers if they would just have some patience.

She would have been billeted, then, even if she had no money. He might have left her to her fate with a clear conscience.

With a clear conscience? He frowned. Why would his conscience be involved in any of this?

He opened the door of his room and stood aside to allow her to step inside first. The noise from downstairs was still very audible, but somehow the room seemed very silent.

"Richard."

She turned to him, her face pale. But she had to wait until the servant had brought in her valise and set it down beside his own bag before leaving and shutting the door behind him.

"Richard," she said again, "I am not your wife."

"You are not?" He raised his eyebrows and clasped his hands behind him. She was still very slender, but the coltishness of youth had gone from her figure to leave it looking more voluptuous.

"No, of course not," she said.

"Of course not." He spoke softly and smiled at her though there was no amusement in the expression.

"I ought not to be here," she said. "This is not right."

She glanced uneasily at the door.

"You would rather go back out there alone?" he said, turning to the door as if to open it for her.

"They were saying something about billets in the village," she said.

"Did you take any hurt from the spill?" he asked her. Perhaps her paleness had a direct physical cause. She looked as if she might faint at any moment.

"I was not in it," she said. "I was not on the coach. I was to board it here."

"You live near here, then?" he asked her.

"Five miles away," she said. "*Lived.* Past tense. I was companion to an elderly lady."

"You were sacked?" he asked her.

"I resigned before I could be," she told him. "It was not pleasant employment. Mrs. Witherspoon is not a pleasant lady."

"I suppose," he said, "it must be difficult for you to knuckle under to authority."

He felt instantly ashamed of himself. That had been a low blow.

She looked steadily at him, some color back in her cheeks.

"I am going to get a billet," she said, taking a step toward him.

"I doubt you are eligible," he told her, "since you were not actually on the coach when it crashed."

She stopped.

"Do you have any money?" he asked her.

"Excuse me, please." She took another step forward. Her shoulders had straightened, he noticed.

"You had better stay here," he said, moving in front of the door. "I will not molest you, if that is what you fear. You may choose whatever piece of floor best suits you for a bed. No one will know whether we are man and wife or not— unless you choose to provide the information. If you know it, that is. And if you do not like accepting charity, do note that I have no valet or other servant with me. If you do not like being my wife, you may be my servant."

"Is there a difference?" she asked, a definite edge to her voice.

He looked as steadily at her as she was looking at him.

"I need to go and assess the damage to my curricle," he said. "And I am hungry. I will perhaps eat first. Do you wish to come with me?"

"Absolutely not," she said. "I am going to ask for a billet."

"Suit yourself." He shrugged, opened the door, stepped through it, and closed it behind him before descending to the taproom and the dining room beyond it, where all was merry din and enticing aromas. It occurred to him suddenly that he had not eaten yet today.

What would she do? When he went back upstairs, would

he find an empty room except for his bag in the middle of the floor? Or would she still be there?

He was feeling considerably shaken.

He took a small table beside a window and ordered ham and eggs with potatoes and toast. He sat deliberately with his back to the stairs. He did not want to see her leave. He did not want to feel responsible for her if she did so.

Good Lord, he was *in no way* responsible for her. Except that a ten-year-old question that had worried at his consciousness for every one of those years was asking itself again.

If she left now, she might disappear forever. She might not even turn up tomorrow morning to take the stage to wherever she was going. He might never see her again.

There was a surprising degree of panic in the thought.

He despised himself for feeling it.

He had worked Nora out of his system years ago. It had not been easy since she had had a very real and permanent effect upon his life. His present and his future would be forever shaped by what had happened between him and her.

But if she disappeared from his life forever, it would still not be long enough.

He *hoped* she would be gone.

He hoped he would not see her for the rest of today or tomorrow morning. Or ever again.

"And send some of the same up to my wife with a pot of tea," he said to the waiter as the latter set his food before him. "If she has already gone out to enjoy the festivities, take the plate back down to the kitchen. One of the servants may eat the food at my expense."

She had not answered his one question. But he knew as surely as if he had raided her purse that she had no money. Her former employer had probably refused to pay her since she had resigned from her position.

It was none of his concern that she might be penniless. Indeed, he hoped she was. He hoped she would starve.

Except that he would feel responsible. Dash it all, he would feel responsible.

All over again.

And except that the thought was spiteful, and it disturbed him to realize that he could feel such a juvenile hatred of someone he had not even seen in ten years.

He picked up his knife and fork only to discover that his appetite had fled.

Chapter Three

She was going to leave immediately. She would ask to be billeted elsewhere. But there were so many problems involved with that plan that she dithered and stood where she was for several minutes after he had left the room.

It might be too late by now. And perhaps he was right—perhaps she would not qualify since she had not yet been on the stagecoach when it crashed. And the fact that she was supposed to be Mrs. Kemp would necessitate some awkward explanations. And perhaps even billets in the homes of villagers would have to be paid for. Even if payment was not required, she would feel obliged to offer something for her keep. Yet she had no more than a couple of small coins left in her purse.

And . . .

And, and, and.

And he was *Richard*. Richard Kemp.

It was as if that realization had only now fully struck her. She sat down hard on the side of the bed and closed her eyes.

Richard was here. He had actually come to her rescue and brought her up to his room. Not that he had looked any too pleased about it. He had looked downright morose, in fact.

Why had he done it, then? She gripped the bedpost with one hand.

Oh, dear God, Richard! What strange, bizarre coincidence had brought them together like this in such a remote corner of England? *Stranded* them together, in fact. He was stranded here until tomorrow just as surely as she was.

How had she even recognized him? He was very different from what she remembered. He had been little more than a boy when she saw him last. He had been tall and slender and lithe, his face handsome beneath the shock of dark hair though his expression was almost always serious. But his blue eyes were warm and even blazed with intensity during certain private moments. She had fallen headlong, passionately in love with him long before he knew.

And he had loved her long before *she* knew.

It was all so long ago that it might have happened in another lifetime.

Though it had been real enough at the time and nasty enough at the end.

Nora turned her head and rested her forehead against the bedpost. She had not wanted to live. She had wanted to die. But death could not be willed upon oneself, she had found. She had lived on anyway.

He was a man now with a man's powerful and perfect body. His face was handsome and cold—those blue eyes were so, *so* cold. And there was a confidence in his bearing that had not been there before. He looked as if he had been born to command, though of course he had not.

He was Lord Bourne now, she reminded herself. A baron. A stranger. She had never known him by that name.

Why, she wondered again, had he come to her rescue? It

was clear he did not like her. Perhaps to gloat? He had told her she might choose whichever patch of floor she wanted for tonight. While he slept on the bed. Gallantry had had nothing to do with his offer, then.

Yes, he had done it to remind her just how much their positions had reversed themselves.

She was going to have to seek a billet somewhere else despite all the problems. She would not be beholden to him. *Him* of all people. She got to her feet and then clutched the bedpost again when someone tapped on the door.

He would come right on in, so she crossed the room and opened the door to find the waiter, carrying a large tray. She could not see what was on the plate, but she could smell the food.

For the first time she realized she was ravenously hungry. She had not eaten since dinner last evening, and she was facing at least two days without food if she were left to her own resources. She clenched the muscles of her stomach to stop it from rumbling.

"Your husband ordered the tray sent up to you, Mrs. Kemp, ma'am," the waiter explained.

She did not have the strength of mind to send it away. Richard would have to pay for the food anyway, she reasoned. She might as well eat it. She stood aside to allow the waiter inside to set his tray down on the dressing table.

And after he had left, she ate every last crumb. She drained the pot of tea. And then she wondered if it would be utterly foolish to leave her last coins beside the tray before she left. Yes, of course it would. And pathetic, too.

Where would she go? It was far too late now to ask for a billet. She could go and mingle with the villagers while they celebrated the holiday. But what would she do tonight? She would have to think about that when the time came, she supposed.

And then she remembered his saying, with a heavy sarcasm

she had never heard in his voice before, that if she did not want
to be his wife, she could be his servant instead.

It was one way to pay for her breakfast. One way to sal-
vage a little of her pride. One way to thumb her nose at him.

She opened his bag. There was not a great deal in it.
Clearly he had not expected to spend long on the road. She
took out a black tailed evening coat, brushed off some lint,
and hung it in the wardrobe. She shook out a white shirt to
rid it of wrinkles and hung it up beside the coat. It was of the
finest linen, she noticed. She ran her hands over the soft
fabric and even lifted it to her cheek for a moment. She was
startled by a faint yet familiar smell though the garment had
obviously been laundered recently. She smoothed out three
starched neck cloths and hung them carefully over the rail
beside the shirt. She set a pair of black evening shoes side by
side at the bottom of the wardrobe. She left the small pile of
undergarments where it was and set out his shaving gear
beside the washbowl.

The water pitcher was empty. She pulled on the bell rope
and then, when no one answered the summons, she took the
pitcher and went downstairs herself to fetch some water. He
was not going to be able to say that she had not earned her
breakfast.

There were a few people in the taproom and dining room
beyond it. Richard was not among them. He must be outside
in the yard, perhaps looking at his curricle. She would have
plenty of time to slip away before he returned.

Since there were no servants about to help her, she walked
right into the kitchen. She caused some consternation there
and much bowing and curtsying. She did not have to wait
long for the kettle to boil and her pitcher to be filled with hot
water. Even so, matters had changed by the time she got
back upstairs. When she opened the door and stepped inside, it was to find Richard in the act of stripping off his
coat.

"Ah," he said, turning to look at her, "I thought you had forgotten to take your valise with you when you left."

"I have returned just for a moment," she said. "I went to fetch some hot water for you. I thought perhaps you would wish to shave."

He was looking at her with raised eyebrows.

The pitcher was heavy. He did not come to relieve her of it. She crossed the room and set it down on the washstand.

If the crash had not happened, she realized, he would have driven on his way and she would have boarded the stagecoach and they would never have realized that they had passed within a few yards of each other. She would be on her way to London and he to wherever it was he had been going.

"I will be leaving now," she said. "Thank you for breakfast."

"You are not going to shave me?"

His tone was hard, insolent.

She turned her gaze on him.

"Are you not afraid," she said, "that I would slash your throat?"

One corner of his mouth lifted in a knee-weakeningly familiar half smile. But there was nothing pleasant about this one.

"You have grown sharp, Nora," he said softly.

He did not mean intelligent. He meant hard, sharp-tongued.

"I have grown *up*," she told him.

"In ways you did not expect, I suppose," he said.

"We none of us know what is in store for us in life," she said. "We have to grow in whichever direction life takes us. It has been kind to you."

"Life?" he said. "Yes, I suppose it has. And brutal to you."

"It might have been worse." She continued to look steadily at him. His mouth lifted at one corner again.

"Sharp indeed," he said. "What do you plan to do?"

She shrugged. "That is not your concern," she said.

"Ah, but it is." His eyebrows rose, and he looked suddenly arrogant—a new look indeed. But he had had almost ten years to perfect it, had he not? "As far as everyone in Wimbury is concerned, Nora, you are my wife. And everyone will have heard the story of how you must have been thrown from the curricle so that no one even realized you had been there until I found you again inside the inn and bore you up here to rest. Everyone will also know that I had breakfast carried up here for you. A tender, romantic gesture, was it not? It will look extremely odd if you now wander off alone, valise in hand, like an unwanted waif."

"I did not ask you to lie for me," she said sharply.

It was his turn to gaze steadily at her.

"Arc you sure it *was* a lie, Nora?" he asked her.

"Of course it was," she said.

"And yet," he said, his voice soft, "I distinctly remember a nuptial ceremony."

"It was not legal or valid," she cried.

"Just because it was performed in Scotland?" he said. "Just because it was not performed by a minister of the church? Just because you ran away almost immediately after?"

"It was not consummated," she said, and then felt her cheeks flame with heat. It was too late to recall the words, though.

"It is a curious fallacy that many people seem to share," he said. "That an unconsummated marriage is an annullable marriage, that is. It is quite untrue."

She offered no response. She swallowed awkwardly instead.

"Besides," he added as she felt she was looking at him down a long tunnel, "it is an irrelevant point, is it not, Nora? You and I know full well that the marriage *was* consummated."

Once. Fumbling and almost inept. Two eager, nervous virgins groping in the near-darkness caused by heavy curtains and gloomy rain beyond the small window of their bedchamber. Performing the act swiftly and inexpertly and painfully—for her anyway.

Hideous beyond belief.

Wonderful beyond imagining.

Young love ought never to be underestimated.

She broke eye contact with him and looked down at her hands.

"There was no marriage," she said. "It was not a real marriage."

"I suppose not," he said with a soft laugh, which sounded more menacing than amused. "Money made it go away. Money can accomplish many things, as I have discovered to my delight in recent years. You were fortunate, Nora, that there was no child."

She had thought there was. She had been more than three weeks late, and then she had bled horribly. She had often wondered since if there *had been* a child, or at least the beginnings of one. She had wondered if she had miscarried.

She had been sick with relief and disappointment.

She had been sick for a long time. Even getting out of bed each morning had been almost too much of an effort. Even setting one foot ahead of the other. Even eating.

"I am going," she said. It was beginning to sound lame even to her own ears. If she meant it, why was she not already long gone?

She *hated* her helplessness. It seemed to her that she had always been helpless. Though she had fought it once in her life—one glorious, short-lived act of defiance and freedom. And even in recent years she had refused to be dependent. She had refused to allow her brother to support her but had taken employment instead. She must not be too harsh on herself. But she *felt* so helpless.

She reached for her bonnet and her valise.

"You had better stay here," he said, his voice brisk and impersonal. "It is just for the rest of the day and tonight. You might as well be safe here. And you *will be* quite safe. I have no wish to repeat our wedding night—or evening, to be more precise. It was really quite forgettable, was it not?"

The words, she believed, were meant to insult and hurt. They did both.

"So much so," she said, looking up at him, "that until you reminded me, I had long forgotten—as you apparently had not. But you are quite right. I believe it really did happen. It was *very* forgettable."

There was a gleam in his eyes for a moment—a gleam of pure amusement, surely. Again, it was an achingly familiar expression. Why should so much about him be familiar? She had not set eyes on him for ten years. And she had spent every day of those years forgetting him.

Richard.

So briefly her husband. And then not.

"It is May Day," he said. "And it looks as if this village is all set to celebrate the holiday in style. The maypole is up and there are booths all about the village green. And the sun is shining. It feels almost like a summer's day. Let's go outside, Nora, and enjoy the fair. We have to fill in the hours of this day somehow."

"Together?" she asked him.

He shrugged.

"Wimbury is not a large village, is it?" he said. "We would have a hard time avoiding each other even if we tried. And it would look odd if we did so, as if we had quarreled. We would draw more attention to ourselves than either of us would welcome, I believe. It would be easier if we stayed together. Besides, you never did answer my question. *Is* your purse quite empty?"

"That," she said sharply, "is none of your business."

He nodded. "I thought so," he said. "You are going to need to eat and drink again today. We will stay together."

She hesitated. But everything he had said made sense. There was going to be no avoiding him for the rest of the day, she supposed. And tonight they were going to be here together in this room—a thought she did not wish to dwell upon. She might as well spend the day in his presence, too, even if only to curb gossip.

"Very well," she said. "But this is *all* your fault, Richard. If you had not hailed me downstairs with your ridiculous claim, we would not now find ourselves in this predicament."

"If you had not tricked me into eloping with you ten years ago, Nora," he retorted, "that ridiculous claim would not even have occurred, would it? I could merely have played Sir Galahad and offered my room to an old acquaintance while I betook myself to a billet elsewhere."

Tricked!

If you had not tricked me.

She felt almost blinded by hurt as her fingers fumbled to tie the ribbons of her bonnet.

Was the keeping up of appearances so important to him, then? Richard wondered as they left the inn together. The sun warmed them immediately.

Or did he really feel responsible for her? But that was ridiculous. He had not set eyes on her for ten years, and surely he had not thought about her, wondered about her, worried about her for every day of those years. Or had he?

Or was it just that he felt sorry for her? She had come as far down in the world as he had gone up. Farther, in fact.

"Shall we stroll about the green and see what the fair has to offer?" he suggested.

It all looked very inviting. Booths shaded with striped awnings circled the green, the thatch-roofed and white-washed cottages of the village beyond them. And in the center of it all the maypole awaited the dancers. It struck Richard that if he had to be stranded for a whole day, he might have been landed in a far worse place and at a far worse time.

But what bizarre type of fate had stranded Nora here, too?

"Yes, let's," she said, and they set off on a clockwise circuit of the fair. He did not offer his arm, and she made no attempt to take it.

There was a large crowd out already—though of course it must be close to noon by now. All the villagers and people from the surrounding countryside for miles around must have turned out for the occasion. Young and old were dressed in their Sunday best, and all seemed to be in a festive mood for this rare treat of a holiday.

He did not go unnoticed, as he had hoped he might. Neither did Nora. Several strangers stopped to ask them how they did, to assure them that the accident had not been their fault, to welcome them to the village celebrations, to exhort them to enjoy the day.

But how could they even begin to do that? They were silent and awkward together. They both smiled and spoke to strangers yet did neither to each other. The day stretched endlessly ahead. And the night . . . Well, he would think of the night when it came. Had he really told her she could take the *floor*? He resented the fact that she had aroused such spiteful bad manners in him.

Nora! He could still scarcely believe it was really she at his side. He turned his head to look at her and was surprised that he had even recognized her. She was no longer pretty and sparkling with exuberance. She was . . . But he did not want to think of her as beautiful. His jaw hardened, and he looked away.

She stopped to examine the embroidery and lace the ladies of the church had made to raise funds for repairs to the bell tower while he talked with the ladies. He bought a linen handkerchief that just happened to have his initial embroidered in one corner, and he bought a lace-edged handkerchief for Nora despite her look of alarm and assurance that she did not need it.

The ladies, though, smiled from one to the other of them, clearly charmed.

"You take it, love," one of them said. "When your husband wants to buy you gifts, you take them and run."

Both Richard and Nora joined the laughter of the ladies.

"You really ought not to have done that," she said softly but sharply as they moved away. "I do not *want* anything from you."

"It was not a gift for you," he said curtly. "It is a gift for them. They have put a great deal of time and effort into producing beautiful items that will benefit only the church."

"You might have made a simple donation, then," she told him.

"But that would not have been the point at all," he said.

She folded the handkerchief and put it into her reticule without another word—not even a thank-you—while he frowned in irritation at the top of her bonnet. And then both of them lifted their heads to smile at an elderly couple who hoped they had not sustained any injuries in this morning's accident.

At another stall Richard hurled balls at a large cabbage precariously balanced on a stand, failed to knock it down with the first set of three, succeeded with the second ball of the next set, and presented the prize length of ribbon to a small girl who was standing beside him, clapping her hands and laughing.

Nora was doing the same two things, he noticed when it was already too late to give the ribbon to her.

"Oh, that *was* good of you," she said as the child went darting off with her treasure. "She was thrilled."

"I had no personal use for the ribbon," he told her. "Though I might, I suppose, have tied it about my hat and beneath my chin to prevent it from blowing away in the wind."

"It would have looked a mite eccentric," she said. "Especially as it was pink."

"And there is no wind," he added.

For an unguarded moment they smiled into each other's eyes as they shared the silly joke. And for that same moment he saw traces of the old Nora in her face. And then they both sobered and turned away in what he guessed was mutual embarrassment.

They paused at the booth of an artist who was sketching portraits in charcoal and doing quite a passable job of it.

"And you, too, ma'am?" he said, looking up at Nora and then at Richard. "Let me sketch your lovely lady, sir. It will be something you will treasure for a lifetime, I promise you."

"Oh no, really—" Nora turned away.

"Oh, go *on*, mum," someone else urged. "It will be something to remember Wimbury by."

"The day both of you might have got yourselves killed but didn't," someone else added.

Other people lent their voices to persuade her, all of them good-natured and jocular. She looked at Richard, her teeth sinking into her lower lip.

"I think," he said, opening his purse again, "you had better sit for your portrait."

"Take your bonnet off, if you will, ma'am," the artist said. "Your hair is too lovely to hide."

Her fair hair gleamed smooth in the sunlight as she sat very still and self-conscious—though she did relax somewhat after a while as the crowd gathered about spoke with her and teased first a smile and then a laugh from her.

Richard watched in silence. She was indeed lovely. Perhaps lovelier than she had been. It was an odd feeling, gazing at a stranger and yet feeling the pull of familiarity—and hurt and resentment and even hatred. He had thought all those sharp, negative feelings long gone. But they had come rushing back at the mere sight of her, as if the old wounds had not healed at all but had merely festered beneath the surface of his consciousness.

Everyone had to gather about the finished portrait and give an opinion as to whether it was a good likeness or not. Most agreed that it was. Finally the artist handed it to Richard.

Her smile fairly lit up the paper. She looked younger. She looked like the Nora he had known ten years ago.

"It is *nothing* like me," she said after they had moved out of earshot of the artist, who was busy persuading someone else to pay his fee. "It grossly flatters me, as of course it is meant to do. He cannot have his subjects demanding their money back, after all, can he?"

"It does *not* flatter you," he said as he rolled up the picture and clasped it in his hand. "It considerably underestimates you, in fact."

She looked up into his face, startled. But he had spoken curtly, even coldly, he realized. If she had been fishing for a compliment from him, she had had it. The leftover smile from her sitting faded, and she turned away. And he felt badly. There had been no need for that tone of voice. She had not asked to have her portrait done.

"You must find somewhere to dispose of it," she said. "You wasted your money."

"That is for me to decide," he said. "It was my money to waste."

"So it was," she said.

They were like a couple of children, irritable and squabbling over nothing.

They moved on to watch a fast-talking man perform a series of tricks with a deck of cards that looked as greasy as his hair. But he was good.

"Oh, how did he *do* that?" Nora asked after one particularly clever sleight of hand. And when she looked up at Richard, he could see that her cheeks were flushed from the heat of the sun despite the shade of her bonnet brim.

She looked as if she were actually enjoying herself, he thought. And he? The festive atmosphere was admittedly hard to resist. He would have enjoyed the day thoroughly if he had been stranded here alone. Or would he? Would he even be out here in the sunshine, participating in all the absurd pleasures of a country fair, if he were alone?

His fingers closed a little more tightly about the charcoal drawing.

When they moved on she laughed outright at the antics of a juggler dressed like a medieval jester. So did everyone else who was crowded about the man. And so, despite himself, did Richard. He looked down at Nora at the very moment she looked up at him, and suddenly the sun seemed very bright and very hot. They both looked away without speaking.

At the next booth a woman was loudly proclaiming to all who would listen that each stone in the jewelry she was selling was precious and priceless.

"But I'll let you have one of those for a bargain, guv," she told Richard when Nora ran her hands through the hanging strings of brightly colored beads. "Special for today, even though they are real, genuine pearls. Every one of 'em."

Nora laughed. "*Bright blue* pearls?" she asked.

The woman winked at Richard. "Extra rare, they are guv," she said. "Suit your lady a treat, they will. Here, I'll cut the price in half and take even more of a loss. They are yours for a shilling."

"That is eleven pence ha'penny too much," Nora protested, still laughing.

"One and six with the matching bracelet," the woman said, still looking at Richard. "Two shillings for the necklace and *three* bracelets. You won't get a better bargain this side of China, you won't, guv."

"Richard," Nora said in sudden alarm, though she was still laughing, *"don't."*

But he did. Just because suddenly he wanted to.

He took the long rope of garish royal-blue beads from the vendor's hand after paying for them and slipped them over Nora's bonnet while she dipped her head. He drew back to admire the effect against the serviceable dark blue of her dress. She lifted her left arm and he slipped the three bracelets over her wrist.

He expected her to look embarrassed and annoyed, as she had with the handkerchief. Instead she waved her hand in the air so that the beads clicked against one another. And her eyes danced with merriment.

"Everyone will see me coming from a mile away," she said. "How silly you are, Richard."

"And how ravishing you look," he said, making her a mock bow.

"You look like a duchess wearing the crown jewels, mum," the vendor said before turning to bargain with another customer, who was admiring a pair of priceless diamond earbobs.

Nora tipped her head slightly to one side—the familiarity of the gesture smote him.

"You really must not keep doing this, Richard," she said, her eyes still bright though the laughter had faded from them. "You are spending a great deal of money."

"I think perhaps all of five shillings so far," he said.

"Five shillings can be a fortune when one does not have it," she said, and then turned sharply away as if she had revealed too much.

"Are you hungry?" he asked.

She sighed. "No."

He inhaled the savory aroma that was coming from a food stall. "That smells delicious," he said. "And it is a few hours since we had breakfast."

"Richard," she said, "I am not—"

"But I *am*," he said. "And I would rather not eat alone."

He gave her the rolled-up drawing to hold and went to buy them a meat pasty each. And he led the way to an empty plot of grass on the green, where a number of people were sitting, either eating or simply relaxing in the sunshine.

They sat side by side, eating in silence except when one family group nodded affably at them and called across to ask about their health and the state of the curricle. Nora had her legs curled up beside her. Her back was straight, her neck arched over her food. His pasty finished, Richard reclined on one side, propped on one elbow so that he could watch all the festive activity going on around them.

"Have you worked all these years, Nora?" he asked at last and then wished he had not. He did not really want to know about the missing years. He did not *need* to know.

"Not all of them," she said. "I stayed with Papa for two years until he died. He always believed his fortunes would come about again. I suppose I did, too. I did not understand how deeply . . . Well, never mind."

She had been a sheltered and privileged girl when he had known her, daughter of a gentleman of vast wealth and political influence—or so it had seemed. Richard had been his secretary, yet even he had not suspected that Ryder's properties were all mortgaged to the hilt, his debts astronomical, his penchant for gambling out of control. Ryder had managed to pay his wage on time most months.

"After his death I lived with Jeremy for a year," she said—Jeremy Ryder was her brother. "But I would not do that indefinitely especially after he married. I have had employment since then."

He opened his mouth to ask a question, closed it again, and then asked anyway.

"You did not consider marriage?" he asked her.

She did not answer for a while. She was looking toward the juggler, who had just provoked a loud cheer from the people in his vicinity.

"No," she said.

"Because no one would have you?" he asked her.

"Because I would have no one," she said.

"Because you were already married?"

He was not sure she had heard. He had spoken quietly, and there was a great deal of noise and merriment going on about them.

"I was *not*," she said just as quietly after a few moments. "I have chosen not to marry because I do not wish to do so. Why have *you* not married?" And then she turned her head to look at him. "But perhaps you have."

"No," he said. He had thought of marrying. Apart from the emotional need he had sometimes felt for one woman—a whole string of mistresses and casual amours had never satisfied that need—there was the duty of begetting an heir. But he had never been able to persuade himself that he would not be committing bigamy by marrying. Yet he had never checked, had never consulted an expert.

They had eloped to Scotland and had married there. They had returned to their inn room and consummated the marriage. And then, five minutes after they had gone downstairs to get something to eat, her father and brother had arrived and she had gone with them. He had been left behind, unable to travel for two whole days until he had recovered somewhat from the severe beating the two men had meted out as both punishment and warning. He had been a studious young man in those days and not at all robust. Certainly he had been no match for two enraged men.

The man who had married them and the innkeeper who had let a room to them had been paid off, he had gathered. All evidence of the marriage had been swept away.

Did that mean they were not married?

He had never known for sure. He still did not.

But for perhaps an hour and a half of their lives, he and Nora had been man and wife. Happily-ever-after had lasted that long.

What would have happened, he wondered, if he had inherited his title and fortune six months sooner than he had? But the answer was obvious. When he *had* inherited— quite unexpectedly—he had suddenly found himself being warmly congratulated and aggressively courted by the very man who had pursued him to Scotland and beaten him within an inch of his life when he had been nothing but a secretary without prospects. Suddenly he had become a very desirable son-in-law indeed. By that time Ryder had been so close to the brink of disaster that his ruin had become common knowledge and creditors were pressing him from all sides. A wealthy son-in-law would have been a godsend—just as it would have been six months earlier when Ryder had been trying to marry his daughter to old Potts, who, true to his name, was very wealthy indeed.

"What I have done with my life in the last ten years is nothing to do with you, Richard," Nora said now, turning to him as she rubbed the last of the crumbs from her hands onto the grass. "Just as what you have done is nothing to do with me. Let us leave it at that, shall we? If you intend to remain out here, I shall return to the inn room to rest. If you wish to rest, I shall remain out here."

If her father had not pursued her, driven on, no doubt, by the deep fear that he would lose his daughter to an impoverished man and thus not be able to use her to lure a wealthy husband to help pay his debts—had he not pursued her, or had he behaved with greater honor after he had, then they would have been married for ten years now, he and Nora.

They would be long familiar with each other. They would probably have children. They—

A few men, all smiling and jovial, were shooing everyone off the grass. Fiddlers and pipers were tuning their instruments on the far side of the green. Two young girls were straightening out the ribbons about the maypole. The dancing was about to begin.

"Stay," he said, getting to his feet and reaching out a hand to help her to hers. "Let's watch the dancing together, Nora. One gets a chance to watch maypole dancing only once a year, after all."

"Oh," she said, her eyes traveling up the maypole and down to note all the activity about it, "it *would* be a pity to miss it."

And she smiled again as she looked about, a bright, warm, happy expression. The sun glinted off her gaudy beads—her rare and priceless blue pearls. And he wondered if after all he was sorry that this had happened today. There was something undeniably seductive—

But he shook his head slightly, pushing aside the thought.

And then girls and young men took the ribbons in their hands, the musicians struck up a merry, toe-tapping tune, and the dancing began.

He stood watching, his shoulder almost, but not quite, touching Nora's. And he felt a sudden welling of nostalgia for his youth, for those days of charmed innocence, when he had had employment that satisfied him and when there had been Nora, his employer's daughter, to admire from afar. To weave dreams about. To fall headlong in love with, long before he knew she returned his feelings. And finally to hold and to kiss and to rescue from an undesirable marriage— rushing her off to the border and beyond like the proverbial knight in shining armor rescuing his damsel in distress.

Except that there had been nothing final about it.

No happily-ever-after.

She was tapping her foot and clapping her hands, as were most of the other spectators about the green. She was smiling again, her eyes sparkling with pleasure.

She looked up at him.

He looked back.

And, God help him, he smiled at her.

Chapter Five

It struck Nora that she had been terribly, terribly lonely for a long time. So long a time, in fact, that it seemed to her she had always been lonely.

She had been a pampered and adored child, it was true, even though her mother had died when she was but a year old. But she had rarely had companions of her own age, and she had never been sent away to school. As a girl she had been taught to expect a glittering come-out Season and a match with a wealthy, distinguished gentleman. But then, before she could even be taken to London to participate in a Season, she had been told that she would marry Sir Cuthbert Potts, who was amiable and good-hearted—but on the wrong side of his sixtieth birthday. She had not understood until she had objected that he was also to be her father's savior—she had not known how close to financial ruin her father was.

She had been a lonely girl.

And for the last several years—well, "loneliness" was not a powerful enough word. Not that she was in the habit of feeling sorry for herself. But now, when she was in the very midst of such exuberant celebrations and watched the dancers weave their colored ribbons about the maypole while the sun beamed brightly down on them all—now it struck her that she was lonely.

For Richard stood at her side, almost shoulder to shoulder with her, in fact. But they were as far apart as if they had been standing on opposite sides of the globe. Her loneliness was worse than if she stood here alone and hungry and homeless, as she would have been if the owner of the crashed curricle had been anyone but him.

And yet a perverse part of her was undeniably happy. This day was like a time out of time, something to be lived and hugged to herself and remembered—even if only with pain. Her cheap, garish, bright blue beads caught her eye as they glinted in the sunlight, and she knew she would keep them and treasure them as if they really were the costliest of jewels.

The human heart was an incomprehensible thing.

Her right foot beat out the time of the music against the grass. She clapped her hands, as most of the spectators were doing, and smiled. It was May Day and she was alive and healthy and . . .

Well, why not be happy when the chance offered itself?

It does not flatter you. It considerably underestimates you. And how ravishing you look.

He had spoken those words to her today, and he was standing beside her now—*Richard* was. It was still an incredible thought. The last time she had seen him was in the dining room of their inn in Scotland. He had not stopped her father from taking her upstairs to pack her belongings. He had not come after her either then or when they left the inn. He had never come after her. She had not heard from him again except for one strange, brief, formal letter in which he had offered to marry her. It was after he had unexpectedly inherited his title and fortune, six months after their elopement, no more than a week after the final horrible crash of her father's fortune and ruin of all his prospects.

It was an offer that had been made out of pity—perhaps. Or out of a desire to gloat over her father, who had pleaded with her to accept.

She had refused.

She turned her head now to look up at him, and he looked back—and smiled.

He had been a serious young man, her father's secretary. She had admired him for a long time before she had walked past the open door of his study one day and he had looked up from his books and their eyes had met and he had smiled at her—and she had plummeted all the way into love with him.

His smile had not changed. It began in his eyes, crinkling them attractively at the corners, and spread to his mouth.

Nora was smitten with a yearning nostalgia that reached back beyond the empty, bitter years since they had last smiled at each other. That had been on their wedding day.

His eyes lingered on hers, and surely—ah, surely—there was an answering longing there.

Why had everything gone so terribly wrong?

The music and the dancing had stopped, and one of the men who had shooed them all off the green fifteen minutes ago was circling it again, beckoning with both hands, urging other people to take the ribbons and dance with the May Day.

"Come along, sir," he called when he arrived close to them. "Mr. Kemp, is it not? Bring your lady and dance, sir. It was a happy chance that stranded you here today. It is said that couples who dance together about the maypole dance together through eternity."

There was a burst of merry laughter and a few cheers from those standing nearby, and then he moved on, calling similar persuasions to other people as he went.

Richard was still half smiling.

"Shall we?" he said, gesturing toward the maypole.

And the yearning was there again, more intense than ever.

"I have not danced about a maypole since I was a girl," she said. But her eyes said that she was ready to try again.

"It has been at least that long for me," he said. "If you get hopelessly tangled up in the ribbons, I will be right there with you. Shall we try anyway? At the very least we will provide these villagers with a good laugh."

And then he did something that fairly took her breath away. He lifted one hand and pulled free the bow of her bonnet ribbon beneath her chin. She felt the warmth of his fingers against the bare flesh of her neck and gazed into his eyes, which seemed very blue and very close to her own.

And then her bonnet was off and being tossed to the grass with his tall hat and the rolled-up drawing, and a laughing young girl was placing a blue ribbon in her hand, a yellow one in his. They were going to dance about the maypole together to welcome the spring.

To welcome all that was new and bright and hope-filled.

They were going to dance together through eternity, if the leader was to be believed. The memory of his words filled her with sudden laughter, and she saw an answering amusement in Richard's face when she looked at him.

Ah, the day seemed suddenly very warm and very bright.

And then the fiddles and pipes began playing again.

The dance took all of Nora's concentration over the next fifteen minutes as she dipped and weaved among the other dancers, following the instructions called out by the leader, taking her ribbon with her and discovering that miraculously it did not become hopelessly snarled even once but plaited itself about others and then unplaited itself again.

Richard, she realized, was laughing out loud.

So was she.

She could hear the feet of the dancers and the spectators

thumping on the ground, hands clapping, children shrieking at play, hawkers calling out their wares.

And this, she thought as colors whirled about her, was happiness.

Just this glorious, fleeting moment of springtime.

This maypole about which she and Richard danced together.

They twirled about each other, twining their ribbons, laughing into each other's eyes, sharing body heat for the merest instant. And then they danced on to other partners before meeting again and twirling in the opposite direction to free the bonds that bound them—until the next time.

By the time the music stopped again, Nora was breathless. She had to stoop forward, one hand pressed to her side, while she laughed and caught her breath. The leader was striding about the green again, coercing more villagers into taking the ribbons for the next dance.

When she straightened up, Richard was standing before her, her bonnet in one hand, the rolled portrait in the other. He looked flushed and happy—and achingly familiar despite all the changes ten years had wrought.

"Oh," she said, taking her bonnet from him, "that was *such* fun. Have you ever had more fun in your life, Richard?"

"No," he said—and something in the one brief word caused her fingers to pause as she tied a bow beneath her chin again.

They could not seem to stop gazing at each other. And suddenly all her carefree happiness was gone, to be replaced by a sadness just as intense.

This was Richard, who had not rescued her or come after her. Who had ultimately pitied her or seen a chance for a type of revenge against her father—but had not persisted past his one brief, chill offer and her refusal. He was Baron Bourne, and she was an unemployed lady's companion. He was in his thirties, she in her late twenties.

Her vision blurred, and she turned her head sharply away and busied herself with tying the bow.

"Nora." His voice was soft and perhaps as full of misery as her heart—or perhaps not.

He had no chance to say more, and she had no chance to turn her head and look back into his eyes.

"Mr. and Mrs. Kemp?" a pleasant, cultured man's voice asked from close by.

They both turned.

"Yes," Richard said.

"We have just heard about your unfortunate mishap," the gentleman said—he obviously *was* a gentleman. "Have we not, Adeline? You were fortunate indeed to have walked away from it without serious injury. I trust neither of you *was* injured?"

"No," Richard said, while the dark-haired lady with him smiled at them both. "Thank you. We escaped unharmed as did everyone in the stagecoach, it seems."

"Winston Bancroft, baronet," the gentleman said, offering his hand to Richard, "and my wife. We live at Ashdown Manor." He gestured vaguely behind him.

He bowed to Nora, and his wife offered her hand.

"If we had known about the accident sooner," she said, addressing Nora, "we would have offered the hospitality of our own home. You may still move to Ashdown if you wish and stay for as many days as prove necessary. We would be delighted to have you. We understand that it was the stagecoach driver who was to blame."

"It was an accident," Nora said.

"Thank you," Richard said. "But the Crook and Staff is a decent hostelry. We expect to be able to resume our journey tomorrow morning."

"Are you by any chance one of the Devonshire Kemps?" Sir Winston asked Richard.

"I am," he said.

"You are not Bourne himself, are you?" the gentleman asked.

"Actually I am," Richard admitted.

And sooner or later, Nora thought, they were going to discover that Lord Bourne did not possess a wife. That was going to be a fine scandal to fuel village gossip.

"Lady Bourne." Lady Bancroft smiled at her again. "We are delighted to discover you enjoying the village festivities, are we not, Winston? Wimbury always has the best May Day celebrations I have come across anywhere. And they will continue this evening. Did you know? We always invite everyone to join us on the terrace and lawns of Ashdown for refreshments and dancing and fireworks. Do say you will come, too. We would be so very pleased."

Richard and Nora exchanged glances.

"We would be delighted," Richard said.

"Splendid!" Sir Winston rubbed his hands together and beamed at each of them in turn. "We will send the carriage for you. You must come and dine with us first. No, please do not protest. I believe we can offer a more appetizing meal than you would get at the Crook and Staff, and we certainly will not permit you to walk all of two miles before you sit down to it. We will send the carriage."

"Thank you," Nora said. "That is kind of you."

"We are on our way to the lace stall so that Adeline can lighten my purse," Sir Winston said. "It is all in a jolly good cause, of course. Would you care to join us?"

"We went there earlier," Nora told him. "The work is exquisite."

"We are on our way back to the inn for a rest," Richard said.

"After watching you dance, I am ready to excuse you," Sir Winston said before touching the brim of his hat to Nora and strolling off, his wife on his arm.

"How terribly awkward," Nora said. "We cannot possibly go, of course."

"You would spurn their hospitality?" Richard said. "We will certainly go."

"Richard." She turned to him, frowning. "They believe we are *married*. And they know who you are."

"I am not sure which would be more of a lie," he said. "To say we are married or to say we are not. But for today at least we are man and wife, Nora."

He offered his arm.

"For *today*," she said, taking it.

"I have already assured you," he said, his voice suddenly cold, "that you are safe from me tonight, Nora, if that is what you meant by your emphasis upon *today*."

The ribbons of the maypole formed moving patterns of bright color against the blue sky as they made their way back to the inn. The music played as merrily as before. The air resounded with the thumping of feet and the clapping of hands. And with happy voices and laughter.

But some light seemed to have gone from the day.

His arm was warm and sturdy beneath her hand.

Two qualities in him she had once trusted—warmth and sturdiness.

Qualities he had turned out not to possess after all.

Chapter Six

Richard spent the next few hours sitting first inside the taproom, nursing a glass of ale rather than draining it off and
feeling obliged to order another, and then outside at one of
the tables set in such a position that one could enjoy the
sunshine and watch the festivities on the green. He did not
want for companionship in either place. There was always
someone—and usually a whole group—with whom to chat.
Most men seemed happy to while away the hours with a
glass of ale while their womenfolk and children amused
themselves at the fair.

Nora had retired to their room, presumably to rest. He left
her alone there until it was time to get ready for the evening.
He found her seated at the dressing table, sweeping her hair
up into a knot high on her head. She had changed into a different dress, a blue-gray silk that was clearly meant for evening wear. It was short-sleeved and high-waisted, he saw at
a glance, and modestly cut at the bosom. It was neither un-
fashionable nor in the first stare of fashion. It was the sort of
garment one might expect a woman to wear when she was

someone's companion and needed to look respectable without in any way drawing attention to herself.

For some reason the dress and all it said about her irritated him.

Her hands—and her hair—remained suspended above her head as her eyes met his in the mirror.

They were slim arms, and it was a delicate, swanlike neck that was revealed to his gaze. Her hair was still thick and shining and wavy. If the soberness of the dress was intended to disguise her beauty, it was having just the opposite effect.

He stepped into the room and looked around. He had brought a change of clothes with him for evenings with his grandmother, but it had struck him on the way upstairs that they would be badly creased.

Not so.

He saw his shoes first when he glanced toward his bag. They were side by side on the floor, and if he was not mistaken, they had just been freshly polished.

"I hope I did not leave any smudges," she said, still looking at him through the mirror. "I have had no training as a gentleman's valet."

"Good God, Nora," he said irritably, "you did not polish them yourself, did you?"

"Since it did not seem likely that you would risk allowing me to shave you," she said, "I had to think of another way to earn my keep."

It might have been a joke, but her tone of voice said that it was not.

He sat down on the side of the bed to pull off his boots one at a time. His shaving things were set out neatly on the washstand, as they had been earlier. It looked as if some steam was rising from the water pitcher. His evening shirt was hanging on the knob of one wardrobe door, his evening coat on the other. Both looked freshly ironed. So did his spare neck cloths, which were draped over the edge of the washstand.

"Did you do all this yourself?" he asked, remembering with an inner grimace how he had told her earlier that she could be his servant if she did not choose to be his wife.

"Yes," she said.

"It looks," he said, "as if you would make someone a good wife."

The words did not come out sounding like a compliment.

"Oh no, thank you," she said, and she leaned forward and continued with the task of pinning up her hair. "Why would I subject myself to *that* sort of servitude?"

He did not attempt an answer. He shrugged out of his coat, removed his neck cloth, hesitated a moment, and then pulled his shirt off over his head. If she did not like being in a room with a half-naked man, then she might leave. He crossed to the washstand, poured some of the water into the bowl—it really was hot—and proceeded to shave.

She finished what she was doing at the mirror, knelt by her valise, and busied herself with tidying its contents. He half watched her through the small mirror above the washstand.

Her hair looked prettier than it had earlier. It was still smoothly brushed back from her forehead and ears, but the knot was higher on her head, emphasizing the length of her neck and the perfection of her profile. She did not need curls or ringlets, both of which she had had in abundance as a girl.

He rinsed off his razor and gave himself a quick wash from the waist up. He washed out his hair and toweled himself dry before reaching for the newly ironed shirt.

"How did they manage to persuade you," he asked her, "that we were not married?"

The question clearly took her by surprise. She looked up from her valise, her eyes coming to rest on his still-bare chest for a moment before looking up into his.

"The man who married us was not a clergyman," she said. "I was not of age. We had not—" She stopped abruptly, and her head dipped to the valise again.

"Consummated the marriage?" he said. "That would have made no difference. It is not a prerequisite for a valid marriage. Did they persuade you it was? And did you tell them we had not yet slept together? Did they ask you?"

"Did they ask *you*?" She flung the question back at him, looking up at him again, defiance in her eyes and the tightness of her jaw.

"They did," he said.

"And—?"

"I told them it was none of their business what I did with my own wife in the privacy of our own bedchamber," he told her.

"But you must have agreed with them," she said, "that we were not really married."

"Must I?" He tucked his shirt in at the waist, as her eyes followed his movements.

"You made no effort to stop me from leaving the inn with them," she said. "You did not come near the room while I was packing my things. And you did not come after me."

It struck him suddenly that perhaps she did not *know*. Indeed, it was very probable that she did not, though he had never considered the possibility until now.

"That would have been somewhat difficult to do," he said. "It was two days before I was fit to travel. By that time you were long gone."

She looked steadily at him as she closed her valise.

"Before you were *fit*?" she said. "What do you mean?"

"I had dared to run off with their little girl," he said. "I, a mere secretary. I had run off with their last remaining hope of avoiding financial ruin. I had married her, moreover. What do you *think* I mean, Nora?"

No, she had not known. That was obvious in the widening of her eyes now and the paling of her cheeks.

"They *beat* you?" she said.

"Two against one were rather powerful odds against me," he said. "Even so, they did me something of a favor, Nora. They made me realize what a sad weakling I was physically. They caused me to turn my attention to fitness. They would not have had such an easy time of it if I had been then what I am now."

"They beat you," she said, sitting back on her heels. "So badly that you could neither stop me from leaving nor come after me."

She was not asking questions.

"It is what men do," he told her, reaching for his coat, "when they are annoyed with one another."

"They did not tell me," she said.

"I am not surprised," he told her curtly.

Though he imagined they must have both been quite raw-knuckled. Had she not noticed? And if not, why not? How upset had she been during that journey back into England? She had not known they had given him a thorough drubbing. She must have expected him to come to their room while she was packing. She must have expected him to stand up for her against her father and brother. She must have expected him to stop them from taking her away. And when he had done none of those things, she must have expected that he would come after her at any minute.

Because he was her husband, and it was what husbands did for their wives.

How soon had hope died?

How soon had she begun to believe her father that theirs had not been a real marriage after all, that he had merely taken advantage of a young, naïve *wealthy* innocent? She had still believed them wealthy at that point.

She had been eighteen years old, for the love of God. How could she have held firm when she did not even know all the facts?

"Nora," he said.

But he was interrupted by a tap on the door. She crossed the room and opened it a little way while he reached for one of the starched neck cloths.

"The carriage is here," she said as she closed the door again. "Oh, here, let me help you with that."

She came hurrying toward him.

"I used to do it sometimes for Papa," she explained to him when he raised his eyebrows. "After he . . . Well, after he no longer had a valet."

Because he could not afford one. Ryder had lost everything. He was fortunate indeed to have avoided debtors' prison before his death. His son apparently had shown some backbone and had acquired employment.

She busied herself about the task while he held his chin up and felt the warmth of her fingers close to his neck and looked down into her face, frowning in concentration and very close to his own.

There was something uncomfortably domestic about this.

"I hope," she said, "you do not favor elaborate knots. But you used not to."

And then she darted a look up at him and bit her lip, presumably at the memory of a long-ago era.

"A secretary," he said, "ought to have no more ambition to outshine his employer than a lady's companion ought to have to outshine hers. But no, my tastes have not changed."

She finished her task in silence, took a step back, and looked up at him.

Was that hurt he saw in her eyes?

"But then," he said, "some companions would outshine their mistresses even if they were dressed in sacks."

Her smile set her eyes to dancing.

"I was about to stamp on your foot for your rudeness," she said. "And you do not even have your shoes on yet."

"Ouch," he said, and for a moment he let his eyes laugh back into hers.

He was thankful suddenly that there was a carriage awaiting them. There was enough tension in the room to cut with a knife.

"We had better be on our way," he said. "Are you ready?"

"I have been ready for at least the last fifteen minutes," she told him. "*I* am not the one who waited until the last possible moment."

He pursed his lips and offered his arm.

Chapter Seven

Once in a long while life offered up a moment, sometimes even a whole day, of vivid and unexpected pleasure, and Nora had learned that such offerings must be grasped and lived for all they were worth lest they be lost forever.

Today was such a day, though it had begun in disaster and quickly progressed to something that had seemed even worse. She had not wanted to be stranded in Wimbury, and she had certainly not wanted to meet Richard there.

But both had happened, and so she had experienced all the joy of participating in a May Day fair and even of dancing about a maypole. And this evening she was being presented with all the seductive illusion of being back in the world she had grown up in. She was dining with a baronet, his wife, and their wellborn guests, and soon she would be stepping outside with them to enjoy the grand finale of the day.

She had thrown caution to the winds and was deliberately, consciously enjoying herself. Tomorrow she would deal with the inevitable emotional consequences.

Everyone at the table was laughing over the garish blue beads and bracelets she was wearing and the story she had just told about them. Richard had bought them for her at the fair, she had explained, and so she wore them this evening rather than any other jewelry. She chose her words carefully so that she did not quite lie. And she smiled at him across the dining table.

It was *not* a lie she had told. Even if she had had a treasure chest full of costly jewels with her, she would have worn the beads tonight. They were part of the magic of the day.

"They are a gift for our tenth anniversary," Richard said. "I was assured by the vendor that they are priceless pearls, and I do not doubt it for a moment."

And his eyes twinkled back into hers as everyone laughed heartily at the joke.

They had indeed married in May. Almost exactly ten years ago.

Oh, Richard!

"But how very charming and romantic," Lady Bancroft said. "What lady would not treasure such a gift forever, regardless of the truth of the vendor's claim?"

"I will remember this when your birthday comes up next month, Adeline," Sir Winston said to another general laugh.

Nora fingered her beads as a servant took her empty dessert plate.

And she realized suddenly that her interpretation of the events of ten years ago had been wrong in more ways than one.

Her father and Jeremy had beaten him so badly after sending her upstairs to pack that he had been unable to come up to her or to follow her when they took her away.

It was not he who had abandoned her. Yet that had been the keystone of her thinking for ten years.

In fact, it had been the other way around. Instead of digging in her heels and refusing to leave without her husband, as she ought to have done, she had meekly reverted to her old self and obeyed her father almost without question.

She had been eighteen years old, old enough she had thought to make the defiant gesture of running away with the man she loved and marrying him. But not old enough to have developed anything like the maturity she had needed to deal with the situation that had presented itself.

And all these years she had blamed Richard.

But why had he not come after her later, when he was able?

As soon as they had all finished eating, the Bancrofts led their dinner guests to the drawing room and out through the French windows to the terrace, where a crowd had already gathered. It seemed to Nora that everyone who had been in the village during the day must have come here tonight, including their children, who were dashing about at play, their shrieks mingling with the animated voices of their elders. The crowd was spread out over the terrace, the formal flower gardens below, and the lawns beyond. On a large square of grass in the middle of the formal gardens, a wooden dance floor had been laid. And seated beside it, the same fiddlers and pipers who had played for the maypole dancing were tuning their instruments.

"We always hope for fine weather for this particular event," Lady Bancroft explained, her arm linked through Nora's. "It is never quite the same if we have to move everything indoors to the ballroom."

Lamps were lit on the terrace and along the paths of the flower gardens. The sky overhead was clear. The moon and a million stars beamed down at them. It was a cool evening, though not cold.

"This has been a wonderful day," Nora said. "One never wishes to be stranded, but I am almost glad we have been today."

"I am entirely glad," Lady Bancroft agreed. "It is such a

pleasure to have met you and Lord Bourne and to have you here with us this evening. Where are you going?"

Nora had no idea where Richard was going, or even in which direction. She knew nothing at all about him, in fact. She had not *wanted* to know.

"To London," she said.

"You are going to be there for the rest of the Season?" Lady Bancroft asked. "So are we. We will be leaving here next week. Oh, we must meet again there. We will have you to dine. Perhaps we can go to the theater together one evening or to Vauxhall Gardens, one of my favorite places in the world. Perhaps you and I can go shopping together."

And so next week, Nora thought, the Bancrofts would discover how they had been duped today. They would not find her there. They might not find Richard, either. But they would learn that Lord Bourne had no wife.

"That will be pleasant," she said.

"We must get the dancing started, Adeline," Sir Winston said, coming up to them with Richard, "or everyone will be growing impatient. Lady Bourne, will you do me the honor of partnering me?"

"Thank you," she said, setting her hand on his sleeve and descending the steps from the terrace with him.

Richard came behind with Lady Bancroft.

It was a fast and merry country dance, as were the two that followed it. Nora danced those with other gentlemen who had been at dinner. She was breathless by the time the third set was at an end and slipped away to stroll along one of the paths through the flower garden. There was a small octagonal summerhouse just beyond it, she had noticed, the perfect place to sit for a while if it was not already occupied. Surprisingly, it was not, and she stepped inside, where the air was comfortably warm, and sat down on the padded bench that circled the inner wall. She was surrounded by windows and looked out over a lawn to woodland beyond. A group of children were performing some circle dance on the grass, their hands joined.

How different her life would have been, Nora thought, if her father had not lost his fortune—if he had not been addicted to gambling. But there was no point in such thoughts. The past was as it was. Nothing could change it. Any of it.

She closed her eyes and touched the back of her head to the glass behind her.

She ought to have rested this afternoon while she had the chance. But her evening dress had needed ironing after being folded up inside her valise. And she had remembered that Richard's shirt and coat and neck cloths were wrinkled. And then she had noticed that his shoes, though clean, were not as shiny as they ought to be.

Besides, she had not been able to persuade herself to make use of the bed even when he was not in the room. And the floor did not have even one small rug on it. She would have to make do without one tonight.

When she heard someone else at the door of the summerhouse, she opened her eyes and turned her head without lifting it.

"I have brought you a glass of ratafia," he said. "I know you do not like lemonade."

He remembered that about her?

"Thank you." She took the glass from his hand and drank from it while he seated himself beside her, even though she liked ratafia even less than lemonade. "Richard, I told Lady Bancroft that we were on our way to London, and she wants us to meet there and do some things together. She will discover, of course, that you have no wife. I am sorry."

"She will discover that I *have*," he said.

"What?" She looked blankly at him.

"The *ton* will tell her that indeed I do have a wife," he said.

"Oh." Her stomach performed an uncomfortable flip-flop. He had lied earlier, then.

"She is reputed to be a reclusive lady who remains all year at Dartwood Close in Devonshire, where I never invite guests," he told her, his eyes on her the whole while. "I suppose she—and my relationship with her—have aroused curiosity and enlivened drawing room conversations for almost a decade."

"But there is no such person?" She frowned.

"As the reclusive wife at Dartwood?" He raised his eyebrows. "No, there is not. But *is* there such a person elsewhere? I honestly do not know, Nora. I have never had occasion to find out for certain either way. But everyone will be most interested to learn that Lady Bancroft has finally seen my reclusive and elusive wife."

She closed her eyes again and inhaled slowly. He had deliberately let the *ton* believe that he was married. He was not even sure he was not.

Were they married? Could they possibly be?

"What has your life been like?" she asked him when the silence stretched between them.

"Better than it would have been if I had had to earn my living as a secretary," he said. "Especially with a wife and family to support."

She had believed the drop in status and fortune would not matter to her. *Love* was all that mattered. She had convinced him, against his better judgment, that she would never ever be sorry. *Would* she have been? If nothing had changed in her father's life? If nothing had changed in Richard's? It was impossible to know.

The change in status had come for her anyway—without the consolation of love.

But he thought his life would have been worse with her.

"How *much* better?" she asked.

"I have money and freedom," he said. "And the work I do now is for myself and those dependent upon me rather than for someone else."

Money and freedom.

"If you ever want to marry," she said, "you will have to dispose of your reclusive wife somehow."

"I daresay she is a sickly creature anyway," he said. "She can doubtless fade away at a moment's notice."

"Except," she said, "that the Bancrofts have seen her. Do I look sickly?"

He laughed softly but said nothing. She did not open her eyes.

"Have you been happy, Richard?" she asked him. "*Are you happy?*"

"Why would I not be?" he said by way of reply. "I have everything I could possibly want in life."

"Including a reclusive wife who does not interfere with your freedom in any way," she said.

"Yes, including her."

The children in front of them shrieked suddenly as they all fell to the grass. Sounds of merriment and laughter came from the flower gardens and the terrace behind them. The music was as toe-tapping as ever. The summerhouse seemed like an oasis of quiet, though it did not drown out any sounds.

"And you," he said. "What has your life been like, Nora?"

She laughed softly.

"I had no taste for being either a governess or a lady's maid or a milliner's assistant," she said, "though I did try that last one after Papa died. My fingers acquired more holes than the pincushions. I was quite relieved when Jeremy's marriage gave me an excuse to resign so that I could move away from London. I have been a lady's companion ever since."

"To the same lady?" he asked.

"No," she said, "There have been . . ." She paused to count on her fingers. "There have been eight, not counting Lady Rushford, who dismissed me after two days because Lord

Rushford, her son, told me quite ridiculously that my hair must have stolen all the sunbeams from the summer sky. One hopes he never has to earn his living as a poet. Oh, and not counting Mrs. Arkenwright, who died one hour before I arrived at her house, having traveled half across England to get there."

"And your latest employer?" he asked.

"Mrs. Witherspoon?" she said. "I endured her whinings and scoldings and miserliness for six months, but when she accused me two days ago of poisoning her horrid little poodle because he had been sick on the floor in her boudoir, I had had enough and not only denied the charge but went farther. Instead of making soothing noises as I usually did and offering to clean up the mess, I told her the truth—that the dog had been sick because of all the bonbons she had fed him and that *she* was always ill because of all the bonbons she fed herself. She threatened to have me hauled before the magistrate and charged with insubordination or attempted murder or some such atrocity. That was the end, I am afraid. I spoke to her quite candidly and unwisely—and enjoyed every minute of my tirade. The result was that I arrived in Wimbury this morning with all my baggage and no employment and no money whatsoever. She refused to pay me."

"One can hardly blame her," he said.

She turned her head sharply to look at him. Even in the near-darkness, she could see that he was grinning.

She laughed aloud.

"It *was* funny," she conceded. "Except that she had not paid me at all in six months. There was always some excuse. I endured all that dreary drudgery for absolutely nothing. Now I will have to begin all over again."

She closed her eyes again, and there was silence between them once more. Not a happy silence. She guessed that his grin had faded. Just as her laughter had died.

She wondered if he was as lonely as she was.

"I think," he said at last, "we had better go and dance, Nora. We have been gone long enough. I came looking for you to tell you there is to be a waltz soon. It would be a shame to miss it. Have you ever danced it?"

She had learned the steps long, long ago from a dancing master. She had never performed them at an actual ball. She had never *attended* any balls. She never did have her Season in London.

"Only with a dancing master," she said. "But that was during some lifetime in the distant past."

"Let us go and see if you remember," he said, taking her hand in his. "If you do not, I will teach you."

He had taken her hand in his. His was large and warm and strong-fingered.

He drew her along a path through the flower beds, weaving their way past other people, several of whom spoke cheerfully to them.

It was a bittersweet happiness Nora felt for the fleeting moment—for this day was really nothing more than that in the context of a whole life.

She felt ridiculously close to tears.

Chapter Eight

Richard had never particularly enjoyed dancing. It was something he did at social events because it was the polite thing to do. He had never thought of it as a particularly romantic activity, though, not even the waltz. Usually he chose a waltzing partner with whom he could expect to hold some sensible conversation while they twirled together about the dance floor for half an hour or so.

It was impossible to hold a sustained conversation with Nora given the volume of the music and the loudness of the voices all about them. And it was almost equally impossible to twirl her about, considering the size of the floor and the number of people who chose to waltz.

They were forced to dance rather more slowly than they would otherwise have done and at somewhat closer quarters than the customary arm's length. And they were forced to dance in near silence. The lamps were all somewhat distant from the dance floor. They danced by the light of the moon and the stars.

It all seemed unexpectedly—and not altogether comfortably—romantic to Richard.

After a few minutes he decided that he could best protect Nora from the crowds by turning her hand in his and holding it, palm in, against his heart. And by sliding his other hand more protectively about her waist. It was still as slender as a girl's, he found, even though she had developed a woman's figure. Her hand moved inward along his shoulder and then to the back of his neck. He could feel the tips of her fingers against bare flesh above his shirt collar.

The proximity of their bodies as they danced would have caused scandal in any fashionable ballroom.

But this, he thought, was surely how the waltz was intended to be danced.

She glanced up into his eyes, he looked back, and their eyes held. She was not smiling. Neither was he. And yet there was warmth in her look, as there surely was in his.

It was curious how one could feel alone with one's partner even in the densest of crowds. Suddenly there was no one in the world but Nora and him, and nothing of any significance in their surroundings except the moonlight and starlight and the sweetness of fiddles and pipes playing and the intimate steps of the waltz.

It was the 5th of May on which they had married. Almost exactly ten years ago.

A lifetime ago.

He had not been allowed to come near her afterward. He had tried, God knew, apprehensive as he had been about being beaten up again. She would not see him, he had been told every time. And she had returned all his letters unanswered—except the last. Her reply to that one had surprised him. Cynically, he had expected her to say yes.

Why had she said no?

He gazed into her eyes and would not ask the question

now. Now was for the waltz and this unexpected moment of happiness.

Happiness?

But he would not analyze tonight. Tomorrow would be time enough. He would have the rest of his life in which to wonder how he could possibly have felt happy today.

Tonight he held a woman in his arms and she felt right there. Tonight he could even believe in romance.

He liked the simplicity of her gown and hair, so different from the Nora of his memories. He liked the depth behind her eyes, the slightly thinner line of her face. She had grown into a beautiful woman. The prettiness of the girl he had known had been largely an exterior thing, he thought now. There had, perhaps, not been much depth of character behind it. He suspected that there was a great deal of it now behind her understated beauty. Indeed, he suspected that it was at least partly depth of character that gave her the beauty.

She had suffered, he did not doubt. But whereas she had crumbled quickly after their marriage, as soon as her father caught up to her, she had not broken a few days ago when her employer had bullied and insulted her. She had left the woman's house even though she had not been paid and had no money left in her purse after buying her ticket on the stagecoach.

She had even laughed about the whole thing a short while ago.

He rather suspected that he might like this Nora more than he had liked her younger self—if he took time to get to know her, that was. But then he had not really known her ten years ago, had he? It had been all romantic passion between them, made more desperate and therefore more appealing, by the differences in their stations, the secrecy of their meetings, and the marriage that was being forced upon her. They had made a dash for the border and had a Scottish wedding with nothing but love—or what they had called love—to sustain them.

Would it have stood the test of time?

There was no way of knowing, was there?

And perhaps young love would have been strong enough and resilient enough to have carried them through. Perhaps they would have grown up together.

Some empty space opened up suddenly beyond them and he swung her into a wide turn, smiling into her eyes as he did so.

She tipped back her head and laughed. Moonlight gleamed on her face and across her throat. Her beads swung to one side and caught the light. Rare blue pearls, indeed!

Then the laughter faded from her face and softened to an answering smile as he drew her closer again, and again they were encompassed by other dancers. But suddenly her eyes glistened in the starlight, and she lowered her head.

Tears?

He drew her closer still until her breasts were almost brushing against his coat.

"You do remember the steps after all," he murmured into her ear.

"Yes," she said. "My first and last waltz. I am glad it has been here today."

And with me as a partner?

But he had not spoken aloud.

Did he want the question asked out loud? And did he want to hear the answer?

What if it was no?

And what if it was yes?

She sighed audibly, and he realized that the music was coming to an end.

He stopped dancing and looked down at her without releasing her.

"I suppose we should make our way back to the village," he said. "I want to make an early start in the morning."

His curricle would be ready. He had ascertained that earlier.

What he ought to do was leave tonight. There was enough moonlight to drive by. Nora could have the inn room to herself. It would be better for both of them.

"Yes," she said, gazing up at him, her hand still on his shoulder.

But he would not leave tonight, he knew. It was too soon. And very much too late—in every imaginable way.

And then, while they still stood together, though all the other dancers had moved off the floor and even the musicians had disappeared, there was a loud bang, and it was followed by a great cascade of colored light shooting into the night sky from one side of the house.

"Oh, Richard!" she exclaimed, turning sharply in his arms to look. "The fireworks!"

Ah, he had forgotten. Sparks of dimming light were falling back to earth.

Everyone else, he realized, was hurrying off to get a closer look. But one did not need to be close to fireworks.

He wrapped both his arms about Nora from behind and drew her back against him. She laid her hands over his at her waist and, after a moment or two, rested her head back against his shoulder.

They watched together, neither of them speaking. But it was a display that set the final, magical touch upon a day that he knew he would always remember, even if he lived to be a hundred.

Perhaps with pain.

But surely also with pleasure.

The sky was alternately bright with colored fire and dim with starlight. The air smelled of smoke. Cheers and applause came from the side of the house with each explosion.

But they were alone together in a world of beauty and wonder, he and Nora.

Whose shattered relationship had surely wrecked both their lives for the past ten long years.

And for the next ten, too?

And forever?

They were questions he was not prepared to explore.

When the last of the fireworks had burned itself out in the night sky, they found the Bancrofts and thanked them for a lovely evening and took their leave, though there was more dancing to come and refreshments were already being brought out onto the terrace.

They walked back to the village and the Crook and Staff Inn even though Sir Winston tried to press the carriage on them. It was only two miles, they protested. And it was a lovely night for a walk.

They walked in silence, her arm drawn through his and pressed firmly against his side.

He tried not to think ahead—to tonight, to tomorrow, to the rest of his life.

Chapter Nine

It was foolish to have enjoyed the day so much, Nora thought when they arrived back at the Crook and Staff and she climbed the stairs ahead of Richard to his room. It was foolish to have reveled in this evening's activities—the dinner, the dancing, the brief interlude in the summerhouse. The waltz . . .

Ah, that waltz! The glorious romance of it all, when she had forgotten everything except the present moment with the music and the moonlight and the man with whom she danced.

And the fireworks. The light and the colors and the sounds and the smells. And the arms of the man who held her as they watched in silence.

Spellbound.

It was foolish to have abandoned herself to it all, to have flung off her defenses. For of course, all the events of the day had been leading to the night—to a night spent in a room with him, trying to sleep on the hard floor, though sleep would be an impossibility even if she had the softest of feather beds on which to lie. And this night led inevitably to tomorrow morning, when he would resume his journey in his curricle and she would go her way on the stagecoach.

The curtains had not been pulled across the window in their room. It was not a dark night outside. It was easy to see without the aid of a candle. She was relieved when he made no move to light one.

"I will lie down over here," she said without turning to look at him. She had picked out the dark corner beyond the washstand. She had a cloak in her valise to use as a blanket. The valise itself would serve as a pillow.

"You will, of course," he said, sounding autocratic and impatient, "sleep on the bed."

"Oh no," she said, turning to him. "There is really no need to be gallant. It is *your* room. I am only grateful that—"

"Nora," he said softly.

She had not realized he was so close. She could feel his body heat. She had to tip back her head to look into his eyes.

She swallowed and left her sentence uncompleted.

His fingertips touched one of her cheeks, feather-light, and she closed her eyes and stood very still.

"Nora," he said again. A mere breath of sound.

His lips were soft and warm when they touched hers, and she was aware that her own trembled against them.

But she did not draw back as she knew she ought.

A great welling of longing held her rooted to the spot.

"Tell me to stop," he murmured against her lips, "if you wish me to stop. I promised that I would not molest you."

She would have preferred to stand where she was and let him decide what was to happen. No decisions. No responsibility. No blame.

The old Nora, dependent upon and subservient to the men in her life—except for the one brief, colossal act of defiance, which she had not been strong enough to sustain—had been like that.

She was no longer that girl. She had a choice, and only she could make it.

She set her hands on his shoulders.

"Don't stop," she said.

She wondered if this had been inevitable from the moment when he had first spotted her this morning. Or from the moment when his curricle had pulled out of the inn yard just exactly when the stagecoach was pulling in. Or from the moment when she had finally walked out on Mrs. Witherspoon with a ticket for today's stage. Or from the moment when—

How far back did causes go?

And what about effects?

She had said, *Don't stop*, and her life would forever be changed in ways she could not even dream of yet. But she had said it consciously and willingly. It was what she wanted. And so there would be the memory of tonight added to that of today—and all of them to set against the memory of their disastrous wedding day.

She would never hate him again after tonight. Whatever happened, she could never hate him again.

His lips moved from hers to kiss a molten path along her throat and then her shoulder. His hands were unhooking her dress buttons and nudging the garment off her shoulders and down her arms.

She shivered, though not with cold.

He raised his head for a moment and lifted her beads from about her neck. They clattered to the floor as he dropped them. In the near-darkness their eyes met, and they smiled at each other.

It was her undoing. For this was no impersonal exercise in sexual passion. This was Richard and she. And she had never—ah, dear God, she had never stopped loving him.

Hating him and loving him.

But always, always the love.

He had smiled at her once upon a time, when she was a girl, and she had fallen in love with him. And now he had smiled at her again in the darkness of the bedchamber they shared.

He lowered her dress to expose her breasts and cupped them in his hands. His fingers played over them while she closed her eyes and tipped back her head. The pads of his thumbs rubbed over her nipples, which immediately hardened. A sharp, raw ache darted upward into her throat and downward through her stomach and her womb to her thighs.

And then her dress and her undergarments were being pushed lower until finally they slid all the way to her feet.

He went down on one knee before her to roll down her stockings, and she set both hands on his head as if in benediction as she lifted her feet one at a time so that he could ease the stockings off.

He kissed the instep of the second foot, her calf, the inside of her knee, her throbbing inner thigh. And then he stood up, trailing his hands up the outsides of her legs, over the curve of her hips and in to her waist before slipping them behind her and drawing her full against him. His mouth met hers again, open this time, hard, demanding, urgent until she opened her own mouth beneath it, and his tongue pressed inside.

As she clung to him, eager and weak with need, it occurred to her that perhaps she ought to have been unclothing him, too. She knew so very little! But there was something gloriously—what was the word?—*erotic*. There was something almost unbearably erotic about being held naked against his fully clothed body.

She sucked his tongue deeper into her mouth, her hand behind his head, and he made a low sound of appreciation in his throat.

"Come and lie down, Nora," he said, turning to the bed and drawing back the covers while he kept one arm firmly about her.

He leaned over her when she was lying on her back, kissing her openmouthed as he shrugged out of his coat and then tugged loose his neck cloth. She helped him then, pulling his shirt off over his head and dropping it to the floor.

His hands worked at his waist, and he stood again to remove his breeches and undergarments.

Ah, but he was beautiful, she thought, gazing up at him in the light of the moon filtering through the window. More beautiful than he had been. He was broader now and more powerfully muscled.

Or perhaps she thought so only because she was looking at him now through a woman's eyes rather than a girl's. She had a sudden, vivid memory of calling him beautiful then because he had been slender and graceful—and of his laughing at her use of the word just before lust had consumed them both. It had been neither skilled nor particularly satisfying, that long-ago consummation, but, ah, they had been happy. They had been embarking upon a happily-ever-after with all the blind optimism of youth.

And now he was on the bed with her and touching her again with hands and lips that she knew with only a moment's pang of sadness were now very skilled and very experienced indeed. She had only raw instinct to guide her as she explored him with eager hands and caressed him with tender fingers and somehow elicited both gasps of pleasure and moans of desire from him.

But soon she was throbbing with a need that was almost pain.

"Richard," she whispered against his mouth. "Richard." His name sounded like a plea.

"Yes," he said. "Yes."

And all his considerable weight bore down upon her at

last before he spread her legs wide with his knees, slid his hands beneath her buttocks, and came inside her all long and hard and firm until she was stretched and filled and was biting down on her lower lip waiting for the pain.

There *was* no pain.

He drew his hands from beneath her, braced himself on his forearms so that some of his weight was lifted off her, and gazed down at her as he withdrew and pressed back in and so set up a slow, firm rhythm.

She slid her fingers up his arms from wrists to shoulders, feeling the soft hairs and the muscles and the life and warmth. She lifted her feet from the mattress and twined her legs about his. And she moved her hips, clenching and un-clenching inner muscles by sheer instinct as she did so and closing her eyes so that she could concentrate upon what was happening *there.*

She could hear the suck and pull of his movements and feel the slippery wetness.

And she could feel, too, the slow building of a dull ache that became gradually sharper and sharper until it was a keen pain and a near agony before she clenched her muscles tightly about it and then, just when it had become too much to bear, unclenched them and shuddered into surrender, only to discover that after all it was not pain to which she had surrendered, but its exact opposite.

She heard a voice crying out in surprised abandonment and realized that it must be her own.

And then, before she could even begin to put the scattered pieces of herself back together, he moved again, fast and hard and deep, and she felt the flow of his hot release deep inside just as he sighed against the side of her face and all his glorious weight came down on her again.

Richard.

Ah, my love, my love.

He was hot and slick with sweat.

So was she.

She lay still beneath his weight, relaxed and listening to her heartbeat return to normal. Her breathing slowed. They had made love. They had *made love*.

He had told her earlier that he was not sure if he was still married or not.

He was not, of course.

They never had been married.

Perhaps.

So her father had assured her.

It did not matter either way now, though, did it?

Tomorrow he would be gone. So would she. But not together. It was probable they would never see each other again.

Richard.

Ah, Richard.

He lifted himself off her and moved to her side, stretching down as he did so to pull the sheet and blanket up over them. He kept one arm beneath her head. With the other he held the blanket over her.

Neither of them spoke as warmth enveloped them.

She could not hear him breathing though he was warm and relaxed.

Was he sleeping?

She closed her eyes and tried to sleep herself.

She felt like crying instead.

Again.

Chapter Ten

Richard was not asleep. But he was content for the moment at least to pretend that he was.

He had hated her for ten years. He had despised her as a weakling.

After swearing over and over again that she loved him more than life, that she would always love him even if they ended up living in a hovel, after begging him to save her from the marriage that her father was urging on her by running away to Scotland with her, after speaking sacred vows to love, honor, and obey him until death parted them—after all that, she had crumbled utterly the very moment her father appeared on the scene. As soon as he had come striding into the inn dining room, Jeremy Ryder on his heels, and had ordered her to go up to her room and pack her bags, she had gone without a word and with only one dismayed glance at Richard even though he had set a hand on her arm and told her to stay where she was.

It was the last he had seen of her until this morning.

She had been weakness itself.

She had also been eighteen years old.

Was it fair to judge her now by what she had been then?

Her breathing was soft and even. It was not, though, the deep breathing of someone who slept.

He had promised not to touch her tonight.

But he had offered to keep that promise. She had absolved him of it.

She was the first to admit to being awake. She turned her head so that her cheek was against his shoulder.

"I will lie on the floor," she said, "if it will make it easier for you to sleep."

He laughed softly, lifting his free hand to brush the hair back from her face. He turned his head so that they could look into each other's eyes. After a few moments she laughed, too.

"I thought perhaps I was disturbing you," she said.

"You were," he said. "You *are*."

"We ought not to have allowed this to happen," she said.

"But we did."

"Yes." She drew breath and released it on a quiet sigh.

He kissed her. Her mouth was soft and warm and moist. Inside, it was hot about his tongue.

She was, he had realized as soon as he started to make love to her earlier, an innocent. She must have made love twice in her twenty-eight years, once ten years ago, and once this very night. Both times with him.

He could not begin to count all the sex partners he had had between those times.

All in an effort to forget.

All in a futile attempt to find ease for his heart as well as his body.

Her hand was smoothing over his shoulder and down his arm. She was kissing him back, suckling his tongue.

He had adored her. He had worshipped her from afar for many long months. And then, when he had discovered that she returned his feelings, he had loved her with the passionate devotion of a very young man who did not even pause to ask himself if she loved him more because she saw in him a means of escape than because she longed for him as a life's partner.

However it was, he had served his purpose. Potts must have got wind of her indiscretion—or of the near-collapse of Ryder's fortune. He had withdrawn his courtship. Perhaps she was sorry when it was too late. Potts could have saved her from all these years of dreary and impermanent employment.

So could he.

But that was all a long time ago. A lifetime ago.

He turned her onto her back and leaned over her, caressing and arousing her with his hands, noting again, as he had earlier, the unexpected familiarity of her slender body with its firm, high breasts and long, slim legs, and the smell of her, half soap, half woman, with enticing overlays of sweat and sex.

He fondled her breasts, suckled them, kissed her rib cage, her flat stomach, the insides of her thighs and knees, her calves, her feet. He drew her legs about him as he knelt between them, kissing her mouth again as his hands moved up her inner thighs to the moist heat between. He caressed her there with light fingertips, and pressed two fingers inside her while with the pad of his thumb he rubbed across the tender spot that had her lifting her hips from the bed and pressing down on his fingers and moaning with need and pleasure.

He kissed her closed eyelids and her mouth again. He withdrew his fingers, positioned himself, and entered her slowly until he was encompassed by slick heat that slowly clenched about him.

It was a moment he might have accepted for the sheer sexual invitation that it was. He might have driven them both to release and thought of her only as a woman, of himself only as a man.

But this was not just about sex.

He drew a slow, steadying breath and opened his eyes. He was still kneeling, her legs drawn over his spread knees, his hands beneath her. Her hands were flat against the mattress. Her flaxen hair was spread in glorious disarray across the pillow. Her eyes were open and gazing back into his, heavy-lidded with desire.

He braced his arms on either side of her head and lowered himself onto her, straightening his legs as he did so. He gave her his full weight, turning his head to lie beside hers.

And he worked her with long, slow strokes until there was almost no energy left and no control at all. With one final inward thrust he released into her. And he knew, even though she neither cried out nor shuddered, that she reached completion at the same moment.

It was, he knew with his last coherent thought before he slid into sleep, the only time he had ever really made love. And it was with Nora.

With his wife.

The beginnings of dawn were already graying the room when he woke up. He was still on top of her, still inside her. Incredibly, considering the obvious discomfort of her position, she was sleeping. She was warm and relaxed and breathing deeply.

He disengaged from her, lifted himself off her, and covered her to the chin with the sheet and blanket before going to stand at the window. The room was at the back of the inn, looking out over fields and woodland. There was no visible sign of life out there yet, though there was a veritable chorus of birds greeting the new day. He could hear them clearly as soon as he opened the window a little.

He braced his hands on the windowsill and gazed out, the morning air cool against his bare arms and chest.

Chapter Eleven

She woke as soon as the weight of his body was gone from her, to be replaced by the sheet and blanket, though she did not open her eyes until she judged that he must have moved away.

She turned her head then and gazed at him as he stood at the window, his back to her, still naked. He was a magnificent man. And a magnificent lover, too.

She still ached where he had been. Her legs were still stiff from having been pressed wide for so long. She could still smell the musk of him on the bedding, on herself.

"Richard," she said softly, "why did you write that letter? It hurt me terribly."

Perhaps she ought not to have admitted that. She would not have done so just yesterday.

He turned his head to look at her over his shoulder. His hands were still braced on the windowsill.

"Which one?" he asked her.

"Which one?" She frowned. "The *only* one. You wrote me only one."

He stared at her for a long time without moving or saying anything. Then he laughed shortly.

"How stupid of me," he said. "How utterly stupid. Of course! You never even set eyes on any of the others, did you?"

"There were *others*?"

But she knew suddenly that there must have been. Of course there had been others. He would not simply have abandoned her—though she had believed it all these years.

He chuckled again, though it was not a sound of amusement.

"We were a precious pair of innocents, were we not?" he said. "I tried to see you, too, Nora, though I was never allowed beyond the gates—you did not want to see me, I was assured each time. I suppose you knew nothing of those visits, either."

She did not answer. She did not need to.

They stared mutely at each other.

He moved away from the window and came a little closer to the bed. He stood looking down at her though she could not see his face clearly any longer—his head was silhouetted against the window.

"Why did that one letter hurt you?" he asked her. "I offered you marriage in it—assuming we were not already married, that was."

"You did it as an insult to Papa," she said. "Suddenly everything had reversed itself. Suddenly you were titled and very wealthy and we were ruined almost to the point of destitution. You did it to rub his nose in the dirt of that fact, thinking he would be only too eager to accept your suit then."

"He had already made overtures to me," he said softly. "It was why I wrote once more. I thought it was what you wanted at last—and what you had been told to do."

She closed her eyes again and kept them closed.

"I was a pawn in everyone's game," she said.

"I was surprised when you refused me," he said. "You had

been so very obedient to your father until then. It was the first time in six months that I felt some respect for you."

Her heart had bled and bled after she had sent her reply—metaphorically, of course. Hearts did not literally bleed or break. Sometimes one wished that they did.

But all that grieving was long in the past. She had discovered that she was a survivor, like it or not. She still was. And she *would be*. She would survive this—this twenty-four-hour interlude in her life.

"I am going to get dressed," he said abruptly, "and go down and see how my curricle and horses are doing. I might as well make an early start since I am up anyway."

She watched him wash and dress. She watched him shave with the cold water from last evening. She watched last night's hot lover transform himself into a cool and brisk and fashionable gentleman.

Soon yesterday and last night—and this moment—would seem like a dream.

Perhaps a nightmare.

He looked toward the bed when his hand was on the door as he was leaving the room.

"I will have breakfast sent up for you in an hour's time," he said.

She was about to protest that she could not afford to pay for it. But it would have been petty.

Why did she have the sense that they had quarreled when really they had not?

Last night they had made love twice.

They had *made love*.

Or was it a measure of her terrible innocence that she could not distinguish between lust and love?

Had it really been just sex?

She supposed it had.

"Thank you," she said.

And he was gone.

Chapter Twelve

Richard's curricle was ready to go. The woodwork was going to need some repairs and a good coat of paint, it was true, but that work could wait until he got to London. The curricle was roadworthy, and he was eager to be on the way. It was time to get back to real life.

The stagecoach had been repaired, too, the damages having proved to be less severe than had been feared at first. It stood in the inn yard, ready for the passengers when they should have finished their breakfast and come from the inn and the surrounding houses where some of them had been billeted.

The sun was shining again, though there was more of a wind today. The colored ribbons were flapping audibly about the deserted maypole in the middle of the village green.

He would, Richard decided, wait to see Nora on her way. He was tempted to leave before her and without seeing her again—he could send a servant up to fetch his bag. But he knew that he must make sure nothing further cropped up to delay the coach—she had no money, and he guessed that she would not willingly take any from him.

It was going to look very strange to a largish number of people when she boarded the stagecoach and he drove off alone in his curricle. They were going to wonder . . .

For himself he did not care the snap of his fingers what anyone thought. But she was going to be traveling for long hours with some of those very people. Would they give her a rough time?

Damnation!

And what had suddenly gone wrong up there in their room this morning? It was puzzling. They had not quarreled, and yet . . .

He had ended their conversation about the past abruptly by announcing that he was going to get dressed, and suddenly there had been a horrible silence between them.

Just when he had discovered that she was an innocent victim of it all. Just when she had discovered that perhaps he was.

And was he now *running away*?

Was she?

The passengers were being called for with some impatience. Some of them had already gathered and were taking the best places by the windows.

He stepped inside the inn. He would go up and fetch her. He would carry down her valise and take a civil farewell of her.

But *why*?

She was already at the foot of the stairs, her valise in hand. Their eyes met as he strode toward her and took the bag from her.

"You heard the call, then?" he asked.

"Yes."

She was looking slightly pale. Her eyes looked enormous.

Her hair had been ruthlessly brushed back beneath her bonnet.

Was he going to let her go without a fight?

He could clearly see those six months following their wedding exactly as they must have appeared through her eyes. He had meekly allowed her father to take her back home with him and declare their marriage invalid. He had made no attempt to follow her or to see her afterward. He had not written to her. And then, after she must have heard about the change in his fortune and after she and her father had become poor, he had written out of the blue to offer her marriage. To gloat. Her father must have done all in his power to coerce her into accepting. Her own common sense must have told her what the alternative would be. She had had the courage to refuse him anyway.

Not because she no longer loved him, but because she believed he had never loved her.

She was staring into his eyes.

"Miss Ryder?" It was the coachman's voice, loud and impatient, calling from the door. "Is Miss Ryder in here?"

"Nora," Richard said, "that letter was not written to insult your father. Or to gloat. It was a last despairing attempt to persuade you to come back to me."

She stared mutely at him.

"Miss Ryder?" The voice was coming from out in the yard now, irritated, angry. "Does anyone know where the blasted woman stayed last night? Does anyone know what she looks like?"

"I wrote to you every day for the first month," she said, her voice little more than a whisper. "Every single day. But not one of the letters was sent. I had nowhere to send them. I did not know where you were. You had simply vanished. Without me. And not a word from you. Not one. I am sometimes lonely now—the life of a lady's companion is not a delightful one. But I have never known loneliness as I knew it during those months. I had been married and then—nothing. And then that letter out of the blue, so cold, so formal."

"Written a hundred times over before that particular draft was sent," he said. "It was my one final chance. I did not want to squander it. But I did anyway."

"Miss Ryder?"

The coachman appeared in the doorway again. He had bellowed the words. "Drat the woman! Where is she? Do you know anything of her, landlord?"

"Not me," the landlord said.

"I am going to have to go without her and serve her right," the coachman said. "I can't keep everyone else waiting. Not again."

Nora looked beyond Richard's shoulder, and for a moment there was something like panic in her eyes.

"Don't go," he said, setting a hand on her wrist. "Don't go, Nora. Stay with me. Stay for the rest of your life."

She shook her head slightly.

"Mrs. Kemp, ma'am." The landlord appeared beside them. "May I have your bag carried out to the curricle? And may I have yours brought down, sir?"

She bit her lower lip and kept her eyes on Richard's.

From outside came the sounds of wheels rumbling on cobblestones and horses' hooves clopping and the deafening blast of a yard of tin being blown to warn other vehicles away from the gateway onto the road.

The stagecoach was on its way.

Without her.

"Yes, if you please," Richard said, and the landlord scooped up the valise and hurried outside with it, calling to someone unseen to go up and bring Mr. Kemp's bag down without further delay.

"You are my wife, Nora," Richard said.

Her eyes were suddenly bright with tears.

"That marriage was not valid," she said. "It was—"

"*Valid*," he said firmly. "Though I do not doubt that some money changed hands and all documentary evidence disappeared. That does not make it less of a marriage, Nora. You are my wife."

"Richard—" she said.

"*I love you*," he told her, his voice low and urgent. "I always have. I have hated you, too, I suppose. But always, always I have loved you. Last night was all about love, Nora. You must know that. Come with me."

"Oh." She sighed. "I ought to go on the coach."

"Too late," he said. "It has gone."

"*Has* it?" Her eyes widened.

Incredibly, she had not heard it leave. She had been too focused on the drama unfolding between them.

"You are stuck here again," he said. "Stranded. With me."

"Oh," she said. "For the rest of my life?"

"For at *least* that long," he told her.

They stood staring at each other—until he smiled at her, and slowly an answering smile first tugged at the corners of her mouth and then lit her eyes.

"But not necessarily here in Wimbury at the Crook and Staff," he said. "I have a curricle and horses ready to go outside."

"Where will we go?" she asked him.

"On a long journey to the rest of our lives," he told her. "But first to London, where I will procure a special license as soon as I possibly can. *We* may know beyond any reasonable doubt that we are not living in sin, but the rest of the world may not be so willing to believe it."

"Oh, Richard," she said.

He took her right hand in both of his.

"Will you marry me, Nora?" he asked her. "Again?"

He was grinning at her. Suddenly he was feeling exuberant with happiness.

"Oh, I will," she said. "But only *once* more, Richard. I positively refuse to make a habit of this."

They both laughed, suddenly giddy with joy, and he leaned forward to set his lips to hers at the exact moment when the manservant who had been sent upstairs came clattering back down with Richard's bag and the landlord stepped in from the yard outside, having just stowed Nora's valise in the curricle.

The manservant hastily and noisily retraced his steps, and the landlord coughed and discovered something else outside that needed his urgent attention.

Richard wrapped his arms about his wife's waist, and she twined hers about his neck. And they indulged in a lengthy and really quite scandalous display of public affection.

For the moment the rest of their lives could wait.

Mary Balogh

MARY BALOGH grew up in Wales, and after graduating from university, moved to Saskatchewan, Canada, to teach high school English. Her first Regency love story, *A Masked Deception*, was published in 1985. She has written more than seventy novels and almost thirty novellas since then, including the *New York Times* bestselling *Slightly* sextet and *Simply* quartet. She has won numerous awards, including Bestselling Historical of the Year from the Borders Group, and her novel *Simply Magic* was a finalist in the Quill Awards. She lives in Regina, Canada.

Only You

Jacquie D'Alessandro

For Mary Balogh, for sharing her fabulous idea during our wonderful Levy adventure. And to Stephanie Laurens and Candice Hern, who, along with Mary, made this project so much fun. And as always, to my fantastic, supportive husband, Joe, who stole my heart one magical night. And to my extraordinary son, Christopher, aka Heart Stealer, Junior.

Acknowledgments

My heartfelt thanks to the wonderful people at Levy Home Entertainment, who brought me, Mary, and Candice together: Pam Nelson, Justine Willis, Kathleen Koelbl, Krystal Nelson, Janet Kray, Emily Hixon, and Devar Spight. Thanks also to Susan Andersen, Sue Grimshaw, and to all the people at Avon Books for supporting this project.

$\mathcal{C}hapter\ One$

"Stop the coach!" Cassandra Heywood, Countess Westmore, demanded, pounding her fist against the carriage ceiling to gain the driver's attention.

"What's wrong, milady?" asked Sophie, her maid's pretty face clouding with concern. "Ye look pale. Arc ye unwell?"

The carriage rocked to a halt, and she heard Mr. Watley, the coachman, clamor down from his perch. "I'm . . ." *Panicked. Unsure. Dear God, am I making a terrible mistake?* ". . . feeling a bit unsettled." A humorless sound caught in her throat at the understatement.

Mr. Watley opened the door, and a blast of cool, sea-scented air swirled into the warm interior. "Somethin' amiss?"

"Lady Westmore is feelin' peaked," Sophie said. "How much further do we have to go?"

"The Blue Seas Inn is less than a mile ahead," reported Mr. Watley.

Less than a mile ahead. Cassandra's gloved fingers tightened their grip on the black gabardine of her mourning gown.

"Perhaps we shouldn't stop at the inn," Mr. Watley said, a frown puckering his weathered face.

Precisely the words that had repeatedly circled through her mind since they'd climbed into the coach this morning for the final leg of their arduous three-week journey to Cornwall.

"Gateshead Manor is only another two hours away," he continued. "I know ye planned to spend the night at the Blue Seas, but if yer gettin' ill, might be best to press on and get ye home."

It wasn't illness knotting her stomach, but she couldn't deny that it might indeed be best to continue. *Coward*, her inner voice sneered. Indeed, she was. But she didn't want to be. Not anymore. Yet old habits died hard.

"I think . . . I just need some air," she murmured. She accepted Mr. Watley's large, callused hand and exited the carriage. Warm sunshine and cool air fanned over her, and she stretched her back. Her muscles ached and her temples pounded from the endless jouncing on the leather seats and the monotonous grinding of the wheels.

Walking several yards away, she peered over the hedges lining the narrow dirt road and drew in a quick, delighted breath at the view. The sparkling wonder of St. Ives Bay greeted her gaze, an expanse of blue that melted into the indigo of the Atlantic glittering on the horizon. Gulls swooped over the sand dunes below, then skimmed over the white-capped waves. Golden ribbons of early afternoon sunshine shimmered over the boats bobbing near the shore, the vessels awaiting men to draw them out to catch pilchards and haul up lobster pots.

Cassandra drew a slow, deep breath and briefly closed her eyes, savoring the hint of salt that scented the summer air. Nostalgia tightened her throat, and for the first time in ten long years, the viselike grip of homesickness for her beloved Cornwall loosened just a bit. Gateshead Manor in Land's

End, the childhood home she hadn't seen in a decade, was only another two hours away. A place she looked forward to seeing with both anticipation and trepidation. A place saturated in memories, the site of some of her happiest days, and her most heartbreaking.

The place where she'd be forced to come face-to-face with her uncertain future.

Yet no matter how uncertain that future remained, it couldn't be worse than the past she'd left behind three weeks ago when she'd escaped from the nightmare into which her life had deteriorated.

But should she continue on to Land's End today? She'd planned to spend the night here in St. Ives, but now that the moment was upon her, misgivings plagued her. Her better judgment, her common sense warned her that stopping here was unnecessary. Was foolhardy. Wrong. Highly improper. And might even prove dangerous. That the past could never be recaptured. Yet despite all those warnings, her heart . . . her heart refused to listen.

And then the single question that had haunted her during the entire three-week journey whispered through her mind once again: *Would he be at the inn?*

She tipped her head back to capture the sun's warmth and squeezed her eyes shut. *There's only one way to find out, Cassandra.*

Opening her eyes, she looked out at the water, and allowed the memories to overtake her. Memories that, after several minutes, dispelled her doubts, making her choice clear. For years decisions had been made for her, regardless of her feelings. This was her chance to find the answers she sought. To finally do what she wanted. What she needed.

God knew when she might have such a chance again.

And what she wanted, needed, was to stop at the Blue Seas Inn.

Would he be there? And if so, would he remember her? A

long sigh escaped her. Of course he would *remember* her. But in what way? With fondness—or indifference? Most likely he hadn't thought of her in years. He undoubtedly had a wife. Children. A happy, fulfilling life. They'd probably run out of conversation within five minutes.

Yet something inside her insisted that if she allowed this opportunity to pass her by, she'd regret it.

And she'd promised herself no more regrets.

Her decision made, she straightened her spine and walked back to the carriage where Mr. Watley and Sophie awaited her with questioning expressions.

"We shall spend the night at the Blue Seas Inn," she said, proud of how sure and steady her voice sounded.

"As ye wish, milady," said Mr. Watley.

He handed her and Sophie back into the carriage, and they resumed their journey. A quarter hour later the carriage jerked to a halt. Slipping on the mantle of outward calm that for years she'd worn like a second skin, Cassandra once again placed her hand into Mr. Watley's and stepped from the coach.

Bright sunshine flooded her eyes beneath the short brim of her bonnet, and she lifted her hand to shade the glare.

Two stories of aged stone, mellowed to shades of soft gray, indicated the Blue Seas Inn dated back at least one hundred years. Yet the building was beautifully maintained, its mullioned windows sparkling clean, the modest flower beds flanking the walkway well tended and blooming with a profusion of colorful wildflowers. A livery, clearly a fairly recent addition, stood directly next to the original building.

As she looked at those stables, a memory flashed through her mind, so strong, so vivid, it nearly stole her breath. Ethan's dark eyes smiling down into hers as they shared a joke while currying her chestnut mare, his strong hands sure yet infinitely gentle with the animal.

She blinked away the image, and her gaze shifted to rest

on the hand-painted sign swinging gently in the salt-tinged breeze. It depicted a gull gliding over white-capped waters, the bird's gray-tipped wings reflecting the shimmering sunshine. "Blue Seas Inn" was scripted in indigo letters, the perfect name for this charming setting, with the smaller letters beneath: "Ethan Baxter, Proprietor."

Her gaze riveted on the name, and she had to grip her fingers together to keep from brushing their tips over the letters.

"Shall I accompany ye inside to arrange ye rooms, milady?" asked Mr. Watley.

Cassandra dragged her gaze from the sign and turned toward the coachman. Her initial reaction was to pounce upon the offer, to grasp the excuse not to venture inside the inn alone. But she firmly shoved aside the *yes* that rushed to her lips. She'd come too far to hide behind anyone now. Still, nervousness had her swallowing to locate her voice.

"No, thank you." She turned to Sophie. "Please show Mr. Watley which pieces of luggage we'll require for our stay."

"Yes, milady." Sophie turned her attention to the carriage, and Cassandra forced her less than steady legs to move up the cobblestone walkway toward the front door, her mind swirling with that haunting question. *Would he be here?*

Ethan Baxter wiped at his sweaty brow with an equally sweaty forearm, then rolled his aching shoulders. Nothing like an afternoon spent mucking out the stalls and currying horses to exhaust the body. But it was a good exhaustion, one that came from an activity he loved, one he didn't do often enough since he'd hired Jamie Browne to run the livery. But when word had come at noon that Jamie's wife's labor had begun, Ethan had sent the young man home. A smile tugged at his lips as he recalled Jamie's expression—a combination of awe, excitement, and complete, utter panic. A fissure of envy suffused Ethan, fading his amusement, echoing through the hollow space inside him, the space that longed for what Jamie and Sara had—a loving marriage. A child on the way. A real family.

His jaw tightened with annoyance. That cursed hollow space. 'Bout bloody damn time he did something about it. And after much soul-searching, he believed he knew just the thing.

Ethan left the livery and walked into the bright sunshine. He immediately noted the unfamiliar carriage outside the inn, the coachman removing a portmanteau from the stack of luggage, a lady's maid pointing to another for him to remove. As the carriage was empty, the rest of the party was clearly already inside to inquire about rooms, of which, based on the coachman and the maid, they'd require at least two. Excellent for business, which he always welcomed. The Blue Seas had a reputation for being a clean, respectable, well-run establishment, and it was a distinction he'd worked hard to establish over the past four years since he'd first opened the inn's doors.

Having no desire to greet the newcomers smelling like horse and feeling gritty with sweat, he headed toward the inn's side door, intending to head immediately for his own room to make himself presentable. Certainly Delia was fully capable of handling things and seeing to their comfort. Indeed, the inn's housekeeper was so efficient, Ethan could probably leave St. Ives for a month and not be missed. Not that he had any intention of leaving for so much as a minute. St. Ives, the Blue Seas, was *home*—a place he'd searched long and hard to find. A place where he'd finally located a measure of the impossible-to-find tranquility he'd desperately sought. And if at times his work didn't exhaust his mind and body enough to forget the past, it at least brought him a modicum of peace he hadn't found anywhere else.

Of course, he suspected that Delia would note his absence if he were to leave. He huffed out a breath and dragged a hand through his sweat-dampened hair. Suspected? Hell, he knew it. Over the past year—and more frequently of late— she'd made comments, looked at him with a certain expression, both of which left no doubt that she wouldn't mind being more to him than an employee, more than a friend. She was an attractive woman, and God help him, he'd been tempted more than once to quit pretending he hadn't noticed her subtle hints.

Up until now he'd ignored them. Delia Tildon was a good, decent young widow who certainly deserved better than him. He was damaged goods, on both the inside and the outside. He liked and respected her too much to take advantage of her kind nature and use her to slake his loneliness.

Yet lately . . . over the past few months the temptation to do just that was proving nearly overpowering. The ache of emptiness eating at him seemed so much more acute lately, the memories bombarding him so hard, so fast, it was a daily struggle not to drown in them. A fact that never ceased to annoy him. Why the bloody hell couldn't he just *forget*?

Yet no matter how strong the temptation, he'd thus far resisted Delia's lure. A woman like Delia would want—and deserved—a man's whole heart. And he simply didn't have one to give. To offer her any less would be unfair to both of them.

Or so he'd thought until he'd spent the last few days pondering the reality that loneliness was also unfair. The thought of having someone to share his life with, someone to talk to, to listen to, had taken root in his mind and in spite of his best efforts to dislodge it, it refused to budge. He didn't want to hurt Delia, but bloody hell, he was so damn tired of being alone. Perhaps affection and respect were enough. Enough to make a marriage. Enough to make him forget. Or at least make him stop wanting, yearning for things he could never have.

It was time to give in to temptation. To discuss the matter

with Delia. Let her decide for herself if affection and respect were enough. And maybe, if he were very, very lucky, they would be. And he wouldn't be alone any longer.

Feeling more lighthearted than he had in a long time, he entered the inn through the side door, closing the oak panel softly behind him. He stood for several seconds to allow his eyes to adjust from the bright sunlight to the sudden dimness, and he heard Delia's voice drift toward him from the inn's front room.

"So it's two rooms ye'll be needin', milady?"

"Yes, please, Mrs. Tildon. One for me, and one for my maid. For one night."

Ethan went perfectly still at the sound of the newcomer's voice, his heart seeming to stall in his chest as myriad images flashed through his mind. Shiny hair the color of freshly harvested honey, laughing blue eyes, a mischievous smile. He blinked away the mental pictures, then with a sound of disgust, he shook his head. Bloody hell, bad enough that even after all these years he couldn't erase the thought of her, but now he was imagining her voice as well.

"The coachman will require a bed as well," continued the soft, slightly husky voice that sounded so much like her, he found his feet moving of their own volition toward the front room. His mind, his common sense knew it wasn't she, that she lived hundreds of miles away, yet he walked toward that voice, drawn to it like a thirsty man to an oasis.

"We've beds available for your coachman in the livery," came Delia's voice. "Finest stables in St. Ives we have here at the Blue Seas."

"With Mr. Baxter as the proprietor, I'm not surprised."

Ethan rounded the corner and halted in the doorway. He vaguely noted Delia's raised brows, heard her ask in a surprised tone, "Do ye know Ethan, my lady?" but his attention was riveted on the other woman.

She stood in partial profile to him, the upper half of her

face obscured by her bonnet brim. But his heart lurched at the glimpse of honey-colored hair, at the curve of her chin, the shape of her lips. The slight indent in her cheek next to her mouth, one that he could almost see deepening if she smiled.

Her head jerked in a nod. "Yes, I know him," she said softly. "Or at least I did, a long time ago . . ."

Her voice trailed off and she seemed to go perfectly still—just as his heart began to pound in hard, fast thumps, as if he'd sprinted across a decade's length of time to arrive from very far away. And then, as if feeling the weight of his stare, she turned slowly toward him. And he found himself gazing into eyes he never thought he'd see again, beautiful blue eyes that reminded him of the sea and that had haunted his nights and days for more years than he could recall.

Cassie . . .

Her name reverberated through his brain, then rushed to his lips, but he couldn't speak. Couldn't do anything save stare.

Her skin paled, then flushed crimson before his disbelieving eyes, and for several long seconds the only sound he heard was the frantic beat of his heart. And then, in that same soft voice he still heard in his dreams, she broke the silence.

"Hello, Ethan."

Chapter Two

Hello, Ethan.

With those two simple words, the years fell away and Ethan was once again a green lad, working in her father's stables, eagerly awaiting the moment she would arrive for her daily ride and greet him with a dimpling smile that could chase even the darkest clouds from the sky and those two words. *Hello, Ethan.*

Hello, Cassie. The reply crammed into his tight throat, and he clenched his jaw to contain it. For she was no longer the Cassie he'd grown up with, the shy, awkward girl who'd blossomed into a beautiful young woman, the best friend with whom he'd shared countless hours. She was now Lady Westmore. A countess.

And by God, she was still beautiful. With her huge blue eyes and pert nose and full, bow-shaped lips, she looked as if the gods had taken extra care when fashioning her. Yet, as he studied her face, he noted subtle differences. The lack of sparkle in those eyes. The slight tightness around her mouth. The thinness of her once apple-round cheeks. The laughing, hoydenish girl he'd once known was nowhere to be seen in this woman. He immediately wondered what had brought about the change.

And then with a jolt he noticed her clothing, the unrelieved black that encased her from head to foot. She was in mourning. But who had died? Her mother or father? Surely not. Lord and Lady Parrish's estate was only a two-hour journey from St. Ives. If either had died, word would have reached him via the gossip grapevine. That left her husband.

For one terrible, ridiculous instant his heart leaped at the thought of her no longer being married, then reality returned with a bruising thump. It made no difference if she had a husband or not. Not now, not ten years ago, not ever. She was so far above his station as to be laughable. The platonic relationship they'd enjoyed as children and young adults was long since over. That his feelings had deepened far beyond mere friendship was his own pain to bear. She'd certainly never given him hope that there could be more between them—the limitations were never questioned. A stable boy and a viscount's daughter? Utterly impossible. Yet that hadn't kept his stupid, foolish heart from falling hopelessly, irrevocably for that which he could never have.

Reality's bruising thump also brought with it a jolt of anger—at himself, for never being able to forget the past, forget her, or talk himself out of his futile feelings. And anger at her, for showing up like this, and still having the power, after all these years, to tilt his world on its axis by simply standing there.

Years ago he'd done everything in his power to hide his feelings, yet part of him had unreasonably resented the fact that she'd never guessed. How could she not have noticed what to him seemed to glow like a beacon from his every pore? Clearly he was an accomplished actor and liar. Of course that last year she'd been too preoccupied planning her Season. And then her wedding . . .

She cleared her throat, and with a jolt he realized he was staring and wondered how long he'd stood there gaping in silence.

"Lady Westmore." The words felt like a knife in his gut. "Please forgive my silence. I'm simply surprised to see you."

Something he couldn't decipher flickered in her eyes, followed immediately by what appeared to be relief. Surely she hadn't thought he wouldn't remember her. A humorless sound rose in his throat. Bloody hell, if she only knew how hard he'd tried to forget her.

Clutching her reticule to her midsection as if a band of thieves were about to burst through the door she said, "Not unpleasantly surprised, I hope."

"No, of course not," he said, not certain that was completely the truth.

"It's been a long time."

Ten years, two months, and fourteen days. "Yes." His voice sounded rough and harsh, as if he hadn't used it during that entire decade.

Her gaze searched his face. "You've been well, I hope . . . ?" Her words tapered off, and he knew the instant she saw the puckered scar that marred his left cheek. He hadn't been handsome before the disfigurement, but the mark had wiped away any vanity he might have foolishly possessed. A daily reminder of the past. His jaw tightened at the shock and sympathy brewing in her eyes. Damn it, he didn't want her pity. Anything but that.

Her gaze lingered for several seconds on his ruined skin, then moved downward, over his clothing to his boots, and he barely suppressed a groan. Bloody hell, how many times had he imagined this scenario in his dreams? Of her coming to his inn, or of them meeting by chance somewhere? Hundreds? More like thousands. Yet in all those fantasies he'd been clean and well-dressed and debonair—not dirty and smelling of sweat and horse, and tongue-tied.

Hands clenched, he bore her brief scrutiny and tersely reminded himself it didn't make any difference what he looked like or smelled like. He was what he was, what he'd always been—a commoner, a man of the working class.

When her gaze once again met his, he lied and said, "I've been well. And you?"

"I've . . . managed." One gloved hand brushed over her black gown, and her bottom lip trembled. "Westmore died. Two months ago."

God help him, he'd wanted to hate Westmore, and he supposed in some ways he did—hated him for his perfect, handsome face and title and wealth that allowed him to have the one thing Ethan had wanted and loved above all else.

Cassie.

Yet how could he hate a man who'd given her everything she deserved? Glittering parties and fancy gowns. A title, wealth, and a place in society. A comfortable, happy life. She clearly deeply mourned his loss, and for that he was sorry.

"Please accept my condolences."

She gave a tight nod, then said, "I'm on my way to Land's End, to Gateshead Manor."

"For a visit, or to stay?"

She hesitated, then said, "To stay."

A muscle in his jaw ticked. She'd be only two hours away.

God help him.

"You're not continuing on today?" he asked, experiencing a sudden, almost desperate need for her to leave. Before he said or did something he'd regret. "This fine weather may not last." *Having you here, in my inn, my home, will be torture. Close enough to touch, yet, as always, untouchable.*

She shook her head. "I need a respite from the long journey before returning home." The ghost of a smile whispered across her lips. "One more minute in that coach and I'd have gone mad."

Understandable, he supposed. Yet was her stopping at his inn by design or coincidence? He didn't particularly believe in coincidence, yet why would she purposely visit the Blue Seas? Surely she didn't want to renew their friendship.

A combination of idiotic elation and something that felt damn close to panic seized him at the thought. For one insane moment he allowed the notion of once again being her friend, of sharing laughter and sorrow, to fill him with a sense of happiness he hadn't known in years. But then dread quickly replaced that momentary euphoria.

Bloody hell, he couldn't possibly be her friend. Couldn't possibly spend any amount of time in her company and successfully hide his feelings. The only reason he'd been able to do so all those years ago was that she'd been so innocent. After ten years of marriage, ten years of maturity, she'd surely guess, would certainly see his hopeless feelings. Oh, she'd be too kind to mock him, but by God, he didn't want her pity. Bad enough that he already had it thanks to his damn scar.

Why had she come here? So she could regale him with tales of her fabulous life and wonderful husband? He didn't begrudge her those things, but unlike years ago, he'd no longer subject himself to the punishment of hearing all about them.

Silence swelled in the room which suddenly felt far too warm. Damn it, where were words when he needed them? Or at least appropriate words, for he could hardly say those that rested at the tip of his tongue: *Go away!* Or even worse, *God, I've missed you.*

"Is your . . . family well, Ethan?" she asked.

"Family?" he repeated, confused. Surely she recalled that his father had died. She'd stood beside him at the grave. "I have no family." A movement behind her caught his eye, and his attention shifted to Delia, whose presence he'd completely forgotten. Noting her dark-eyed gaze resting on him, he collected himself enough to shoot her a quick smile, then said to Cassie, "Although my friends here at the Blue Seas make me feel as if I do."

Something again flickered in Cassie's eyes. She appeared about to speak, but the front door opened and the young woman he'd seen outside, who was clearly her lady's maid, and the coachman, who carried two portmanteaus, entered. After Cassie performed quick introductions, she accepted two brass keys from Delia.

"Yer rooms are numbers five and six, just up the stairs," Delia said in her usual brisk manner. "Dinner's served at seven in the main room. Will ye be needin' help with yer bags?"

"I can handle them," Mr. Watley said.

"Will you be here for dinner this evening, Ethan?" Cassie asked, her huge blue eyes spearing him to the spot.

"Dinner?"

One brow shot upward. "Yes. The meal that is served at seven in the main room."

He blinked, then realized she was teasing him. Just as she always had. Bloody hell, it felt like . . . coming home. And bloody hell, he didn't like that one bit. Crossing his arms over his chest, he said brusquely, "Man's gotta eat."

She looked uncertain, then said, "Excellent. I'll see you at seven."

With Mr. Watley leading the way, Cassie and her maid climbed the stairs. Seconds later they disappeared from view, leaving only the murmur of their voices behind.

Ethan drew a deep, careful breath. He'd be sharing a meal with her this evening. She'd be spending the night under his roof. He wasn't certain if the heart-pounding sensation surging through him was elation or dread. A bit of both, he suspected.

It was just one night. He'd hidden his feelings for so long, kept them in check for so many years, surely another mere twenty-four hours wouldn't matter.

And then, as she had ten years ago, she'd say good-bye and leave.

He didn't know how he was going to survive her staying here.

And he sure as hell didn't know how he was going to survive watching her go.

Chapter Three

Cassandra walked slowly around her cozy bedchamber, trailing her fingertips over the neat dark blue counterpane. Her avid gaze took in the oak night table, wardrobe, single chest of drawers, and washstand, all serviceable pieces without frills, but the furniture and the mantel gleamed with polish. The walls were unadorned, painted beige, their pale color giving the illusion of space in the small chamber. Plain blue curtains flanked the open window, through which a warm, sea-scented breeze wafted. Everything in this room spoke of Ethan's ownership—strong, functional, tidy, and no fuss.

Ethan . . . She closed her eyes and drew a long, slow breath. Seeing him, hearing his voice had brought back a plethora of memories that had threatened to render her speechless. And while she would have recognized him anywhere, he was undeniably different. Physically, he was bigger, broader, more muscular. She'd had to tear her gaze from the fascinating display of brawn showcased by his snug black breeches and dirt-streaked shirt. His disheveled appearance had in no way detracted from his masculine appeal.

His ebony hair, which he'd always cropped ruthlessly short, was longer now, touching his collar, and looked as if he'd just run his fingers through the thick, shiny waves. The urge to touch those silky-looking strands had seized her with such stunning force, she'd had to press her hands to her midsection.

And his eyes . . . those fathomless deep brown eyes she'd seen twinkle with teasing laughter and glow with intensity, were different as well. The warmth was gone. There were secrets behind those eyes now. And suffering.

His scar had shocked her. How had he come by such an injury? Clearly whatever had happened had caused him great pain. And she hadn't known. Hadn't been there to comfort him, help him, as he'd comforted and helped her so many times. Although Ethan no longer looked like a man who required comfort. No, now he looked like a fortress. Dark, grim, impenetrable. Forbidding.

Now she had the answer to the question, *Would he be here?* Yes. He was here. And for this one day, their paths touched again. And she intended to make the most of it. Tonight they would share a meal, catch up with each other's lives. And she'd find out the answers to the questions that had plagued her all these years.

Unless she saw him even sooner.

Yes. No time like the present.

After making use of the washstand to refresh herself, she changed into her riding habit and headed down the stairs. When she entered the main room, Mrs. Tildon looked up from the ledger in which she was writing.

"Goin' riding, milady?" she asked, her gaze skimming over Cassandra's attire.

"If there's a mount available. If not, then a walk will suffice." She offered the woman a smile. "After spending so many hours inside that carriage, I long to be outdoors."

"Stables are just outside. Ethan can saddle a mount for ye."

Precisely the words she wanted to hear. "Thank you."

She turned to go, anxious to be off before Mrs. Tildon might think to question her about her intention of riding alone, but before she could escape, the other woman said, "Milady . . ."

Cassandra paused and swiveled her head around, and noted that Mrs. Tildon was studying her with an expression that made Cassandra feel as if she could see into her soul, an unsettling sensation, to be sure. She was an attractive woman, Cassandra realized, probably no older than thirty, with brown hair and dark, intelligent eyes, her trim figure apparent even beneath the apron she wore over her plain gray gown.

Turning fully around, she said, "Yes, Mrs. Tildon?"

"I couldn't help but overhear what ye said to Ethan earlier, about yer husband passin' on. I lost my husband, John, two years ago. 'Tis a hurt that never quite goes away. I wanted to extend my sympathies to ye."

A hurt that never quite goes away. Yes, that described it very well. "Thank you. Please allow me to extend the same to you for your loss."

She nodded her thanks. "Ye said ye knew Ethan years ago . . . ?"

The way her voice trailed off made it clear she hoped for more information, and Cassandra saw no reason to deny her. "He worked in the stables at my family's estate in Land's End."

"That'd be Gateshead Manor?"

"Yes. He's mentioned it?"

"Said he worked there. Grew up there, actually."

"Yes, he did. He was only six when his father was hired

as stable master. They lived on the estate, above the stables."

"Got a gift with horses, Ethan does."

Cassandra couldn't help but smile. "He always had, even as a young boy. His father possessed the same gift."

Again Mrs. Tildon nodded, her steady gaze never straying from Cassandra's. "He's a good man, Ethan is."

Something in Mrs. Tildon's tone, in the intensity of her expression, stilled Cassandra. Although she didn't add the words "*my* man," they seemed to hang in the air between them. And Cassandra realized that the woman was doing more than making a simple observation. She was, very subtly—or perhaps not so very subtly—staking a claim.

Cassandra wasn't certain what in her manner had given Mrs. Tildon the impression that such claim staking was necessary, but she had no intention of repeating the mistake.

Lifting her chin in the manner employed by generations of Westmores, she met the woman's gaze straight on and said, "A very good man, indeed. I bid you a good afternoon, Mrs. Tildon." Then she turned and exited the inn, ignoring the gaze she felt boring into her back.

Yet she couldn't ignore the tension churning in her stomach. *Had* she said or done something to bring out Mrs. Tildon's clearly possessive feelings for Ethan? Or did the woman merely feel the need to warn off every female who visited the Blue Seas Inn? Was there something between her and Ethan, or was Mrs. Tildon just a concerned friend? Or perhaps she'd mistaken the woman's tone and misinterpreted her words.

She covered the short distance to the livery and entered through the opened double doorway. She blinked several times to acclimate her eyes to the shadowed interior. The air inside was cool and redolent with fresh hay, leather, and the earthy scent of horses. Dust motes danced on the ribbons of golden sunlight filtering through the shadows.

The stables were spacious and scrupulously neat; not that she would have expected anything less from Ethan. He'd always taken great pride in his work, and she'd never met a man with a greater affinity for horses. Indeed, he had loved all animals.

As if the thought of Ethan conjured him up, he strode through a side doorway, one she guessed led to the tack room. A large black dog trotted at his heels. At the sight of her, Ethan halted, but the dog continued toward her, tail wagging, tongue lolling.

She pulled her gaze away from Ethan, who was staring at her with an unsettling intensity, and looked down at the approaching dog. She noted the animal's white-tipped tail, and her eyes widened with recognition.

Crouching down, she scratched behind the dog's ears, then looked up at Ethan, who still hadn't moved, and asked, "Is this . . . could this possibly be T.C.?"

The dog, who obviously knew his name, answered by emitting a deep woof, then running in a circle to chase his tail, his favorite trick, which had earned him his name—Tail Chaser.

A laugh escaped her at the dog's antics, surprising her, and she realized that it had been a long time since she'd indulged in laughter. Since she'd had any reason to do so. After successfully capturing the snowy end between his teeth, T.C. released the offending bit of white fur, then flopped onto his back and presented his belly for rubbing—his second favorite trick.

"Oh, you were barely more than a baby when I saw you last," Cassandra said with a chuckle, tickling her fingers over the dog's thick fur, much to his squirming delight. "What a big, handsome boy you are now."

She heard Ethan's boots shifting against the rough wood floor, and seconds later he stood next to her. The fresh scent of soap wafted toward her, and she looked up, taking in his scuffed black boots—clearly old favorites. Clean fawn breeches hugged his long, powerful legs—in a most distracting way. Forcing her gaze to continue upward, she noted his snowy white shirt, casually open at his throat, the sleeves rolled back to reveal strong, tanned forearms dusted with dark hair.

Then she found herself staring into ebony eyes that pinned her in place with an inscrutable expression. Fathomless eyes that were both familiar and those of a stranger. From this angle he appeared impossibly tall. And ridiculously masculine.

Warmth raced through her, and she was about to rise when he suddenly crouched down. Her relief that he no longer towered over her was tempered by the unsettling realization that he was now so close she could feel the heat emanating from his large body. His face, less than two feet from hers, remained streaked in shadows, his scar barely visible.

For several long seconds they simply looked at each other, and her fingers stilled on T.C.'s warm fur. It seemed as if all the air had left the room. She searched her mind for something, anything to say, but apparently she'd forgotten how to speak. How to breathe.

"It appears T.C. remembers you," he finally said.

She had to swallow to locate her voice. "I doubt it," she said, pleased that she managed not to sound as breathless as she felt. "I'd wager he flops onto his back like this for anyone who appears willing to pet him."

"Obviously you remember him, too," he said in a dry tone. He shifted his gaze to the dog and patted the animal's sturdy side. "You remember Cassie, don't you, boy? She's the one whose handkerchief you stole. The one you pulled into the lake."

Cassie. The name reverberated through her mind, swamping her with memories. And relief that Ethan obviously remembered those times as well, a fact that made him seem somewhat less forbidding.

Adopting a mock-haughty tone, she informed him, "T.C. didn't pull me into the lake. I had every intention of wading in."

"With your shoes on? I think not. As I recall, he grabbed the hem of your gown between his teeth and dragged you in."

"Hmm. No doubt because you sat in the rowboat in the middle of the lake calling out, 'C'mon boy! Bring her here!' "

He glanced at her, and for an instant he was the mischievous young man she remembered. "I don't recall doing any such thing," he said, perfectly straight-faced. "You must have me confused with someone else."

Before she could refute his claim, their fingers brushed, sending a heated jolt up her arm. Her hand stilled and her gaze dropped. Ethan's large hand rested only inches from hers. She'd always admired his hands, so strong and capable. They were browned from the sun, and hers looked small and white in comparison. Fragile and useless.

Silence fell between them, and again she searched for something to say. And when she looked up and met his gaze, the words simply spilled out of her.

"I haven't heard the name Cassie since the last time I saw you. You're the only person who ever called me that."

A curtain seemed to fall over his expression. "Forgive me. I shouldn't have—"

"Oh, but you should have. You have no idea how wonderful it sounded. But I don't know . . ." Her voice trailed off, and she dipped her chin.

"Don't know what?"

She drew a bracing breath, then again met his gaze. "I don't know what happened to her. To that girl you called Cassie."

"She's right here. Petting my zany dog."

She shook her head. "I haven't seen her in a long time. But I'd like to. Before she's lost forever."

A frown bunched his brows. "What do you mean?"

"Only that . . . I'm not that same person anymore, Ethan. Are you the same man you were ten years ago?"

He raised his hand and ran his fingers over the left side of his face. "I think you can see that I'm not."

"I'd like to know what happened, if you'd care to tell me. About that, and everything else that has occurred in your life." Summoning her courage, and with her gaze steady on his, she said, "We have this one day together. This one beautiful summer day before I have to leave. We could walk along the beach and reminisce about Gateshead Manor. Tell each other about our lives these last ten years." She gave a half smile. "I'd love to see more of this lovely town you've made your home. Will you spend the day with me, Ethan?"

For several long seconds he regarded her with an unreadable expression. Then what looked like anger flashed in his eyes. With an impatient sound he rose and strode several feet away, as if he couldn't wait to put distance between them. Then he halted, his back to her, his shoulders straight with a tension she could almost see radiating from him.

With a sinking feeling she realized she'd made a mistake. He clearly had no desire to spend time with her, to talk about the past with someone he hadn't seen in years. Still, she somehow hadn't anticipated his rejecting her request. Rejecting her. She foolishly hadn't braced herself for the hurt.

Skin prickling with embarrassment, she rose, intending to return to her room with as much dignity as she could muster. She'd barely taken a step, however, when he turned around and shot her a dark glare that halted her. With his gaze locked on hers, he moved slowly toward her, and she instinctively backed up several paces, until her shoulders hit the wall, ending her retreat. His advance continued until a mere arm's length separated them.

"You've had a wonderful life," he said, his voice low and intense. "Why would you want to hear the sordid details of mine?"

She froze, staring into eyes that smoldered with an unmistakable animosity she didn't understand. Yet it was one that sparked her own anger and resentment. One that had her lifting her chin to glare right back at him.

"Wonderful life?" A bitter sound escaped her. "You know *nothing* of my life since I saw you last."

A muscle ticked in his jaw. He leaned forward and planted his hands on the wall on either side of her head, caging her in. She sucked in a breath, and her head filled with his scent. Clean soap and something warm and masculine she couldn't name other than to know it made her heart beat faster. Or perhaps the frantic pounding was the result of his nearness.

"I'm not the same man I used to be, Cassie," he said softly, his warm breath touching her lips. "If we spend the day together, I can't guarantee I won't do something we'd both regret."

"Like what?"

Fire seemed to kindle in his eyes, and his gaze wandered down to her lips. Her mouth tingled under his scrutiny, but before she could so much as form a thought, his lips covered hers, in a hot, hard kiss that tasted of passion and suppressed need and dark hunger.

Heat whooshed through her, melting her knees, but then as quickly as he'd started the kiss he ended it, lifting his head and staring down at her with glittering eyes that seemed to breathe smoke.

Dear God. Shock rendered her immobile. Except for her heart, which thundered hard enough to echo in her ears.

Never, in her entire life, had any man looked at her like this. Like he was starving and she was a banquet feast. Like he wanted to devour her. Certainly she'd never inspired her husband to look at her in such a way.

"Like *that*," he said, his voice a husky growl.

Oh. Like *that*. Except he thought it was something they'd regret. Perhaps *he* did, but she didn't, although she knew she should. Yet how could she possibly regret experiencing something so bold and fiery and darkly arousing? Especially when it had been so long since she'd felt anything except emptiness?

"Different than last time," he said softly.

She knew what he meant, and fire heated her cheeks. Shortly before her marriage, she'd asked Ethan to kiss her. Westmore had finally kissed her, a momentous occasion she'd dreamed would thrill her, but one she'd found oddly disappointing. When she asked Ethan to offer up a comparison, he'd looked angry and initially refused. But after she persisted, he relented and brushed his lips gently over hers. The contact lasted only seconds, but she'd felt as if lightning had struck her—a reaction Westmore's kiss had most emphatically not induced. She'd desperately wanted him to kiss her again, but couldn't summon the courage to ask. Indeed, her strong reaction had deeply unsettled her. Ethan had stepped away, then made light of the situation with a joke, and they'd never mentioned it again. Two days later he was gone, leaving only a brief note behind.

Now she sensed the tension gripping him, and knew without a doubt that he wanted to kiss her again. And God help her, she wanted him to. Just as she'd wanted him to years ago. Was it possible that he'd wanted to then as well, but unlike now had held back?

She swallowed, then agreed in a shaky voice, "Different than last time."

"Still want to go for that walk with me, Cassie?"

His voice was edged with challenge, his eyes daring her to say yes. And she realized that he hadn't lied—he wasn't the same man.

But neither was she the same woman.

"Yes, Ethan. I still want to go for that walk with you."

Chapter Four

With T.C. leading the way, Ethan walked next to Cassie along the trail that led through a thick copse of trees toward the beach, and tried his damnedest to shove aside the memory of the kiss they'd just shared. But he might as well have attempted to push back the tide with a broom.

Part of him was deeply irritated that after only a few minutes in her company he'd allowed himself to lose control like that. Allowed his anger and resentment to get the better of him. But another part of him was darkly pleased that he'd finally acted on his long-suppressed desires. Still, another part of him cursed him for doing so. Because instead of satisfying his desire, that brief taste had unfortunately only whetted his appetite for more. Just as it had ten years ago.

The memory of the chaste kiss they'd shared that summer day in the stables flashed through his mind, burning as brightly as if it had taken place a moment, rather than a decade, ago. In that brief instant he'd discovered what she tasted like. Heaven. And no longer had to wonder if her lips were as lush and soft as he'd suspected. They were.

Her request for a kiss had stunned him. And angered him—because he knew damn well she only wanted to compare it to her bloody fiancé's kiss. But in the end he couldn't deny her. Or himself. And after he'd experienced that perfect taste of that which he could never have, he'd wanted to kiss her again more than he'd wanted to draw his next breath.

And ten years later he felt the exact same way after kissing her in his stable.

Damn it, she should have slapped his face. Stormed from the stables in a fit of outrage. He'd hoped she would. Instead she'd looked at him with those damn big shocked eyes, making him feel like a bastard. While he grudgingly admired the fact that she'd held her ground and accepted his challenge, he still wished, for both their sakes, she'd scurried off. But he should have known she wouldn't. His Cassie had never been a coward.

His Cassie. Foolish words that he needed to thrust from his mind. She wasn't his—never had been, never would be. Yet still, she was here, and they'd been friends, and he was acting churlish. It wasn't her fault he'd fallen in love with her and never gotten over his feelings. But bloody hell, how could he stand an entire afternoon of being regaled with stories of London society and fancy soirees and her perfect husband?

You know nothing of my life since I saw you last.

Her words had sounded angry, although he couldn't imagine why. Surely Westmore had worshipped the ground she walked on. Most likely his recent death was the source of her embitterment.

They continued along the path, and in spite of the tension he sensed between them, it felt as if the years had slipped away. They'd explored the grounds of Gateshead Manor countless times, sometimes on foot, sometimes on horseback. Sometimes they talked, barely pausing for breath, as if there weren't enough hours in the day to say all that needed to be said. Other times, as now, they remained silent.

Of course back then it was a comfortable silence, one steeped in being with someone who knew you well. Someone with whom you'd shared your deepest thoughts and hopes. Discussed your fears and disappointments. Someone with whom you'd laughed and cried.

He'd loved her for as long as he could remember, but after the realization when he was fifteen that he was *in love* with her, he'd often spent those silences wondering what she was thinking, fantasizing that her thoughts ran along similar lines to his—that he was a titled gentleman who'd come to court her. Who would lavish her with jewels and gowns and ask her to marry him. That he could spend every day with her. Draw her into his arms and kiss her. Touch her. Make love to her. Sleep beside her. That she belonged to him. And now, years later, he found himself again wondering what she was thinking.

"It's beautiful here."

Her soft voice yanked him from his brown study and he turned toward her. Sunlight dappled through the thick leafy cover overhead, glinting off her shiny hair. Her bonnet hung down her back by its ribbons, reminding him how she'd always remove her headwear the instant she was out of her mother's sight. She'd often regaled him with her mother's frequent warnings about allowing the sun to freckle—or as her mother called it, *ruin*—her skin, but he'd always liked the pale gold dots that marched across her nose.

With his gaze drinking in her profile, he agreed, "Very beautiful."

"How long have you lived in St. Ives?"

"Four years."

"And before that?"

"Lots of places, looking for somewhere to call home. I finally found it here."

"You never married?"

"No."

He hoped his brusque tone would discourage her from asking him why not, as he wasn't about to admit the truth. Thankfully she fell silent, and for several minutes the only sound was that of the leaves rustling overhead and the twigs snapping beneath their feet. Then she said, "You say you were looking for somewhere to call home . . . but Gateshead Manor was your home."

"For a time. But then it was time for me to go."

"You left very abruptly." She paused, then added, "Without saying good-bye."

And it was the hardest damn thing I've ever done. "I left you a note."

"Revealing only that you'd received a lucrative offer to work on another estate and that they wanted you to begin immediately."

"There wasn't anything else to say."

From the corner of his eye he saw her turn to look at him, but he kept his gaze steadfastly straight ahead. "After all these years I suppose there's no reason not to tell you that you leaving like that hurt me. Deeply."

What hurt you all but gutted me. "I don't see why. You were leaving Cornwall in less than a fortnight to marry Westmore."

"Because you were my friend. My *only* friend. I suppose I expected more of you than to simply abandon me without any explanation or good-bye other than a hastily scribbled note. I never would have done that to you." There was no mistaking the hurt and anger and confusion in her voice.

Shame filled him. He'd hated himself for leaving that way, but at the time he hadn't had any choice. "I'm sorry, Cassie," he said, and God knew he meant it. "It wasn't my intention to hurt you."

"I kept expecting to hear from you, but I never did."

"I wasn't much good at sending letters." Guilt slapped him, although he hadn't actually lied. He was bad at *sending* letters. But he'd certainly *written* them. Dozens of them. Pouring out his heart to her on pages he knew he'd never mail. "Actually, I thought it best not to write. Stable boys don't correspond with countesses."

Her silence indicated she knew he was right. Just as he knew it. Unfortunately, that didn't make the harsh facts of life hurt any less.

Finally she said, "I asked my father which estate you'd gone to work on, but he didn't know."

"I didn't tell him."

"Why not?"

"He didn't ask."

"Why not?"

"You'd have to ask him."

His shoulders tensed, sensing she was about to ask him another question, but he was saved when they rounded a corner. She halted, drawing in a quick breath at the sudden unexpected and spectacular view. As many times as he'd rounded that corner and beheld the vista, it always stopped him as well.

The ocean was spread before them, an indigo blanket of white-capped waves that rushed onto golden sand. Soaring cliffs protruded into the water at one end of the expanse of beach, jutting rocks that broke the ocean's inexorable flow, shooting fountains of seawater toward the sky, to fall in a sheet of droplets that caught the sunlight in glittering bursts of rainbow brilliance. Gulls screeched, some swooping low, others soaring high, still others floating on the brisk breeze as if suspended in midair.

"Oh, Ethan," she whispered. "It's magnificent." Her eyes slid closed and she tipped her head back, the sun's rays reflecting off her beautiful face. "It's been so long since I've seen the ocean, breathed in the salt air, felt its soothing coolness upon my skin. I'd forgotten the sense of peace it could bring. I've missed it so. I've missed so many things . . ."

She lifted her head and opened her eyes, and her face bloomed into a full smile that coaxed the dimples flanking her lips to appear. As it always had, her smile dazzled him, skewering him in place, making his heart pound.

"Isn't it just the most wonderful thing you've ever seen?" she asked with a laugh, spreading her arms to encompass the panorama.

"The most wonderful thing I've ever seen," he agreed, unable to pull his gaze from her.

"I must feel the sand," she said. "And the water. And collect some shells and stones to skip." Then she grabbed his hand and dashed forward, tugging him along.

At Gateshead Manor she'd frequently touched him like that—clasping his hand, giving him a playful shove, or brushing bits of hay from his hair and clothing. Casual gestures he'd simultaneously loved and hated for the contrast of pure pleasure and jaw-gritting torture they provided.

Now the unexpected sensation of her palm nestled warmly against his shot a bolt of heat up his arm, and he nearly stumbled. But he quickly recovered and, unable to resist, ran beside her, the air whipping at their hair and clothes, the sun warm against their skin. T.C. ran ahead, kicking up sand in his mad scramble across the beach. The sound of Cassie's laughter enveloped him like a soft blanket. He couldn't recall the last time he'd felt so carefree, but he did know that whenever it was, it had been with her. With Cassie.

They halted near the shore and she released his hand, and he instantly missed her touch. Flinging her arms wide, she turned in a circle, breathless and laughing, her dark blue skirt swirling around her legs. When she stopped, her eyes glittered like sapphires from her exertions, and several tendrils of tawny hair clung to her flushed cheeks.

Facing her, he wished he knew how to paint so as to

capture her in this moment, with the sea and cloud-studded azure sky behind her, the gilded sand beneath her, and all of her bathed in golden sunlight and tousled by the breeze.

Unable to stop himself, he reached out and brushed back one of the windblown curls from her cheek. A simple, casual gesture that felt neither simple nor casual to him. Nor to her, he'd wager, given the way she went perfectly still. Never had he touched such velvety smooth skin, and he lingered for several seconds, allowing the breeze to entwine the silky strands around his fingers before lowering his hand.

"If you've been looking for Cassie, she's right here," he said softly, "laughing in the sunshine."

Closing her eyes briefly, she drew a deep breath, then slowly nodded. "I feel her. Deep inside. She desperately wants to come out."

"As far as I can see, she already has." Something flickered in her eyes, something he couldn't decipher. Something that prompted him to ask, "What are the other things you've missed, Cassie?"

The light faded from her eyes and she turned toward the water, leaving him to study her profile. She was silent for so long, he wondered if she intended to answer him. Finally she looked at him, her expression unreadable. "I've missed walking along the shore. Skipping stones and splashing in the water. Collecting shells and capturing crabs. Having someone to talk to, someone to listen to me, someone to listen to. I've missed laughter and gazing at the stars and building castles made of sand. Riding a horse just as dawn breaks. Sharing silly dreams and making up stories and impromptu picnics."

He stared. Those were all things they'd done together, memories they'd shared, steeped in the unlikely friendship they'd forged out of loneliness and a surprising number of common interests. Before he could say a word, she reached out and pressed one of his hands between both of her own. "You, Ethan," she said softly. "I've missed *you*."

Her words, the warmth of her soft hands surrounding his callused ones rendered him speechless. Before he could recover, she asked, "Have you missed me?"

Bloody hell, if he'd been capable of it, he would have laughed. Missed her? Only with every breath. Every heartbeat. Every day.

He had to swallow to locate his voice. "Sometimes."

Her bottom lip trembled, threatening to smite him where he stood. And damn it, if he allowed himself to continue looking into her eyes, he'd fall on his knees before her and confess his ridiculous, impossible love. Probably beg her to love him in return.

That scenario all but made his blood run cold. And this damn conversation suddenly felt too personal and intense. Forcing himself to heave a put-upon sigh, he teased, "Even though you were horribly girly."

"Girly?" She sounded outraged, as he'd known she would. She released his hand and planted her fists on her hips. "I was no such thing. Was I afraid to bait a fish hook?"

"Well, no. But then you rarely caught a fish."

"Only because you splashed about so. Was I afraid to climb a tree?"

"No. But I recall you required rescuing on more than one occasion when your *girly* gown became caught in the branches."

"Humph. I wouldn't have required rescuing if you'd lent me a pair of your breeches as I requested."

Most likely not. But *he* would have required rescuing. The mere thought of her wearing his clothing had all but stopped his heart.

"Very well," he conceded. "You weren't the least bit girly. Indeed, you were practically a man. Why, I'm surprised you didn't grow a beard and take up smoking cigars."

She wrinkled her nose. "I don't care for either, thank you very much." Then she raised her chin. "Of course there's nothing wrong with being girly."

"Especially if one is a girl."

"You should have loaned me your breeches."

"Your mother would have fainted."

Eyes twinkling with amusement, she gave an elegant sniff. "Mother always had her hartshorn at the ready, and even if Father were to grab a weapon, he had dreadful aim."

Not always. With a jolt he realized his fingers were brushing over his scarred cheek, and he lowered his hand. Shaking off the memories hurtling toward him, he crossed his arms over his chest and adopted his sternest expression. "Young ladies do not wear breeches. Ever."

She heaved an exaggerated sigh. "If I'd known you were such an authority on deportment, I'd have simply pinched them from your room."

"Young ladies do not steal. Ever."

"Stick-in-the-mud."

"Impudent hoyden."

Her lips twitched. "Guilty as charged."

"Then it's off to the gallows for you."

"You'd have to catch me first."

"Hardly a problem given your"—he gave her garment a pointed look—"*girly* attire."

A quick laugh escaped her. "Hoist on my own petard."

Her beautiful eyes glittered with amusement and his heart thudded, pleasure suffusing him just because she was near him. Ten years faded away, and he was once again twenty years old and simply enjoying the company of the girl he loved.

He inhaled and caught a subtle whiff of roses. And barely suppressed a groan. No matter what messy adventure they'd undertaken, whether it involved mud or sand or sea or lake water, she'd always smelled as if she'd just wandered through the flower garden.

Bloody hell, how many late night summer hours had he spent in Gateshead Manor's rose garden, sitting with his eyes closed, breathing in the scent that to this day instantly called her to mind? Spinning useless dreams, imagining a make-believe place where a stable boy magically turned into a prince so as to court a viscount's daughter.

The laughter slowly faded from her eyes and her gaze lowered, settling on his scar, a forcible reminder of what he'd momentarily managed to forget—that he looked very different now. And not for the better.

She reached out and brushed her fingertips over his ruined skin, and his every muscle tensed, bracing himself for the pity he knew he'd see in her eyes.

"Does it hurt?" she asked softly.

Not trusting his voice, he shook his head.

"You must have suffered a great deal." Her gaze met his. "I'm so sorry, Ethan."

As am I. For so many things . . .

Unable to speak, he simply stood still while her fingers continued to lightly stroke his cheek. It required a Herculean effort not to turn his face and press a kiss into her palm. Snatch her into his arms and kiss her until he couldn't think any longer. Couldn't remember all the reasons that he shouldn't.

"How did this happen?"

"I was cut," he said, his tone curt. He stepped away from her and started walking along the shore. She fell into step beside him, with T.C. trotting at her heels. In an effort to forestall further questions about his face he said, "I have others."

"Other what?"

"Scars."

"And how did you come by those?"

While he didn't particularly want to have this conversation, she'd said she wanted to know about his life, so he might as well just get it over with. "After I left Gateshead Manor, I joined the army. I was injured at Waterloo. In a fire."

Memories he'd firmly locked away bombarded him. The screams of men and horses. Weapons discharging. The roaring blaze, men trapped. Rescuing one . . . but then the flames too hot, the smoke too thick. His coat catching fire. Shocking, scalding heat.

He glanced toward her and found her looking at him with a combination of horror and sympathy. "Dear God, how awful." She paused, then said, "You never spoke of a desire to join the army."

Because he'd never had one. Since he hadn't much cared if he lived or died after he left Gateshead Manor, he figured he might as well die doing something useful, and the army seemed the quickest way to accomplish that. And by God, he'd done every reckless thing he could think of to get himself killed, volunteered for every dangerous assignment, but instead of dying, he'd survived and received damn medals and commendations.

"I decided someone had to put that bastard Napoleon in his place."

"You succeeded."

"Finally. But the cost was . . ." He shook his head and shoved back the encroaching memories. "Many good men died. Too many."

"I'm grateful you weren't one of them."

"I wasn't." The words slipped out before he could stop them. And just as he always had, he ended up confiding things to her that he'd never shared with anyone else. "Between the bone-deep exhaustion and the pain from my injuries, I prayed more than once to go to sleep and not awaken."

A lengthy silence followed his words. Finally she broke it by asking, "How did you manage to go on?"

He debated how honest to be with her, then shrugged. No point in not telling her—she'd be gone tomorrow. *Yes—*

taking another slice of your soul with her, his inner voice sneered.

"I thought of you. Of all the times you'd convinced me I could do things I was sure I couldn't. Like when you taught me sums. And how to waltz. And sew a button on my coat. And learn all the flowers in the garden."

He paused to pick up a small rock, toss it into the waves, then continued, "I remembered what you said, what you did, when my father died. How you held my hand and told me, 'You're not alone, Ethan. Your father will always live in your heart. And I will always be your friend. And both he and I know that you are the very best of men.'" He looked at her. Saw her staring at him through huge eyes. "Those words helped me through some very difficult times over the years."

"I . . . I'm glad. And surprised. And touched that you remembered."

"I remember everything, Cassie." *Every touch. Every smile. Every tear. Every heartbreak.*

Her gaze didn't waver. "As do I."

He forced himself to look away, to concentrate on the sand in front of them, and they walked in silence for several minutes, not pausing until she found a shell she liked. After brushing the sand off the pale pink treasure, she asked, "How did you come to own the Blue Seas Inn?"

"When I was in the army, I helped out a friend, another solider. He left me some money, and I used it to buy the inn. The building needed some renovations, and when they were done, I opened for business. Things have gone well, so I added the livery two years ago."

"How did you help your friend?"

Another image, of an earlier battle, flashed through his mind. "Billy, Billy Styles was his name. He was trapped beneath his fallen horse. I dragged him free." And then had used his last lead ball to put down the suffering animal. And hadn't even realized tears streamed down his face until Billy had told him they were there.

"You saved his life."

"He was a good man. His leg was broken bad enough that he was finished with the army. Went home to London, but he died two years later from a fever—right around the time I was injured. A solicitor located me and told me about the money. After I healed, I started looking for a place I could call home."

"And found the Blue Seas Inn."

"Yes. And now it's your turn." Doing his damnedest to keep all traces of bitterness from his voice he said, "Tell me all about your wonderful life as Countess Westmore."

Several long seconds passed. Then she said quietly, "If it's something wonderful you wish to hear, then I'm afraid I have nothing to say."

Chapter Five

Cassandra glanced toward Ethan and saw the bewilderment clouding his dark eyes, the frown bunching his brows.

"Are you telling me you haven't been happy?" he asked slowly, his voice laced with both confusion and disbelief.

She jerked her gaze from him to stare straight ahead. "Yes, Ethan. I haven't been happy."

She felt his gaze boring into her, but didn't turn to look at him. "Because your husband died?"

Until this moment she hadn't quite known how much she would tell him. But his question seemed to burst a dam inside her, releasing a flood of suppressed anger and bitterness. "No. Because my husband *lived*. And for ten years made my life a living hell. Those feelings you described, about wanting to go to sleep and never wake up? I know those feelings. All too well." The words were tight. Clipped. And somehow cathartic to say out loud.

"My marriage was a disaster. A nightmare that thankfully ended when Westmore died." A shudder ran through her. She turned toward him, knowing he'd see the hatred, the anger in her eyes, and not caring. "I do not mourn him."

He halted and stepped around to face her, his gaze searching hers, looking for answers. "A nightmare in what way?"

Unable to remain still or look him in the eye, she shook her head and resumed walking with quick, agitated steps, her gaze steadfastly fixed on a tall outcropping of rocks ahead. He fell into step beside her, silent, waiting.

"As you know, I had high hopes for my marriage . . ." Of course he knew—she'd shared all her hopes and dreams with him. He'd patiently listened to her expound on her desire for a caring husband and lots of children with whom she'd share the sort of warm, loving relationship she'd always craved. The sort denied her by her parents, who'd been bitterly disappointed their only child was a girl—a fact they never tired of pointing out to her. Indeed, she'd known from childhood that the only thing she could possibly do to please them was marry well. When her father had announced that the handsome, charming, and much-sought-after Earl of Westmore had offered for her after her first Season, she'd believed herself most fortunate.

"My duty was to marry well and in accordance with Father's wishes. Westmore's duty, of course, was to produce an heir. Our relationship began to deteriorate after I failed to conceive during the first six months of our marriage. Things grew progressively worse as time wore on."

The words began to rush from her now, as if she'd lanced a festering wound and allowed the poison to run free. "After three years of me failing to conceive, Westmore announced he was finished—that he couldn't stand to touch me again. From then on, our relationship consisted of little more than icy silence. When he did bother to speak to me, it was merely to remind me of how useless I was. How disappointing and stupid. And of how much he loathed the very sight of me."

She paused, needing to shove back the painful memories that rose up to thicken her throat.

"Bloody bastard," Ethan muttered. "Did it not occur to Westmore that the fault might be his?"

"It wasn't," she said, her tone utterly flat.

"How do you know?"

"Because over the next seven years Westmore impregnated a half dozen of his paramours. Perhaps more. I stopped counting."

For several seconds silence swelled between them. Then he said in a tight voice, "He was unfaithful to you?"

She couldn't suppress the humorless sound that escaped her. "Almost from the beginning. At first he was at least discreet, and I had no idea. But after it became apparent that I wasn't able to provide him with his heir, he made no effort to conceal his indiscretions. By then all my hopes and illusions for my marriage were shattered, yet part of me still clung to the wish that our relationship wouldn't deteriorate into hatred. So I foolishly made an attempt to reason with him. Reiterated how grievously sorry and disappointed I was that I couldn't have children. Asked if we couldn't at least be civil with each other."

"What did he say?"

"He made it abundantly clear he wasn't interested."

"Abundantly clear how?"

A chill shivered through her and she wrapped her arms around herself. "He . . . hurt me."

Ethan halted and grasped her arm, swinging her around to face him. A storm brewed in his eyes and a muscle ticked in his jaw. "Hurt you?" he repeated in a low, awful voice. "He . . . forced himself on you?"

She shook her head. "No. He'd left no doubt he didn't want me . . . in that way . . . ever again."

Relief flickered in his eyes, then he frowned. "Then what . . . ?" His expression turned thunderous. "He *hit* you?"

There was no mistaking his shock. And outrage. Both of which were balms for her soul and tightened her throat. It had been so long since anyone had shown the least concern for her. Hot moisture pushed at the backs of her eyes and she fiercely blinked it away.

"He hit me," she confirmed in a deadly calm voice that seemed to come from far away, and his gaze raked over her as if to check for bruises. "Beat me, actually. It took me weeks to recover."

Looking him in the eye, she stated the bald truth, one she'd never before admitted out loud. One that would certainly prove to him that she wasn't the same young girl he'd known. "I think he suspected I'd kill him if he ever touched me again. He never did. But I was tempted to do so anyway."

She fell silent and realized she was shaking. Breathing hard. And couldn't bear to look into his eyes any longer. In spite of her trembling knees, she stepped back, and his hands fell to his sides. Wrapping her arms around herself, she began walking again. He fell into step beside her, saying nothing, for which she was grateful, as her throat was too tight to speak. By the time they reached the outcropping of rocks, she felt mentally and physically drained, and she paused in the sheltering shade the promontory provided.

Ethan moved to stand in front of her. Afraid of what she might see, she had to force herself to look into his eyes. When she did, she found him watching her with an intensity that was at once darkly fierce and utterly tender.

"Cassie . . ." Her name whispered past Ethan's lips, the only word he was capable of pushing past his constricted throat. A rage unlike anything he'd ever known roiled through him. Bloody hell, she looked lost and alone, her eyes so desolate and bleak. Something inside him seemed to break, leaving a gaping wound through which all the anger and bitterness he'd nursed leaked out to spill at her feet.

He knew she spoke the truth, but somehow his mind couldn't seem to reconcile her words. How, *how* could anyone hurt her? He'd lain awake countless nights in an agony of jealousy, imagining her husband making love to her, lovingly claiming that which Ethan could never have. Never, not once, had it occurred to him that she was anything less than happy. Cherished and pampered. Loved and cared for. God *damn* it. The thought of that bastard treating her badly, hurting her, beating her . . . he squeezed his eyes shut to dispel the red haze that filmed his vision.

He'd killed men in battle, and even though those men were his enemies, he'd still lost a piece of himself with each fatality. But by God, he knew in what was left of his soul that if given the chance, he'd kill that bastard Westmore and not feel a ripple of regret. Indeed, his only regret was that the bastard was already dead, thus denying him the pleasure of snuffing out his miserable life.

Opening his eyes, he drew a deep, careful breath, then lightly clasped her upper arms, felt the tremors running through her. "Why didn't you leave?"

"And go where?"

"Home. To Gateshead Manor."

She shook her head. "My parents would not condone me leaving my husband."

"If they knew how he treated you—"

"They knew."

Another spurt of outrage rippled through him. "And they did nothing?"

"No. Father fully sympathized with Westmore's distress that I couldn't have children. As for the beating, Father declared it an aberration from a man who'd never before exhibited violent tendencies, who had simply lost control when faced with the crushing blow of being leg-shackled to a useless, barren woman."

An image of Cassie's father loomed in Ethan's mind.

Bloody bastard. He'd disliked the man ever since his first conversation with Cassie, when they were little more than children and he'd just arrived at Gateshead Manor, where his father had been hired as stable master. He'd found her huddled in the corner of a stable stall, crying over some cutting remark her father had uttered. His dislike had grown over the years, culminating in a deep loathing.

"Surely you had friends—"

"No. Westmore forbade me to leave the estate grounds and did not provide me with any funds. His household staff was completely loyal to him and watched me constantly. The few servants I attempted to befriend were summarily dismissed. My only refuge was in my daily walks and rides—always accompanied by a silent footman or groom— and the occasional letter from my mother. My surroundings were beautiful, but a prison just the same."

"And you lived like that for ten years." He nearly choked on the words, on the fury that tensed his every muscle. "By God, if I'd known—"

"There's nothing you could have done."

"The hell there wasn't. I'd have seen to it that he paid for the way he treated you."

"He would have had you thrown in prison."

"Dead men don't throw other men in prison."

Her eyes widened, then shimmered with tears. "No. You'd have hanged instead."

A price he'd have gladly paid. He lifted unsteady hands and framed her face between his palms. And fought to push his voice around his clogged throat. "Cassie . . . all these years I imagined you enjoying life. Surrounded by laughing children. Happy." Bloody hell, it was the only thing that had kept him sane.

"That's exactly how I imagined you. Ethan, it was those thoughts that made life bearable."

Before he could even think of a reply, she said, "When

you returned from the war, you were able to start again. As a man, you are in charge of your own destiny. You can start a business, earn money. You have *choices.* I thought Westmore's death freed me, but I was quickly proven wrong. He left me nothing. His brother inherited the title and moved into Westmore Park." Fresh anger kindled in her eyes. "My choice was to remain and become my brother-in-law's paramour or leave. As I have no money and nowhere else to go, I'm returning to my parents' home. Father informed me I may do so."

She lifted her hands and laid them across his wrists. "Mother mentioned in a letter I received just after Westmore's death that she'd heard you'd purchased an establishment called the Blue Seas Inn in St. Ives. When I made the decision to return to Cornwall, I vowed to stop here. To see you. The dear friend whom I missed so much."

A single tear slid down her cheek, smiting him where he stood. There were dozens of things he wanted to say, but sorrow and rage from all she'd suffered slammed his throat shut. Instead he drew her into his arms and tried to draw into himself all the pain she'd suffered. Her arms went around him, clutching him tight, and she burrowed against his chest, reminding him of a wounded animal searching for warmth.

Ethan held her against him, absorbing the shudders that wracked her shoulders and her tears that wet his shirt, each one a whip's lash. Feeling utterly helpless, he whispered what he hoped were soothing words against her soft hair and gently rubbed his hands up and down her back.

Finally her sobs tapered off and she lifted her head. Their gazes met, and the area surrounding his heart went hollow at the sight of her pale, tear-streaked face, and her eyes, twin pools of distress surrounded by wet, spiked lashes.

Keeping one arm around her, he pulled out his handkerchief and handed it to her. She nodded her thanks, then said in a shaky whisper as she mopped her eyes, "I'm sorry. I didn't mean to cry all over you."

"You've nothing to be sorry for. And you're welcome to cry all over me any time you wish."

"Thank you." A tremulous smile touched her lips. "You've always been the kindest, most patient person I've ever known."

"Because you're the kindest, loveliest person I've ever known. I've thought so since the day we met."

A flash of humor lit her eyes, filling him with relief that the worst of the emotional storm appeared to have passed. "What did you know—you were only six years old and knew all of ten people."

"More than ten," he said, one corner of his lips curving upward. "You'll recall my father worked at Baron Humphrey's estate before we came to Gateshead Manor. The baron's children didn't like me." He lowered his voice to a conspiratorial whisper. "They told me I smelled."

"I liked the way you smelled. You smelled of . . . adventure."

And she'd smelled of roses, even as a child of five. A little sprite with gangly legs, huge eyes, tightly plaited hair, and a freckled nose. After he'd discovered her crying in the stables, she'd swiped at her eyes with her small fists, then studied him through those big, serious eyes. He'd braced himself for another rejection, but instead she'd asked, "Would you like to be my friend?" Not wanting to appear too eager, he'd frowned and tapped his chin, as if giving the matter great thought. Finally he'd shrugged and agreed. She'd then flashed him a dimpling grin that was missing her two front teeth, grabbed his hand, and ran, leading him to the lake on the estate where they'd sat and talked for hours.

"Thank you for the use of your handkerchief . . ." Her voice yanked him back to the present, and he noticed her staring at the cotton square she held out.

He looked down and stilled, watching as her thumb slowly stroked over the initials embroidered with blue thread in the corner. "This handkerchief . . . it's mine," she said softly. "The one T.C. stole from me when he was just a puppy."

"Yes."

"You've kept it all this time?"

"Yes."

"And had it in your pocket this afternoon?"

He lifted his gaze, saw that hers was filled with questions—ones he couldn't avoid. "It's in my pocket *every* afternoon. Every day. A good luck charm of sorts, I suppose."

"I'm . . . honored, Ethan." She cleared her throat. "I have a good luck charm of my own."

Keeping her gaze on him, she reached beneath her fichu and pulled out a slender leather cord. A flat, oval gray stone, the length of her thumb, dangled from the end of the cord that had been threaded through a small hole drilled near the rock's edge. Ethan reached out for the stone, which still bore the warmth from her skin. And recognition instantly hit him. "It's the skipping stone I gave you."

She nodded. "The day we walked along the beach after your father was buried. You told me this stone would guarantee me a win in any skipping contest."

"And you've kept it all this time?"

"Yes. I drilled a hole in it and wear it around my neck. Every day." A self-conscious-sounding huff escaped her, and she repeated his earlier words. "A good luck charm of sorts, I suppose."

His heart seemed to shift in his chest, as if whatever anchored it in place had lurched free of its moorings. Then just as she'd repeated his words, he repeated hers. "I'm honored, Cassie."

He watched her tuck the necklace back into her bodice, imagining the stone nestled warmly between her breasts, then slipped his handkerchief back into his pocket.

"Thank you for holding me, Ethan," she said. "I . . . I haven't been held in a long time."

Bloody hell, how many times could his heart break in one day? His arms instinctively tightened around her, and she responded in kind. And suddenly he was very much aware of the fact that they touched from chest to knee. That with every breath his head filled with the subtle scent of roses rising from her soft skin. That her lips were only inches from his.

Desire hit him with a low, hard, visceral punch that threatened to buckle his knees. His inner voice warned him that in spite of his earlier intimation that she risked more than a walk by accompanying him, only a cad would take advantage of her obvious vulnerability. His conscience demanded that he release her and step away. And he would have, surely he would have, but then her gaze lowered to his mouth.

He felt that look like a caress, and his gaze riveted on her lush lips. In his fantasies he'd kissed them countless times. There were reasons . . . so many reasons why he shouldn't, yet suddenly he couldn't recall one of them.

Unable to stop himself, he lowered his head, slowly, certain she would push him away, tell him to stop. But instead she raised her face and closed her eyes.

As if in a dream, he brushed his lips over hers, a whisper of a touch that jolted heat to his every nerve ending. With his heart thundering hard enough to crack his ribs, he kissed her slowly, gently, with infinite care as if she were a fragile treasure, circling his lips over hers, lightly touching the corners of her mouth, then returning to her lips. And surely that's all he would have done, all he'd intended to do— but then she whispered his name, a soft, breathy, husky sound that unraveled him. Her lips parted beneath his, and with a groan that drowned out the sound of his good intentions crumbling to dust, he sank deeper into the kiss.

His tongue slipped into the silky sweet warmth of her

mouth, and everything faded away except her. Her delicious taste. The delicate scent of roses wafting from her skin. The feel of her lush curves pressed against him. The sound of her husky moan. They all inundated his senses, and he gathered her closer. She rose up on her toes, straining against him, and with a growl he lifted her straight up, then stepped deeper into the cool shadows, into a curve in the rocks that shielded them from the wind and prying eyes, should anyone venture onto the deserted beach.

Without breaking their kiss, he turned, propped his back against the rock wall and spread his legs, drawing her into the vee of his thighs. Where she fit as if made just for him.

One deep kiss melted into another, filling him with an overpowering need to simply devour her. And he damn well might have except she kept distracting him. Squirming against him. Tunneling her fingers through his hair. Rubbing her tongue against his. Clutching his shoulders. As if she craved him as much as he craved her.

He slid one hand down her back and splayed it against her bottom, pressing her tighter against his aching erection, while his other hand came forward to cup her breast. Soft fullness filled his palm and her nipple pebbled. Mentally cursing the material that separated their skin, he teased the aroused tip between his fingers.

But again she distracted him, this time running her hands over his chest, kneading his muscles, flashing fire through him. His pulse roared hot through his veins, pounding in his ears, throbbing between his legs. Helpless to stop himself, he rubbed himself against her. The taste of her in his mouth, the feel of her hands on him, her body undulating against his, stripped him of his last bit of control. If he didn't stop now, he wouldn't be able to.

He managed to drag his lips from hers, but couldn't keep from exploring the temptation of her slender neck, savoring the vibrations against his lips when she expelled a long, husky groan. God, she felt so good. Smelled so good. Tasted so good. And he'd wanted her for so damn long.

After pressing one last lingering kiss to the satiny skin behind her ear, he drew a shaky breath and forced himself to straighten.

Looking down at her, he bit back an agonized groan. With her eyes closed, hair wildly mussed from the wind and his impatient hands, cheeks flushed cherry-red, and lips moist and parted, she looked aroused and thoroughly kissed and more beautiful than anything he'd ever seen.

Her eyes slowly blinked open, and she gazed at him with a dazed expression. He lifted one unsteady hand to brush back a stray curl from her flushed cheek, then gently glided the pad of his thumb over her plump lower lip. The need to say something gripped him, but words failed him. All he could do was look. And feel. And want.

"Ethan . . ." The sound of his name, uttered in that husky, aroused rasp, tightened his every muscle with need. She framed his face between her hands, and he felt the slight trembling of her fingers as they feathered over his skin. As if she were trying to memorize his features with her fingertips.

"So *this* is what kissing is supposed to be like. I was married for ten years and never knew."

She sounded as dazed and bemused as he felt. If he'd been able to form a coherent sentence, he would have told her that he didn't know kissing could be like that, either, although he'd always known it would be like that with her. How could it not with a woman who made his heart pound with a mere look? He knew in his soul he'd never be able to erase the taste of her, the feel of her—every detail was burned into his mind, branded in his senses.

And tomorrow she would be gone.

Taking his heart with him.

Just when he'd decided that perhaps there was a tiny piece of it left to give to Delia.

Half of him wouldn't trade the last few moments, this entire day, with Cassie for anything.

The other half wished she'd never come back. Because now he craved her even more. He could barely contemplate dredging up the strength to unwrap his arms around her and set her away from him so they could return to the inn. How the bloody hell was he going to stand watching her leave tomorrow?

He didn't know. But one thing he did know.

They still had tonight.

"Cassie—"

She touched her fingers to his lips and shook her head. "Please don't say you're sorry."

Reaching up, he lightly clasped her hand and kissed the soft, pale skin of her inner wrist. And enjoyed her quick intake of breath. "I'm not sorry. I'm . . ." His voice trailed off, and he brought her hand to his chest, then pressed her palm to the spot where his heart thudded in hard, fast beats.

"You're what?" she asked in a breathless voice.

"Hungry for more. Cassie, you asked me to spend the day with you. Now I'm asking you to spend the night with me."

Chapter Six

Cassandra paced the length of her bedchamber, her insides knotted into a jumble of nervous expectation. In less than thirty minutes, she'd be joining Ethan for dinner—which would lead to . . . after dinner. *I'm asking you to spend the night with me.*

His words reverberated through her mind. Words she couldn't deny she'd secretly hoped, prayed to hear. Words that deep in her heart she knew were the ones that had driven her to stop at the Blue Seas. So that for one night she wouldn't be alone. And so that Ethan, who had lived in her heart all these years, would be the person to banish the loneliness she'd lived with for so long.

Tonight he would do just that.

Tonight she would shove aside the respectability that suppressed her deeply buried desires, desires she'd give free rein to for this one night. Tonight she wouldn't have to lie alone in the dark and pretend it was Ethan's hands touching her rather than her own.

After returning to the inn an hour earlier, she and Ethan

had parted company—but not until he'd pulled her into a shadowed corner of the stable and kissed her with that same intoxicating, knee-weakening perfection, leaving her aroused and breathless and aching for more. On her way to her own room, she'd stopped by Sophie's chamber. One look at her maid confirmed she was still exhausted from the journey, so Cassandra arranged with Mrs. Tildon for a tray to be brought to her room, an offer Sophie had gratefully accepted.

Guilt pricked Cassandra at how quickly she'd offered to arrange for that dinner tray. And at how selfish she felt for wanting to dine at the table alone with Ethan. She'd buried her conscience, reminding herself that there was nothing improper about a widow dining in a public place with an old friend, especially as there would surely be other guests in the main room. And she ignored how completely improper her plans for after dinner were.

Walking to the oval cheval glass, Cassandra heaved a sigh at her reflection. For just this one night she dearly wished she had something beautiful to wear. She'd done the best she could with her appearance given her severely limited wardrobe—Westmore had refused to fund anything more than the barest necessities—but the most that could be said for her drab gray gown was that it wasn't the hated and hypocritical black of mourning.

A knock roused her from her musing, and she crossed the room to answer the summons. A broad-faced, pink-cheeked young woman dressed in servant's garb, holding a tray from which delicious aromas wafted, bobbed a shallow curtsy. "Yer dinner tray's arrived, milady. Yer bath as well."

"Dinner? Bath . . . ?" her confused voice trailed off as the maid entered, followed by a quartet of sturdy young men hefting a copper tub partially filled with steaming water. The maid set the tray on the bed while the men moved toward the hearth. "But I didn't—"

"Here's a towel and soap for ye," the maid continued, setting the items next to the tub. "I've also a note for ye, milady." She slipped a folded piece of paper sealed with a blob of wax from her apron pocket and handed the missive to Cassandra. "Sorry to hear yer journey tired ye so, milady, but a warm meal and hot bath will set ye back to rights." After another quick curtsy, she followed the young men out, then closed the door quietly behind her.

Cassandra immediately broke the wax seal, unfolded the paper, and scanned the brief note.

Enjoy your bath. I'll join you soon.

Ethan

Her gaze shifted from the generously laden dinner tray to the steaming tub, and tears sprang to her eyes at his thoughtful gesture. Clearly he'd decided they should dine in the privacy of her room rather than in the inn's main room—a plan that quickened her pulse into an erratic beat.

She undressed as quickly as she could without Sophie's help, then lowered herself into the heated water. With a blissful sigh, she bent her knees and slithered her back down until she was submerged to her chin. Her eyelids had just drifted closed when she heard a muffled sound near the window. She opened her eyes, and her heart jumped at the sight of a shadowy figure on the small balcony. A shadowy figure she immediately recognized. One that opened the French windows, then silently slipped into the room.

She stared in amazement as Ethan walked slowly toward her, his eyes gleaming like twin ebony braziers. In one hand he held a large worn leather satchel. Her avid gaze drank in his imposing height, the breadth of his shoulders, the strength of his long legs outlined by his snug black breeches. His midnight hair gleamed in the golden glow from the crackling fire, which cast his rugged features in an intriguing display of shadows and light. He looked big and strong, masculine and darkly attractive, and everything inside her heated with awareness, tingled with anticipation.

"H-how did you get onto that balcony?" she asked.

"My room is directly above this one. It's a reasonably short drop."

Her eyes widened. "*Drop?* You could have injured yourself!"

He reached the edge of the tub and halted. His gaze skimmed slowly over her, leaving a trail of heat in its wake. "A small risk given the reward."

"Why didn't you simply use the door?"

"Too ordinary for an extraordinary woman like you. And I intend to see to it that everything about tonight is extraordinary for you."

Her heart stumbled at his softly spoken words. Before she could even think up a reply, he continued, "My timing is perfect, I see."

"Perfect for what?" Her voice sounded positively breathless.

"For helping you bathe—the first step in my plan."

"If that's the first step, I'm burning with curiosity to know what the second step entails."

He set the satchel on the floor, then crouched down next to the tub. His white shirtsleeves were rolled up to his elbows, exposing muscular brown forearms which he leaned on the tub's copper edge. Dipping his fingertips in the water, he lightly stirred the surface, his serious gaze resting on hers. "The second step—and every step afterward—is to give you the sort of evening you deserve. The sort you've been denied all these years. One filled with happiness and smiles. Romance and passion."

"Oh . . . my." To her mortification, hot tears rushed into her eyes.

He traced a single wet fingertip over one of her upraised

knees, skittering tingles along her skin. "Since our time together is so short, I didn't want to waste a moment of it dining in the main room. I hope you don't mind."

Cassandra shook her head and tried to speak around the
tightness in her throat. "I can't recall the last time anyone
has done something so thoughtful for me."

"You deserve to have thoughtful things done for you all
the time, Cassie. But I have to admit my intentions are also
selfish. I want to spend what time we have together in private. I don't want to share you."

The heated way he was looking at her, the velvety seduction of his voice wrapped around her like a warm blanket. "I
don't want to share you, either." She craned her neck and cut
her gaze toward the floor. "What is in the satchel you
brought?"

His lopsided grin flashed. "Surprises."

"What sort of surprises?"

"Curious, are you?"

"Extremely."

A devilish gleam danced in his eyes. "How badly do you
want to know?"

Laughter bubbled in her throat at his exaggerated leer.
"Name your price."

The fire that flared in his eyes nearly scorched her. "A
kiss will do. For now." He leaned forward, and she raised
her face, pulse pounding in anticipation. His lips brushed
softly over hers, once, twice, whispers of touches that teased
and tantalized and left her aching for more. On his third
feathery kiss, she ran her tongue over his bottom lip and was
rewarded with a low growl. He sank deeper into their kiss,
his tongue gently swirling around hers. She lifted her wet
hands and threaded her fingers through his hair, feeling
utterly wanton and luxuriously decadent. When he finally
lifted his head, he looked dazed and was breathing hard.

"You've completely distracted me," he said.

"I did nothing save sit here," she said as primly as she could, given she was naked.

"That's all it takes. You're . . . potent."

A feminine thrill such as she'd never known rushed through her. "If so, it's because you're . . . inspiring."

"You're distracting me again," he said with a mock frown. "Do you want me to open the satchel or not?"

"I do."

He turned his attention to the leather bundle. She suddenly detected the scent of roses, and seconds later he handed her a bouquet, the stems tied with a length of twine.

"Ethan, they're beautiful," she said, taking the offering and bringing it to her nose to breathe deeply. She ran her fingertips over the delicate petals of vivid red, buttery yellow, snowy white, and blush pink. "Such lovely colors. We only returned from our walk less than an hour ago. How did you manage to get these?"

"I cut them from the inn's rose bushes."

She looked at him over the top of her bouquet. "Roses are my favorite flower."

"I know. Which is why I wanted you to have them."

She dipped her chin, burying her face in the fragrant blooms, so he wouldn't notice her bottom lip quivering or the fresh moisture threatening to spill from her eyes. "No one has ever brought me flowers," she whispered. "Thank you, Ethan."

"You're welcome. You deserve to receive flowers every day." He took the bouquet from her and set it on the floor. Then he reached out to once again draw a slow circle over her knee before his fingers dipped lower to glide sinuously down her calf. His heated gaze moved over her with the same lack of haste, and she marveled that he could make her feel as if she were on fire even while submerged in water. His attention lingered on her breasts and her nipples hardened under his intense regard. Sudden shyness assailed her and she made to cover herself, but he shook his head and captured both her hands in one of his, bringing them to his lips.

"Don't hide from me, Cassie." Each word was a heated breath against her skin. "Are you enjoying your bath?"

Warmth suffused her cheeks, but she couldn't bring herself to look away from his compelling eyes. "It's lovely."

"From the moment I ordered it, I thought of you—naked and wet."

His words acted like a spark to dry kindling, shooting fire straight to her womb. "From the moment I was naked and wet, I thought of you."

Stark, raw hunger smoldered in his gaze, and Cassandra found herself wishing for a cool breeze. *So* this *is what true desire feels like.*

Without a word, he plucked the small bar of soap from atop the towel. After dipping the square in the water, he slowly worked a lather between his large hands. When they were coated with soap, he moved behind her. "Lean forward," he instructed softly.

She did as he bid her, wrapping her arms around her upraised knees, her skin tingling in anticipation. At the first pass of his soap-slicked hands down her wet spine, she gasped, a soft sound that turned into a long purr of pleasure as he slowly kneaded every inch of her back. A sensation of warm relaxation suffused her, melting away years of tension, melting away everything except him, his hands stroking her, scooping warm water over her.

"Lean back, Cassie."

With a soft sigh, she obeyed, resting her head against the curved lip of the tub. To her delight, he slowly lathered his way down first one arm, then the other, massaging each bit of her skin, each sensitive finger, reducing her to a breathless, boneless mass.

"That feels so . . . ummm . . . marvelous," she said, her voice a husky sigh.

"Your skin is the softest thing I've ever touched," he said, drizzling a handful of water over her upper arm.

"Your hands are the most magical thing I've ever felt."

Once again he lathered his hands, this time working his way over her collarbones, his fingertips dipping into the hollows there and at the base of her throat before inching lower on her chest. When his hands slipped below the water to smooth over her breasts, she gasped, then arched into his touch. She watched his hands curve around her breasts, his thumbs glide over the aroused peaks that seemed to beg for his touch.

She arched again, this time raising her arms up and back to encircle his neck. Turning her head, she pressed a series of nibbling kisses along his jaw.

"You're distracting me again," he said, his hands descending to skim over her abdomen.

She sucked in a quick breath. "You're driving me mad."

His hands eased between her thighs, and he spread her legs as far apart as the confines of the tub allowed. "Do you want me to stop?"

"God, no," she whispered against his lips. "Please, no."

Her eyes slid closed, and with a pleasure-filled sigh she surrendered her inhibitions and allowed herself to simply *feel*—the desire to do so was something she'd never experienced with her husband. One of Ethan's large hands skimmed back up to tease her breasts, while his other hand glided deeper beneath the warm water, between her splayed legs. At the first touch of his fingers over her feminine folds, they both groaned. His mouth settled over hers and he kissed her deeply, his tongue slowly mating with hers in a lazy rhythm that matched the leisurely caress of his fingers around her sensitive flesh.

She moaned into his mouth and shifted restlessly against his hand, wanting, needing more, with a growing desperation she'd never before experienced, one she couldn't control. Her hands clutched at his shoulders, urging him to kiss her deeper as she raised her hips in silent plea for him to touch her deeper.

Yet when he slipped a finger inside her and gently stroked, it still wasn't enough. She wanted to feel his entire weight on her, his skin next to her. All of him against all of her.

He eased another finger inside her and pressed his palm against her, slowly rotating his hand in a manner that ripped a groan from deep inside her. Exquisite sensations pulsed through her, leaving her awash in currents of pleasure. Mindless, she lifted one leg, hooking it over the edge of the tub to open herself more fully to his touch, then arched upward, straining for the next intoxicating caress. The coil of tension inside her tightened, propelling her toward a dark edge of something . . . something she desperately wanted that remained elusive, just out of reach, filling her with an edgy pressure that demanded relief.

But then he quickened his rhythm, the gentle tugging on her nipples roughened, the strokes of his tongue and thrust of his fingers deepened, and suddenly her entire body convulsed, dragging a surprised cry from her. Wave after wave of intense pleasure throbbed through her for endless seconds when the only thing that existed was Ethan, the way he was touching her. The way he made her feel. The spasms tapered off and an unprecedented feeling of the most delicious languor stole over her entire body.

She felt his fingers slide from her body, his lips pressing kisses along her jaw.

"Cassie," he whispered, his teeth lightly grazing her earlobe.

"Ethan . . ." His name came out as a pleasure-filled sigh. Before she could say anything else, such as thank you, he scooped her up into his arms. Heedless of the water sluicing from her body, soaking him, for several long seconds he simply held her against him, his gaze so hot upon her, she felt as if she were glowing.

"Hold on," he said.

After she tightened her arms around his neck, he bent down and snatched up the towel, which he wrapped around her. Snuggled between his warm body and the fire-warmed towel, she pressed a kiss to the side of his neck.

He walked to the bed, then slowly lowered her until her feet touched the floor. Taking the towel, he gently blotted the water from her skin. She reveled in his ministrations, and when he finished, she framed his face between her hands, then rose up on her toes to kiss him. His arms clamped around her, and she felt the heat of his body along the entire length of hers. The hard ridge his arousal pressed against her belly, and her womb clenched in response.

"Ethan," she murmured, leaning back to look at him, "I've never felt that way before."

His eyes darkened with some emotion she couldn't decipher. "The pleasure was mine."

"Not entirely, I assure you."

A hint of humor whispered over his features, then he raised his hands and slipped the pins from her chignon.

"Your hair is beautiful," he said, slowly sifting his fingers through the strands. "Just like the rest of you." He stepped back, and his gaze raked over her with barely suppressed hunger. "So beautiful," he murmured, cupping her breasts, his fingers lightly tugging her nipples, eliciting a low moan of pleasure from her. She leaned into him, then gasped when he lowered his head to draw one tight nipple into his mouth.

"This is hardly fair," she said, arching her back, offering more of herself. "I want to see you, touch you as well, Ethan."

At her words, he gave her nipple one last long lick, then lifted his head. "Very well," he said, raising her hands to his shirt. "Undress me."

She immediately applied unsteady fingers to the fastening on his shirt. She fumbled a bit and forced aside her nervousness that she would fail to please him as she'd failed to please her husband. As if he'd read her thoughts, he said, "There is nothing you could do that will displease me, Cassie. You are the most beautiful thing I've ever seen. The softest I've ever touched. Believe me when I say that it is only by exerting an extreme amount of will that I am keeping myself from devouring you. Even so, my control is severely tested."

A dark thrill raced through her at his admission, and she pulled his shirt open. "I don't want you in control," she said, skimming her hands over the hardened slopes of his chest. His body was that of a laborer, thick with muscle, browned from the sun—strong, masculine, and profoundly arousing. Dark hair dusted the broad expanse of sun-kissed skin, narrowing to a dusky ribbon that bisected his torso, a silken trail her fingers itched to explore.

She breathed in and savored his scent. He smelled of soap and clean linen and, just as he always had, deliciously of adventure. The mere sight of him made her feel daring and reckless, and giddy with a sense of boldness that, despite its unfamiliarity, couldn't be denied.

Dragging her gaze back up to his, she said, "I want to be devoured. I want to *feel*. Everything. I want to touch. All of you."

His eyes darkened, and with her help, he shrugged out of his shirt. Stepping closer to him, she pressed her lips to the center of his chest, then dragged her open mouth to his nipple. She suckled him softly, absorbing the hard beat of his heart against her palm and the growl vibrating from his throat. Her hands moved lower, over his abdomen, her fingers tracing, investigating the captivating ripples of hard muscle and that alluring ribbon of dark hair that cut down the middle of his torso. When her hands reached his breeches, she raised her head. "I want these off, Ethan."

She stepped back and watched him remove his clothing, first his boots, then his snug breeches. When he finally stood before her naked, her mouth went dry at the sight of him. That enthralling ribbon of hair continued lower, spreading at the apex of his thighs where his arousal jutted forward, thick and fascinating. His legs were long and powerful, and his entire body appeared tensed with expectation.

She walked slowly around him, halting when she stood behind him, her gaze riveted to the scarred skin on his back.

"This is from the fire?" she asked softly, coasting her fingers over the pale, puckered marks.

"Yes."

She wrapped her arms around his waist and rested her cheek against the old injury, then sprinkled gentle kisses over every bit of it she could reach. "It must have hurt terribly," she whispered between kisses, her heart aching for what he'd suffered. "I'm so sorry."

"It doesn't hurt anymore."

After pressing a last lingering kiss to his back, she moved to stand in front of him once again. Reaching out, she brushed her fingers over the head of his erection, and he sucked in a harsh breath. "You are extremely well made, Ethan. So very strong."

He swallowed, hard, and she basked in the hunger that darkened his eyes, flushed his skin.

"I'm not feeling very strong right now," he said, his voice resembling a low growl.

"Oh? How do you feel?"

"Conquered."

She wrapped her fingers around his arousal and gently squeezed. His eyes slammed shut. "Vanquished," he whispered.

"Do you want me to stop?" she asked, repeating his earlier question.

"No. God, no. Don't stop."

She couldn't suppress the smile of pure feminine satisfaction that curved her lips at his rough tone. "If you insist," she murmured, and stroked her fingers down his length, exploring every inch of the taut flesh, first with one hand, then two, cupping and stroking him, becoming bolder and more confident with each of his increasingly ragged breaths.

A long groan escaped him, and he tipped his head back and squeezed his eyes shut. "You cannot possibly know how incredible that feels."

When she dragged a single fingertip through the pearly drop glistening at the tip of his erection, spreading the warm wetness over the swollen head, he made a strangled sound, then scooped her up in his arms.

"Can't take anymore," he muttered, his eyes all but breathing fire. He laid her down on the counterpane, then climbed onto the bed. He urged her knees apart and knelt between her splayed thighs. Breathing harshly, he reached out and teased her swollen folds, which felt wet and heavy and ached with need. His gaze tracked up her body until their eyes met, then he lowered his body onto hers.

His first stroke was a long, delicious glide that elicited a wordless gasp of wonder, from both the glorious friction and the profound intimacy of his body sliding into hers. When he was buried to the hilt, he stilled for several seconds, and she absorbed the indescribable sensation of him filling her, stretching her. Wrapping her legs around his waist and her arms around his shoulders, she pulled him tighter against her.

"So *this* is what passion feels like," she whispered.

"Yes." He withdrew nearly all the way, then slowly sank deep once again, a silken caress that ignited the same fire inside her he'd lit earlier. "And this . . ." Another long, slow stroke, another wet, satiny slide of his body into hers. His smooth thrusts quickened, deepened into driving jolts, each one edging her nearer to release. Her fingers bit into his shoulders, then with a startled cry, she arched beneath him as sweet, hot pulses of pleasure washed through her. She felt his entire body tighten, then, gathering her close, he buried his face in the crook where her neck and shoulders met and he poured himself into her.

When his shudders subsided, he drew in several shaky breaths, then raised his head. Cassandra's eyes fluttered open. He looked as dazed and sated as she felt, and an aching tenderness pervaded her system.

She rested one hand against his cheek. "So *that* is what making love feels like."

He turned his head to kiss her palm. "I'd have to say yes, but in truth I've never known it to be like that."

"Like what?"

"Exquisite."

He moved, as if he intended to roll off her, and she tightened her arms and legs around him. "Don't go. The feel of you on me, in me, is, to use your word, exquisite." Her gaze searched his, then she said softly, "My . . . relations with Westmore were very . . . impersonal. He never made love to me as you just did. He considered coming to my bed a chore and merely spilled his seed in me as quickly as he could get it over with in order to beget his heir."

Unmistakable anger flared in his eyes. "Any man lucky enough to have you who would do less than worship you is an ass," he stated in an emphatic voice.

Her bottom lip trembled, and he leaned down to lightly run his tongue over it. She gasped softly and pulled his head down for a slow, deep kiss. When he lifted his head, she said in a tentative voice, "The skill with which you touched me . . . clearly you've had . . . much experience."

For the space of several heartbeats, he regarded her through serious eyes, then said quietly, "No one, ever, has touched my heart as you have, Cassie."

Her fingers lightly traced his scar. "Jealousy is not an emotion I've had cause to experience for a very long time, but I find I'm jealous of every woman who's ever touched you. Of every woman who will touch you in the future." Indeed, the thought of him being with another woman like this, buried inside her, sharing confidences, cramped her insides and dulled her vision with a red haze.

"Cassie . . . let's not waste what little time we have thinking of any future beyond the next few hours."

He was right, of course. "Very well." She stretched sinuously beneath him and smiled when he skimmed one hand down her torso. "I find the inexhaustible nature of your interest in my body very enjoyable," she said.

"Excellent, because my interest is far from slaked."

"I was just thinking something similar with regard to you."

He brushed a light kiss to the corner of her mouth. "I don't know when I've ever heard better news."

She drew a long, deep, contented breath, and caught the faint whiff of roses, which prompted her to ask, "What else do you have in that satchel?"

"A blanket, a bottle of wine, and some strawberries—to combine with your dinner tray to make a picnic for us."

Moisture dampened her eyes at his thoughtfulness. "The picnics we used to share were some of the happiest days of my life."

"Mine as well. Then, after I feed you, I intend to make love to you—properly now that the edge is off." He nuzzled the sensitive skin behind her ear. "Next time will be even better. Less rushed. And the third time better still."

"Show me," she said, seeking his lips for another open-mouthed kiss. "Show me everything."

He did. Until she finally fell asleep in his arms just as the mauve of dawn broke through the window. And when she awoke, he was gone, a single slip of paper resting on the pillow that still bore the indent from where he'd lain. With shaking fingers, she picked up the missive and read the brief message.

I will never forget last night. Forgive me for leaving this way, but I cannot bear to say good-bye.

Her vision blurred, and a tear plopped onto the paper. Ethan was gone. And the empty loneliness was back.

Chapter Seven

Ethan reined in Rose, and after giving his winded, sweaty mare an affectionate pat on the neck, he stared across the beach at the glittering blue expanse of St. Ives Bay. He'd been riding hard since the muted shades of dawn lit the sky, trying in vain to exorcise the memories of last night from his mind. Now, several hours later, bright sunshine gleamed, without a cloud in sight to break the endless azure. Yet how could the sun possibly be shining? Cassie was gone. Surely the weather should have been gray and gloomy, topped off with a cold drizzle—to match his mood.

His gaze slowly tracked down the beach, along the route they'd walked yesterday, pausing for a long moment at the outcropping of rocks where they'd kissed. An emptiness and longing such as he'd never known twisted inside him, one that intertwined with fingers of anger. At himself—for allowing her to stay. For sampling that which he would never have again. For inflicting upon himself this gut-wrenching agony. Maybe it was better to never experience paradise than to do so and know in your soul that nothing would ever again be that good.

He'd missed her before yesterday—with a deep ache that never completely subsided—yet it was an ache he'd learned to live with.

But now, now that he'd held her, tasted her, laughed with her, made love with her, held her while she slept, how could he hope to learn to live with *this* ache? This debilitating pain that made it feel as if his heart had disintegrated into dust and blown away. That left a hollow space in his chest that nothing could ever hope to fill.

He withdrew her handkerchief from his pocket and stared at the embroidered initials, dark blue letters that matched her eyes. His fingers curled, crushing the material in his fist, and he squeezed his eyes closed. How the bloody hell was it possible to feel so numb, yet hurt so badly?

How could he ever hope to erase her from his memory now? She used to live only in his mind. His heart. His soul. But now the scent of her, the taste and feel of her, were all branded under his skin. So deeply that no other woman would ever be able to erase the imprint—not that any other woman ever had, but at least part of him had always held out hope that perhaps someday he'd find someone who could. Who'd be able to offer more than a fleeting encounter that only served to temporarily ease his loneliness.

Yet now that hope had been trampled. Because he'd discovered the difference between having sex to relieve a physical need and making love to the woman who owned his heart. And soul.

Even worse, all the places that he used to consider his sanctuaries were now steeped in recollections of Cassie. His inn. His stables. This stretch of beach he frequented nearly every day. There was now nowhere to go to escape the memories.

After a final look at the white-capped water, he turned Rose—named for Cassie's favorite scent—back toward the stables. After currying the mare, he returned to the tack room. He'd just finished putting away his supplies when a voice behind him asked, "May I have a word with ye, Ethan?"

He turned and saw Delia regarding him from the door- way with an indecipherable expression. Based on her pale face and the way her fingers pleated her gray work gown, he suspected something was amiss.

"Of course. Is something wrong at the inn?"

She shook her head and stepped into the room. "Not at the inn." She pressed her lips into a tight line, then said, "I want to talk about Lady Westmore."

Ethan's hands involuntarily clenched at the sound of her name. "What about her?"

Delia's gaze skittered away for several seconds, then re- turned to his. "I suspected there was someone who held yer heart. Someone from yer past. Figured that were the reason ye pretended not to notice the broad hints I tossed in yer di- rection." She lifted her chin. "It's her. Lady Westmore. She's the one who holds yer heart."

Bloody hell. Was his lovesick yearning scrawled across his face for everyone to see?

When he didn't reply, Delia jerked her head in a tight nod. "Well, at least yer not denyin' it. No point in doin' so. I saw the way ye looked at her."

"And how did I look at her?"

"The way I'd hoped ye'd look at me someday."

Ethan expelled a long breath and dragged his hands down his face. "Delia, I'm sorry."

"Ye've nothin' to apologize for. Ye never gave me false hope that we'd be more than friends." She dipped her chin and stared at the floor. "Yer a good man, Ethan. Honorable. Not yer fault that I wish ye were *my* man."

He crossed to her and gently clasped her upper arms. "You know I care about you, Delia."

She looked up, and he saw the sheen of moisture in her eyes. "I know, Ethan. But not in the same way I care about you. I knew it, but I convinced myself that the woman who held yer heart was either gone from yer life or dead. And that one day ye'd wake up and be ready to move on. And I'd be waitin'."

She drew a deep breath and stepped back, and his hands fell to his sides. "But knowin' she exists and actually meetin' her are two different things. I'd never be able to look at you and believe ye were thinkin' of me. Ye'd be thinkin' of her, and I'd know it. She's not some phantom ghost in my mind anymore. I met her. Saw you lookin' at her. Smilin' at her. Laughin' with her. Second place is one thing, but with you, there'd never be a first place. There's only room for her."

Bloody hell, he wished he could deny her words. Wished he could transfer his feelings from Cassie to Delia—a woman of his own class with whom he could share a future. Unfortunately, his love for Cassie lived in his bones. Always had. He knew it, and Delia knew it. And he wouldn't dishonor her by telling her anything less than the truth.

"I never meant to hurt you, Delia."

She shrugged. "I hurt myself. But now it's time I stop. I'm leavin', Ethan. Leavin' the Blue Seas, leavin' St. Ives. Plannin' to go stay with my sister in Dorset. She had twin babies a few months back and could use the help." She twisted her hands together, and what looked like a combination of confusion, pity, and anger flashed in her eyes. "Ye know yer feelin's for her are hopeless. Grand ladies don't take up with folks like us."

A muscle ticked in his jaw. "I know."

"Well, yer feelin's for her won't keep ye warm at night. Any more than my feelin's for you will keep me warm. And I'm tired of being cold. And alone. I miss havin' a husband. I want someone to share my life with. I wish ye luck, Ethan. I hope ye find happiness. And love."

He stood rooted in place and watched her walk away. Half

of him wanted to go after her, beg her to stay, tell her he'd try to forget Cassie—at least enough to attempt making a life with someone else. But the other half knew it wouldn't happen. The last ten years—and last night—proved that.

Feeling as though he'd been pummeled with ham-sized fists, he stared at the empty doorway through which Delia had left. It couldn't have been easy for her to have faced him like that—told him she cared for him, especially knowing her feelings weren't returned. She'd exhibited a courage that he never had. He'd never admitted his feelings to Cassie. Never told her he loved her.

He froze, then, as realization sank in, he slowly raked his hands through his hair. Just yesterday he'd been prepared to shove the past aside and discuss the future with Delia. Had been ready to confess his feelings of friendship and respect, and let her decide if the little he had to offer was enough. If he was willing to do that with Delia, why the bloody hell wouldn't he do that with the woman he'd loved his entire life?

I want someone to share my life with. Delia's words reverberated through his mind. Damn it, *he* wanted someone to share his life with, too. And that someone was Cassie. He had nothing to offer her but himself. There were no titles and estates. But by God, he sure as hell would never hurt her. Plus he could offer her something that bastard Westmore hadn't given her.

His love. And heart. And soul.

Maybe she'd simply look at him with kindness. Or worse, pity. But maybe for a woman who'd spent the last ten empty years unhappy, lonely, and unloved, the little he had to offer might be enough. If nothing else, at least she'd know she was loved. And by God, she deserved to know that.

Of a certainty she'd turn him down, but it was a chance he'd have to take. As things stood, she was gone from his life, so he had absolutely nothing else to lose by declaring himself. And maybe, just maybe, the little he had would be enough.

He could at least let her decide.

Cassandra sat in the drawing room at Gateshead Manor and tried to concentrate on the conversation bouncing back and forth between her parents, but her mind kept wandering. Luckily Mother had commenced one of her long-winded descriptions of a recent musicale they'd attended, which required nothing more from Cassandra than the occasional nod.

She sipped her tea, using the delicate china cup as a shield to hide her misery, although the effort was most likely wasted, as she doubted either of her parents would have noticed had she taken it into her head to jump upon the table and scream, *I'm miserable!*

Hmm . . . that wasn't truly accurate, she decided. They'd notice. And then Mother would say, *You're nothing of the sort and I'll hear no more such nonsense.* And Father would shake his head and say, *You wouldn't be miserable—none of us would—if you'd cooperated and been born a boy.*

Well, she couldn't argue with that. If she'd been born a boy, she certainly wouldn't be suffering a broken heart over Ethan.

Ethan . . . Dear God, she thought she'd experienced pain and emptiness and loneliness over the past decade. How ironic to learn that those years would prove to be merely practice for the future. Nothing she'd suffered at Westmore's hands could compare to the eviscerating pain of leaving Ethan, a pain squeezed around her so tightly, she couldn't draw a breath without hurting.

She'd wanted to know what spending time with him, his kiss, his lovemaking would be like, and now she knew. It was everything she'd dreamed. Everything she'd been denied her entire marriage. Everything she'd always wanted—passion and laughter and caring. He'd given her those things for one magical night, one magical night she wouldn't trade for anything on earth. But one that would render all the following nights that much more hollow.

She took another sip of tea and closed her eyes, and instantly a parade of images flashed through her mind. Of Ethan smiling at her. Feeding her a strawberry. Looking at her with heated desire. Leaning forward to kiss her. Lowering his body to cover hers.

He'd wanted to make their one night together perfect and he'd succeeded. So well that she despaired of ever again being able to close her eyes and not see him. Of ever drawing another breath that didn't hurt the now vacant area of her chest where her heart used to reside. Of ever being free of the deep ache of wanting him so much. Needing him so deeply.

Of loving him with all her heart.

She'd known she missed him, loved him, but hadn't truly comprehended or realized the immeasurable, fathomless depths of those feelings until she'd seen him again. Hadn't understood that "missed" was a lukewarm description for the gut-wrenching, enervating yearning now settled in her soul. Hadn't conceived the vast difference between loving someone and being struck by the irrefutable realization that you are deeply, intensely, insanely *in* love with that person.

Now she knew.

And God help her, she didn't think she'd ever recover from that brief taste of paradise. Because she would crave it with her whole heart and soul, every day for the rest of her life. With Ethan. Only Ethan.

And Ethan was gone.

Hot moisture pooled behind her eyes and she quickly blinked it away. She then set down her teacup and slipped her hand into the deep pocket of her gown where her fingers brushed over the note he'd left her. *I cannot bear to say good-bye.*

When she'd first read those words, her heart had crumbled that she wouldn't see him again before departing the Blue Seas Inn. But then, as she'd sat in the carriage and watched the inn fade into the distance, she realized he'd done the right thing. She wouldn't have been able to say good-bye, either. Wouldn't have been able to force her legs to step into the conveyance that with each turn of its wheels would take her farther away from him. And she'd had to leave.

Hadn't she?

Her brows furrowed into a frown. Of course she'd had to leave. Her place was here. At Gateshead Manor.

Wasn't it?

Her frown deepened, and her gaze scanned the beautifully appointed, luxurious room. She'd grown up here, among the rich furnishings and multitude of servants, enjoying the comforts her family's wealth provided. Yet the manor itself hadn't been what she'd loved best. Her favorite part of the estate had always been the vast grounds. Which she'd explored with Ethan. And the stables. Where she'd spent time with Ethan.

"Don't you agree, Cassandra?"

Her mother's imperious question broke into her reverie, and with an effort she dragged her attention back. "Agree?"

Her mother pursed her lips in the display of vexation Cassandra remembered all too well. In the three hours since she'd arrived at Gateshead Manor, she'd already been treated to that look several times.

"That when Lord and Lady Thornton visit next week, it would be acceptable to host a small musicale in their honor."

"Of course, if that is what you wish. Why wouldn't it be acceptable?"

"Because of you, of course." She shot Cassandra's black gown a pointed stare. "Your state of mourning."

Cassandra had to press her lips together to contain the bark of bitter laughter that rushed into her throat. "I won't be the least offended, Mother," she managed in a dust-dry tone.

"Damn mourning period," her father said in his gruff voice. "An inconvenient nuisance is what it is." He pinned Cassandra with the frosty, narrow-eyed glare that had never failed to freeze her in place as a child. His pale blue eyes had always reminded her of shards of ice. "Damn inconsiderate of Westmore to leave you with nothing, but of course the man had his reasons." He didn't actually say the words, *Because you failed to provide him with an heir,* but given the way they permeated the air, he didn't need to. "Yet all will be as it should as soon as your mourning period is over. I've arranged everything."

"Arranged? What do you mean?"

"Your next marriage."

A deafening silence filled the room. One that seemed to suck out all the air. For several seconds Cassandra could do nothing save stare at her father. Surely she had misheard him. She had to swallow twice to find her voice. "I beg your pardon? It sounded like you said, 'your next marriage.'"

"That's precisely what I said. The Duke of Atterly has expressed interest. I recently purchased an estate in Kent he covets. In exchange, he's agreed to settle a good sum on you and a nice bit of land in Surrey on me. His first wife, rest her soul, provided him with three sons, so your barren state is not a deterrent, thank God. The only possible problem is this bothersome mourning period of yours. What with the duke's advanced age, being forced to wait these next ten months is a gamble. Hopefully he won't cock up his toes before the deed is done."

The wave of stunned disbelief that swept over Cassandra nearly drowned her, and she had to fight to compose herself so that the next sound she uttered wouldn't be a laugh, a cry, or a scream. Or a combination of all three. She glanced at her mother, who nodded and said, "You're very fortunate, Cassandra. It's an excellent match."

Stomach heaving, she returned her attention to her father. After clearing her throat she said carefully, speaking each word very precisely so there would be no misunderstanding, "I'm afraid you've made a mistake. I have no intention of marrying again."

Her father's eyes turned from frosty to frigid. "Your intentions do not enter into this, daughter. You'll marry Atterly immediately upon the end of your mourning period, provided he's still alive. If he should die in the interim, Lord Templeton—whose first wife also provided him with sons—is my second choice."

Cassandra pressed her hands against her midriff in a vain attempt to calm her jittery insides. Then she raised her chin and met her father's glare. "I will not marry either gentleman."

Crimson flushed her father's cheeks, and his eyes narrowed further. "You will do exactly as I say. The arrangements have already been made."

"Then you'll need to unarrange them."

"I'll do nothing of the sort." He rose and crossed the short distance between them in two angry strides, then glowered down at her. "A match between you and Atterly is more than you deserve. You'll be a duchess."

Cassandra's insides trembled, not with fear, but with revulsion and icy rage. She slowly stood and faced her father, locking her knees so he wouldn't detect their trembling. "Thanks to the last marriage you arranged for me, I'm already a countess—a title that has not brought me a moment of happiness."

"Happiness?" The word exploded from her father in an incredulous bark. "This has nothing to do with happiness."

"Obviously. It has to do with you gaining the piece of land you covet. Just as my first marriage you arranged had to do with several thousand acres in Dorset."

"Which is precisely the sort of advantageous mergers marriages should be based upon."

"Advantageous for you, but not for me."

"Making you a duchess is certainly an advantage. Whether you want to marry him or not doesn't matter. You will do as I say. God knows you owe me that much—you've not been of any other use."

She'd heard various themes on those words so many times, first from her father, then Westmore, that they should have ceased to hurt by now. And although they still stung, they mostly filled her with an icy, quiet calm. "I paid whatever debt you feel I owed you by agreeing to the first marriage you arranged. I'll not agree to another."

His arctic eyes bored into her with pure disgust. "You are living in my home, without any means, and will therefore do as I say. I'll not hear any further arguments regarding the matter. You have ten months to accustom yourself to the idea, and you'd best do so, as you have no choice." He jerked his waistcoat into place and raked a scathing scowl over her. "You'd best retire to your bedchamber until dinner. You're looking more peaked than usual." With that he returned to his wing chair and picked up his teacup as if nothing had just transpired, secure in the knowledge that his every word would be obeyed.

For several seconds Cassandra remained frozen in place, scarcely able to breathe, her heart thundering so loud she could hear it pounding in her ears. Her gaze shifted to her mother, whose countenance bore the same look of utter unconcern as her father. Not that she'd expected to find an ally in the woman who'd never once taken her side against her father. Still, it just brought to the fore with bone-jarring intensity the stark realization that she was, once again, completely alone.

Feeling as if her blood had chilled to ice, Cassandra forced herself to hold her head high and walked stiffly from the room. She made her way down the corridor to the foyer, each step tightening the coil of misery and anger twisting inside her. By the time she gained her bedchamber, her breathing had hitched into broken, furious sobs, and tears ran down her face unchecked.

Why had she not anticipated this turn of events? How was it possible that after all she'd been through, she possessed enough naïveté to believe she'd be able to return to her childhood home and quietly live out the rest of her life?

You have no choice. Her father's words rang through her mind like a funeral knell, the most hated words she'd ever heard. Words she was sick to death of hearing. Of living by. Words she never wanted to hear again.

She paced across the Axminster carpet in small, jerky steps. Dear God, how was it possible that only a few hours ago she'd felt so euphorically happy, and now she felt such profound emptiness and despair?

Because a few hours ago, you were with Ethan.

Ethan. She halted her pacing and squeezed her eyes closed. Dear God, she loved him so much. He made her happy. Made her laugh. Made her feel wanted. Needed. In a way no one else ever had. While she wasn't certain of the depth of his feelings, he obviously cared for her. And desired her. She didn't doubt she'd made him happy, at least for one night.

She opened her eyes and drew in a shaky breath, her mind suddenly racing. *You have no choice.* But she was filled with the realization and hope that perhaps she *did* have a choice—if she had the courage. The courage to consign convention to the devil, to disregard the rules of society that had governed her entire life, and return to the Blue Seas Inn. To tell Ethan how she felt about him. To ask what he felt for her. If his feelings amounted to even a fraction of what she felt for him, then there was the chance that he might want her to stay. And if so, she would. Not because she had nowhere else to go, but because she wanted to be with him—wherever he was.

The scandal would ruin her, cut off any hope of ever re-entering society. Her parents would surely disown her. She'd forfeit any possibility of ever returning to Gateshead Manor.

And none of that mattered one bit.

She had nothing to offer Ethan except herself. But perhaps, if she was very, very lucky, that would be enough.

I can't bear to say good-bye. Well, neither could she. At least not without a fight.

Filled with a sense of elated hope she couldn't recall ever before experiencing, she crossed the room and pulled the bell cord. A moment later a knock sounded on the door, and Sophie entered the room.

"Yes, milady?"

Cassandra crossed to her, then said, "I know you and Mr. Watley are departing tomorrow to return to the Westmore estate, but—"

"Oh yes, milady," Sophie broke in quickly. "I accept."

"Accept?"

"I'd be honored to remain here with you instead." A shy smile curved her lips. "Yer the kindest lady I've ever served. Truth be told, I wasn't lookin' forward to returnin' to Westmore. The new earl's wife ain't half as nice as you. Nasty temper, she has."

Cassandra's hands clenched at the thought of Sophie being subjected to anyone's nasty temper. "Thank you, Sophie. You're the best lady's maid I've ever had. But what I wanted to tell you is that I'm leaving Gateshead Manor. Today. And I'm not coming back."

Sophie blinked. "Leavin', milady? But ye've only just arrived. Where are ye goin'?"

"Back to the Blue Seas Inn. Where I intend to remain."

Sophie's eyes widened. "Oh . . . I see," she said, although

it was clear she didn't see at all. Indeed, the young woman looked . . . lost.

An idea hit Cassandra, and she said slowly, "If you would like to come with me, you are welcome to do so, Sophie, although I cannot promise what the future holds. I completely understand that a village inn cannot compare to this estate—"

"I'd be honored to accompany ye, milady," the maid cut in, her voice filled with obvious relief. "I'd rather be with ye there than without ye at Westmore." She offered Cassandra another shy smile. "I wouldn't be surprised if Mr. Watley decided to inquire about work at the Blue Seas. Quite taken with the fine stables there he was. Westmore's stable master is a nasty piece, and Mr. Watley weren't lookin' forward to being under his thumb again."

Reaching out, Cassandra squeezed Sophie's hands and returned her smile. "It's all settled then. If you'll see to the packing, I'll go to the stables and inform Mr. Watley of our plans."

And then she'd tell her parents she was leaving. And then she'd be on her way to Ethan. And hopefully he'd want her to stay.

Chapter Eight

After arranging with Mr. Watley to have the carriage brought around as quickly as possible, Cassandra entered the house through the French windows at the rear terrace. She'd just stepped into the black and white tiled marble foyer when she heard her father's voice, laced with frigid anger, coming from the library door, which stood ajar.

"Get the bloody hell out of my house."

"Not until I've spoken to Cassie."

She froze in shocked disbelief at the sound of Ethan's voice—filled with a cold determination she'd never before heard.

"When I booted you from Gateshead Manor ten years ago I told you to never return."

"And I'll gladly leave as soon as I've seen Cassie."

"You'll leave now or I'll carve up your right cheek the way I did the left one."

Everything in Cassandra froze—her blood, her breath, as if an unseen icy fist constricted her. Several long seconds of silence followed, and the awful truth of her father's words sank in.

"I assure you, you'd have one hell of a time doing so," came Ethan's quiet reply, no less threatening due to its softness.

"Ten years ago you thought you could get away with kissing my daughter—you who are worth even less than what you mucked out of my stalls. I saw the way you looked at her. Given the chance you'd have lifted her skirts, and she was just stupid and useless enough to let you."

"You won't talk about her that way in my presence."

Her father gave a bark of harsh laughter. "I'll do exactly as I please, which includes not listening to any more from you. Get out. Now. Before I have you thrown out."

"Again, I assure you you'd have one hell of a time doing so before I speak to Cassie."

Another short silence followed, during which Cassandra snapped out of her stunned state. She started toward the library, but before she'd taken even two steps, the door opened, hard enough for it to bounce back on its hinges, and Ethan strode into the corridor, his face set in grim lines, looking large and dark and dangerously determined. He halted for several heartbeats when he saw her, then moved swiftly toward her. Seconds later he clasped her shoulders.

"Cassie," he said, his gaze anxiously searching her face. "Are you all right?"

God help her, she didn't know. The things her father had said, the ramifications of those words . . . but she'd have to think on that later. She jerked her head in a nod. "I'm fine. I cannot believe you are here."

"I need to talk to you—"

"Take your hands off my daughter."

She and Ethan turned. Her father was advancing on them, his eyes iced with fury. Ethan stepped in front of her, but she moved to stand next to him, feeling strong with him near and her anger further fueling her courage.

Her father stopped an arm's length away. He didn't even spare her a glance, instead fixing his glare on Ethan. "This is your final warning. Get out of my house."

"No." The word erupted from Cassandra. She was so angry she was shaking. "I heard what you said in the library, Father. That you ordered Ethan away ten years ago. That you caused the injury to his face." Her voice vibrated with disgust. "You're a cold, evil man, and I'm ashamed to be your daughter."

He whipped up his hand, clearly intending to strike her, but in the blink of an eye Ethan deflected the blow, then lifted him up by the front of his shirt. In two long strides he thumped her father's back against the wall. Her father gasped, but before he could utter a word, Ethan shoved his forearm against his throat.

"This is *your* final warning," Ethan said, his voice low and deadly calm. "First, if I ever see you raise a hand to her again, I'll break your damn arm. For starters. Second, I'm going to talk to Cassie, and there's nothing you can do to stop me. Not with a knife, not with a pistol, not with a battalion of your servants, or anything else you might think of. I'm not the same green youth I was ten years ago, and believe me, if you try to interfere again, I won't hesitate to carve up your face to match mine."

Her father's face resembled a beet, and a combination of fury and fear blazed from his eyes. He tried to jerk out of Ethan's grasp, but he might as well have been attempting to move a granite boulder.

"Someday you'll rot in hell," her father spewed in a strangled voice.

"Maybe. But if you attempt to hurt her in any way or interfere again, I'll make certain you get there first." Ethan released her father, so abruptly he crumpled to the floor, clutching his throat and breathing hard.

Ethan moved to stand before her. "Are you all right?"

"Y-yes." This time she grabbed his hand, anxious to get away. They exited the house, and when she hesitated, not sure which way to go, Ethan led her to a beautiful chestnut mare tethered to a gatepost. After he mounted, he reached down and plucked her off her feet as if she weighed no more than a daisy, and settled her across his lap, wrapping his strong arms around her. She leaned back against his chest, and his warmth and strength surrounded her. She didn't ask where they were going as his heels set the horse in motion at a brisk pace. It didn't matter. She was with him, and that was enough.

He said nothing, and she had to press her lips together to keep from asking him the plethora of questions racing through her mind. A quarter hour later he slowed the horse when they arrived at the stretch of beach on the estate's grounds, a place where they'd spent many hours together. He swung down from the saddle, then reached up for her, clasping her waist. With her hands braced on his shoulders, he lowered her, her body dragging slowly along his. When he set her on her feet, he continued to hold her, for which she was grateful, as her legs felt less than steady.

She looked up at him, and a swell of love washed through her. His hair was wildly windblown, his skin browned from the sun . . . except for the slash of white on his left cheek. She reached out with unsteady fingers and brushed them over the marred, puckered skin.

"Why didn't you tell me?" she whispered.

"It happened a long time ago."

A fresh spate of anger arrowed through her. "I'll never forgive him for how he treated you."

"I'll never forgive him for how he treated *you*."

"The way you stood up to him, the way you defended me . . . you were magnificent. No one has ever taken up my cause like that. Thank you."

"You're welcome. I'm only sorry I wasn't around to do so for the past ten years."

Dear God, so was she.

"The way you defended me was also quite magnificent," he said, his voice solemn. "Thank you." He clasped her hands, entwining their fingers, then regarded her through very serious dark eyes. "Before I arrived . . . did he hurt you in any way?"

"Not physically." She quickly told him of her father's plan to marry her off to the Duke of Atterly.

His expression tightened, and a muscle ticked in his jaw. "What did you say?"

"That I refuse to marry again."

Something flickered in his eyes. "I . . . see." He gently squeezed her hands. "He was wrong when he said you don't have a choice, Cassie. You do. Come with me. Come back to the Blue Seas Inn."

The relief and love that swamped her snatched her breath. "I'm so glad you said that, Ethan, because I was planning to return to the Blue Seas Inn today."

His brows shot up, and he seemed momentarily at a loss for words. "Because of your disagreement with your father?"

"No, although in the end that proved the spark which fired my decision, so perhaps I should thank him." She drew a bracing breath, then plunged ahead, "I was returning to the Blue Seas to tell you that I love you, Ethan. But not just that I love you—I've known that for years—but that I'm *in love* with you. Painfully so." The words came faster, spilling out of her like water pouring from a widemouthed pitcher, afraid that if she so much as paused for breath, she'd lose her courage. "In the course of one magical day and night you erased ten years of empty loneliness. And you made me realize not only things that I want, but things that I don't want. I don't want to live at Gateshead Manor without you. I don't want to live *anywhere* without you. As for what I *do* want—I want you. Every day. Every night. For as long as you want me."

She paused for breath, but found she could barely draw air into her lungs as she searched his stunned gaze, waiting for his reply. A muscle ticked in his jaw, and he squeezed his eyes shut. Good God, what did that mean? The silence dragged on until she wanted to shake him. Why didn't he *say* something?

Finally he opened his eyes, and the heat flaring in them instantly gave her hope. "For as long as you want me," he murmured, repeating her words. "Cassie, you realize that's forever."

Relief nearly buckled her knees. "Dear God, I hope so. But Ethan, I must remind you that I have nothing. No money. And I'm barren. You'd make a wonderful father—"

He cut off her words by laying a single fingertip over her lips. "The one benefit of not being titled is not having to produce heirs."

"It would only be you and me."

He yanked her against him and touched his forehead to hers. "You're all I've ever wanted."

She framed his face in her hands and leaned back in the circle of his arms until their eyes met. Joy rushed through her, so swift it threatened to sweep her off her feet. "Ethan, will you marry me?"

Again he squeezed his eyes shut, and then his mouth was on hers in a hard, hot, passionate kiss that stole her breath. When he finally lifted his head, she felt utterly and deliciously dazed. "Is that a yes?" she whispered.

He kept one strong arm wrapped around her and lifted his other hand to brush back her disheveled hair. "Before I answer you, don't you want to know what I came here to tell you?"

"If you still wish to tell me."

"Oh, I do. I came here to tell you that I love you. I've always loved you. Only you. You've held my heart in your hand since that first day when you asked me to be your friend. I always believed there could never be anything between me and a countess, but after seeing you again, hearing about your marriage, I realized I couldn't let you go without at least telling you how much I love you. And letting you decide if the very little I have to offer is enough. I'll never be able to afford the sort of luxury you've always known, but I'll make sure you're always warm and well-fed. I don't have much, Cassie, but all I have I offer to you."

Her lips trembled, and a half laugh, half sob escaped her. "The estates, the title, the place in society—none of it has ever brought me happiness. All I want is your love, Ethan."

"You've always had it. You always will. For a long time I believed that loving you was mistake. But now I know it wasn't—my error was in letting you go." Clasping both her hands, he dropped to one knee before her. "Cassie, will you marry me?"

Tears of pure joy rolled down her face and plopped onto their joined hands. "I asked you first."

A grin curved his lips. "My answer is yes."

"*My* answer is yes."

"Thank God." He rose and gifted her with another heated, passionate kiss, then lifted her off her feet and twirled her around until they were both breathless and laughing.

After he set her down, Cassandra looked up at him and saw all the love she'd ever dreamed of beaming at her from his beautiful dark eyes. "So *this* is what happiness feels like," she said, smiling into those eyes.

"My sweet Cassie, this is *exactly* what it feels like."

Jacquie D'Alessandro

Growing up on Long Island, New York, I fell in love with romance at an early age. I dreamed of being swept away by a dashing rogue riding a spirited stallion. When my hero finally showed up, he was dressed in jeans and drove a Volkswagen, but I recognized him anyway. We married after both graduating from Hofstra University and are now living our happily-ever-afters in Atlanta, Georgia, along with our very bright and active son, who is a dashing rogue in the making. I love to hear from readers! You can contact me through my website at www.JacquieD.com.

From
This Moment On

Candice Hern

*Dedicated with thanks to all the readers
who wrote to me asking for Wilhelmina's story*

Chapter One

October 1814
Buckinghamshire

The crunch of wheels on gravel and the clip-clop of a slow-ing team heralded the arrival of yet another coach. Captain Samuel Pellow, late of His Majesty's Royal Navy, nursed a tankard of ale in the public room of the Blue Boar, and watched from the little windowed alcove overlooking the inn yard as the new carriage pulled to a stop. The innkeeper rushed out to welcome yet another unexpected party compelled to halt their journey due to the downpour.

Sam had pulled into the yard driving his own curricle not half an hour earlier. After so many years at sea he didn't mind getting wet, but he was much more comfortable on a rolling quarterdeck in a high storm than he was navigating sloggy, uncertain roads with an irritable team. He'd decided to ride out the squall in a dry taproom with twenty or thirty like-minded travelers.

Grissom, the innkeeper, was quite obviously delighted to

have so many customers, as the village of Upper Hampden was between regular stops on the coach road, and Sam guessed the Blue Boar did not often have such a full house. It was an old inn, had probably been built over two hundred years ago: black and white timbered, steep-pitched gables, with projecting stories leaning drunkenly over the inn yard. Even so, it was a surprisingly well-appointed and comfortable inn for such a small village. The stables, though, were already overcrowded with carriages and carts and gigs, and more horses than they were built to handle. The situation did not dim the innkeeper's mercenary smile as he stood holding a large umbrella, ready to escort the new arrivals inside.

Through the rain-streaked mullioned window, Sam could see that there were actually two carriages in the yard, each of them large and elegantly appointed, with a crest on the doors. He couldn't make out the crest—not that it would make any difference if he could; one coat of arms looked much the same as the next to him—but it was clear from his deferential attitude that Grissom was aware he had a member of the aristocracy in his inn yard.

A liveried footman, soaked to the skin, jumped from his perch on the back of the first carriage, pulled down a portable set of steps, and opened the door. Shielded by the innkeeper's huge umbrella, a lady stepped down and was rushed inside the inn. Another woman followed, obviously a maid as she didn't warrant the courtesy of an umbrella. Pulling a cloak over her head, she made her way indoors, carrying a leather box tight against her chest. A bull of a man stepped from the second carriage, conferred with the other footmen and the ostlers who were seeing to the horses, then rushed inside.

Sam settled back in his chair and proceeded to enjoy his ale in peace while the entry hall became a frenzy of activity. He could hear Mrs. Grissom, somewhat less delighted with today's parade of customers than her husband, shouting out orders to her small staff. Her voice rang out with an authority that made Sam smile, thinking she might have done quite well as a gunnery officer during a close action.

Amid the bustle and shouting he caught the words "best room" and "Your Grace." So, the newcomer was a duchess. The tiniest twinge of anxiety gripped the muscles of his abdomen. He had met a few duchesses in his day, but there was one who still held a tiny corner of his heart, though he had not laid eyes on her in many years. And their last meeting had not been one of his better moments. He was foolish to hope that this particular duchess was *his* duchess. She was a creature of London, which was one reason he'd avoided going up to Town whenever he was in England. He hadn't wanted to meet her again. Their last encounter had been too awkward. He never quite knew what he felt for her, and that uncertainty always tied him into knots. No, this far from London, it would be some other duchess. England was crawling with duchesses.

But he could not tear his eyes from the doorway that opened into the entry hall. Several figures were crowded into that tiny space. It was easy enough to identify the duchess. She was the center of attention. The innkeeper's wife was bobbing up and down like an anchor buoy in front of the lady, when she wasn't shooing a maid in one direction or another to prepare for their grand guest. And the bullish fellow from the second coach was hovering close and keeping the riffraff at bay.

The lady herself seemed unperturbed by the fuss and bother. Her back was to Sam, but there was that indescribable something about her bearing that marked her as Quality. She wore a full-length pelisse of deep blue velvet with several short capes at the back, in imitation of a man's greatcoat, and a matching bonnet. Sam knew next to nothing about ladies' fashion, but even he could see that this was a very stylish ensemble, and no doubt very expensive.

She nodded to the innkeeper, then turned to speak to the bullish man. In doing so, her face came partially into view, and Sam sucked in a sharp breath. Dear God, it *was* his duchess. Or rather, the Duke of Hertford's duchess. Sam had no claim to her at all. Except that they had once loved each other, a very long time ago. Almost twenty-five years ago. Gulfs of time and experience separated them, and yet she still had the ability to set his heart beating to quarters.

Almost without thinking, he rose from the bench, stepped down from the raised alcove, and walked toward her. Toward Wilhelmina, Duchess of Hertford.

Blast the rain! Wilhelmina had hoped to make it home tonight. But there was nothing more dismal and uncomfortable than traveling in a rainstorm. It was only just past noon and the storm might pass in an hour or so, but the delay would mean an even later arrival in London. Instead, she preferred to take advantage of whatever accommodations could be had in this quaint little village and settle here for the night. They could start out for London in the morning when the weather would hopefully be more cooperative.

She was giving Smeaton, her long-suffering factotum, instructions to arrange rooms for her small entourage of servants when, out of the corner of her eye, Wilhelmina saw a movement in the adjacent public room. Something, some inexplicable pull, compelled her to turn and look. A man was walking toward her. He was silhouetted in shadows against the bright blaze from the large open-hearth fire behind him, and she could not make out his features. But in less than an instant, she assessed what she could see of him with a practiced eye.

He was tall with broad shoulders and a trim waistline, his straight-backed posture lent him a military air. His purposeful stride in her direction made Wilhelmina think she must know him.

Who was he? If he was one of her former paramours, she might find some pleasure in this pokey old inn by reminiscing with a friend. She hoped to God that it wasn't some fellow she'd once rejected—and they were legion—who would make the day even more miserable than it already was.

As he came nearer, a jolt of familiarity shot through her insides. By the time his face came into the light, knocking the breath clean out of her, she had already guessed who he was.

He smiled, that crooked smile she had once known so well, and said, "Willie."

She was no longer a young girl who swooned with emotion, but Sam Pellow always managed to make her feel unsteady on her pins. He was still good-looking. In fact, he seemed to have grown handsomer over time, or maybe it was her own notion of handsome that had changed. A man of years and experience, with wisdom and character in his face—that was what Wilhelmina now found attractive. It was a mark of her own years, she supposed, that fresh-faced, untried young men no longer held much appeal for her.

Sam's hair was still thick and dark, though cut short, which was a surprise. He'd worn it long, tied in a queue the last time she'd seen him. The hint of silver at his temples had not been there before, either, and somehow made him even more attractive. And there was a small scar she did not remember, that cut through one eyebrow.

His eyes had always been a changeable sort of brown, sometimes dark as coffee, sometimes sherry-colored. But now they seemed more golden than she remembered, as if they'd been bleached and polished by the same sun that had darkened his skin.

That face, so familiar and yet so changed, still had the power to make her weak in the knees, and to set off an explosion of emotions she'd thought long buried.

Composing herself, she reached out a hand to him. "Sam. How good to see you again."

"And you," he said, and took her gloved fingers to his lips. "It has been a long time, Your Grace."

"If you are going to 'Your Grace' me, then I must call you Captain Pellow. It is Captain, is it not?"

"It is. I made post a few years back."

"Congratulations, Captain."

"Thank you. But I'd rather you called me Sam."

"Only if you call me Willie. No one has called me that name for years. I rather like it. Sometimes Wilhelmina is too grand."

"Isn't that why you chose it?"

She chuckled. "Indeed. Plain Wilma Jepp just did not have the right note of . . . panache. But I'm older and wiser now and no longer trying to impress anyone. Willie will do quite well, thank you."

"Willie, then."

He smiled again, and it took some effort for her to breathe properly. That smile did not belong to a man of mature years, but to a boy of eighteen who'd delighted in teasing her and making her laugh.

"Since we both seem to be waiting out the storm," he said, "would you care to join me?" He gestured toward a small alcove set slightly above the main floor, where there was a table and two facing benches with high sides, like box pews, that provided a measure of privacy. The rest of the room—it appeared to be a combination taproom and dining room, probably the only public room at the inn—was filled with people, mostly men, crammed shoulder to shoulder around long tables, talking and laughing, tankards clanking, utensils clattering. There were a few other separate alcoves along the windowed walls, all occupied.

"At least it's removed somewhat from the general hub-bub," he said. "I was one of the first to arrive—the blasted bonnet of my curricle began to leak like a sieve—so I managed to claim the best seat. I'd be pleased to share it with you. And the duke, too, if he's with you."

Ah. He didn't know. "His Grace passed away four years ago."

"Oh. I am sorry. I hadn't heard." An odd expression crossed his face for an instant and was gone. Then he sighed. "I can tell you every maneuver of every battle on land and sea during the late wars, but I confess I did not keep abreast of society news. My condolences, Willie. I know how happy you were with him."

Did he? The last time she'd seen Sam—could it truly be ten years ago?—she had been married to Hertford for less than a year. Sam had approached her at a rout party, and she'd been rather stunned to see him there. He was almost always at sea and seldom in London. Plus, he did not approve of her, of the choices she'd made in her life, and so it surprised her when he had deliberately sought her out. He'd seemed at loose ends, a bit uncertain, but nevertheless pleased to see her, which made her heart lurch. She'd politely asked about his voyages and his family, and learned that he'd recently lost his wife. When she told him of her marriage to the duke, the conversation spiraled into a painful awkwardness she'd never quite understood. Had he disapproved? Had he thought she was reaching too far above herself? Or was he disappointed for some other reason? She had never known why, but it had been a decidedly uncomfortable encounter.

"I was indeed happy with Hertford," she said. "I could not have asked for a better husband or champion. I miss him. But life goes on, as you know."

"Yes, it does, sometimes with the most surprising turns. Like bumping into you here, in the middle of nowhere, after all these years. We have a lot to catch up on, Willie. I'd be honored to share my table with you while we wait for the storm to pass."

Wilhelmina smiled. "I'd love nothing better. A nice pot of tea would be just the thing. Thank you, Sam. Just give me time to shake off the dust of the road. I'll join you shortly."

She turned and found her ubiquitous factotum at her side. His thuggish face often struck fear in the best of men, with its large, crooked nose, heavy brow, and a long scar running down one cheek and across his chin. It was, though, a comfort to Wilhelmina, who relied so much on him. Smeaton, who'd once been a pugilist, had been in her employ for more than fifteen years and was now indispensable. Part butler, part steward, part man of affairs, and part bodyguard, he managed everything in her life, whether at home in London or on the road.

"I have ensured that you have the best room in the inn, Your Grace," he said in the soft, cultured voice so at odds with his face. "I inspected it myself and believe it will be suitable."

"Thank you, Smeaton." He had no doubt made sure that anyone who might have occupied the room had been moved elsewhere. The dear man tossed around her rank and fortune much more than she ever did. He was a great snob, Smeaton was.

"I am afraid there is no private parlor to be had in this inn, Your Grace," he said, his tone dripping with incredulity at such an omission, "but there is a decent table in the bedchamber where you might dine in private."

"I am sure it will do quite well for one night," Wilhelmina said. "But as soon as I have changed out of these clothes, I shall be going down to the public room."

A look of horror gathered in his eyes. "The public room? Are you *quite* sure, Your Grace? I noted a few unsavory-looking fellows in there, and I dislike to think of you exposing yourself to such company."

Wilhelmina laughed. "One of those fellows is a captain in the Royal Navy and an old friend. I am going to have tea with him. With your approval, of course."

"Your Grace!" He reared back, looking offended. "I would never presume to approve or disapprove of anything you chose to do."

"I am happy to hear it. Now, be so good as to direct me to my room, and then send Marsh to me."

"This way, Your Grace. And I believe Miss Marsh is waiting for you." He led her up a narrow flight of stairs that turned back on itself twice before reaching the next floor.

The bedchamber she'd been given—or that Smeaton had commandeered—was clean and spacious, with a simple stone-fronted fireplace, solid oak furniture, and a bank of diamond-paned windows overlooking the inn yard. The bed—large and plain, hung with old damask bed curtains—dominated the room. Ginny, Wilhelmina's maid, was making up the bed in the fine linen sheets they'd brought with them. The inn's sheets lay in a heap on the floor. Marsh, her dresser, was unpacking a trunk and draping dresses over chairs in front of the freshly made fire so the heat might loosen any wrinkles or creases. They both bobbed curtsies when she entered the room.

"I have laid out a few dresses for you to choose from, Your Grace. I had thought this one . . . ?" Marsh indicated a plain jaconet dress with a high standing collar of Vandyke lace. It was simple enough for a day indoors at a country inn, but not what Wilhelmina had in mind. She shook her head, and Marsh held up another simple dress of sprigged muslin. No, that wouldn't do, either. Marsh seemed put out of countenance that Wilhelmina should reject her advice for dresses that were perfectly appropriate.

But Marsh wasn't having tea with Captain Sam Pellow. Some might think the dowager Duchess of Hertford was past her prime—they would be wrong—but she still wanted to look her best when meeting a gentleman. And this was no ordinary gentleman. This was Sam. Her Sam. Her first love.

She selected a dress of French figured muslin with long

sleeves and a crossed bodice and a neckline that provided a hint of cleavage. Wilhelmina was proud of her figure, which did not, she believed, show the matronly sags and bulges one might expect from a woman her age. She might as well show Sam that she still had the makings of a desirable woman.

Or perhaps she was being foolish. Sam would never desire her again. She might be a duchess now, but there had been a time when her favors had been for sale. And that was something he would never be able to forget, or forgive.

Ginny helped her out of the bonnet and pelisse while Marsh tried to smooth wrinkles out of the French muslin. Wilhelmina stood like a mannequin and allowed them to minister to her, as her thoughts drifted back to simpler times, when she and Sam were children in the Cornish village of Porthruan Cove.

Wilma Jepp, as she'd then been called, was the only daughter of the local blacksmith. Sam had lost his parents as a boy and had supported himself as a fisherman from the time he was about twelve. When he was sixteen, he'd suddenly shot up to a great height and become what Willie and the other local girls thought to be exceedingly handsome. But he'd only had eyes for Willie, the village beauty. They fell madly, wildly in love, as teenagers do, and talked of marrying one day when Sam had saved enough money to build a cottage.

Willie's mother, a strict Methodist, had not approved of the impertinent young fisherman who lived by his wits and had nothing to recommend him. She had once caught Sam and Willie kissing, and had beaten Willie mercilessly for it. But that hadn't stopped Willie's youthful passion for the handsome young fisherman. When she was sixteen and Sam eighteen, they finally gave in to their desire one day and made love in a hayloft in her father's barn.

A week later, he was gone.

Sam had not returned from fishing one day, and the next day his empty boat had washed ashore, damaged, with his gear still on board and a scrap of fabric caught on a nail. Everyone in the village assumed he'd had an accident in the boat and drowned.

Willie had been distraught with grief and ready to die, until she was befriended by a visiting London artist who was obsessed with her face and painted picture after picture of her. When her mother learned she was posing for a painter, she'd been livid, and eventually threw Willie out of the house. Some months later, having lost her love and her home and figuring she had nothing left to lose, Wilma Jepp had become Wilhelmina Grant and the artist's mistress. Her face became her fortune, and soon she left the artist for another man's protection, and then another, until she was courted by some of the highest men in the realm.

For five years she had cherished memories of the boy she had loved and lost, often dreaming of what might have been. But all those sentimental fantasies had been shattered in an instant when he'd walked into her box at the theater one night—alive, angry, and accusing.

Wilhelmina had been shocked to the core to see him. She had very nearly swooned, thinking at first she'd seen a ghost. Sam was then a midshipman in the Royal Navy, and she learned that he had been taken by a press gang back in '89 when she thought he'd died. Though he claimed to have written her, she never received his letters. All that time he'd been alive and she'd never known.

And so Wilhelmina, by then a well-known demirep, had to face a furious Sam who didn't understand why she had not waited for him. Even when she explained, he could not forgive her for the life she'd chosen to lead, for giving herself to other men. He had broken her heart when he'd walked away from her, shocked and angry and unwilling to forgive, and had taken a piece of that shattered heart with him. Five years after the wrenching pain of losing him, she lost him a second time.

Wilhelmina had never forgotten the boy she'd loved, and saw him a handful of times since that awful first reunion. Though she regretted having lost him, she could not turn back the clock. She had to live with the choices she'd made. And she'd done well for herself. She'd been with ambassadors and princes, generals and poets, even a prime minister. And her last protector, the Duke of Hertford, had loved her, and scandalized society when he married her.

All things considered, she'd had a wonderful life. A better life than she could ever have had if she'd stayed in Porthruan Cove. She had money and position, and now even a degree of respectability.

But she had sacrificed her first love for it, though she had not known so at the time.

Many years had passed, and she and Sam had mellowed with age. He no longer seemed to scorn her, and she no longer countered his scorn with arrogant condescension. They were mature adults who'd taken different paths but could perhaps meet in friendship, for old times' sake.

Wilhelmina had hardly noticed the actions of Marsh, who'd removed her traveling clothes and dressed her in the French figured muslin dress with the deep vee neckline and the pretty rows of lace at the wrists and the hem. There was only a small dressing table mirror in the room, but it was enough to tell Wilhelmina that the dress flattered her, and she was satisfied. Her hair was still flattened from the bonnet, however, and she sat at the small desk that doubled as a dressing table while Ginny worked her magic. She unpinned the shoulder-length locks that were still golden—nature's gold, not artifice, as some people believed—brushed them out, then deftly refashioned a French knot at the back, tied up with a ribbon of lace, and teased loose curls over the forehead and temples.

Wilhelmina nodded her approval as she studied her reflection in the mirror. She would be damned before she'd be caught in a matronly cap, which any right-minded woman of her age would don, and preferred to flaunt stylish coiffures instead. Not too youthful—there was nothing worse than a woman of a certain age trying to look like an ingénue—but fashionable and perhaps a bit dashing. Is that what Sam saw when he looked at her? An older woman with a bit of dash? Or an aging shell of the girl he'd once known?

"Shall I bring the jewel box?" Marsh asked, eyeing the deep neckline.

"Yes, please. The cameo necklace and earrings, I think."

"Are you certain, Your Grace?"

Wilhelmina sighed. Marsh was right. She was trying too hard to impress Sam. "No, I suppose not. Something simpler." She opted for a gold lyre-shaped pendant set with seed pearls, on a delicate gold chain, and plain gold hoop earrings.

She was ready. Or was she? Would she ever be ready to face his judgment of her? To stand before him without shame?

How foolish. Shame had never been a part of her nature. She had long ago ceased to regret the life she'd chosen. There was no going back, no reclaiming of innocence or virtue, and to lament the impossible seemed a pointless waste of time. But on each occasion she'd seen Sam over the years, she'd experienced momentary pangs of uncharacteristic regret. If only she'd known he was alive, if only she had received his letters, if only . . . if only . . .

But this time was different. Hertford had made her his duchess and given her back a modicum of respectability. Some high sticklers would never accept her completely; some doors would always be closed to her. But her rank and fortune opened most doors, and in a few of them she'd found good friends whose unwavering support and love had opened even more doors. When she'd married Hertford, Wilhelmina had determined to cast off her old life entirely, to become an asset to the duke rather than an embarrassment. For the seven years of her marriage and the four years of her widowhood, Wilhelmina had become as close to a pillar of society as was possible for a former courtesan. There was no need for shame and regret when facing Sam. She was able to face him proudly, finally, after all those years.

Wilhelmina glanced out the window as she left the bedchamber. The rain had not let up. It looked as though the storm would last a while longer. Which meant she might have an entire afternoon with Sam.

She could not decide if the fluttering in her belly was anxiety or anticipation. Or just the idiotic girlish reaction she had whenever Sam Pellow, however briefly, walked back into her life again.

Chapter Two

Sam was glad he had not ordered tea right away because, as he ought to have expected, the duchess had not yet returned after half an hour. He'd spent the greater part of his years living in close quarters with men, and sometimes forgot how long it took a lady to "shake off the dust of the road." It was one of those things about women that tested the patience of many men, but that Sam always found rather endearing. He liked the idea that ladies always wanted to look their best. But today it only gave him more time to ponder this unexpected encounter. He was encouraged by their brief exchange, which had been neither awkward nor strained. She had been perfectly open and friendly; none of her protective hackles were up, as they sometimes had been in the past. But those hackles had always been thrown up in defense of his own undisguised disdain. It had taken many years for Sam not to feel betrayed by her decision to lead such an infamous life. Discovering what had become of Willie had changed his own life forever. He no longer harbored romantic illusions of any kind where women were concerned. Willie had cured him of that weakness. Or so he'd always thought, until he found himself in London seeking her out. Not once, but twice. It had been a fool's errand each time, but he'd never been rational where Willie was concerned.

By the time he'd come to terms with the fact that she had only done what she could to survive after her shrew of a mother had tossed her out on her ear, it was too late to effect the sort of reconciliation he'd wanted. She had married and become a grand lady, a duchess.

She was widowed now, though. That piece of news had been something of a jolt. This serendipitous meeting at an old country inn might have been an opportunity for that reunion he'd once dreamed about. Except that Sam's destination, once the storm passed and he was back on the road, put a damper on the various wild fantasies that had been spinning around in his head.

No, today it would simply be two old friends who hadn't met for years, catching up with each other's lives. He would enjoy that. And when they'd grown easy in their conversation, perhaps she would allow him to apologize for his past behavior, for judging her so harshly.

A lull in the noise and general conversation in the room allowed Sam to hear bustling in the entry hall. When he saw the duchess through the doorway, escorted by Grissom, the innkeeper, he signaled to one of the serving maids to bring the pot of tea he'd ordered. He rose as she crossed the room, and drank in the sight of her as she approached the alcove.

By all rights, a woman of her age should not look so appealing, and yet a brief surge of sexual desire crested and broke like a wave inside him. It was pure stupidity, of course. They were both too old for such nonsense. His only excuse was that he had been without a woman for too long.

But damn it all, she looked good. Without the bonnet, it was easier to study her. Willie's face still held much of the beauty she'd had at sixteen. Good bones, he supposed. She would always have classic good looks, he imagined, even in her eighties. Her hair was still blond but more honey-gold than the bright guinea-gold of her youth. Were there silver strands among the gold? He couldn't see any, but she was only two years his junior, and he had more silver in his hair than he'd like.

But it was the way she moved that stirred his loins. A sort of feline grace that drew all eyes to her as she crossed the public room. The skirts of her white dress flowed elegantly as she walked, hinting at the curve of thigh and hip beneath, and the bodice dipped into a deep vee that revealed a tantalizing glimpse of bosom. Even at her age she radiated an irresistible sensuality. Was it a performance, well practiced, or had it always been there, drawing him from the start, all those years ago?

"Duchess," he said as he held out a hand to her.

"Thank you, Sam." She took his hand and allowed him to guide her up the two steps to the alcove. When she was seated, she looked up at him and smiled. "I am sorry to have been so long. You have no idea how complicated a process it can be for ladies to dress, even with help."

"It was worth the wait," he said as he took the seat across from her. "You look beautiful."

She chuckled. "Sam! You have become a flatterer."

He smiled and shrugged, a bit embarrassed that he had spoken his thoughts aloud. He was saved from responding by the arrival of no less than Mrs. Grissom with a pot of tea and a serving girl with a tray of crusty bread and butter and jam. The tea service was obviously her best china—not the heavy blue and white dishes that lined the old deal dressers flanking the fireplace, but delicately thin-walled pieces such as Sam had brought his wife from the East Indies.

"Here you are, Your Grace, a nice pot of my best Bohea. And more ale for you, Cap'n." Mrs. Grissom and the girl unloaded their trays and arranged everything on the table just so, as if they were in the finest restaurant in London instead of the old Blue Boar in Upper Hampden. "The bread's fresh baked, and there's good local butter and my own blackberry jam. If there's anything else you need, you just ask Lizzie here to fetch it for you."

The duchess offered effusive thanks and the innkeeper's wife beamed, bobbed several curtsies, then tugged the girl Lizzie with her as she left them. While Willie set about preparing the tea, Sam marveled at how easily she wore the mantle of her high rank. She truly was a duchess, every inch of her. The blacksmith's daughter had done very well for herself.

"What brings you to this part of England?" she asked. "I confess I was astonished to see you here."

"No more astonished than I was to see you. I somehow imagined you never left London."

"Oh, I sometimes follow the beau monde to Brighton or a country house party. I have just come from one, in fact, and was on my way home when this wretched storm broke through. But this is a charming old inn, is it not? A fine place to stay the night and hope for sun in the morning. And you?"

"I am a more intrepid traveler, I fear. I am simply waiting for the rain to stop and I will be on my way."

"To . . . ?"

"I am to visit friends who live a bit north of here. But I must say, Willie, that I am delighted to have met you here. It has been such a long time since I've seen you."

"Ten years."

His brows lifted in surprise. "Sink me, has it been ten years?" Could it really be that long? Yes, it had been 1804, during that long leave after Sarah's death, before Trafalgar. It was the last time he'd visited London, in fact. He had not even come to town for Nelson's funeral in 1806. Oh yes, he remembered his last meeting with Willie quite vividly. It was when he learned she had married the Duke of Hertford, and he had barely avoided making a prime fool of himself.

And yet she knew exactly how long it had been. Lord, he hoped the date wasn't burned in her memory because of his bumbling behavior.

"How have you been, Willie?"

"Very well, thank you." She looked up from pouring tea and caught his eye. "That was not merely an idle question, was it? Yes, I am indeed very well. I have a good life. I have become quite a respectable widow, you see. But what of you? With the wars over, have you come home to stay a while?"

"More than a while. With Boney confined to Elba, there is little activity for the navy in Europe. And I have no desire to join the war in America. Instead, I have retired."

"Retired? I rather thought you'd stay on until you'd made admiral, at least."

"The navy wasn't my choice as a career, you may remember. I have enjoyed it, though, and would not have missed it. But I'm tired of bouncing about the world and want to plant more permanent roots. I have a little place on the Sussex coast that I am rather fond of. I'd like to live quietly for a while and watch the sun rise and set over green instead of blue."

"You will miss the sea."

"Perhaps. Many of my fellow officers are bored to the bone and secretly praying for a new war. As for me, I am ready to enjoy a long peace. To spend the rest of my days on dry land, in Sussex. It's a fine house with a small park, a view of the sea from the front and the south downs from the rear." He grinned at her and winked. "Perhaps I'll become a gentleman farmer."

She laughed, and the sound took him back to that hayloft in Porthruan, where they had gifted each other with their virginity. It was the same musical laugh. A touch lower in timbre, but still the same. "Do you know anything about farming, Sam?"

"Not a bit. But I can hire people who do, while I sit by my fire with my pipe and my dogs and grow to a crusty old age. But for now, I'm going to enjoy the peace and collect my half-pay—"

"Half-pay? But I thought you retired."

"One never retires from the Royal Navy, Willie. There is no provision for it. Once you join, you're in for life. But you can opt to go on half-pay and live as you please until you are called to duty. Then you must report or lose your half-pay, which is precisely what I intend to do."

For the next half hour she peppered him with questions about his naval experiences, and they talked easily together about the places he'd been, the battles he'd fought, the occasional foray into the East Indies, and the tedious blockade duties that had kept him busy the last half-dozen years.

He watched her closely as they talked. She was still an uncommonly handsome woman. No, "handsome" was too bland a word for the duchess. She was beautiful. Not in that fresh-bloom-of-youth way that had so captivated him as a boy, when she was soft and round and pink-cheeked. Now she had the sort of timeless beauty of antique marble statues he'd seen in Greece. Every plane and angle was perfect, even if etched with a line or two.

And yet, beneath the elegant and no doubt expensively maintained veneer, the pretty young girl he'd once known still lurked, catching him off guard now and then and robbing him of breath: in the way the merest hint of a dimple winked at one corner of her mouth, or the way she tilted her head as she listened to him speak, or the way she wrinkled her nose when she laughed. In such moments, decades rolled away and he was back in Cornwall. In the hayloft with his girl.

He had to wonder if things had gone as they'd planned, if

he'd never been taken by the press gang and they'd married, would she have retained her beauty? Or would she now be haggard and worn out at forty-one, her looks long faded, bowed down by a hardscrabble life of drudgery and child-bearing? Or would they have been so happy together that life would never have seemed too difficult?

There was no way to know what might have been, and no way to change the past, so there was no point in dwelling on it. Sam had always been forward-looking, making the best out of what life brought him.

But what was he to make out of this chance encounter? How was he to make the best of it?

"And what of you, Sam? I mean on a personal level. When we last met you had lost your wife. Have you remarried? Had more children?"

He shook his head. "No. I've been away too much. I took leave when I could to see Tom, of course."

"Your son?"

"Yes. But no time for wooing a wife. A blockade captain's life is not his own."

"I never understood how an impressed seaman managed to rise to the rank of captain."

"Mine was not a typical path, I assure you. In fact, my career has been quite out of the ordinary. I have always been a good sailor, as you know."

She did know. Wilhelmina smiled and remembered the young Sam, scampering about on the cove, more at home on a fishing boat than on shore.

"My natural abilities were noticed and utilized from the start," he continued. "Once I realized there was no going home for me, that I was stuck in the bloody navy against my will, I decided to make the best of it. I enjoyed the life, learned quickly, and put myself forward at every opportunity. After a few years, I was rated able seaman and made it known that I aspired to the quarterdeck. I was fortunate in my captain, who went against tradition to eventually assign me a midshipman's rating."

She poured another cup of tea, only to find the pot empty. Looking about, she caught Lizzie's eye across the room and lifted an eyebrow. The girl bobbed and hurried off. Wilhelmina wanted to sit here for hours and listen to Sam, to allow that voice, still colored with the long Rs and rolling vowels of Cornwall, to wrap around her like a soothing blanket. But she could see that the rain was easing up and he would be wanting to resume his journey, and she didn't want to let him go just yet. It was the first time they'd had more than a brief conversation in years, and most of those had been either unpleasant or awkward. Talking together like old friends was something she'd never imagined for them, and she savored every moment. Perhaps if she kept him talking, he would never notice if the rain stopped.

"I don't know much about how the navy works," she said. "Achieving a midshipman's rating was unusual?"

"For an impressed seaman, it certainly was." He shook his head and gave a soft chuckle tinged with self-mockery. "I was three-and-twenty, the oldest midshipman on board, but I was proud as a peacock, and already mapping out a career as an officer. It was just then that we returned to England, after five long years at sea. And I was bursting my buttons with pride in my new assignment, eager to track you down and lay my paltry little fortune, my hoarded bits of prize money, at your feet."

Ah. At last they'd arrived at the topic they were bound to address, but she had hoped they would not. It had been inevitable, she supposed. But perhaps it was time they talked it out. "And instead you found me gone."

He frowned and fell silent for a long moment. When he finally spoke, there was a dark, bitter edge to his voice. "I was so angry when I learned you'd run off with that artist fellow and become . . ."

"A whore."

Sam grimaced. "That wasn't the word I was going to use."

"I have no doubt my mother used it when she told you I'd gone." She had flung that word and worse at Wilhelmina when she'd cast her out, accusing her of sharing her favors with the artist, James Benedict, and with Sam and others. Martha Jepp would have no hesitation in using the same language when Sam had come back looking for her daughter.

"You did what you had to in order to survive," he said, his tone softening. "It took me a long time to come to grips with it, but I understand now. Truly I do, Willie. I want you to believe that." He reached out and touched her hand briefly. "But all those years ago . . . Well, when I came home in '94 a newly rated midshipman, puffed up in a crisp new uniform paid for with my own prize money, the news devastated me. And I lashed out in pain."

She had been in the theater, holding court in her reserved box, when he found her. It had taken less than an instant to recognize him, and the sight of him had her reeling, this ghost from her past walking toward her.

"So, it's true."

He glared at her with such anger that another wave of dizziness almost overwhelmed her. If she had not been seated, she would surely have collapsed. Her emotions were a turmoil of surprise, joy, and shame. Thoroughly dumbfounded, she could not manage to speak.

"I dared not believe it," he said. "I kept hearing tales of the infamous Wilhelmina Grant and knew that woman, that lightskirt, *could not be the sweet Wilma Jepp I had known. I had to see with my own eyes that it was not true. And look what I find instead." His glance had swept over her court of admirers. "The woman I once loved surrounded by men who've had her, who've paid for the fancy clothes and the fine jewels. Perched up here like a queen in your box, flaunting your indecency for all the world to see." His mouth*

twisted, and he looked like he might become ill. "God, Willie. How could you?"

"Sam." The single syllable had almost choked her. She was sick with joy that he was alive, he was really alive, *and devastated that he'd found her like this. He was only half right about the other men in the box. They'd all sought her favors. Only a few had been successful. Wilhelmina Grant was an exclusive item, not easily purchased. Her current protector, Sir Clive Binchy, hovered behind her, his hand on the back of her chair. She could feel him about to make a move toward Sam, but she held up her hand to stop him.*

"How could you do this?" Sam asked, the anger in his voice tinged with a plaintive note. "I thought I'd find you in Porthruan, waiting for me. I thought . . . But instead you've come to this? Damnation. Your mother was right. You're nothing but a—"

Before he could hurl the vulgar word she knew was on the tip of his tongue, a word she had accepted years ago but had no wish to hear from Sam, she quickly composed herself and donned her usual public manner, flippant and condescending.

"Don't be such a prig, Sam. This is the real world, not that rustic little fishing village in Cornwall. I love all my 'fancy clothes' as you so quaintly call them, and my jewels and carriages and more. If you do not like how I came by them, feel free to leave."

His face fell into a look of such wretchedness it had torn at her heart. But this was for the best. She had to drive him away or she surely would fall apart.

Without another word, he turned on his heel and left.

"I'd hoped you would wait for me." His voice brought her back to the present.

"I thought you were dead!" Her voice rose, colored with the emotion of that memory. "Your boat washed ashore without you. No one knew what had happened."

"The press gang commandeered my little boat and forced me to go with them. I told them I was no sailor, just an ordinary fisherman, but they either didn't believe me or didn't care. They needed seamen and I looked close enough to one, so off I went, leaving my boat abandoned in the cove."

"When it was found the next day, empty and shattered against the rocks, we all assumed you'd suffered some sort of accident and drowned."

"But I wrote you. Once I made land, I sent letter after letter." At her frustrated sigh, he said, "I suppose your mother didn't pass them on, did she?"

"No, of course not. She probably burned them."

They were interrupted by the arrival of the serving girl with a kettle of hot water that she poured into the teapot.

"C'n I gets yer anyt'ing else, Yer Grace?"

"No, thank you, Lizzie. But could you tell Mr. Smeaton I'd like a word with him? Tell him to bring paper and pen."

Lizzie nodded, bobbed a quick curtsy, and hurried back to the kitchen with her steaming kettle.

"Paper and pen? Gad, Willie, I hope you're not going to ask me to re-create those letters for you here and now?"

He looked so abashed that she laughed. "Nothing of the sort, Sam. I just realized that I need to note down some instructions for the staff regarding our return to London. It won't take a moment, I assure you. I just want to do it before I forget."

"I am relieved." He heaved a theatrical sigh. "I couldn't do it. I'm sorry you never got my letters, Willie. You'd have been devilish impressed."

She laughed again. "I have no doubt of it."

"No, really. You would have been. They were damned fine letters."

"I wish I'd seen them, Sam. You cannot imagine how much I wish it." She laid a hand over his, and he captured it, lifting it to his lips. The warmth of his skin and his breath

against her knuckles sent a wave of such yearning through
her body that she almost moaned aloud. She had not wanted
a man this badly in a very long time. And because it was
Sam, the wanting was even more powerful, all tangled up
with first love and heartbreak. As she looked into his eyes,
she could feel his desire as well.

"Those letters kept me going," he said, stroking her fingers, "gave me purpose when I thought I would die of missing you. I wasn't much good at reading or writing, as you
will remember, but soon after being pressed, I was fortunate
to find a friend in the master's mate, a fellow Cornishman.
He took me under his wing, taught me everything about the
service. He gave me nautical books to read, but when he saw
me struggling—I swear the words looked like a foreign language to me—he gave me lessons in reading and writing. If
I wanted to rise in the service, he said, I had to be able to
compose dispatches and logs, and read and understand con-
tracts and orders and regulations.

"I practiced my penmanship in letters to you. Page after
page, filled with details of my life at sea, and full of longing
for you. It really is too bad your mother never sent them to
you. They were masterpieces, those letters, worthy of Byron
himself. No, don't laugh, they were pure poetry, I swear it."

"I'd give anything to have read them, Sam. But I never got
them and assumed you were dead until you walked up to me
that night at the theater. I thought you were a ghost. An angry ghost. Lord, I was so ashamed for you to find me like
that."

He lifted an eyebrow. "You did not put on a show of
shame, as I recall."

"No, I flaunted my circumstances proudly in hopes you
would go away. I couldn't go back and change things, I
couldn't reclaim a virtuous life, so I knew I could never be
with you. It was too late for that. The best thing would be a
clean break. So I made it easy for you to leave."

"And set me on a new course."

"Did I?"

"You planted a new level of ambition in me. I was determined to prove that I would never stoop to . . . well, that I could make a fortune without, um, compromising my honor. I even found myself a rich wife." He shrugged. "I doubt I'd have married in such an all-fired hurry if I hadn't still been smarting from learning you'd become some other man's mistress."

He spoke of the artist, James Benedict, but they both knew he meant more than that. Dear Sam, he still could not bring himself to name what she'd truly been. But she had never imagined that her career had pushed him into marriage.

"It was not a love match, then?" she asked.

"Not at first, but it was a good match. Her father was a planter in the West Indies where I'd spent a lot of time. Somehow I managed to convince him that I had a bright future and would be a worthy husband to his daughter. She was a pretty girl, and I was very fond of her. That affection grew into something deeper over time. I loved her. She was a good woman, my Sarah." Sam smiled wistfully, and Wilhelmina knew he still felt her loss.

"You sent for me, Your Grace?" Smeaton stood at attention beside the alcove, awaiting her pleasure. He held a small silver tray with her traveling writing set and a sheet of paper. The writing case was open, and a silver nib was screwed onto the slender sterling pen, ready to use.

Wilhelmina turned to Sam, reluctantly drawing her hand away from his. "If you will excuse me for a moment, Sam, I will just write a quick note." She nodded for Smeaton to place the tray on the table. He did so, then took the two steps back down and waited stoically, never giving away any hint of surprise that she had made such an odd request.

Covering the sheet with her arm so the words could not be

seen, she scribbled a few lines, blew on it, folded the sheet in half, and held it out for Smeaton. "Please take care of this for me."

He stepped back up to the table, retrieved the tray and the note, and said, "Will that be all, Your Grace?"

"Yes, Smeaton. I will leave all the arrangements in your capable hands."

"Your Grace." He bowed sharply and took his leave.

"I've seen that face before," Sam said, his gaze following Smeaton out of the room.

"He acts as my butler in London. Perhaps you remember him from the time you came to visit me there."

"Ah yes, when I was on leave in '99, when all London was still basking in our victory at Aboukir Bay six months before."

"Considering our previous encounter, you could have knocked me over with a feather when Smeaton gave me your name."

He lifted his hands in a helpless gesture. "I'm not sure why I came. I had seen you from a distance at a reception for Nelson, and some imp of mischief compelled me to see you again. To show you how I'd prospered."

"You lost no time in telling me about your lady wife."

"I will confess to you, Willie, that it pained me to see you again, and to see you with no less than a duke on your arm. I thought how equally ambitious we were, you and me. My competitive nature compelled me to boast to you of my successes: my fortune, my rise in the ranks on display in the white lapels of my new lieutenant's uniform, my new home in Sussex, my rich wife, and my strapping son."

"It pained me, too, Sam, to see you again. And to hear of your wife and son. Oh yes, that was a blow. I kept thinking how it might have been me, tucked away on that Sussex estate with you."

"You did?"

"But I quickly realized it would never have been like that for us. If you hadn't been taken by that press gang, we'd have carried on as planned, living in a one-room cottage near the sea with a slate roof, no glass in the windows, and the constant smell of fish permeating the stone walls. Neither of us would have found our fortunes. I was as determined in the competition as you, Sam, determined to show that I had reached higher. And so I flaunted my jewels and my duke. And more."

"And the last time I saw you . . ." He paused, and a pained look crossed his face. "I was back home for a long stretch, and both our lives had taken new turns. I was widowed and you had married your duke."

"We've come a long way," she said, "on our separate paths. At sixteen, I could never have imagined this life, where I have rank and fortune and want for nothing."

"Yes, it's ironic, is it not? That a dreaded press gang should change both our lives for the better?"

Chapter Three

Sam glanced out the window and was astonished to see sunshine. When had the rain stopped? He'd been so entranced with Willie that he hadn't noticed. God, it was good to see her again, and finally to speak of all the things that had kept them apart. It had been almost twenty-five years since they'd spoken at such length. Yet somehow, despite all that had happened, despite the opposite paths their lives had taken, despite hateful words spoken by both of them long ago, they had fallen into easy conversation as though they'd never been estranged, getting through even the most painful subjects without constraint. Like old times.

Perhaps their lives had come full circle, and with the wisdom of age and the forgiveness of time they could now be together again. At last. They were both unmarried. And the air between them crackled with unspoken desire. It was almost as though it was meant to be, their meeting like this.

Except that it could not be. Some sadistic fate had brought them together just at a time when he was not entirely free. If it was not so cruel, it would be laughable.

But Sam was not laughing.

"The rain has stopped. I'm afraid I must be on my way." He rose from the bench, reached for his greatcoat and hat on a nearby peg, then walked around the table to Willie's side. He lifted her hand from where it rested on the table, took it to his lips again, and then kept hold of it while he spoke. "It has been an unexpected pleasure, Willie, and absolutely splendid to see you again. I don't get to London often, so we may not run into each other for another ten years, who knows? But I wish you well, my girl." The old endearment came easily to his lips, which brushed her hand once more before releasing it.

A frown puckered her brow. "Must you leave? It has been such a long time since I've seen you and there is so much to catch up on. So much more to say. Could we not share a dinner? For old times' sake?"

The look on her face almost made him change his plans. That, and the way her fingers touched the edge of her neckline, drawing his eyes to the soft swell of her bosom. Was she flirting with him, trying to seduce him into staying? The very idea made his groin tighten, and his heart pitch and roll in his chest like a sloop in a high wind. He forced himself to say, "I'm afraid I cannot stay. I am expected at the home of friends, only a few hours north, near Clophill. I can get there before dusk if I set out now."

"Surely they will not mind if you are late." Her fingers continued to play with the lace at her bosom. "They will understand that the rain delayed you."

He looked down and brushed a speck of lint from his sleeve, unable to meet her blue eyes. "I am expected," he said. "Expected to . . ." His voice trailed off, and he gave a shrug. "I'm sorry, Willie, but I must go."

"They must be very important friends that you are so determined not to disappoint them."

He did not look up, and an awkward silence fell between

them. Their easy camaraderie was gone. Damn. He might as well tell her the truth and be done with it.

Finally, he said, "They are a family I got to know while in the East Indies. John Fullbrook was chief aide to the governor of Penang, but has retired to his family estate in Bedfordshire, near Clophill. His son is a good friend, Captain Fullbrook of the *Valiant*. And . . . there is a daughter. Mary."

"Ah." She gave him a rueful smile. "So you are to marry again?"

He shook his head. "I don't know. Perhaps. It is, I believe, expected. It is why I have been invited."

"You sound reluctant. Not exactly the eager bridegroom."

"No, I am ready to make an offer. Mary is a fine woman. And I have been alone these eleven years. With the wars over, I am content to settle down in Sussex and get to know my land. I am ready to be married again."

"Well, then. I must wish you happy."

"I haven't made an offer yet, Willie."

"Then I wish you luck."

He smiled sheepishly. "Thank you."

"May I walk out with you? I'd like to enjoy a bit of sunshine after such a gloomy day."

"Of course. Though it's likely to be muddy. And chilly."

"I'll dash upstairs for a shawl and my old half boots. They are not remotely stylish, I warn you, but eminently practical and impervious to mud. Perhaps I'll have a walk about the village after I wave good-bye as you drive away."

He backed down the steps and held his hand out to her. She took it and allowed him to guide her to the main floor. When they stood together beside the alcove, mere inches apart, he suddenly realized—or remembered—how small she was. The top of her head barely reached his shoulder. It somehow made her seem younger, as though she was still that sweet girl in Cornwall. Except that she smelled like a woman. She wore a spicy, slightly musky fragrance that reminded him of some of the exotic plants he'd seen in the East Indies. For an instant, he wanted to wrap himself up in that fragrance, to taste it on her skin.

It was a good thing he was leaving. Sam was very close to making a fool of himself. Again.

Instead, he gave her his arm and escorted her out of the public room, which was only half filled now. He'd been so wrapped up in Willie that he hadn't noticed how many customers had left.

"I'll only be a few minutes," she said when she left him at the bottom of the stairs. "I'll look for you in the yard."

Sam shrugged into his greatcoat, put on the cocked hat he still wore even when not in uniform, and walked outside. The main entrance to the Blue Boar opened onto the inn yard, just beyond the arched carriage entrance. His boots scrunched in the wet gravel of the yard as he made his way toward the stables in the rear.

His curricle was one of several vehicles parked beneath a long, simple, open-front structure beside the stables that served as a carriage house. Two ostlers were standing nearby, one of them gesturing at Sam's curricle.

"Look lively, lads," Sam said in his booming quarterdeck voice as he approached. "I need this rig made ready to go. If you'll be so good as to harness my team, I need to be on my way."

One of the ostlers touched his cap and said, "Clemmons, at yer service, Cap'n. This here be yer curricle?"

"It is. Now, if you'll see to bringing 'round the horses, I'd appreciate getting this ship ready to sail."

"Beggin' yer pardon, Cap'n," the ostler said, "but you got yerself a problem here."

"What problem?"

"Me and Jim, here, was just talkin' 'bout it. Looks like

yer left wheel's broke. See, this here spoke is clean split from the hub, and the next one be loose. Can't put no weight on this wheel without bringin' the whole carriage down."

Sam bent to examine the wheel. Damn and blast. The wheel was shot. The ostler was right; there was no way it could be used. "How in the name of Old Harry did this happen while I was inside tipping a tankard? The wheel was fine when I drove in."

"Yer sure 'bout that, Cap'n?" Clemmons asked. "Might've come loose when it hit a rut. Roads here 'bouts get right pockety with the rain."

That was certainly true. He'd had the devil of time nego-tiating ruts and potholes along the last stretch of muddy road, and once or twice had taken a fairly hard bounce. It had been pouring buckets when he turned into the Blue Boar's yard, and he'd flung the reins to an ostler while he dashed inside. He might not have noticed anything wrong in his haste to get out of the rain. But it wasn't like him not to notice something as obvious as a broken wheel. He rather suspected it was one of the ostlers who'd been too rough in handling the curricle in the flurry of activity that brought so much unexpected custom to the stables.

"I suppose it must have been a rut," Sam said, skewering both men with a glare that had sent many a midshipmen scurrying with fear, "though I still find it hard to imagine how I didn't notice the wheel had split."

"Happens often enough, Cap'n," the second ostler, Jim, said as he tested the other spokes. "Most folk don't notice nothin' till it's too late an' the carriage turns 'em top over tail. It's lucky we noticed it afore yer drove off an' tossed yerself in a ditch."

"Yes, well, I thank you for your keen eye. Now, what—"

"We can get it fixed up fer yer right an' tight in no time," Jim said. "Wheelwright's just across the green. I'll take it over meself and have a couple o' new spokes fitted up. Shouldn't take long."

Sam tossed him a few coins and thanked him. Another delay meant he would likely not reach Clophill until after sunset, but it couldn't be helped. He turned to walk back to the inn, and when he entered the yard saw Willie coming toward him, wrapped in a large Paisley shawl and wearing sturdy brown boots that somehow managed to look fashionable on her. She smiled as she stepped carefully on the slippery gravel, and there was something about that smile and the way her eyes seemed to dance with mischief—another flash of the Cornish girl lurking beneath the worldly sophisticate.

"You are looking at me with the oddest expression," she said when he reached her side.

"Because you remind me of a girl I once knew."

She laughed and cocked her head to one side, peeking up at him from beneath the brim of her bonnet. "Was she pretty, this girl?"

"The prettiest girl I ever saw. She was beautiful. And still is."

"Sam! You will make me blush. At my age. But where is your carriage? I have come to see you off."

"You will have to wait a bit. It seems I've got a broken wheel and it must be repaired."

"Oh, what a bother. But at least we can spend a bit more time together. That is, if you're not bored to death with me already."

He took her hand and tucked it in the crook of his elbow. "I shall contrive to stay awake if you will walk with me a while. Since we're both dressed for outdoors, and the sun is shining again, let's see what Upper Hampden has to offer."

Wilhelmina bit back a smile as they strolled through the carriage way toward a small village green. She had hoped he

would stay. In fact, she hoped Sam would remain at the Blue
Boar for the night. She wasn't ready to give him up just yet. It
was selfish, to be sure, but, dear God, it was pure pleasure
just to look at him. And to remember those long-ago days in
Cornwall when she thought she would die for loving him.

But this was not the gangly youth she'd once known.
When he was a boy, Sam had grown tall seemingly overnight. Unaccustomed to his new long limbs, he was sometimes rawboned and clumsy in his movements. Now he had
impeccable posture and a sure-footed grace—no doubt a result of years of shifting his weight against the rolling decks
beneath him. And he had filled out rather nicely over the
years—broad-shouldered and solid. Just the way she liked a
man. In his greatcoat and hat, he was a large and formidable
presence. And sinfully attractive.

Wilhelmina never played games with herself where men
were concerned. There was no sense in denying it: She
wanted Sam. One night together might heal a world of hurt
between them. She could be honest with herself about it, but
she was not ready to be that forthright with him. If there was
any seducing to be done, Sam would have to take the lead.
She did not want him to see her as a seasoned courtesan,
skilled at seduction. That would only serve to reopen old
wounds. No, it would have to be a simple coming together of
a man and a woman who'd once loved each other.

They had made a good start today in coming to terms
with all that had torn them apart, and kept them apart, for so
many years. There was still much to be said, and, God and
Smeaton willing, time to say it. Afterward, if they gave in
to a mutual attraction—and there was no doubt it was mutual; no one knew how to read a man's interest better than
Wilhelmina—it would be a final act of healing. A closing of
the circle of their lives.

Then he could go off to his Miss Fullbrook and make his
offer.

In the meantime, she would enjoy being at his side, having her arm in his, as they explored what little there was to see in the tiny hamlet of Upper Hampden.

It was a pretty, picturesque village enveloped on all sides by dense woodlands, now brilliant with the colors of autumn. Houses were scattered in clusters off the central green, mostly black and white half timbered, some with thatched roofs, some with red tile. An ancient weather-beaten cross stood in the center of the green, flanked by two enormous beech trees, their bright red and darker orange leaves spreading in wide masses of graceful branches over the green.

They spoke of inconsequential matters as they walked past a bakery, a cobbler, a blacksmith, a grocer. They spoke of favorite books and plays as they wandered out to a nearby mill, sidestepping puddles and mud, and of Sam's travels as they entered the lych-gate of St. Mary's, the broach-spired old church at the north end of the village.

Wilhelmina found tales of Sam's life at sea fascinating, and realized that having been impressed, which must have been frightening and frustrating, had ultimately been the making of him. "You speak with such pleasure about your days aboard ship," she said as they meandered through the churchyard. "But it cannot have always been enjoyable. There must have been rough times as well, dangerous times."

"Yes, there were days when I'd have rather been almost anywhere else. During illness, which is never easy on ship, or when stores ran low and we dined on ship delicacies you'd rather not know about. Or during heavy storms when it seemed you'd be pitched clear off the deck, never to be seen again. Or during battle, when the shuddering report of guns made your ears ring for hours afterward, and the powder and smoke threatened to choke you. But for the most part, I felt at home on board ship. It was hard work and rough living, but I thrived on it."

"I suppose, then, that press gang was a blessing after all. It gave you a life you'd never have known otherwise."

"That's true. Years later, I would thank them for taking me, though at the time, I could not have been more wretched. I thought I'd landed in a nightmare."

"Poor Sam." She squeezed his arm, and he brought his hand to rest over hers. "But you managed to survive. You were stubborn enough in those days that I imagine you forced yourself to make the best of it."

He nodded. "In those early days, when the misery of the lower decks was something I could never have imagined, it was pure dogged determination that kept me going. There were more than a few villainous characters among the crew, each of them ready to make a new boy's life a living horror. But I ignored them, and occasionally stood up to them, and they finally left me alone. Many boys younger than me, much younger, would shinny up masts with the ease of monkeys during the days and at night were slung shoulder to shoulder in narrow hammocks, like bats hanging from the rafters. None of them complained, and neither did I. It's astonishing, really, how quickly one can adapt to conditions so alien. Within a month, I was perfectly at home on board. Soon enough, I found I actually liked it."

He stopped walking and turned to face her. "And while some other pressed men deserted at the first opportunity, I never once thought of bolting. As much as I missed you, I had my honor. I couldn't abide the idea of presenting myself to you as a deserter."

"How disappointed you must have been to learn how easily I had discarded honor while you held on to yours so tightly."

"Willie. Stop berating yourself."

"But it is true, is it not? I will never forget the look on your face when I first saw you after thinking you dead. Shocked disappointment, and anger, was writ clear in your eyes." And in his words.

"It was not only that, Willie. I reacted in anger, to be sure, but inside my heart was breaking. I had been at sea many years by then and seen my share of . . . of women who sell themselves to men. I hated to think of you as one of them."

"I wasn't, Sam." No, she had never been a common whore. She'd been much more exclusive.

"I know you weren't. But at the time, it was an image I could not get out of my mind. Whenever we were in port, whores showed up in droves. The dock whores love a sailor on shore leave. They know as well as anyone that a sailor with a bit of prize money in his pocket will spend the lot of it on drink and women before the night is through. So whenever we dropped anchor in port, they massed on the docks, ready to take their share."

He frowned and looked over her shoulder into the distance as he spoke, as if he could still see those wretched women. "Sometimes they didn't even wait on shore, but took boats out to the ships—large boats filled to bursting with a cargo of doxies. Mind you, some of the men had been at sea as long as eighteen months and seen almost no females. The sight of those boats caused a general furor as seamen scampered down the ropes and brought the women up to ply their wares on shipboard. It was never a pretty sight. Poor, ignorant, desperate women who'd long ago discarded shame or modesty."

He returned his gaze to her, those golden-brown eyes filled with sorrow. "When I heard you'd taken up the trade, all I could think of was those horrid, coarse, pathetic women who'd tup the oldest tar to the youngest third-class boy and everyone in between within the span of a few hours."

"It was never like that for me, Sam." Her voice was barely a whisper. "I promise you, it was never like that."

"I know. But it was the first thing that entered my foolish head, so you can imagine how upset I was, to imagine you in a similar situation. I hated to think that you had become that desperate."

"I never was."

"I know. Forgive me, my girl. It was a long time ago and I was a foolish, heartsick youth." Sam looked down at her troubled face and wondered if she would ever tell him the truth of how she started her career as a demirep. It was none of his business, but he'd always wanted to know.

He retook possession of her hand and tucked it back in the crook of his arm. "Come. There were a couple of old stone benches on the village green. Let's go park ourselves on one and enjoy the rest of the day's sunshine."

Walking together in companionable silence through the churchyard and down the high street toward the green brought back sharp memories of long-ago walks along the Porthruan shore and the cliffs above the cove, when a smile or the squeeze of a hand was all that was needed to feel utterly content. All at once a vision came to mind of him and Willie—not the sixteen-year-old girl, but this Willie, the mature, beautiful, sensual woman at his side—walking over the grounds of his estate in Sussex. The idea taunted him like the hint of a sail in the distance blinking in and out of the mist, beyond his reach, and with it came a pang of longing that he quickly checked. Even if there could be a future for them—as unlikely a notion as ever entered his head— Willie was a creature of Town, one who'd known dukes and princes and prime ministers. She would never be content in an isolated country house with a mere post captain. He must remember that and stop spinning fantasies.

Besides, despite his wish for it to be otherwise, this Willie—Wilhelmina—was not someone he knew. Though there were still occasional haunting flashes of the young Willie, this woman was virtually a stranger—self-possessed, shrewd, knowing. And damned desirable.

When they'd reached the green, Sam removed his great-coat and spread it over a stone bench, still damp from the rain. After they were seated, Willie was the first to break their long silence. "I'm sorry, Sam," she said, placing a hand over his, "but I still feel badly about that heartsick young man. I'm sorry I hurt you. I want you to know that."

He lifted her hand to his lips and kissed it. "I know, my girl. It was just that I'd thought of you as mine. I'd been very possessive of that memory of your father's hayloft."

When he had sought her out at the theater that first time, back in '94, that sense of possession had driven him to believe she could not be what the rumors claimed. But everything changed the instant he saw her surrounded by her court of admirers.

He'd been surprised at her looks. She'd been only twenty-one, but looked older. Not in a haggard way. No, she had still been beautiful, take-your-breath-away beautiful. But all hint of graceless youth, of girlish roundness, was gone, replaced by a willowy slenderness that brought out the strength of her features: the high cheekbones, the straight nose, the elegant curve of jaw set upon the slim white column of her neck. And more than the physical change, the inevitable casting off of youth, was the expression in her face. Worldly. Sophisticated. Smart. It suited her, and certainly suited her chosen profession. The girl he'd left behind had become a woman. Almost too much of a woman. She was not his Willie anymore. She'd even somehow managed to lose every hint of Cornwall in her voice. She was a lady of London now. The notorious Wilhelmina. And no longer his.

"I could see all those memories of Cornwall, and a hayloft, beneath the anger in your eyes," she said. "The same memories flooded through me at that moment, I assure you. But I sent you away with my show of disdain and hoped never to endure that pain of regret again, hoped that you would stay away." She laughed softly. "And then five years later, you showed up on my doorstep. The proud lieutenant."

Sam joined her rueful laughter. It really was an embarrassing memory. He never quite knew why he'd gone to see her.

"There I was, shoe buckles sparkling, Nile medal gleaming on my chest, dressed for a king's levee and standing in line at your door with a dozen other hopeful chaps clamoring to be allowed in. Finally, when that damned fearsome beast of yours let me enter—"

"Smeaton. He's very protective. But when he said there was a Lieutenant Samuel Pellow who wished to see me— well, my heart leapt a little at the thought of seeing you again. I convinced Smeaton to let you in, though he would have preferred to toss you down the front steps, thinking a mere lieutenant beneath my notice. But I longed to see you, despite our less than friendly encounter years before, and asked to have you shown in to my private sitting room."

"My fellow suppliants at the front door were green with envy when that hatchet-faced butler led me inside. And I followed him past rooms filled with well-dressed gents who I knew in my gut, though I did not know any of them by sight, were some of the highest men in the realm. Beautiful girls in dresses that left little to the imagination sat with them in animated conversation, or more. When I happened to see Admiral Blackwood with a plump little blonde on his lap, I almost turned and bolted. I didn't like to think of you in such surroundings, but it was in fact what I'd come to see. To reassure myself that you had turned out badly and I was better off with my Sarah.

"But then there you were, ensconced on a chaise like an odalisque, looking beautiful and sophisticated and far above my touch. Your Smeaton was right about that. I had come to gloat, and yet words dried up in my throat and I did not know what to say."

"Your first blurted words, as I recall, were: 'I am married and have a son.'"

Sam groaned. "I can't imagine what you must have thought of me, the perfect idiot. I was no longer a callow youth, and ought to have had more finesse. Better yet, I ought to have stayed away. But I had come to gloat, after all, so I just launched into my speech without preamble."

"And I accused you of coming there to be unfaithful to that wife I'd just learned about. I can't imagine what you must have thought of *me*, saying such a hateful thing as that."

"We both drew our lines in the sand that day," Sam said, "establishing clearly who we were and the very different lives we led. You knew exactly what you were doing, Willie, establishing boundaries between us. I figured that out much later, and realized that you were a wiser person than I'd ever be. And despite pretending to despise your life, I found I admired you." And even still loved her a little.

"Did you, Sam? Oh, I am so glad you told me. It means a lot to know you haven't been hating me all these years."

No, he hadn't hated her. Never that. Sam had seen Wilhelmina casually a few more times after that meeting at her salon in '99. Whenever he came up to London to visit the Admiralty or take care of other business, he always heard of her and sometimes ran into her at a social function. Once, after he'd exchanged a few polite words with her at a rout party, several of his fellow officers teased him, wondering why he never mentioned that he knew the infamous Wilhelmina Grant and wanting to know all about her. He skirted their questions and said little. He kept to himself the fact that he'd never known the great courtesan, but had once loved the blacksmith's daughter.

"I could never hate you, my girl." He kissed her hand again, and she gave him a smile that shot right through to his vitals. It emboldened him and, without thinking or giving himself time to change his mind, he bent his head and kissed her on the mouth. It was a simple kiss, nothing elaborate, but the sensation of his lips on hers, on the lips of the girl he'd loved, finally, after all these years, was filled with a sweet poignancy that made him feel young again.

He put his arms around her and deepened the kiss. Her lips parted beneath his, and he savored the strangely familiar warmth of her mouth. When he lifted his head, she looked at him with eyes wide with wonder. Had she, too, been momentarily transported back more than twenty years?

He trailed a knuckle along her jaw. "Never think that I have hated you, Willie. You will always be special to me. My first love."

"You have surprised me, Sam."

"By kissing you?" He smiled. "Let's just say it was for old times' sake."

"For old times." She moved out of his arms. "Thank you, Sam. You have relieved my mind. I did think you had hated me. I never thought you would be able to get beyond the life I led, to forget who I'd become."

"Oh, I never forgot," he said, shooting her a grin. "How could I when your every move was reported? I heard rumors . . ."

She sighed and scooted farther away on the bench. "I have no doubt of it."

"It was said that even the Prince of Wales—"

She rolled her eyes. "I have been the object of rumor and gossip since I was sixteen. I long ago stopped listening. Or commenting. I am quite certain that many of the rumors you heard are true. Or based on truth. But I am equally certain that just as many of them are pure invention. People love to spread tales of women like me, whether they are true or not. You may choose to believe what you want, Sam. I will not go down a list with you and say yes to this one and no to that one."

"Fair enough. It is none of my business, in any case."

"Because of what we once meant to each other, I will tell you about two of the men in my life. The two men who changed my life."

"Really, my girl, you need not tell me anything."

She dismissed his concern with a wave of her hand. "No, I want to. But I will only tell you of two men and no more. The first was James Benedict, who was touring the West Country coast when he found his way to Porthruan in '89, shortly after you went missing. He was a member of the Royal Academy and had come to paint the sea and the cliffs and the Cornish sunlight. He always said we had our own special kind of light in Cornwall."

"Pixie light."

"That's what I told him. He always painted outside, even when he painted people. Whether portraits or allegorical paintings, he most liked to paint faces, and he took a liking to mine."

"How could he not?"

Willie smiled at his flattery, then continued. "He paid me to pose for him, and he did a series of classical allegories where I was depicted as each of the nine Muses as well as various goddesses. It was easy work and I liked having my own money, which I tucked away without telling Mama. But most of all, James was kind to me at the lowest point of my young life. I was heartbroken and adrift, having lost all purpose when I lost you."

She paused and took a slow, deep breath before she went on. A frown puckered her brow. "Mama found out about the posing, of course, and raised the roof. She railed and railed against my sinful ways. Papa seemed more sympathetic at first, but he was never a match for Mama's temper, or her Methodist morality, so he did not fight her when she cast me out."

"She really threw you out of the house?"

"Yes. A girl who posed for pictures, even with all her clothes on, had no place in the pious Jepp household. I went crying to James, and he said he'd take care of me. I was to return to London with him where he would make a proper artist's model of me. I jumped at the chance to escape

Porthruan Cove, which had too many memories of you. So
I went to London, and my life changed forever. Even my
name changed. I became Wilhelmina Grant. James's paintings of me drew a lot of praise for his talent, as well as a
great deal of attention to me. Suddenly I was an object of
interest for many gentlemen, several of them members of
the nobility."

Sam knew those paintings well. One in particular, he
knew very well indeed. "I saw some of Benedict's paintings when I first came to London to find you, back in '94.
They were beautiful. You were as luminous as moonlight on
a dark sea."

Willie nodded. "They brought him a great deal of notice.
After the allegories of the Muses were exhibited, commissions
began to pour in. And I drew more interest as the model, and
not just from other artists. I did not enjoy all that attention, I
assure you. I thought it would anger James, and I was fiercely
loyal to him. But one day he came to me and said that a certain gentleman was prepared to become my protector, that
he would set me up in style, that I would have everything I
ever wanted. When I demurred, he said I had to go, that he
could no longer keep me. I soon discovered that James had
passed me on to this new gentleman in order to secure
several very important commissions. It was only then that I
realized I had never meant anything to James, except as a
face he liked to paint. It was my first lesson in the life of the
demimonde. I left James without a backward glance, and
began my notorious career."

At last he knew how it had begun. It was sad, but not sordid. "I'm sorry, Willie."

"Don't be. I may not have led what most people would
call a respectable life, but I prided myself on being selective.
And expensive. I became rich, and was courted by some of
the highest gentlemen in the land. I established a salon
where I entertained artists and poets and politicians, and

invitations were prized. It was an exciting life. I have no regrets."

"And who was the second man who changed your life?"

"Hertford, of course. He pursued me for quite a long time before I gave in to him. He wanted exclusivity, and I was not willing to grant it at first. But he was so ardent, and so charming, that I soon capitulated. We spent a few happy years together, during which I was publicly acknowledged as his mistress. He loved me, the duke did. He truly loved me." She spoke as though she still could not believe it, as though she was not worthy of a good man's love. "But when his wife died and he asked me to marry him, I thought he'd gone mad. But he was quite serious. He was determined to legitimize our love affair. How could I refuse such a magnanimous, extraordinary offer? So I bid farewell to the demimonde and became a duchess."

"Did you love him?"

"The dear man laid the whole world at my feet. He cared more for me than for what people would think of him. Of course I loved him."

"Were there . . . difficulties? Socially, I mean."

"Was I accepted in society? Not entirely. I never will be. But I had rank and fortune that could not be denied, and many doors were opened to me, sometimes reluctantly, sometimes with kindness. I have made wonderful friends who accept me, unsavory past and all, and that has given me the greatest happiness."

It was an extraordinary story. Sam was glad she had told him, at last. He understood her now, he thought, and admired her more than ever.

"How has life been for you since the duke passed away? What have you been doing? Not sitting home in your widow's weeds, I have no doubt."

"No, I have been out of full mourning for over three years. I still enjoy being out with people, and keep a very full social calendar. But I do some charity work as well. I'm a trustee of the Benevolent Widows' Fund, which has been a gratifying experience for me, in so many ways. I found some of my dearest friends in working with the Fund, high-ranking, respectable ladies who never once showed scorn for my low birth and notorious career. I was just visiting one of them, Lady Thayne, in Northamptonshire. She recently presented her marquess with a healthy baby boy, and I have just come from the christening. Can you imagine: I was the god-mother!"

"Godmother to a future marquess? Good God, Willie, you really have changed your life around. And charity work? How noble of you, my girl. And what else?"

She arched an elegant eyebrow. "*Who* else, do you mean? Still judging me, Sam?"

"No, no, I was just wondering if . . ." He hunched a shoulder and shook his head, never finishing his thought aloud. The thought she had read so clearly.

"You want to know if there is another man in my life."

He flashed a sheepish grin. "You can't blame a fellow for being curious. You're still a damned fine-looking woman, Duchess. There must be gallants of all ages cluttering your doorstep."

Her eyes narrowed. "Just like that time you came to call and elbowed your way to the front of the line?"

"No, I didn't mean that. I know you are not in that life anymore. But that doesn't mean all the men of London have been struck blind. You will always draw the appreciative glance, Willie. And more, I should think."

She smiled again and said, "Such blatant flattery, Sam. No, don't apologize. I like it. I will confess that it pleases me all the more because it comes from you. And no, I have not led the life of a nun, as you well know. But I am older now and find that I quite enjoy my own company. I no longer feel the constant need for a man at my side. Or in my bed. There have been one or two since Hertford's death. The last one was so besotted that I fully expected an offer from him—an offer of marriage—but it wasn't long before a younger, prettier woman caught his eye, and he fell out of love as quickly as he'd fallen in."

"I'm sorry, Willie."

"Don't be. It was a fling, nothing more. I would never have married him."

A fling. She had the occasional fling. But would she want to have one with him?

Sam wondered where the devil that idea had come from, and quickly put it out of his mind. It must have been that kiss. He ought never to have kissed her. He was on his way to make an offer to Mary Fullbrook that very evening. Now was not the time to be kissing another woman and thinking of flings, even for old times' sake.

And yet . . .

Chapter Four

A movement across the square caught Wilhelmina's eye, and she looked up to see a man rolling a wheel toward the Blue Boar. It must be Sam's wheel. Damnation. So soon? Things were going so well between them—he had kissed her!—and she hated to think of him leaving now.

Sam noticed the wheel, too, and said, "Ah, no doubt that is mine. It must have been an easy repair to be done in just over an hour. We should head back to the inn so I can be on my way to Clophill at last."

"And Miss Fullbrook."

"Her, too." He stood and took her hand to help her up, then frowned at the greatcoat they'd been sitting on.

"Oh dear," she said. "I hope it is not ruined."

He picked it up and shook it out. "No, it has been through worse. Just a bit creased here and there, nothing serious." He did not put it on, though, but draped it over one arm instead, offering the other to her.

"I've enjoyed our afternoon, Sam," she said as they walked back to the inn. "Are you sure you cannot stay? We could have dinner together. I do not have high hopes for the food, but the company would be welcome."

"Ah, Willie, I wish I could. It has been a delightful surprise to see you again, and finally to have a chance to talk with you, really talk, not just polite conversation. But I am expected at Clophill. I am late enough as it is. I'm sorry, my girl."

For the merest instant, she had an urge to plead with him to stay, but she did not wish to appear so abjectly, and uncharacteristically, needy. The broken wheel had been a blessing, the perfect excuse to keep him with her a little bit longer. But there was nothing now to stop him from leaving. She forced a smile and kept her voice even. "No need to apologize. You must not disappoint Miss Fullbrook and her parents."

She accompanied him to the stables, skirting puddles of mud that had been churned up by the tracks of carriages, creating a crisscross of deep ruts in the yard. Wilhelmina almost slipped more than once, and held on tightly to Sam's arm.

One of the ostlers stood with the wheelwright, examining the wheel. Sam released her arm and walked over to join the two men. "Is it ready to go?"

"Yes, it's good as new, Cap'n. We can—" The ostler stopped, his eyes grew wide, then angry. Raising his voice, he shouted, "Benjie Lovitt, yer young fool, get them animals outa my yard!"

Just then, two enormous pigs came running into the stable yard, with more speed than one would expect from such behemoths—and on muddy ground, too—followed by a young boy waving and shouting for them to stop. Wilhelmina barely had time to form the thought that mud was apparently second nature to the pigs when one of them came to a screeching, sliding halt, smack into Sam's wheel, knocking it to the ground, then crushing it beneath its hooves as the pig stepped over it. His porcine partner in crime simultaneously plowed straight into Sam, knocking him off balance so that he lost his footing and fell backward on his bum.

It had happened so fast, Sam seemed stunned speechless as he sat in the mud, his eyes round with disbelief. Wilhelmina pressed a hand to her mouth to hide the laughter that threatened to overtake her. The ostler continued to yell at the boy, who continued to yell at his pigs as he tried to round them up, though they seemed more interested in exploring the carriages lined up in the yard. The wheelwright began cursing about the state of the wheel he'd taken such care to repair. Every ostler and stable boy came out to see what all the commotion was about, some of them shouting at the boy, some trying to help him control the pigs, and others doubled over in laughter. And Grissom came running out from the inn yard, arms flapping, aghast to find his customer in the mud, and began shouting at all and sundry for causing harm to the good captain.

It was a scene straight out of a farce, Wilhelmina thought. Or a Hogarth painting.

"Get those bloody animals away from my curricle before they do any more damage!" Sam's booming voice finally brought a halt to all the shouting. Seated in his mud puddle, he bellowed out orders to the boy, the ostler, and the wheelwright, in an authoritative voice that brooked no reproach, making it clear he was not amused, and that they had better look sharp in rectifying the situation.

Wilhelmina thought this must have been what it was like to be dressed down on the quarterdeck by Captain Pellow. What a formidable man her Sam had become. Formidably desirable, even plopped down in the mud.

Grissom helped Sam to his feet and launched into a stream of obsequious apologies. Sam dismissed them with a wave of his hand as he gazed down in disgust at his ruined pantaloons and coattails. Finally, he looked up and caught Wilhelmina's eye. Her hand still covered her mouth, for she was having trouble suppressing the mirth that gurgled up from her throat. Sam glanced down again at his mud-covered clothes, then back up at Wilhelmina, and broke into laughter. That was all she needed for her own merriment to burst forth, and the two of them stood in the stable yard and laughed and laughed.

Grissom, his glance darting from one to the other, offered a tentative chuckle. When their laughter had eased a bit, the innkeeper jumped into the breach and said, "Come inside, Captain, and let's get you cleaned up. The wheel can be repaired again, though I'm told it will take longer this time since more spokes are broken and the rim is bent. Blasted pigs! Begging your pardon, Your Grace. It's getting on to dusk, so you'd better stay the night, sir. I'll see about a room for you and have Mrs. Grissom see to your clothes. We'll find you something clean to wear in the meantime."

Sam directed Grissom to retrieve his portmanteau from the boot of his curricle so he could change into his own clothes. Wilhelmina accompanied him back to the inn, where she found Smeaton in the hallway, eyebrows raised in question. Wilhelmina nodded and shot him a wink, then turned her attention to the innkeeper's wife, wild-eyed with outrage at what had happened, muttering under her breath about that wretched boy and his pigs. She offered to give up her own bedchamber for the captain, as there was only one small attic room available. But Sam would have none of that and accepted the tiny room with gratitude. "I am accustomed to cramped quarters on ship," he said, "so any hole in the attic will suit me fine."

Mrs. Grissom thanked him and took his muddied greatcoat and hat, promising to have them cleaned. "And I'll send up a chambermaid to take away your dirty clothes. We'll take care of 'em, don't you worry. You'll have 'em back all cleaned and dried by tomorrow morning. Now, if you'll follow me . . ."

Before heading off for his attic room, Sam turned to Wilhelmina and smiled. "Looks like I'll be able to share dinner with you after all."

"I'm glad, Sam." It was too soon to part. She wanted a few more hours with him. That was all. Just a few more hours. It was selfish of her, but there it was. Miss Fullbrook would have to wait another day for her offer. For tonight, Sam would belong to Wilhelmina. Or so she hoped.

Sam looked across the table, laden with platters of roast mutton, game hens, potatoes with butter sauce, pickled onions, French beans, and crusty bread. Mrs. Grissom had done her best to compensate for the mud and the pigs and the cramped attic room by making sure he did not also go hungry. Sam had dug into the hearty meal with relish, but noticed that the duchess ate very little.

"What's the matter, my girl?" he asked. "You do not like Mrs. Grissom's cooking? No doubt you have become accustomed to finer cuisine."

She looked up and smiled. "I employ a French chef who would swoon at the sight of that leg of mutton and those soupy potatoes. In fact, he often travels with me, but since we were visiting Lord and Lady Thayne, who keep an excellent chef, I sent him on a well-deserved holiday."

"And so you are forced to endure a plain meal without elegant French sauces or exotic seasoning. Poor Willie."

She laughed. "I am not so spoiled as all that. I can manage an indifferent meal from time to time. I'm just not very hungry."

"The food may seem indifferent to you, Your Grace, but after so many years of salt pork out of a beer keg and hardtack biscuits that could chip a tooth—once you'd first banged them on the table to chase out the weevils—I can assure you that a good English roast leg of mutton is nothing short of heaven to me."

His comment steered the conversation back to tales of Sam's life at sea, which seemed to fascinate her. Wilhelmina peppered him with questions throughout the meal, and even the grinding monotony of the blockade began to take on a more adventurous turn in the telling. She showed a particular interest in his rise through the ranks, something even she recognized as unusual for an impressed seaman.

"I had been sublieutenant until Aboukir Bay when more officers were needed," he said, slicing an apple into sections and offering her one. "I had the honor of serving as a full lieutenant in that great battle, under Captain Lewis of the—"

"The *Alexander.*"

His eyebrows lifted in surprise. "How do you know that?"

Willie clicked her tongue. "Really, Sam, do you think I do not read? The Battle of the Nile was second only to Trafalgar in importance. It was written about in great detail in all the newspapers and magazines. I even decorated my drawing room in the Egyptian style. It was all the rage."

"But how did you know that I served on the *Alexander*? Surely a pup of a lieutenant was not mentioned in the *Morning Chronicle.*"

"I saw your name in the navy lists."

He gazed at her in astonishment. "You read the lists?"

She smiled sheepishly. "I have followed your career ever since you showed up alive, and full of vinegar, that night at the theater, five years after I thought you'd died. I know you sailed on the *Alexander*, then the *Pegasus*, I believe. You were given command of the *Libra*, and one more I think, but the *Dartmoor* was your first post ship, as full captain. And your last ship was the *Cristobel.*"

Sam sat back and stared at her. "Well, I'll be damned."

"You see, I never forgot you, Sam. You carried a piece of my heart, whether you knew it or not, and I always liked to know where it was."

His own heart swelled a little and flooded him with warmth. "You never cease to surprise me, Willie. With your full life—the salons, the gaiety, the luxury—I never imagined you spared a thought for me."

"You have never been far from my thoughts, Sam. Just as you said earlier this afternoon, one never forgets one's first love."

Her words moved Sam more than she could possibly imagine, and the fact that she had followed his career so closely must mean that she still cared for him, even a little, despite all that had happened between them. But it was the way she looked at him when she said it, the melting heat in her eyes, that was almost his undoing.

He looked around at the other occupants of the room. A group of four men sat at one end of a long table, laughing and talking loudly, clanking their tankards together as they proceeded to get drunk. A quieter pair at the opposite end played a game of backgammon, and two elderly chaps had pulled chairs close to the hearth, where they sat and dozed. A middle-aged couple of matching stout proportions in one of the other alcoves silently shared a large currant pudding.

Sam and Willie had been private enough in their own alcove, but there were some things he wanted to say, and do, without the possibility of an audience. He could not in good conscience ask to go to her bedchamber, though God knew he wanted nothing more. Since his own room was little more than a garret with a narrow bed and a thin pallet, the best he could do was to take her outside, into the moonlight.

She accepted his invitation, and within a few minutes, under the bright full moon, they were seated on an old tomb in the churchyard where they had walked earlier. He wanted to kiss her again, but kept thinking of tomorrow and Miss Fullbrook and her family's expectations. But that was tomorrow. For tonight, he was with Willie. And she looked so beautiful in the moonlight that he was not sure he would be able to keep his hands off her.

Every time he'd seen her, even that first time when he was so furious and heartsick at how she had degraded herself, he'd still wanted her. He'd wanted to possess her, body and soul, just as he had at eighteen. But too many others had possessed her, and his pride—and pain—would not allow him even to consider it.

Until ten years ago, when he'd been prepared to toss aside all his fine scruples for her.

And here he was now, wanting her again, on fire for her again, and a whole new set of scruples niggled at the edges of his conscience. Those scruples kept him talking. Talking was safer than kissing. And so their conversation, which had continued with few interruptions since shortly after noon, the conversation that had been more than twenty years in the making, continued as they sat side by side on the tomb of some poor unknown soul.

"Tell me about Tom," she said.

He smiled, and was sure his pride gleamed bright in his eyes. "He's a wonderful boy. A young man, I should say. He's nineteen, and already a lieutenant making a name for himself in the lists. He was active in the blockades, and is now in the East Indies, the Java Sea."

"Do you see him often?"

"Not often enough. The problem with a naval career is that one is never in one place for very long. I missed so much of his childhood. After his mother died, he went to live with her sister's family in Somerset. But he was sea-mad even then, and bristled at being away from the shore. He wrote plaintive letters begging to be taken aboard ship, to train for a midshipman's berth. I finally capitulated when he was twelve. Within two years he was wearing a midshipman's jacket. And passed the lieutenant's exam when he was seventeen. His will be a more traditional career than my own. He will no doubt achieve admiral before he's forty."

She smiled wistfully. "You should see your face when you speak of him. You are such a proud papa."

He laughed. "I am indeed. He's a good son. A good-looking boy. As tall as me, though still too thin. All elbows and knees, long-legged and lanky."

"Just like his father was at that age."

Sam smiled and nodded. "He even has my coloring. Not a trace of poor Sarah in him, except now and then about the mouth. I wish we'd had more children, perhaps a daughter with Sarah's fair coloring. But it was not meant to be, I suppose. And what of you, Willie? Any children tucked away somewhere?"

Her face paled slightly, save for two bright splashes of color high on her cheeks, and he felt her stiffen beside him. A frown marked her brow, and Sam knew he had said the wrong thing. They had once talked, in the way young lovers do, of having a brood of perfect children, pretty little girls and mischievous boys. Willie had wanted children. But perhaps she had discovered she was barren. Or had lost a child. Or, because a child would have been an inconvenience in her style of life, she might have had children and given them away to be raised by others. Whatever the reason, he had certainly trod on unwelcome ground. Damnation. He would have bitten off his tongue if he could, for he might have just ruined a near-perfect evening with his clumsy inquiry.

"I'm sorry, Willie. I should not have asked. It is none of my business. Let us talk of other things. Tell me about this charity you're so involved with."

Uneasiness showed in the tightening of her jaw and the nervous fidgeting of her hands. She held her mouth in a grim line for a long, uncomfortably silent moment, and then, in a voice barely above a whisper, said, "I had a child, once."

Ah, Willie. Had?

"But she was born early and did not live even an hour."

"I'm so sorry, Willie."

"I named her Samantha."

He suddenly felt the blood drain from his face, and his throat went dry. "Samantha?" he choked.

"After her father."

He buckled, as though punched in the stomach, and a sound like a wail poured out of him. "Noooooo. Oh no, Willie, my love. It was our child?"

She nodded.

"Oh God." He wrapped his arms around his waist as though to hold in the pain. "That's why you left Porthruan, isn't it? That's why your mother chucked you out of her house? Because you were pregnant with my child."

She nodded again.

He grabbed her roughly into his arms, buried his face against her neck, and held her tight. For several long moments, they each gave in to pain and grief—silent, sorrowful, heartbreaking grief for a child whose death they ought to have mourned together twenty-four years ago.

And Sam grieved for more than the loss of a child. Against the smooth skin of her neck, he muttered, "It pains me that you went through all that alone, Willie. I wish more than anything that I had been with you, that I could have shared the burden of grief with you."

"I wanted that baby so much," she whispered, "for it was all I would ever have of you. To lose her so soon after losing you was almost more than I could bear."

"And because you had lain with me, because I made you with child, you were thrown out into the world without resources. Ah, Willie. No wonder you took the course you did."

She lifted her head from his shoulder and backed away slightly so that he had to loosen his arms. But he did not let go. He wasn't ready to let her go.

"Do not blame yourself for my scandalous career, Sam. It was my choice to become a demirep. When I recovered—it was a difficult, premature birth that might have killed me if I hadn't been so young and healthy—I clung to James as the only friend I had in the world. He had been kind to me, extraordinarily kind, and I repaid him by becoming his mistress. There was no turning back after that."

"But you would never have been forced to make that choice if I hadn't seduced you in that damned hayloft."

"It was a mutual seduction, as I recall. I was a very willing participant." She smiled up at him, and though a trace of sadness still colored her eyes, she gave him a look that spoke of something else altogether. Attraction. Seduction. Invitation? Was she signaling that she would be a willing participant again? Or was that merely wishful thinking on his part? Perhaps it was just the moonlight.

"Besides," she said, "I probably would have run off in time, away from Porthruan and Mama. I was miserable there. I count myself lucky that I found a protector in James. If I'd gone off on my own, I'd likely had landed in the stews and been even more miserable. As it was, I fell into a life of affluence and luxury."

She wriggled out of his embrace but allowed him to keep an arm around her shoulders. They sat in silence for a while, Sam lost in his thoughts of young Willie being cast out and then losing the baby, of his role in her downfall. Yet he had to agree with her that things might have been worse. He ought to thank that damned artist for making sure she did not land in the streets. And she had certainly led an interesting life.

"Were you happy?" he asked.

"Most of the time. Were you happy at sea?"

"Most of the time. I certainly grew to love it. But at first I was merely frantic to get back to you. But the *Calliope*—the ship where the press gang took me—set sail the next morning for the West Indies and there was nothing for it but to hope to get a letter to you at the first port."

Her head dropped onto his shoulder. "What a time that was, the two of us pining after each other in our different ways. At least I was in a world I knew. You were thrust into something relatively unknown. It must have been horrid."

"In those early days, I used to be frightened to death when the guns were run out and we rammed their charges. That's when I'd think of dying and never seeing you again. And many a night I'd be standing watch up in the foretop roost, freezing my jiggers off, and the only thing that kept me warm was thinking of you and me curled up in that hayloft like two inkle weavers."

Sam ran his hand up and down her arm, tucking her close, thinking again of that hayloft. "But he was good to you? Benedict? He treated you well?"

"Yes, while I was with him he treated me with great kindness and affection."

"Do you still see him?"

"Occasionally, but not often. He used to be a fixture at my salons. And even all these years later, we are still linked in many minds because of those early allegorical paintings."

"His work is very different now, I think."

"Yes, though he is still sought out for portraits. Hertford loved James Benedict's work and was mad for the Muses. More for the model than the art, I always thought. He was determined to own all nine paintings, and went to great expense tracking them down and convincing the owners to sell them. He only managed to obtain seven of them. The Prince Regent refused to part with Erato. And he never could locate the owner of Terpsichore. I was sorry for that, because I'd always liked that one best."

"So did I."

Willie leaned away and looked up at him. "You saw it?"

"I bought it."

She threw her head back and laughed. *"You?* You are the elusive owner of Terpsichore?"

He nodded, grinning. "I bought it shortly after I saw you when I returned to England for the first time. Your mother had told me about the artist you'd run off with, but she didn't know, or wouldn't reveal, his name. But it was easy enough to learn his identity, especially when inquiring after his famous model. I was angry at you and heartsore, determined to carry on without you. But I was hell-bent to see those paintings. Benedict still had most of them, and was pleased to display them for me. They held me spellbound, and I couldn't take my eyes off Terpsichore, with the movement of the drapery and the way you held the lyre. I fell in love with it. We negotiated a price, and I spent every remaining shilling of my prize money on that painting. I carried it from ship to ship, until I finally bought the house in Sussex, where even now it hangs in the drawing room. Poor Sarah never knew why I loved that painting so much, and I never told her, although it is clearly the work of a master. You see, I never forgot you, either, Willie."

She reached up and stroked his cheek. "What a pair we are, two old fools still carrying our youthful torches. My navy lists and your painting."

He wrapped his arms around her again and said, "Maybe it's time we let those torches burn again." He smiled into her eyes, bent his head, and kissed her.

Chapter Five

Instinctively, she melted into his arms—arms still familiar even after all those years—and ignored the small voice in her head warning her that, despite how much she wanted it, she was making an enormous mistake to give in to her desire for Sam. He would never truly be able to forget or forgive her shady past, which would only lead to pain for both of them. But she silenced the traitorous voice and allowed the kiss to deepen. For just this moment, this single moment, she wanted him with a yearning deeper and more powerful than she'd ever known. Because this was Sam. Her first love.

Was it still for old times' sake? Was he kissing the Willie of his youth, or the woman she'd become? She would never really know, and all that truly mattered was that he *was* kissing her. And she kissed him back for all she was worth, matching each circle and thrust of his tongue with her own.

When they broke apart at last, each breathing roughly, Wilhelmina looked up to see that his golden-brown eyes had darkened with pleasure.

"God, Willie. I am on fire for you. I don't think I've ever wanted a woman more than I have wanted you."

"Oh, Sam." She cupped his cheek in her hand. "Seeing you again is like a tonic. I am humbled, surprised, and delighted to know that you desire me."

"Why should that surprise you? Because you're not twenty any longer?"

"I'm not even thirty. And though I may skirt the issue of my age with others, you know full well that I won't see forty again, either. But no, that is not why your desire surprises me. I had thought my way of life had squashed every warm feeling you ever had for me."

"Never."

"The last time we met, ten years ago—"

He held up his hand to stop her. "Please. Don't remind me of that embarrassing encounter. I was mortified."

"Why? I never understood what happened. You sought me out, then bolted after exchanging an awkward word or two. Was it because you disapproved of my marriage to the duke?"

"No, of course not. It was just . . . an unexpected surprise."

"Because I had reached too far above myself? Or because the duke had sunk too low?"

"Neither, Willie. It was never that. Deep in my heart, I was glad for you. Glad that you would be out of that other life at last and into something more conventional. No, I did not disapprove. But I was . . . disappointed. I thought you knew why."

"But I didn't. I don't."

"Truly?"

"Sam, I have no idea what you're talking about. I simply assumed you thought I was getting above myself, or that I had somehow tricked the duke into marriage. In any case, I knew you disapproved. Or so I thought. Tell me the truth. What were you thinking that evening? Why were you so uncomfortable?"

He looked down at his feet. "Nothing. It was stupid. You will laugh."

"Perhaps I will, but tell me anyway."

He groaned. "This is devilish embarrassing. But all right, I will tell you. I had thought . . . I had hoped . . . Damn. The thing is, Willie, I was ready to make you an offer."

Her jaw dropped open in astonishment. "To marry you?"

He shook his head. "No."

"Aha. I understand." Of course he would not have thought to marry her. She smiled. "You hoped to be my next protector."

He shrugged. "I told you it was stupid."

Wilhelmina laughed. "Sam Pellow, you hypocrite. You, who had once railed at me for degrading myself as a demirep, wanted to set me up for yourself? My, my. How things change."

"It was the ultimate hypocrisy. I was ashamed ten years ago and still am. I'm sorry, Willie. It was beastly of me to want that from you."

"Is that what you still want, Sam?"

"No, Willie girl, I would never ask that of you. Besides, you're too good for me now. A highly respectable woman. A duchess!"

"I'd be anything for you, Sam."

"Ah, Willie."

And he kissed her again. Despite all the years gone by, despite the opposite directions their lives had taken, despite the very different person each of them now was, it was nevertheless a hauntingly familiar sensation to be held in his arms. Back in Porthruan, though, they'd both been innocents, both virgins. Now each of them was more experienced in the ways of passion, and desire flared fiercely between them.

Sam tried to ignore the drops of rain that began to fall on his face, not wanting anything to interrupt this moment with Willie. But when it suddenly began to pour in earnest, he was forced to end the kiss.

"Damnation. We'll have to make a run for it, my girl. Follow me."

He took her by the hand and rushed to the door of the church, but it was locked. Tugging her with him, he hurried into the nearest shelter: an open stable behind the church.

"Damn and blast." Sam shrugged out of his wet coat and began to shake it out. "It seems I am destined to ruin all my clothes this day." He looked up to find Willie flicking her damp skirts. "Here, take my coat. At least it's dry inside."

He placed the coat around her shoulders, then wrapped his arms around her waist beneath it. Bending his head to hers, he said, "Now, where were we?"

Wilhelmina pushed him away playfully. "No, where *are* we? Sam, you old sea dog, did you plan this?"

"The rain? I may be a good sailor, but I cannot control the weather, my girl."

"Not the rain. This." She swept out an arm to indicate their surroundings.

A slow grin quirked his mouth as he looked around. When his gaze took in the hayloft above his head, he laughed. "Well, I'll be damned."

"If you did not plan this, please do not tell me. It is much too romantic to be coincidence. Are you going to make love to me in the hayloft, Sam?"

He pulled her close. "There is nothing I want more, Willie. But only if you want it, too."

"You know I do. I have wanted it almost since the moment you invited me to join you for tea in the taproom. I have been determined that we should catch up with each other in more ways than simple conversation."

Sam arched an eyebrow. "Willie, what instructions did you give to that hatchet-faced factotum of yours when he came to our table?"

She smiled sheepishly, and the merest hint of a blush colored her cheeks. "Why do you ask?"

"I have a hunch that wheel was in perfect condition when I arrived. What did you say to him?"

"I asked him to do whatever it took to keep you from leaving tonight."

He laughed and brushed a kiss against the top of her head. "You cheeky wench. And the blasted pigs? Were those his doing as well?"

"Smeaton is very thorough and very resourceful. And I wanted this night with you, Sam."

"Then you shall have it, my girl." His heart soared with delight that she had orchestrated his delay. He took her hand and led her toward a wooden ladder leading up to the loft. "Come. Let us pretend to be eighteen and sixteen again, when life was simple and love was new. Just for a few hours, let's recapture our youth, and each other."

He'd been dashing up stepped ladders between decks for years, but he went slowly this time, guiding Willie in front and taking each step with care. When they reached the loft, it was as though years had melted away and they were back in Cornwall in her father's barn. But Sam had been an awkward, inexperienced youth in that hayloft. He trusted he could perform with more skill and polish in this one.

He took the coat from her shoulders and spread it out on the hay, then laid Willie down upon it. He untied his neckcloth and joined her, and took her in his arms and kissed her. He slid his mouth to the sweet, vulnerable skin of her throat, then allowed his lips to cruise the elegant length of her neck. His hands slid over the silky fabric of her dress, tracing the feminine curve of hip and thigh as his lips continued their exploration. She purred like a kitten, and Sam's blood heated at the sound. He wanted to invade her, to possess her, to transport her to the heights of pleasure . . .

"Ouch!"

He stiffened. "Did I hurt you, my girl?"

She wriggled beneath him, and not seductively but as though she was uncomfortable. "No, I was just being poked in the neck by a sharp bit of hay. It was nothing."

He kissed her mouth again, then buried his face in her slender neck, running his lips and tongue against the base of her ear while his hand took possession of her breast. As he worked his mouth along to the nape of her sweet-smelling neck, silky golden curls tickled his nose and lips. And then something not at all silky. Muttering a curse, he reared up and spat out bits of hay and brushed more from his nose. "Damnation."

She looked up at him, blue eyes twinkling with mirth, and soon they were both laughing.

"How did we ever manage this before?" he asked as he sat up, brushing the hay from his shirt. "It's like making love on the back of a hedgehog, for God's sake."

"I think we must have been so young that we never noticed how uncomfortable it was."

Sam helped her to sit up, all the while thinking what a mess he'd made of this seduction. She must think him the clumsiest and most unsophisticated of men. No better than the callow youth she'd once known.

"Don't look so forlorn, Sam." She smiled and stroked his cheek. "I know it seems very romantic to think we have come full circle, from one hayloft to another, with two decades and more in between. But it doesn't have to be a hayloft, you know. I have a perfectly comfortable bed back at the Blue Boar."

Hope flared in his chest. "Are you inviting me into that bed, Willie?"

"Yes. I want to make love with you. Not for old times' sake, but for now. For tonight."

He kissed her. "For tonight. Come on, then. Let's behave like two adults, get out of this damned prickly hay, and find that bed of yours."

Once in her bedchamber, they lost no time in renewing their passion. They each plucked impatiently at the other's clothes, and their own, until every garment had fallen into a tangle at their feet.

Wilhelmina was rather vain about her body. Indeed, she was quite proud of it. Because her face and figure had been her fortune, she had taken good care of both. She exercised to keep her muscles taut and youthful, riding and walking regularly, and working in her small garden. And she did not allow herself to overindulge in either food or drink, which helped to keep her waistline trim. It was not a girl's body—there was only so much one could do to hold back time—but neither was it matronly. She felt no shame in displaying it to Sam.

And he had no cause for shame, either. He was no longer the beautiful young boy she'd known, but a magnificently beautiful man.

She stroked the hair on his chest. "There was a lot less of this on the boy I knew back in that other hayloft."

"And a lot less girth around the waist."

"Nonsense. You're remarkably trim. With girth in all the right places." Her hand traced the muscles of his chest and shoulders.

"I could say the same about you, my girl. In fact, you look better than you have any right to."

"I wish you'd gone bald and run to fat, Sam. You'd be much easier to resist."

"Running up and down riggings keeps one fit."

"But I didn't realize captains did that. I assumed you had young boys to climb up the masts for you."

"I did, of course. Some officers give it up. I never did because I enjoyed it. There's nothing like riding the give and
spring of line rigging to make you feel like a boy."

"Let me see if I can make you feel like a man." She led
him to the bed, where her own clean linen sheets were turned
down. But they did not crawl under the covers. Willie lay on
top of them and pulled Sam down to her. He took her in a
torrid kiss, while she entwined her legs with his, putting
every possible inch of her skin in hungry contact with his.

They kissed for long moments, and then Sam broke the
kiss and looked deep into her eyes.

"You terrify me, Willie. I want you so badly, but I keep
thinking of all those other men—"

She pushed him away, frowning. Hell and damnation. She
had known in her gut that this was wrong. She should have
listened to that nagging voice in her head. "Don't," she said,
moving away from him. "This will never work. It was foolish of us to think it could. You will never be able to forget or
forgive who I've become."

He tugged her back to him. "Silly woman. I've told you
more than once that I understand about all that. I stopped
blaming you years ago."

"And yet you can't stop thinking about all those other men.
I'm sorry, Sam. This won't work. We can't be together again. It
sounded like a terribly romantic idea, but it's too late for us."

"It's not too late. We have to try, Willie. If we don't do it
now, when at last we're both alone and unencumbered, we
may never get another chance. And it *is* romantic. Two lovers sharing passion again after all these years."

"How can we, when you can't stop thinking about all
those other men? And how they made my life a disgrace in
your eyes?"

"It's not the other men in your life I'm worried about, my
dear girl. It's the life in *this* man. I fear I may not measure
up to your worldly expectations."

Her anger and disappointment evaporated in an instant. "Ah, Sam. You could never disappoint me."

And he didn't.

He loved her with hands and mouth and tongue as skillful as the most practiced London rake, without the edge of cynical hedonism. He gave pleasure and took it, in an honest expression of passion and desire. This was not the remembered innocence of their first youthful coupling—uncertain and bumbling—but the knowledgeable and unashamed sensuality of experienced maturity.

Sam's lips trailed down her neck and along her shoulder, and lower still to the curve of her breast until, finally, he took her nipple into his mouth and curled his tongue around it. Her low moan of pleasure echoed through the room. Sam's mouth became hot and greedy in response. His hands skimmed over her bare flesh, creating little sparks of erotic fire everywhere he touched. Wilhelmina kneaded his back and shoulders with restless desire, and in turn explored him more intimately with lips and teeth and tongue.

When at long last he drove himself into her in a single deep thrust, she welcomed him with inner muscles that closed tight around him.

There was no awkwardness between them, even after all these years. There was only ease and rightness as their bodies joined. Wilhelmina could not be certain what his thoughts were, whether or not he was still thinking of all those other men, but her thoughts were on Sam alone, and no one else. A potent warmth rushed through her, welled up, and filled her. She almost became lost in the drugging sensuality of his powerful thrusts, the way he lifted her hips for deeper access, but she never forgot that it was Sam who was inside her, Sam who was loving her.

He prolonged the loving, keeping himself in check, sometimes stilling inside her with a visible effort not to climax before she did. When her body finally stiffened, then convulsed

into a succulent crescendo of passion, he followed close behind with his own release. Burying his face in her shoulder
and his hands in her hair, he pumped faster and faster, calling out her name, until he collapsed on top of her.

Panting and wet, they melted into each other in sheer sati-
ated bliss. After several long moments, Sam rolled off her
and gathered her against him. He kissed her so tenderly, it
made her want to weep. Within a moment, he fell into a deep
sleep, but not before whispering in her ear: "I love you, Willie. I've always loved you."

The cock's crow woke him. Or maybe it was the barking
dogs or the church bell. Sam soon became aware of a morning's chorus of activity. The clank and clatter of harnesses
being set to teams. The crunch of wheels on gravel. The
whinny of horses anxious to be moving. The creak of windows being thrown open and people shouting to others
below.

Sam was exhausted, but sublimely happy. Willie was snuggled beside him, still sound asleep. There had been little
sleep for either of them last night. They had made love three
times during the night, something he'd not done since he was
a very young man. In truth, he felt like a boy this morning,
ready to take on the world. With Willie at his side.

Sam thought of kissing her awake and making love to her
in the golden light of morning, but it seemed greedy and
selfish. They would have a lifetime of mornings. Instead, he
would let her sleep a while longer.

He slid carefully out of bed—dear God, he could easily
get used to those crisp linen sheets—and found a pitcher of
water on a washstand. It was freezing, but he splashed his
face and washed up a bit before unearthing his clothes from
the heap on the floor. He was almost dressed when he heard
Willie stir. He sat beside her on the bed and kissed her.

"Good morning, Willie girl."

"Sam." She sat up and smiled, but her eyes seemed wistful and almost sad. "Thank you for waiting to say good-bye."

A tiny knot twisted in his gut. *Good-bye*?

"Last night was wonderful. Glorious. It has been such a pleasure to see you again, Sam, and to talk out all that was between us. And to make love with you. What a night you have given me! I will never forget it."

Her smile became a bit unsteady and her eyes looked over-bright. But her voice was even, and her intent clear.

"Thank you, Sam. And God's speed to you."

Did she really think he was going to leave her after finally finding her again? After loving her again? "I'm not going anywhere, Willie."

"Yes, you are. You must go to Clophill and the Fullbrooks."

He took one of her hands and caressed it. "Do you think I can walk away from you after last night?"

"Yes. You must."

"No, I must not." Sam could not understand why she was saying such things. After she'd slept naked in his arms. "God, Willie, I want to marry you. I want to spend my life with you. I was your first love, my girl, and I want to be your last love."

She sat up straighter, wrapping the coverlet around her breasts. "What we had together back in Porthruan, the love we shared, was a very special thing, Sam. But what I did—"

"Willie, stop! I don't blame you for—"

"—what I did with my life changed everything, irreparably. I am not the girl you once loved and never can be. We cannot go back, either of us. It is impossible."

"Then let us go forward."

"We can't. There's too much behind us."

He took both her hands in his, willing her to trust him. "Willie, sweetheart, this could be a second chance for us. We don't often get second chances in life."

"I'm sorry, Sam, I can't. It won't work. There are no second chances. I'm sorry."

The stubborn woman! Why was she being so difficult? He made an effort to keep anger and frustration out of his voice. "Why? Why won't it work? It may have been impossible once, when there was too much guilt and pain, on both sides. But that's long past. There is nothing now to keep us apart."

She shook her head and met his gaze squarely, though a glimmer of what looked like sadness shone in her eyes. "The past will always keep us apart. Despite last night, I will always be damaged goods to you, irreparably soiled, and I could not live with the disdain your eyes. It might not be there at first perhaps, but it would come eventually, and I could not bear it. No, Sam, you are better off following your original course, to marry Miss Fullbrook. She will give you no cause for regrets."

He dropped her hands and rose from the bed. Could she really be sending him away? He could not believe it. "You disappoint me, Willie. I thought you were beyond regrets. But it's more than that, isn't it? You say you are afraid I cannot forgive you, and yet I did so years ago. No, the real problem is that you cannot forgive yourself. For not knowing I lived. For not waiting for me. For breaking my heart. I think it is the disdain in your own eyes that troubles you, Willie, not mine."

She threw back the covers and swung out of bed, gloriously naked. Good Lord, she was beautiful. And not just for a woman who'd passed forty, but for a woman of any age. How was he supposed to walk away from her, out of her life? There was a stubborn tilt to her chin as she donned a wrapper and tied it about her waist.

"No, you're wrong, Sam. You believe yourself to be above it all now, with your mature tolerance and liberal-mindedness. But how will you tolerate wondering if every man you meet in London has shared my bed in the past? How long before you are asking for names? And once you've heard them all, how long will you continue to be able to touch me without disgust?"

"Oh, Willie, my love, I—"

"Stop." She raised her hand, palm out. "I never cared what other men thought of me. They knew who and what I was, so it didn't matter. Even with Hertford, because I was his whore before I was his wife. But you're the only man who knew me before I entered the demimonde. Who knew my innocence. My pure heart. I will always care what *you* think of me, Sam. How *you* judge me. Which is why I cannot be with you. I can never be good enough because I cannot erase the past."

"Willie." She was breaking his heart.

She smiled, this time with more conviction. "But I am so very pleased that we had last night. It is a memory I will cherish forever. You will always be my first love, Sam. Even if we never see each other again, I will never forget you. Or last night. You were quite splendid."

"And so you are sending me away?" His voice choked with emotion.

She stood before him, reached up, and placed a hand on his unshaven cheek. "You were on your way to another woman. Go to her. And be happy."

Dear God, she was serious. Where had he gone wrong? Why was he unable to convince her that the past did not matter to him anymore?

Bewildered and bereft, confused and confounded, he kissed her and took his leave.

And what the devil was he supposed to do with his life now?

Wilhelmina collapsed against the door when he'd gone. It was the hardest thing she'd ever done. He was the biggest temptation she'd ever faced, but she'd forced herself to be strong and do the right thing, no matter how much it hurt.

And dear God, how it hurt. She'd never loved anyone the way she'd loved Sam. She had loved him, or the memory of him, for years, and now she had come to love the fine man he'd become. What a difference one night could make. But everything she'd said to him was true. She would rather live with the memory of their one lovely night than face a lifetime of his scorn. When she had entered into the life of the demimonde all those years ago, she'd known there was no looking back. Even marrying the duke did not wash away the stain of her past. To some people, she would always be a whore.

If she went with Sam, people would think of her as *his* whore, and she could not do that to him. She was accustomed to the label, but it would be a constant source of pain for Sam. He was better off without her.

But she'd had one night with him. One magical night. It would have to be enough.

She took her time getting ready to depart, lethargy and sorrow slowing every movement. She was strangely reluctant to leave this quaint old inn where she had reconnected with the one great love of her life. Ginny and Marsh were patient with her, though she sensed their frustration. Perhaps they were wiser than she. Perhaps it was best to get back to her life in London as fast as possible and forget about Captain Sam Pellow.

Smeaton managed the other servants and the luggage while Wilhelmina sat quietly in the carriage, nursing her heartache. At Wilhelmina's request, they left her to ride alone. Ginny sat up with the driver, and Marsh rode in the other carriage with Smeaton. Wilhelmina wanted to sort out her thoughts in solitude during the drive to London.

It was late in the morning when the carriages finally pulled out of the Blue Boar's yard and took to the road. Wilhelmina did not look back at the old inn. She kept her gaze forward, on the road to London.

Less than a half mile down the road, the carriage lurched and came to a noisy and jarring halt. She felt Trevitt jump down from the driver's bench. Wilhelmina rolled down the window and saw him and George, the footman, examining one of the horses.

"What has happened?" she asked, leaning her head out the window.

"One of the team has thrown a shoe, Your Grace," Trevitt said in an exasperated tone. "Fortunately we have not gone far. I'll walk him back to Upper Hampden and have him reshod."

He muttered under his breath as he began to remove the harness from the shoeless horse. Wilhelmina watched the operation with resigned indifference. Despite the sunny skies, it was already a miserable day, and one thrown shoe could hardly make it worse. She had settled back into the velvet squabs when she heard the approach of another vehicle.

A curricle slowed and pulled up right beside her. Sam held the reins and flashed a smile at her through the window.

Wilhelmina tamped down the jolt of pleasure at the sight of him, but was unable to stop herself from opening the carriage door and stepping out to see him. "What are you doing here?" she asked, eyeing him suspiciously.

"Just passing through. What's the problem?"

"I believe one of the horses has thrown a shoe."

"Indeed." He looked at the horse being removed from the harness. "Sorry, old chap."

Wilhelmina glared at him, round-eyed. "You? *You* did this?"

He winked at her. "You are not the only one with a few tricks up a sleeve." He reached out a hand to her. "Come, Willie. I'll take you the rest of the way. Your entourage can follow later."

"But—"

"No buts, Willie." He was not going to let her talk him out

of it this time. He'd made his excuses to the Fullbrooks, and so there was nothing to stand in his way, save Willie's own mule-headedness. And by God, she was no match for a man who never let ferocious winds or treacherous seas or enemy broadsides keep him down.

"Let me take you up in my carriage, Willie. It's not as grand as yours, but it has a certain dash that should suit you."

"But I'm going to London."

"I know."

"You would be going in the wrong direction."

He smiled and shook his head. "No, for once I will be going in the right direction. To you. With you."

"Sam—"

"You almost convinced me to go, Willie, but none of your idiotic, mulish arguments will hold water. And by God, you won't get rid of me that easily. Don't condemn us with another mistake, my girl. The first time, you thought I was dead. This time, you think I can't love you because I can't forgive you. But you would be wrong to believe that. I fell in love with you when I was seventeen, and despite all the years and all that's happened, I've always loved you and always will. If you can't believe that, you'll be making another life-changing mistake, like I almost did with Miss Fullbrook. Bilged by your own anchor. Don't do it, Willie. Don't walk away from me . . . from us. Come with me to London. Marry me."

"But—"

"Life is too short, Willie," he said, determined not to allow her a word of disagreement, "and we're not getting any younger. Let's make the best of the years we have left to us, which, God willing, are many. No more excuses. No more regrets. We shall have a lifetime of love and happiness instead. And I won't be convinced by any more of your flimsy arguments this time, or let you sacrifice yourself to them,

either. Come, let's see what sort of life we can make together."

"And what about all those scandalous years behind me?"

He grinned, thinking the question was little more than
one last salvo, and a weak one at that, before surrender.
"Frankly, my girl, I'd rather concentrate on the scandalous
years ahead. When all of society is reeling in shock and
outrage that a duchess would give up her title for a lowly sea
captain on half pay."

Wilhelmina smiled. "You are making quite a leap, Captain, from a roll in the hay to a lifetime commitment."

"Take my hand, Willie, and we'll make that leap together."

She studied him for a long moment, a moment during
which Sam ceased to breathe. Then she reached up to take
his hand, and his world changed again, forever.

When she was settled beside him, he kissed her softly on
the mouth. "No looking back, Willie."

"No looking back."

"I mean it."

"I know."

"Say it again."

"No looking back."

He took her in his arms and kissed her more thoroughly.
"I'm proud of you, my girl. I knew you could not be so
hen-hearted. You always had spunk." He smiled so broadly,
he thought his face might crack. "Dear God, I am surely the
happiest man alive! I love you, Wilma Jepp. I always have.
And I always will. I'm hoping you love me a little, too."

"More than a little."

He grinned like an imbecile at her words. "I don't care
that it took almost twenty-five years to finish what we started
in your father's hayloft. It was worth the wait. But from this
moment on, it's full speed ahead."

"Then what are you waiting for, Captain? Let's get this pitiful excuse for a carriage to Town and start that new scandal you were talking about."

Sam threw back his head and laughed with pure joy, gave the horses their heads, and set sail for London and a new life with the only woman he'd ever truly loved.

Candice Hern

CANDICE HERN has always enjoyed escaping into the history and literature of Regency England. After years of re-reading the novels of Jane Austen and other women of the period, she by chance discovered the great Georgette Heyer—and all her contemporary stepchildren—and was instantly hooked.

Candice lives in San Francisco in a house cluttered with African violets, orchids, Regency-period antiques, and mountains of reference books. She loves to hear from readers. Contact her via email at candiceh@candicehern.com, or the old-fashioned way at PO Box 31499, San Francisco, California 94131. Please visit her website at www.candicehern.com.